DECLARED HOSTILE

JACK STEWART

Copyright © 2025 by Jack Stewart

All rights reserved.

No part of this book may be reproduced in any form or by any electronic or mechanical means, including information storage and retrieval systems, without written permission from the author, except for the use of brief quotations in a book review.

Severn River Publishing
SevernRiverBooks.com

This is a work of fiction. Names, characters, businesses, places, events and incidents are either the products of the author's imagination or used in a fictitious manner. Any resemblance to actual persons, living or dead, or actual events is purely coincidental.

ISBN: 978-1-64875-631-3 (Paperback)

ALSO BY JACK STEWART

The Battle Born Series
Unknown Rider
Outlaw
Bogey Spades
Declared Hostile

To find out more about Jack Stewart and his books, visit
severnriverbooks.com

For my mom,
Who always knew I would fly.

PROLOGUE

Fallon, Nevada

Nikolai Voronov pulled into the gravel lot and shifted the Mercedes sedan into park before allowing himself to finally relax. After what felt like years of navigating potential pitfalls, he sighed with contentment and sank into the plush leather seat. And with the enormity of what they had just accomplished weighing down on him, he closed his eyes and listened to the final notes of Rachmaninoff's Second Concerto. Its haunting melodies were imbued with a somber pathos that seemed oddly fitting for the moment.

As the song ended, he opened the door and stepped out into the retreating sunlight. He slipped on a pair of dark Ferragamo sunglasses and gazed contemplatively into the cloudless sky, knowing that he had only one final task to complete before he could return home.

Viktor had promised him that much.

Voronov stretched out his left arm and brought his Poljot watch up to his face. Its elegant steel case was adorned with Swarovski stones and attached to his wrist by a black leather strap. Beautiful in its simplicity, it was a fitting timepiece for the Russian intelligence operative.

Seeing the time, he grunted.

They should be here by now.

He lowered his watch in disgust and straightened his coat before leaning back against the Mercedes to present an air of nonchalance that was counter to how he actually felt. Every nerve ending was on fire, and his heart raced with anxiety. He just needed to hold out a little while longer. Once his team arrived, he could complete the job and return home. For good.

Voronov took a deep breath and inhaled the dry desert air. Even its smell grated on him. The gravel lot was like so many others in this dismal town—vacant with an utterly unattractive appearance—but had one redeeming quality that made it ideal for what they needed to do: It bordered a stretch of track that ran through the center of town and linked Fallon to the rest of the world.

Even in the twenty-first century, trains still served a vital role.

The sound of steel grinding against steel drew Voronov's gaze westward toward the setting sun. He couldn't see the train yet but knew it was the one Viktor had arranged. He glanced at his watch again and swallowed back his ire.

At least the train is on time.

He pushed off from the Mercedes and began walking across the crushed gravel toward the raised embankment lined with steel rails resting atop wood sleepers. Voronov knew this stretch of track was the terminus for a line that was seldom used, and it was unlikely they would be disturbed while transferring their cargo from the van to the rail car. But that didn't mean he was comfortable with sitting idle while he waited on a van full of thieves and murderers to arrive.

The Russian climbed the shallow embankment with some difficulty, limping closer to the tracks with gritted teeth. The dry desert air seemed to have aggravated his oldest wounds, especially those to his knees and hip that brought forth memories of Alkhan-Yurt—memories he had spent a lifetime trying to forget. He gave a little shake of his head and rested his foot atop the rail, feeling it tremble as the train pulled nearer.

Voronov looked over his shoulder at the main road cutting through town. He was two blocks north of Lincoln Highway, separated by only the gravel lot and Stockman's Casino, and he felt completely exposed.

"Damn fools!"

No sooner had he finished cursing the incompetence of the men Viktor had foisted on him than he saw a white panel van pull into the lot from the south with its engine roaring. But his feelings oscillated from relief to frustration as he watched the van jostle from side to side and careen over the curb, kicking up a cloud of dust as it raced across the gravel toward the Mercedes.

"This is why we should have used professionals," Voronov grumbled before turning to limp down the slope and greet the new arrivals.

The van skidded to a halt next to the Mercedes and its two front doors opened. Even through the growing darkness, he could see their prison tattoos clearly and again lamented Viktor's decision to hire criminals. They were reckless and untrained, and it would be a miracle if they managed to load the cargo onto the train without the local police descending on them.

"You're late," he said to the driver.

"We're here, old man."

Even with two decades on the heavily muscled thug, Voronov wasn't afraid. He had spent his entire life engaged in combat and waging war for the Rodina—first as a paratrooper, then as a soldier in the Spetsnaz GRU. Feckless criminals like the ones Viktor had hired didn't scare him.

The two locked eyes and stared at each other in silent defiance as the van's sliding door opened and two more thugs stepped out onto the gravel lot. The stalemate stretched on as the train rolled into position and came to a stop with the large side door on the nearest railcar already open in silent beckoning. At last, Voronov broke the silence.

"Load the cargo in there."

The passenger looked to his comrade expectantly, and the two men standing behind them grinned in quiet expectation. Voronov instinctively knew what was about to happen, but he gave no outward indication that he was anything more than mildly annoyed by their tardiness.

"Our price just went up," the driver said.

Voronov nodded slowly but lowered his eyes to the ground between them. "How much?"

"Ten thousand," he replied.

"Each," the passenger added, apparently emboldened by his partner's moxie.

Voronov looked up at the passenger, then shifted his gaze to the driver and the two men behind them. "Very well."

He reached into his coat but kept his eyes fixed on the men who practically licked their lips and salivated in anticipation of an increased payday. But with lightning speed, Voronov drew his PSS-2 silenced pistol and aimed it at the driver. The criminal's eyes went wide in disbelief a split second before the pistol coughed in Voronov's hand.

Thwap!

The wedge-shaped bullet caught the tattooed and heavily muscled thug in the bridge of his nose, spraying the air behind him in a dark mist as he collapsed to the ground. But Voronov had already shifted his aim to the passenger, leveling his sights on the space between his frightened eyes.

"Load the cargo in there," Voronov repeated.

The passenger stood frozen in place, unable to look away from the miniature handgun in the Russian intelligence operative's hand. But the two men who had exited the rear of the van nodded anxiously, eager to complete their task and flee. After several seconds, the shock of what had just happened wore off, and the passenger turned to help his comrades.

Good dog, Voronov thought.

He'd be damned if a ragtag group of criminals prevented him from returning home. He held the pistol in a loose grip at his side and watched the men struggle to carry the pallet from the rear of the van to the waiting train.

Over the men's grunting, Voronov heard the unmistakable sound of a large jet aircraft in the distance, breaking free from the earth and climbing into the sky. He turned and saw the faint outline of a twin-engine passenger jet with its nose pointed at the heavens. He couldn't see its details beyond its blue-and-white livery, but he knew that had he been closer he could have seen the vertical stabilizer flag and prominent "UNITED STATES OF AMERICA" cheatline markings.

Air Force Two.

"I'll see you soon, Mr. President."

1

Marine Corps Installations—West
Camp Pendleton Base Brig
Camp Pendleton, California
Two years later

The sterile light of the interrogation room poured over Special Agent Emmy "Punky" King's dark hair and cast angular shadows across the metal table. She leaned forward with her eyes fixed on the former Marine corporal. Adam Garett, the traitor once known to her only as *KMART*, sat in the chair opposite her with rigid posture.

But the tension in his shoulders betrayed an unease his stoic face tried to mask.

"The orange looks good on you," she said.

"Why are you here?"

His tone was flat and emotionless, as if the months leading up to his court-martial had sapped him of his strength. But she couldn't care less if he thought she was only harassing him at this point. Still, she needed some level of cooperation, and it would only benefit her by being at least somewhat cordial. "Listen, Garett," she began, her voice steady and piercing. "I need you to tell me about the Russians."

He rolled his eyes. "This again?"

She nodded. "This again. Details matter."

Adam's hands were clasped tightly on the table, and he glanced down at his white knuckles. "I've already told you everything I can remember."

Punky could sense his words were deliberate and weighed with a caution bordering on defiance. She gritted her teeth before responding. "Everything except for the link between you and President Adams."

The inmate's head snapped up. She could see the fear in his eyes as the accusation knocked him off-balance. "There *is* no link. I only met him that one time in Fallon. I already told you that."

Punky smirked at him as her hand gently patted the file in front of her. It was thick with surveillance photos, phone transcripts, and printouts of cryptic messages between Adam and the woman she had known as *TANDY* —the Ministry of State Security handler he had given secrets to. The woman was long dead, but that didn't mean Adam hadn't still been working for the enemy when he sat down with Jonathan Adams.

"Coincidences don't interest me, Garett. Patterns do." Punky opened the folder and removed a surveillance photo she had taken of a simple mid-century home in the San Jose neighborhood of Willow Glen. "Whose house is this?" She already knew, but she needed him to say it.

"Ma'am, I swear to you—"

Punky cut him off. "Swear to me later. Convince me now."

Her words were like bullets, precise and meant to hit their mark. She pushed the photograph in front of him, then flipped through the pages of her notes, pointing out dates, locations, times—each one highlighting connections that were invisible to untrained eyes but glaring under her scrutiny.

Adam's jaw clenched, and his eyes darted away momentarily.

She moved on to keep him off-balance. "Let's talk about why you went AWOL and fled from the Marine Corps."

"I already—"

"Is it because you killed Shi Yufei?"

He shook his head emphatically. "I didn't kill him. I swear to you!"

She shifted again. "What are the Russians after, Garett? What's their game here?"

Silence hung heavily between them and stretched thin the thread of patience holding Punky's composure in check. Every second that ticked by without an answer was a tightening of the vise around her resolve to crack this case wide open.

"Look," Adam finally said. "I was just a pawn, alright? They never told me what it was all about."

"Then start with what you know." Her keen eye caught a slight tremor in his hand and the faint sheen of sweat on his brow. "Pawns see things, even if they don't play the whole board. Start talking."

"Alright." He let out a faint sigh, then began recounting the fragmented memories of leaving San Diego behind for his family's cabin in Lake Tahoe. He told her how he'd left the serenity of the mountains for the flash and fast pace of the "Biggest Little City" to drown out the voices of self-doubt.

As Punky listened, she dissected each word for the telltale signs of truth and deceit. In the dance of espionage, she knew every player masked their steps. But it was her job to peel away the layers and reveal the choreography of betrayal and allegiance beneath.

"Keep going," she urged. "Every detail can shine a light on the bigger picture, and your cooperation is crucial, Garett. Don't forget that."

The clock on the wall seemed to tick louder as the seconds became minutes, and Adam continued sharing his tale of being abducted in front of the Nugget Casino before his captors whisked him away into the Nevada desert. He told her of the shed they had locked him in, and the surprising parole his captors had given him.

His voice was heavy with the weight of consequences he was just now beginning to feel.

"Details, Garett, I need more details!" Punky's voice cut through the stale air of the interrogation room like a scalpel. The stark fluorescent lights hummed overhead and cast a harsh glare on Garett's drawn face.

He shifted in his seat with discomfort written across his features as if it were just another part of his prison uniform. His eyes darted to the door and back, his instinct to flee visibly warring with the knowledge that there was no escape from either her or his prison sentence. "Look, I've told you everything," he stammered in an anxious rush. "I don't know what else you want from me."

Punky leaned forward and ran her fingers through her thick hair before pulling it back into a ponytail. "What I want," she said, her voice lowering to a simmering threat, "is the truth. Every hesitant pause or sidestepped question is just another thread I need to pull. You're my *only* link to understanding what happened, and I won't let you shut down on me now."

Punky leaned across the table and waited for Adam to speak. But he only fidgeted in his seat as his eyes scanned the photographs and documents she had scattered on the table between them. Then she noticed something. She wasn't sure what it was exactly, but his eyes had narrowed as they paused on a photograph just a little too long to be a coincidence.

"Recognize someone?" Punky prodded, her instincts razor-sharp.

On the table between them was a photograph of President Jonathan Adams shaking hands with an unassuming figure at a crowded fundraiser during the recent campaign.

Adam swallowed but shook his head. "It's nothing. Just another handshake."

"Sure," Punky said, her voice flat. "But that handshake seems special to you."

He hesitated, and the silence stretched as Punky waited. Finally, he spoke. "I—I can't."

"Can't or won't?" Punky pressed.

But before he could elaborate, the door burst open, and a non-commissioned officer dressed in the Marine Corps Combat Utility Uniform entered and fixed her with a grim and resolute expression.

"Special Agent King," he said, glancing briefly at Garett. "You're needed outside."

"Can't you see I'm in the middle of something?"

"Right now."

The interruption had cut through the room's tension like a guillotine blade, and Punky shot a glance at Garett. Her chair scraped across the floor when she stood. "Fine. But we're not finished here. Not by a long shot."

As Punky turned to leave the interrogation room, the image of the handshake haunted her thoughts. *Whose hand was the president shaking? Why did that one mean something to Garett?*

2

Punky reined in her emotions and walked calmly from the interrogation room. Her pride prevented her from giving Garett the opportunity to see her as anything other than the person in charge. But when she heard the door click shut, she wheeled on the Marine correctional specialist. "Just who the hell do you think you are, Sergeant?"

He hesitated before removing the key from the door, then turned to face her. "This wasn't my call, ma'am."

She stared incredulously at the stone-faced Marine sergeant as he calmly stepped around her and began walking down the hall. She felt her frustration at being interrupted threaten to boil over into anger at being dismissed. "Then whose was it?"

"Special Agent Camron Knowles," he replied over his shoulder. "He said you'd be pissed."

That's an understatement.

She shook her head in disbelief. "What? Why?"

"He's on the phone. You can ask him yourself."

She groaned and charged down the corridor after the sergeant, her boots echoing off the sterile walls. There were too many secrets still locked inside Garett's head, and she needed to get them out before the Marine

Corps shipped him off to Kansas to the United States Disciplinary Barracks in Fort Leavenworth.

Or before the Russians put into motion whatever scheme Adam had been a part of.

She rushed past the correctional specialist and burst through the door into a cramped room filled with desks lining the walls on all sides. It was just as drab as the interrogation room, and she scanned the desks for the one with a phone that had her supervisor waiting on the other end. She spotted it almost immediately.

"Camron, I don't have time for this right now—"

"Quantico's not happy, Punky," he said, cutting her off. "They're asking questions."

She knew what he meant. The headquarters for the Naval Criminal Investigative Service was located in the Russell-Knox Building aboard Marine Corps Base Quantico in Virginia. That meant her boss's boss's boss had taken exception to her interrogating a prisoner already found guilty of treason. "Let them ask. I need answers."

"It's been almost two years, Punky. Maybe it's time you accepted that there's no bigger conspiracy here." It was the same thing he'd been telling her for months as he made his case for her to return to working on any one of the dozens of cases piling up on her desk.

But she just wasn't wired that way.

"Camron, Adam Garett is the adopted son of the former head of the West Coast network for China's Ministry of State Security. He actively committed espionage and delivered secrets that exploited a weakness in our most advanced stealth fighter, directly resulting in an attempted attack on a nuclear-powered aircraft carrier off the coast of California."

"Yeah. And now he's in the brig where he belongs."

She closed her eyes and kneaded the tension from her temples. *How can he not see it?*

"Only until they transfer him to Leavenworth," she protested. "Then I'll never get access to him."

"Punky!" Camron sounded even more exasperated than normal. "Sometimes, you can be so relentless—"

"You mean stubborn," she said, cutting him off.

"Yeah, a real pain in the ass. But now you're ignoring your other cases and chasing after phantoms. He can't do anything from the brig. Come back to the office and let's put more bad guys behind bars."

Their relationship had always been one of constant tension. He gave her just enough leash to hang herself with, and she constantly tugged at it and tested the limits of his patience. But this time she knew she was right. There was a reason the Russians had abducted Garett and arranged for him to meet in private with then Vice President Jonathan Adams.

"Just because something bad hasn't happened yet doesn't mean it won't."

"Punky—"

"Camron, he was found guilty of treason for giving secrets to the Chinese. But the Russians put him in the same room as Adams for a reason. I need to find out why."

The supervisory agent sighed loudly over the phone. "Fine. Find out the reason and close this case for good—"

"I'm on it, Camron."

"And Punky?"

"Yeah?"

"No more interviews with Garett—"

"But Camron—"

"Your focus should be on the Russians. Not the Chinese."

"But they're all connected," she said, then hung up the phone a little harder than she had intended, earning her disapproving looks from the Marine correctional specialists gathered in the small room. She knew Camron's next call would probably be to the commanding officer of the Security and Emergency Services Battalion when he'd ask the colonel to bar her from access to the brig. She knew the clock was ticking on her ability to question Garett further.

Turning to look at the Marine who had summoned her, she gestured to the door. "Take me back."

"But, ma'am—"

"Now, Sergeant."

He might eventually receive orders to stop her from questioning the inmate. But he didn't have them yet. The sergeant reluctantly opened the door to the hallway and gestured for her to lead the way.

When they were alone in the hall, he turned to look at her. "What's so special about this guy anyway?"

Nothing.

And that was the truth. There was nothing special about Adam Garett. He was just a guy who turned his back on his country and knowingly gave secrets to the enemy. But she was certain he had seen something or heard something that would help her uncover what the Russians had planned. And that mattered.

"He's the key."

"Then maybe you should just turn him," the sergeant replied.

Punky stopped walking. *If only it were that simple*, she thought.

She waited for the Marine to unlock and open the door to the interrogation room, then walked inside. Garett didn't even bother looking up at her and stared at the table with a blank expression of defeat. "Please, just leave me alone. I've told you everything I know."

Punky walked to the table and stabbed at the photo. "Except for this."

The image, innocuous to most, screamed volumes to her trained eye. She knew she had finally found the thread that could unravel the entire fabric of lies entwining Adam Garett and the president. And she intended to pull it, no matter the cost.

His gaze flicked to the door and back at her, a silent plea for escape. She could feel him teetering on the precipice between fear and the need to tell her what it was he had seen. "I already told you—"

"Look again," she said, sliding the photo closer. "This isn't just another grip-and-grin, Garett. And you know it."

Adam's throat worked as if trying to swallow stones. "You don't understand—"

"Make me understand," she cut in. The room seemed to constrict around them as she lowered herself into the chair.

"I…" His voice cracked, and he clamped his mouth shut.

"Time isn't on your side," Punky reminded him.

A heavy silence fell upon the room, thick and suffocating. Then he whispered so softly she might have imagined it. "Check… the watch."

Punky leaned forward. "What watch, Garett? Describe it."

"Silver... or steel," he murmured. "Old-fashioned like."

"Keep going," she said, her thoughts racing ahead to piece together the fractured image of a puzzle only she could see. "How is the watch connected to the president?"

Adam's throat worked silently as his gaze clouded with memories he wished to forget. He clenched his hands into fists. "I—I'm not even sure it is."

"Then what did you see?"

For a second time, the door to the interrogation room opened, and the Marine sergeant walked in with an almost apologetic expression on his face. She shook her head and lifted a hand to silence him before he could deliver the message she feared he had been instructed to give.

"Not yet," she said.

"Ma'am—"

"Not yet, Sergeant!" Punky slammed her palm on the table, startling Adam from his silent brooding. "Time's up, Garett. *What* did you see?"

"Look for the watch," he said.

The Marine sergeant stepped forward and placed a hand on her shoulder. "Ma'am, I have orders to stop you from asking the inmate additional questions and escort you from the brig."

This time, it was Punky whose head drooped toward the table in defeat. Camron had pulled the plug on her access to *KMART*, and now she had no choice but to comply. She shrugged the sergeant's hand off her shoulder, slid her chair back, and stood.

"I hope you can live with yourself," Punky said to Adam, one final barb to elicit cooperation, then turned to follow the sergeant from the room.

"It's the same watch," Adam muttered, barely loud enough for her to hear.

She spun back, hoping he would elaborate, but the Marine had already closed the door. He twisted the key and locked her out for good.

Click.

3

Fallon Range Training Complex
Fallon, Nevada

The endless desert floor stretched out beneath them in a patchwork of brown-and-tan hues. Dust swirled in the wake of the propeller-driven aircraft and created a hazy, shifting view as Lieutenant Commander Colt "Mother" Bancroft piloted his A-29 Super Tucano just beneath the thick, low-hanging clouds. In tight formation to his left and right, Lieutenant Commanders Carlton "Cubby" Elliott and William "Jug" McFarland mirrored his every maneuver with precision.

"Keep it tight, Cubby," Colt said, his voice terse but steady over their tactical frequency. His wingmen were among the most talented aviators he had ever flown with. But it was his job to train them in the new aircraft and prepare them for combat operations. "Jug, we're turning into you. Watch those mountains."

Cubby's acknowledgment was a grunt. Jug's, a sharp, "Copy that."

Colt banked hard to the right and led the formation in a steep dive, allowing their planes to accelerate in the thin desert air as the ground rushed up to meet them. At the last second, he snatched back on the stick and leveled off mere feet above the surface, causing a group of jackrabbits to scatter in panic.

"Show-off," Master Chief Dave White said from the backseat.

Colt ignored the SEAL's comment. His heart kept beat with the thrumming engine, and adrenaline laced each measured breath, but he wasn't in a playful mood. This was serious business. He glanced briefly over each shoulder, then banked hard left and felt the G-forces press him into his seat, rolling out to set up for the next pop attack over the barren landscape.

"They need to be ready," he replied before keying the microphone switch to address his wingmen. "This ain't your daddy's Super Hornet."

"Yeah, no shit," Cubby replied.

"We'll be operating at low altitude and relatively low airspeeds. So high-G turns in close proximity to the terrain will be our bread and butter downrange." He knew there was a fine line between motivating them and discouraging them, but the skipper had entrusted him with the task of getting them ready.

"We're right there with you, boss," Jug said, almost as if challenging him to push them harder.

The entirety of Colt's focus was on the mountains looming large on either side of his nose. With each pass over the target complex, he demonstrated not only the maneuvers that would keep them safe but the necessity of anticipation and foresight that came from years of experience.

He was completely at ease. His body melded with the machine—a testament to his time in the sky.

"As you begin your pop, add throttle but ease it off before rolling over into the dive. Smooth transitions, people, smooth transitions," he instructed, his voice betraying none of the strain against the rising G-forces. He pressed forward on the throttle and yanked the stick back into his lap.

Without even looking, Colt knew Cubby and Jug had followed suit and were piloting their aircraft like loyal hawks. They were good pilots, but Colt knew that just one misstep, one lapse in focus, could turn even a routine training mission into disaster.

Not on my watch, he thought.

Colt craned his neck to look over each shoulder at his wingmen as they adjusted their angles to maintain a tight formation, weaving a pattern of discipline and precision through the dry air. He nodded with silent approval as the trio of dark gray Super Tucanos cut across the sky.

"Looking good, boys," Colt said, though he still saw room for improvement. They weren't training for a game. It was his job to ensure they flew better and fought smarter. Lives depended on it. Their own most of all. "Alright, let's tighten it up on this next run."

Neither pilot replied as Colt's clipped and authoritative tone left little room for doubt. He had put aside their years of friendship and donned the mantle of the squadron's relentless taskmaster. He would accept nothing less than absolute perfection from the other pilots.

"Don't you think you're driving them a bit hard, flyboy?" Dave asked.

Colt glanced in the mirror at the Navy SEAL in his backseat and shook his head. "They're not ready yet, and it's my job to—"

"Pony One, Pony Base," a voice said over their tactical frequency.

"Go ahead," Dave replied.

"Wrap it up and return home." The voice was unmistakable. Commander Andy "Freaq" Wood was the commanding officer of Light Attack Squadron Four. He was ultimately responsible for the Black Ponies' readiness.

"Roger that, Skipper."

Saved by the bell, Colt thought.

"Alright, boys, this next run will be our last," Colt said, his voice steady and clear.

He looked over his right shoulder and saw Jug give a thumbs-up from the cockpit of his own A-29 Super Tucano. "Copy that," Cubby said.

"Stay sharp, hold your lines. Make each movement count," Colt said, his eyes scanning for any sign of weakness in their formation.

"Roger," Jug acknowledged.

Colt guided the trio into a steep dive, then leveled off with a smooth pull and G-forces that tested their physical limits and skill. "Discipline. Precision," Colt reminded them as they raced westward mere feet over the desert floor. "That's what sets us apart. That's what keeps us alive."

Colt's eyes darted across the terrain in front of them, hugging an invisible line he had drawn in his mind. He was the conductor orchestrating a symphony of turbine engines and wind. His two wingmen operated in seamless harmony and demonstrated their trust in Colt's leadership with every turn and climb.

"Nice work." Colt pulled back on the stick and guided them higher into the sky. His Super Tucano sliced through the air like a blade through silk. "Now, let's bring it home. Wedge formation."

At the initial, Colt glanced over his shoulder and watched Cubby cross under from his left wing to Jug's right side. By the time they reached the runway numbers, the trio was in a tight echelon formation and ready to enter the carrier break and bring their Super Tucanos back to earth.

He brought his right hand up to the side of his mask and made a "kissing off" gesture to his wingmen, then slapped the stick to the left and pulled it back into his lap. The rapid onset of G-forces caused him to grunt as he sank lower into his seat, but he was focused on carving an arc through the sky and remaining level with the horizon in a tight break turn.

Colt pulled back on the throttle to slow the Super Tucano, lowered his gear and flaps, and rolled wings level only moments before his main wheels squeaked down onto the tarmac. No matter how many times he had flown this plane or others, there was always an instantaneous moment of relief when he returned safely to Mother Earth.

"You're starting to make a habit of this," Dave said.

Colt shook his head at the backhanded compliment. "Get used to it."

He slowed the turboprop to a crawl, then exited the runway and waited for his wingmen to take up position on either side of him. Looking through his forward windscreen, he watched a line of FA-18E Super Hornets taxi past, their pilots turning to study the secretive dark gray airplanes idling in relative silence.

Colt waited until they had moved on, then taxied south to their squadron's hangar. He pulled into his parking spot and popped the canopy. The wind carried the scent of jet fuel and burnt rubber—a scent that had long been a backdrop to his life. With deliberate movements, he removed his helmet but still felt the weight of his responsibilities bearing down on his broad shoulders.

"They're looking pretty good," Dave said.

Colt nodded. "They're getting there."

He swung his legs over the side of the cockpit and dropped down off the wing onto the tarmac. His shadow stretched long on the ground, mimicking the day's end. The world around them seemed to move in slow motion as the tension of the day's training mission lingered like a prelude to something greater.

"Colt," a firm voice called out, cutting through the hum of distant hangar activity. He looked up and saw Freaq striding confidently across the ramp to greet him.

He acknowledged his boss with a respectful nod. "Skipper."

"How'd they do?"

Colt looked over his shoulder at Cubby, Jug, and their SEAL backseaters climbing down from their own planes. "They're getting there," he said, repeating the same assessment he had given Dave.

His CO's eyes were steely and unreadable. "Let's hope they're already there."

A twinge of curiosity piqued Colt's interest, though his face remained an impassive mask. "What's that supposed to mean?"

"I just heard from the Beach that we're being mobilized to support a critical operation."

"Where?" Colt asked.

"Ukraine."

4

Camp David
Frederick County, Maryland

Samuel Chambers lowered himself into his chair and fidgeted with a fold in the armrest's floral fabric. He looked across the coffee table at the most powerful man on earth. Jonathan was visibly tense, and Sam knew what was coming. But he patiently passed the time by studying the rustic decor that didn't appear to have changed much over the last several administrations. Their decades-long friendship was the only reason he was even sitting in the Aspen Lodge living room.

"I knew this was going to happen," the president finally said.

Jonathan Adams was a soft-spoken man and not quick to anger, but Sam could tell by the timbre in his voice that he was pissed. So, he wisely kept quiet.

"This is just the first time your mistake has backed me into a corner."

"Jonathan—"

The president whipped his head in Sam's direction, visibly seething at his chief of staff. "Don't."

"I can fix this," Sam said. Though, in truth, he wasn't sure he could.

"How? How can you *possibly* make this okay?"

Sam took a deep breath and leaned forward. Aside from the specters of each president who had made Camp David their retreat, they were alone. But some things demanded they spoke only in hushed tones. "Let me speak to Viktor."

The president shook his head. "You speaking to Viktor is the reason I'm in this mess in the first place."

"Don't you mean *we*?"

The president clenched his mouth shut and flexed his jaw muscles, an obvious sign that he was angrier than Sam had ever seen him before. But they hadn't made it all the way from the California legislature to the White House because Sam was as timid as a church mouse. He had always been fiercely protective of Jonathan, but the reason *they* were in this mess wasn't because he had spoken to Viktor.

When the president refused to answer, Sam spoke. "You're wrong." His tone had a quiet edge to it. "*We're* in this mess because *you* couldn't keep your dick in your pants and knocked up an underage girl. Or did you conveniently forget that part?"

Jonathan recoiled as if Sam had struck him. "Who do you think you are?"

Sam didn't hesitate. "The only person who can fix this. Now, snap out of it."

The president closed his mouth again, but his jaw seemed to relax. Sam knew Jonathan was unaccustomed to being dressed down like that, but he had made his point. Always delivering the unfiltered truth was the earliest pact they had made while still students at UC Berkeley, and he had never wavered from that commitment.

Even when Jonathan was pissed.

"Frank's going to need an answer soon," the president said, reminding him what was at stake.

"The SECDEF can wait."

Before flying out to the presidential retreat, Jonathan's director of national intelligence had briefed him on a report filtering through the intelligence communities that, if true, posed the greatest threat to national security in decades. He had immediately convened his National Security Council and listened impatiently as his most trusted advisors discussed how best to address the situation before it spiraled out of their control.

Coverage of the Russian invasion of Ukraine was no longer a centerpiece in the nightly news, but that didn't mean the United States had backed down from supporting the former Soviet republic. Jonathan's predecessor had committed their country to monetary support more than double every other country combined, but he had avoided wading into the quagmire by establishing the policy of not committing actual American forces. There would be no troops on the ground.

But an obscure intelligence report seemed poised to end that.

"Let me meet with Viktor," Sam said again. "If I can't get him to back down from this foolish plan of his, then you can give Frank the green light."

Jonathan chewed on the inside of his cheek. "We're talking about nukes here, Sam."

"Allegedly," he countered.

Jonathan leaned back with an exasperated sigh. "Now you sound like all the others—too afraid to take meaningful action just because you don't want it to be true. I don't have that luxury. Maybe if the intelligence had come from only one source, I could buy the Agency some time to corroborate the claims. But multiple sources?" He shook his head.

Sam understood Jonathan's point of view, but the science was questionable. Even if the RA-115, or so-called "suitcase nuke," had actually been produced during the Cold War, most experts believed its useful shelf life had already expired. "It's a phantom, and I think you're playing right into Russia's hands by committing troops to Ukraine."

"Not *troops*... Christ, it's not like I'm sending an entire brigade or anything."

"No, just a team of Navy SEALs and an unproven light attack squadron," Sam shot back.

Jonathan closed his eyes for a moment, then leaned forward and spoke with a firm tone that left little doubt who was in command. "I've ordered them to stage in Poland under the guise of participating in a joint NATO exercise. But if you can't get me assurances that Viktor's men aren't planning on trying to recover these *suitcase nukes* from Ukraine, then I'm going to give Frank the okay to execute."

Sam started to protest, but Jonathan held up a hand to stop him.

"Portable nuclear weapons falling into the hands of terrorists isn't something I'm willing to risk, Sam. I'm giving you twenty-four hours."

"You know what's at stake—" Sam said, still trying to reason with him.

But Jonathan had heard enough. "I do. The lives of countless innocent men, women, and children."

Sam finally fell silent. The president had made up his mind that he wouldn't be coerced into allowing Viktor's men to recover the Cold War–era nuclear weapons that had gone missing inside Ukraine. He wasn't going to be blackmailed into ignoring his oath and allow them to find their way into the enemies' hands. Jonathan had made it perfectly clear that he had donned the mantle of responsibility and wouldn't be swayed.

"Twenty-four hours, Sam."

Sam gritted his teeth. "Yes, Mr. President."

When Sam exited the president's cabin, he made his way around to the lower terrace and nodded at each secret service agent he passed. Even tucked away within the secluded 125-acre retreat in Catoctin Mountain Park, a team of dedicated professionals stood ready to protect Jonathan from harm. But Sam was the only one who could protect the president from himself.

He casually descended the steps to the pool deck and circled around to the far side before removing his phone. Scrolling through his contacts, he found the listing where he had hidden the one number he had hoped never to need. But Jonathan had left him no choice.

He tapped on the number and brought the phone to his ear, inhaling the fresh mountain air to calm his anxiety and channel a fraction of the retreat's tranquility. Located in the northeastern rampart of the Blue Ridge Mountains, the property was home to an abundance of trails, sparkling streams, and panoramic vistas of the Monocacy Valley. There were few places on earth more peaceful.

But it might as well have been a prison for as trapped as it made him feel.

"Samuel," the Russian said. "To what do I owe this pleasure?"

"We need to meet," he replied, swallowing back the instant taste of bile in his mouth as he recalled the last time they had met in person at the Jefferson Memorial. It had been the first time Viktor Drakov had asked him for a favor, but he knew it wouldn't be the last.

"Can you perhaps be a little more specific?"

Sam couldn't be sure, but it sounded like the former Russian intelligence officer was almost amused. But Drakov had always favored himself a puppet master who manipulated events to serve his needs. He probably did find it amusing that the chief of staff to the president of the United States had called to request a meeting.

"Not over the phone," Sam said. "But you need to make the time."

The Russian chuckled quietly. "I think you might have confused our relationship, Samuel."

Drakov sounded confident, but Sam dealt with his kind every single day. He wasn't easily intimidated and made it a point not to back down, facing strength with strength. "I know you still need me to grant you access to the president—"

Drakov's chuckle grew into uproarious laughter. "Please, Samuel. You and I both know I can end Jonathan Adams with one phone call. I do not need you to grant me access… I need you to keep him in his place and make sure he barks for his master like a good dog."

The Russian whistled as if calling an obedient pet, then laughed again.

"Viktor—"

"Calm yourself, Samuel. We can meet at our usual place and time." The Russian's voice turned serious. "But do not make me regret this."

The call ended, and Sam composed himself before slipping his phone back into his pocket and turning back to the lodge.

5

REACH 23
C-17 Globemaster

Colt opened his eyes, surprised he had fallen asleep on the uncomfortable bulkhead seat. But to call it a seat was really an insult to seats. It was more or less a padded box frame with an emergency flotation device pinned to the wall behind a thin piece of canvas for lumbar support. On the bright side, since most guys hated them, he had plenty of elbow room.

Take that, Southwest!

The C-17 had a spacious cargo hold—large enough that it could transport three AH-64 Apaches—but it could only carry two of their Super Tucanos along with the detachment's personnel and support equipment. Still, the Globemaster seemed almost luxurious compared to other transports Colt had flown on.

He glanced up and watched an Air Force captain in a standard-issue green flightsuit climb down from the cockpit and cross the darkened cargo bay to where Freaq rested on a Big Agnes inflatable sleeping pad. The skipper saw the captain approaching and propped himself up on his elbows.

Dave saw his expression and got up from his foam sleeping pad to sit next to Colt. "What's that all about, you think?"

They watched the captain shake his head, look at his watch, and say something else that made Freaq's face turn sour. "Fuck if I know, bro. But it doesn't look like good news."

The Air Force pilot patted their skipper on the shoulder, then stood and returned to the Globemaster's flight deck. "Go do some of that officer shit and find out."

He eyed the SEAL with suspicion, but Freaq's booming voice saved him. "Hey, Master Chief."

Dave groaned.

"Let me know what's up," Colt said with a wink.

Dave stood and walked over to their skipper, who was now on his feet. The men spoke in hushed tones and moved aft toward the cargo ramp, stepping over SEALs and pilots who were just beginning to wake in preparation for their descent into Virginia Beach. After a few minutes, the skipper turned and walked past Colt to the front of the plane where he followed the captain up the steep ladder. Colt turned back to Dave and saw him taking his sweet-ass time talking with the others scattered around the cargo hold.

His curiosity got the better of him, and he couldn't take it any longer. He unbuckled from his seat to walk aft to where the master chief was already spreading the word. With waning patience, he reached up and turned off his Bose QC-45's noise-cancelling feature in time to catch the tail end of what Dave was telling Todd and Ron, two of their other SEAL WSOs.

"...skipping Virginia Beach and going straight to Poland."

Fuuuuck.

Dave turned and gave a look of mock surprise when he saw Colt standing there. "Oh, I'm sorry, Commander," he said with a playful smirk on his face. "You wanted me to tell you what was going on too?"

"Uh, yeah, asshole."

Dave smiled, and Colt struggled to keep a disgruntled look on his face. The SEAL was the kind of guy who could defuse a fight by telling a corny joke and then laugh at himself while staring into the distance with a dumb smile on his face. It wasn't a mystery how he had survived the never-ending, teeth-chattering torture in the cold surf of Coronado.

He waited for Dave to fill him in, but the older SEAL seemed content with making the pilot feel increasingly awkward as the silence stretched on.

"Well?"

"Might want to make yourself a nest, brother. The other alert birds are already in the air and headed east. We're meeting up with a KC-135 to drag us across the pond. We're flying all the way there."

Colt shivered as mention of the Stratotanker forced him to recall the times he'd spent behind the boom of an Iron Maiden. Unlike when Air Force fighters refueled, Navy fighter pilots had to guide retractable probes into baskets that were towed behind the tanker. When the KC-135 was configured to support Navy aircraft, an impossibly short length of hose was attached to its stinger-like boom and ended with an unforgiving basket.

Navy pilots often joked that they were the man in the fighter-tanker relationship. But there was no question that tanking on a KC-135 was a more stressful evolution than on a KC-10, known for its softer hose and wide, pillow-like basket. Colt's old skipper had once described it like "falling into the arms of a well-seasoned whore."

But the Iron Maiden was just a bitch.

"Something happen to move up the timeline?" Colt asked, knowing they hadn't even received a full intelligence briefing on their mission in Ukraine yet.

"Not that I know of. But if I had to guess, I'd say we have a strike window that could narrow over time, and they want to put us into play sooner rather than later."

It made sense. Their squadron had been resurrected to provide air support to the Navy's JSOC task force—a unit that existed for the sole purpose of executing high-priority missions that were too difficult or too high profile for their more conventional brethren. Whatever it was they were being asked to do had to be pretty damn important for the president to reverse existing policy and authorize military forces to put boots on ground in Ukraine.

"Wish you were on the other bird?" Colt asked.

Dave was silent for a moment, and Colt wondered if the master chief secretly wished he was deploying as an assaulter instead of being confined to the small cockpit of a light attack plane orbiting overhead the target. He knew it hadn't been that long ago when all four of the squadron's SEALs had been called on to parachute into communist China and rescue a captured Agency officer. But Dave shook his head, and his trademark smile cracked behind his thick beard.

"Nowhere I'd rather be, brother."

Colt appreciated the sentiment, and they clasped hands.

"How much longer?"

"Oh, only about ten hours."

"Seriously?"

Dave slapped him on the back. "'Fraid so."

"Got any of those no-go pills?"

Dave nodded. "Get your nest all set up and I'll come tuck you in."

"Read me a bedtime story too?"

Dave pinched his cheek. "I'll tell you the one about the ugly little caterpillar that became a beautiful frogman. You'll like that one."

"Rise and shine, flyboy."

Colt heard the voice but ignored it, hoping it would just go away and leave him be—nestled inside his sleeping bag and swaying gently from side to side. He hovered just beneath the surface of consciousness and wanted desperately to fall back into the deeper slumber he had been enjoying, courtesy of the pharmaceuticals Dave had provided.

Dave...

"Open your eyes, Colt."

Still, he resisted. The warm embrace of his hammock held him immobile.

Slap!

Colt's eyes shot open, and he stared up at a maze of cables and hydraulic lines snaking across the cargo jet's ceiling. He sensed the presence of a person hovering just out of view, and he turned to see the bearded SEAL smiling at him.

"Did you just slap me?"

Dave's grin grew, and he nodded like a mischievous teenager who had just pulled off his greatest prank. "It's time to get up."

Colt turned away from Dave and closed his eyes. "Leave me alone."

But before he could regain his grip on the invisible thread that would lead him back to blissful sleep, the world suddenly flipped upside down. Colt's eyes shot open a second time as he fell from his hammock and crashed down into the steel decking of the cargo jet.

Fully ensconced in his sleeping bag and unable to break his fall, Colt turned his head at the last moment and winced at the sudden impact along his cheek. He was still coming out from under the sedative's influence, and his reactions were slowed. But after only a second, he scrambled to free himself from his sleeping bag and staggered to his feet.

"What the hell?"

Dave remained still but didn't back down under Colt's withering anger. "It's time to get up."

Colt shook his head to clear away the lingering effects of sleep before replying. "I thought we were going all the way to Poland."

"We did," Dave replied.

"Wait—"

"You've been asleep almost nine hours."

Colt's mouth fell open in shock as Dave patted him on the shoulder and turned to resume his procession around the cargo hold to wake the others who had made nests of their own. Colt watched the master chief making his rounds, then slowly turned back to pack away his hammock and sleeping bag.

His ears popped as the cargo jet started its descent into Lask Air Base, and the last remnants of his fatigue evaporated with the sudden realization that he was no longer preparing to fly the Super Tucano in combat. That time had come, and the Black Ponies were about to be put to the test.

"Pony up," Colt muttered, then he made his way forward to take his seat along the bulkhead for landing.

6

Reagan National Airport
Washington, DC

Punky stepped through the automatic double doors and exited Terminal One for the curved drive in front of the historic end of the airport. Dulles or Baltimore-Washington International would probably have been easier for her to get in and out of, but the proximity of the smaller airport to the people she needed to see in the capital made Reagan the ideal choice.

With phone in hand, she checked her ride-sharing app for an update on the status of her driver. Mohammed's red Toyota Prius was one minute away. She switched over to her contacts and dialed the number for the first person on her list to visit. The phone rang several times before a tired voice answered.

"Hello?"

"Connor, it's Punky. Were you sleeping?"

She heard commotion on the other end as if the intelligence officer was in fact waking up. "Sorry. Been a rough couple weeks."

Then she remembered. "Of course. How's the new baby?"

"Jax is great," Connor said, though his tone carried a hint of sadness.

Punky understood. Connor Sullivan and his wife had named their newborn after Jax Woods, his former colleague who had been killed by a Chinese operative at an Agency safe house in Valley Center, California. She thought it was a beautiful tribute for the man who had paid the ultimate sacrifice while trying to prevent a horrific biological weapon attack in the South China Sea.

"If today's not a good day—"

"No, it's fine," Connor said, sounding more alert. "But I'm at home today. Any chance you can come out here?"

Punky looked up just as a red Prius pulled up to the curb. "Yeah, my Uber just arrived. Text me the address, and I'll meet you there."

Connor ended the call, and Punky waved at Mohammed to catch his attention. The driver stopped the car and jumped out, beaming at her from ear to ear as he raced to collect her suitcase and deposit it in the hatchback's cargo area. She thanked him when he held the door open for her, then climbed into the backseat and waited for Connor's text message.

"Where did you fly in from?" Mohammed asked as he slipped in behind the wheel.

"San Diego," Punky replied, just as her phone vibrated with an incoming text.

"Sunny San Diego," the driver echoed, then put the Prius into gear and pulled away from the curb.

Punky scrunched up her face when she read the address Connor had sent her. "How far away is Annapolis?"

Mohammed glanced at her in the rearview mirror and shrugged. "An hour, give or take."

"I need you to take me there."

McGarvey's Saloon and Oyster Bar
Annapolis, Maryland

Punky had spent the hour-long drive to the Maryland capital flipping through pages of notes she had taken during dozens of interviews with Adam Garett. The former Marine had been surprisingly candid about his involvement with Chen Liling, the Ministry of State Security operative who had recruited him to spy for the People's Republic of China, but he was tight-lipped when it came to his connection to the president.

Maybe because there isn't one.

But Punky was unwilling to believe Camron was right. There was definitely a reason the Russians had abducted Garett from the Nugget Casino Resort in Reno and arranged for him to meet with Jonathan Adams during his visit to the naval air station in Fallon. And that was why she found herself sitting alone at a table on the second floor of the historic saloon staring at a photo of the president shaking hands with a stranger.

"Penny for your thoughts?"

Punky looked up and smiled at the intelligence officer standing over her. "Hey, Connor. Not sure they're worth that much."

"What's that?" He leaned over and placed a hand on her shoulder as he stared at the photograph. "Is that the president?"

She nodded but didn't answer. "Thanks for meeting me."

Connor took the seat opposite her and leaned back in his chair. "Something big must be going on for you to get on a plane and fly all the way out here."

Punky dropped the photo and rubbed her eyes. "I feel like I'm staring the answer right in the face, but I can't see it."

"Okay. What's the question?"

She slid the photo across the table to Connor, spinning it around to give him a closer look. "Who do you see there?"

Connor glanced at the photo, then back up at Punky. His forehead was creased with confusion. "President Adams?"

"Who's he shaking hands with?"

He glanced back down and squinted. "I don't know."

Her shoulders slumped in defeat. "Neither do I."

"What's this about?"

It was a little early for the saloon's dinner rush, but Punky still surveyed the room to make sure they were alone. There were a handful of young midshipmen dressed in dark blue double-breasted uniforms gathered around a table downstairs, but otherwise nobody was around to hear.

"You know about Adam Garett?" Punky asked.

Connor squinted in thought. "Isn't he that Marine convicted of treason?"

She nodded. "I spent months on a joint task force with the FBI trying to identify him and his Chinese handler. I provided most of the evidence used to convict him at his court-martial."

"Sounds like he got what he deserved."

"The part most people don't know is what happened leading up to his arrest," she said.

Connor folded his arms across his chest. "It was at one of the president's first campaign stops, right?"

She nodded. "Several days before his arrest, I followed Garett in the middle of the night from Marine Corps Air Station Miramar to a man-made lake, expecting to catch him meeting with his Chinese handler."

"And did you?"

She shook her head. "I found his handler, though. Dead."

"He killed him?"

Again, she shook her head. "The next day, he went AWOL from the Marine Corps and fled to Nevada. I followed him to Reno, where I witnessed a group of Russians kidnap him in broad daylight."

This caught Connor's attention, and he leaned forward and fixed her with an intense stare. "How do you know they were Russian?"

She waved off the question. "That's not important. What's important is that he slipped through my fingers and disappeared for several days, only to resurface when Jonathan Adams came to town. At the time, I thought the Russians had arranged for Garett to assassinate the frontrunner to the presidency."

"A reasonable assumption," Connor said, urging her to continue.

"But the Secret Service found no explosives, no weapons, no poisons—"

"The Russians are fond of their poisons," he agreed.

"They found nothing to explain why his captors had suddenly released him and put him in the same room at the same time as the next president of the United States."

Punky could tell by the look on Connor's face that she had piqued his curiosity. "Why do you think?"

"I don't know," she admitted. "But that's why I've been visiting him in the brig. I need to understand what the Russians are up to before something bad happens."

Connor nodded at the photo sitting on the table. "And somehow that photo came up as significant during questioning?"

Punky remembered Garett's words.

Check... the watch.

She looked at the picture upside down and immediately thought back to something she had learned during high school art class. Her teacher had once told the class that drawing upside down trains the eyes to recognize lines and shapes and their relationship to one another without focusing on the finished product. She cocked her head to the side and studied the picture from that different angle.

"Punky?"

"He said it was the watch," she said, more to herself than to Connor.

"What watch?"

Then she saw it. Neither the president nor the man whose hand he was shaking wore a watch prominent enough to warrant Garett's comment. But the figure in the bottom left of the photo—or top right from Punky's upside-down perspective—had his sleeve pulled up to reveal a unique-looking timepiece.

Silver... or steel.

Old-fashioned like.

Punky reached across the table and stabbed at the upside-down figure. "Who is that?"

Connor glanced to where she pointed. "Samuel Chambers. He's the president's chief of staff."

7

Thomas Jefferson Memorial
Washington, DC

Samuel Chambers parked his Rivian in a parking lot along the Potomac, then climbed out and walked back under the interstate overpass. He popped the collar on his overcoat to block the wind but kept his eyes fixed in front of him, trying to spot hidden dangers lurking in the shadows.

You're being paranoid.

Paranoid or not, Sam knew he was playing at a very dangerous game and couldn't afford to be lax. His relationship to the president was the only thing keeping him alive, but it was also the one thing keeping him embroiled in a world of deceit and treachery. He was a target, but he was also a weapon. Woe is the man who underestimated him.

Sam kept his hands in his pockets and trudged onward, passing the George Mason Memorial without so much as a glance, and crossed the road to follow the walking path along the tidal basin. His gaze lifted to the domed roof built in the neoclassical style, only casually finding it ironic how the memorial anchored the National Mall while segregated by a body of water.

The memorial stood apart from the others as if Jefferson's teachings on life, liberty, and the pursuit of happiness were too radical to be enshrined within reach of the great George Washington or Abraham Lincoln. But as Sam climbed the steps on its north side, he was keenly aware of Jonathan's unobstructed line of sight from the Oval Office.

But Jonathan's not there, he reminded himself.

Reaching the top step, Sam walked through the columns and stopped in front of the bronze statue. He knew Viktor was already there and watching from the shadows to make sure Sam had come alone before stepping into the light and exposing himself. It was a fitting reminder of what was at stake.

"So, what has you so worked up, Samuel?"

Even though he had been expecting it, Sam still startled. Like always, the older man was finely dressed in a three-piece suit and matching fedora, presenting an appearance that almost overshadowed the fact that his right eye was a prosthetic.

"Please tell me it's not true."

The Russian's lips pursed together, neither a smile nor a frown. "I'm afraid you'll have to be more specific."

He had rehearsed what he was going to say several times on his way back from Camp David. But he felt his stomach twisting with anxiety as he stood only feet away from the Russian intelligence operative. They locked eyes, and Sam stared at the twitching prosthetic for several seconds before finally speaking.

"The suitcase nukes?"

Viktor's expression didn't change. Not even a flinch.

"In Ukraine?"

Viktor held his hands out to his side in a placating gesture. "I'm afraid you have me at a disadvantage, Samuel. I'm not familiar with what you're speaking of."

His rehearsed entreaty vanished in an instant as a wave of frustration washed over him. The words came out in a rush. "Agency assets in Europe have uncovered a plot by several former SVR operatives to manipulate the chaos caused by Russia's invasion of Ukraine and use it as a cover to reclaim multiple RA-115 nuclear devices that have been in storage inside the former Soviet republic for decades."

Again, Viktor gave no indication he was privy to any such scheme. "I've heard rumors of these devices."

But Sam wasn't fooled. "Our assets further allege that the Russians intend to sell *these devices* to the highest bidders in the Middle East. Al-Qa'ida. Al-Nusrah. Hamas. Hezbollah. I'm sure you can appreciate the president doesn't intend on allowing that to happen."

This time, Viktor flinched. It was barely perceptible but enough that Sam couldn't miss the Russian's obvious surprise at Jonathan planning to prevent the rumor from becoming reality.

"Where does this information come from?" Viktor asked.

Sam was satisfied he had knocked the Russian off-balance. "Our reach is wide, Viktor. Did you really think you were going to be able to get away with it without us knowing? Did you really think the president was going to allow this to happen on his watch?"

Viktor's head drooped in subtle deference. "Why did you ask to meet?"

Sam's back stiffened at feeling the tide shift in his favor. "Call it off."

The frail-looking older man slowly lifted his head and met Sam's gaze. "No."

He took a step back as if the Russian had shoved him. But when he saw Viktor's lips curling upward in a sinister smile, he wondered if he had misread the entire situation from the start. His mouth suddenly dry, he swallowed with some difficulty before speaking. "No?"

Viktor clasped his hands behind his back and angled his chin upward as he studied the inscriptions surrounding the bronze statue at the center of the room. "I'll admit I was somewhat surprised you were able to come by this information so quickly, but it changes nothing."

Sam stared at him. "Of course it does. You have to call off the operation."

As if Sam had just said something embarrassingly obtuse, Viktor gave a little shake of his head. "I'm sorry my friend, but I will not do that."

"If you don't, the president will—"

Viktor wheeled on Sam and darted forward with surprising speed. "The president will *what*? Commit American forces to action in Ukraine, when he has tried everything to appease us and prevent the war from spilling over into a global conflict? No, but I'm sorry. He will do no such thing."

Sam swallowed again but refused to back down. "But he has."

For the second time, Viktor appeared surprised by something Sam had revealed. But he quickly shrugged it off. "No matter. You will just have to convince him that would be a very unwise move on his part. Remind him that I can ruin him with one phone call if he doesn't back down."

Sam knew Jonathan would never acquiesce, but he nodded anyway. "Splendid."

Sam walked back to the parking lot as if on autopilot while Viktor's words echoed in his mind. Part of him had always known that accepting the Russian's help all those years ago meant he also had to accept the strings that came attached. He had rationalized it by convincing himself it was for the greater good—that the country needed a man like Jonathan at its helm.

But now, he wasn't so sure.

Damn!

He reached the Rivian R1S and climbed inside, but he sat frozen with indecision. For the first time in his career, Sam couldn't visualize a clear path forward to achieve the desired results. He had negotiated complex labor agreements with union leaders and closed high-stakes backroom deals in each legislative body Jonathan had been a member of. But a single one-eyed Russian had confounded him and left him feeling more helpless than ever before.

Damn! Damn! Damn!

He was caught between an unstoppable force and an unbreakable object and could side with neither. Jonathan wouldn't back down from demanding that Viktor recall his men from Ukraine, but Viktor wouldn't hesitate to reveal what Sam had kept secret for two decades if the president continued to resist him. In either case, he was being forced to choose sides in an untenable conflict.

But sitting idle wasn't an option either.

Sam put the Rivian into reverse and backed out of his parking space, already thinking about the seeds that needed to be planted in case he was unsuccessful and needed to resort to damage control. He just needed an excuse to begin laying the groundwork.

Teddy's always good for happy hour.

Sam pulled out his phone and tapped on one of the most frequently dialed numbers, then shifted the Rivian into drive. As he pulled out onto Ohio Drive, he listened to the phone ringing through the car's audio system and predicted the forthcoming conversation.

Teddy's voice reverberated through the car's speakers. "Well, isn't this a treat."

Any other day, Sam would have found humor in the good-natured ribbing. But he really wasn't in the mood. "Are you busy?"

The trademark jovial tone vanished from the reporter's voice. "What do you got?"

"Let's talk about it over a drink."

"What's going on, Sam?"

Sam followed Ohio Drive across the bridge onto the peninsula separating the Potomac River from the tidal basin. He could have plugged the address for Old Ebbitt Grill into the Rivian's navigation system, but it really wasn't necessary. He had spent enough time in the iconic tavern across the street from the White House to make it feel almost like home.

"You know where I'll be, Teddy."

The *Washington Post* reporter didn't hesitate. "I'll be there in ten minutes."

8

Lask Air Base
Lask, Poland

Colt shook his head to clear away the last remnants of fatigue and brought a fist up to his mouth to stifle the yawns that just kept on coming. He thought he had managed to get enough sleep on the flight over from the States, but the time difference was kicking his butt. And from the droopy eyes and lethargic demeanor of the others in the room, he didn't think he was alone.

"So, where's this thing going down anyway?" Cubby asked.

"Where do you think?" Ron replied. The SEAL zipped up the survival vest over his two-piece flightsuit and began checking the gear in his combat kit, including a personal defense weapon with spare ammunition. It wasn't their first time flying with the gear, but Colt thought it suddenly felt more real.

Todd seemed skeptical. "I know the skipper said Ukraine, but do you really think POTUS will authorize an operation there."

"If it's important enough, he will," Ron countered.

Their mission was scheduled as a benign post-maintenance check flight of the reassembled Super Tucanos, but they still dressed out with their full combat load. Knowing that the squadron had been ordered into theater for an imminent high-priority operation, Colt tended to side with Ron on this one.

"Well, one thing's for sure. We won't launch from here," Colt said. "We're too damn far to do anything meaningful."

"Think they'll stage us at a Ukrainian air base?" Cubby asked.

Colt thought about it, then nodded. "Most likely."

"Yeah, well, do we even know how the assaulters will get to the objective?" Todd asked. "I didn't see any Ospreys sitting out there on the ramp. Did you?"

Todd had a good point. The CV-22 Osprey tiltrotor was the ideal platform for transporting the assault force to the objective—wherever that was—but the closest ones were stationed at RAF Mildenhall in Suffolk, England.

Colt zipped up his survival vest, then picked up his combat pack and helmet bag. "You guys ready to do this or what? We need to get in the air before I fall asleep."

"Hey, Ron," Todd said. "Wanna swap pilots today?"

Colt smacked him on the shoulder. "Pony up, brother!"

The four men carried their gear from the room they had converted into a makeshift paraloft and pushed open the door leading out into the early morning darkness. Colt turned and looked at several US Air Force F-16CJs from the 480th Fighter Squadron sitting dormant on the ramp, and he couldn't help but feel relieved at seeing American aircraft capable of going supersonic. As much as he loved the Super Tucano, he knew they were going to be isolated wherever they ended up.

Seeing the Wild Weasels comforted him.

Colt advanced the throttle slowly while pressing on the brakes to rein in the A-29 Super Tucano as the Pratt & Whitney Canada PT6A-68C turboprop engine roared and spun the five-bladed Hartzell propeller in violent arcs around his nose. The plane seemed to prance like an untamed pony, as if waiting to be released from its earthly bondage.

He looked over his shoulder at Cubby, who gave him a thumbs-up, then gave his wingman the signal to "kiss off" before releasing his brakes. His plane bucked before accelerating down the runway, and Colt watched the speed tape in his Heads Up Display tick upward toward the calculated nose wheel liftoff number. With one more glance at his engine parameters displayed on the EICAS, or Engine Indicating and Crew Alert System, Colt pulled back on the stick and broke free from Earth's gravity.

As the ground fell away beneath them, Colt raised the landing gear lever to retract the plane's three stubby wheels into the body. Without the gear hanging in the wind, the plane increased speed, and Colt banked to steer toward their designated operating area for the post-maintenance check flight.

"Pony One One is switching," Todd said, letting the tower controller know they were changing to their pre-assigned departure control frequency.

Colt leveled off at one thousand feet and looked over his shoulder as Cubby maneuvered inside the turn on a forty-five-degree bearing line. Rolling out on the assigned heading, Colt watched Cubby continue to close to a standard tac wing formation.

Nicely done, Colt thought.

All those reps in the Fallon Range Training Complex seemed to have paid off. At just inside half a mile from each other, there was enough separation between the planes that they could maneuver independently without worrying about hitting the other. But they were still close enough to maintain formation and provide mutual support with little to no effort.

Colt turned his attention back to the array of displays at his disposal to begin verifying his aircraft was combat ready. The Super Tucano came in as many cockpit layout variations as there were countries flying them, but the Navy had spared no expense in giving the Black Ponies a cockpit that rivaled even the most advanced strike fighters.

On his left display, Colt had pulled up a digital moving map to use as his primary navigation reference. They could preload the map with mission-specific waypoints to outline a route of flight or an operating area. While his radar warning receiver could populate the map with threats, he could also receive them via datalink from off-board sensors—like the F-16CJ Wild Weasels he had seen at the air base.

On the middle display, Colt had pulled up the ADHSI, or Attitude Direction and Horizontal Situation Indicator. The top half provided a digital representation of the standard aircraft gyro, showing his pitch, bank angle, heading, altitude, and airspeed. The lower half provided a top-down view of the aircraft's current position.

But the right display was where the rubber met the road. When the SEAL WSO in his backseat lowered the fuselage-mounted sensor turret, it would display images in high-definition television or thermal and infrared. They had come a long way since the Special Forces covey riders in Vietnam who had often fired their carbines from the backseat of similar-sized planes.

Though Colt suspected the squadron's SEALs secretly would have preferred that.

"Up for a little tail chase?" he asked over their tactical frequency.

"Let's do it," Cubby replied.

Colt snapped the stick into his left thigh and rolled his plane inverted, then pulled it back into his lap as the dense forest raced up to meet them. He rolled upright with the nose still thirty degrees below the horizon and twisted in his seat to keep sight as Cubby scrambled to follow in his wake.

"Five hundred feet," Todd said calmly from the backseat. "Four hundred... three hundred..."

Colt snatched back on the stick again and lifted the nose in ten-degree increments to level off just over one hundred feet above the trees. Technically, Naval Aviators were prohibited from flying lower than two hundred feet, but the Black Ponies had received special authorization to deviate from the regulation based on the unique nature of their mission.

Not that any of their pilots would have thought twice about breaking the rule if needed.

Despite the air-conditioned cockpit, Colt felt beads of sweat that had formed under his helmet run down his head each time he pulled on the stick and increased the G-forces.

"Ninety feet," Todd said coolly from the backseat. For somebody more accustomed to being on solid ground or in the water, he was remarkably relaxed flying at close to three hundred miles per hour at treetop height.

Colt acknowledged the call and bumped back on the stick to bring them above their pre-briefed no-lower-than altitude. Though he had spent most of his career flying single-seat aircraft, he was thankful to have the SEAL's second set of eyes while he focused his attention on the undulating terrain in front of their nose.

"Alright, let's knock-it-off," Colt said over the radio.

"Copy, knock-it-off," Cubby replied.

Colt glanced over his shoulder as his wingman maneuvered to return to a tac wing formation on his right side. He eased back on the stick and returned the flight to a more comfortable altitude where they could focus on their systems and ensure the Super Tucanos were ready for combat.

"Guess it's time to get to work," Todd said. "Deploying turret."

"Copy." Colt felt the sensor pod lower into the slipstream beneath their airplane.

Their plan had been to transit to the working area and perform a myriad of basic maneuvers to ensure the airworthiness of their planes. But the impromptu tail chase had assured both pilots of that. All that remained was to employ ELGTRs, or Enhanced Laser Guided Training Rounds, and verify that their weapons systems were up to snuff.

"Cubby, you're up first," Colt said.

"Pony One Two."

9

Lask Air Base
Lask, Poland

Colt hung his survival vest on the peg in the makeshift paraloft, unable to hide his smile from the others. After being cooped up in the back of an Air Force transport for the trip halfway around the globe, yanking and banking in their nimble planes for an hour and a half felt good.

"Dude, that was fun," Cubby said.

"Hell yeah," Todd replied. "Will be even more fun when they let us put warheads on foreheads."

It sounded crass, but Colt knew that was the nature of the business. The men and women who went into tactical aviation weren't warmongers, but they weren't pacifists either. And the SEALs who volunteered to ride in the backseats were cut from the same cloth.

"How'd Nuts fly?" Colt asked.

The Navy and Marine Corps identified specific aircraft within a squadron with a two or three-digit number known as a modex that was part of the visual identification system. The Black Ponies flew airplanes with a one hundred series modex, meaning that the first was Aircraft 100, known as "double nuts" or just "nuts" for short.

"She flew great," Cubby replied. "Triple sticks?"

Aircraft 111 was the newest Super Tucano in their fleet and one of special importance. While most of the Black Ponies' planes weren't adorned with the names of their pilots and weapon systems officers on the side like in other squadrons, Triple Sticks was different. It paid tribute to a Naval Aviator who had lost his life during operational testing of the Super Tucano—a pilot both Colt and Cubby knew personally.

LT Chris "Bueller" Short.

"Better than ever. Hard to believe she was in the back of a C-17 over the Atlantic Ocean only yesterday." He had the same level of awe he remembered having the first time he had landed on an aircraft carrier in the T-45 Goshawk. As the purple shirts pumped him full of gas following his first arrested landing, he had looked out across the flight deck and thought, *I'm in a jet. On a boat. In the middle of the ocean. Un-frickin-believable.*

"Think Freaq knows what the mission is yet?" Cubby asked.

Colt had wondered the same thing. "Let's go find out."

While they had been evaluating the airworthiness of their airplanes, the skipper, Dave, and the rest of the squadron had been busy establishing a TOC, or Tactical Operations Center. If there was any chance of learning why they had been flown halfway around the world without advance notice, it would be there.

When Colt walked into the corner of the hangar where they had built the temporary TOC, he was surprised by the level of activity in the cramped space. He ignored the buzz and walked over to where the skipper was holding court with Jug, Dave, and Graham.

"...four or five possible locations, but our latest intelligence suggests this is the most likely target."

Colt's heart rate increased at hearing that last word.

Target.

"How soon do they want us to push forward?" Dave asked.

"Unsure," Freaq replied. "When we get the word, we'll send two crews to ride on the Herc down to Voznesensk and go into crew rest—"

"Where's that?" Colt asked, unable to stop himself from interrupting.

The skipper turned to look at him. "Mykolaiv Oblast in southern Ukraine."

"Which two crews?"

Whether flying a Super Hornet onto a deployed aircraft carrier or a Super Tucano into Ukraine, no pilot wanted to give up his spot at the controls to become just another passenger. The skipper also knew this, and he took his time before answering.

"You, Cubby, Todd, and Ron will fly down on the Herc—"

"I'd like to go with them, Skipper," Dave said.

Freaq considered the suggestion for a moment. "Okay, Master Chief. You can go in Todd's place. He can go with me when we escort the assault force."

Colt still hadn't seen any transports on the ramp. "And how are they getting there?"

"Ospreys from the 7th Special Operations Squadron in the UK will be here any minute," Freaq replied, patiently addressing Colt's concerns.

Colt glanced over and made eye contact with Jug. He had already interrupted the skipper twice and didn't want to a third time, but he still didn't know what was going on. "Skipper, what's the target?"

Before Freaq could answer, a commotion near the front of the TOC caught his attention, and he turned just as the ISR battle watch captain announced, "Ghost Three Two is on station."

Every head in their group turned to look at the monitors mounted on the wall as the oncoming Reaper shifted its sensor and centered on what looked like a warehouse surrounded by dense forest.

"That is," a stranger said, stepping forward to join their quorum.

Colt eyed the man up and down, noticing that he didn't wear a uniform but reeked of current or former military. He suspected the stranger worked for a three-letter agency, but that didn't explain the smug look on his face. "And what exactly is *that*?"

"A KGB cache site," he replied.

This time, Jug was the one who spoke up. "KGB? I thought they disappeared with the fall of the Soviet Union."

Apparently satisfied at being given center stage, the stranger stepped into their circle and nodded. "They did. This site has remained largely untouched in the forest north of Yuzhnoukrainsk since the Cold War."

"What was its purpose?" Colt asked.

"The Soviet Union used it and other sites inside its satellite states to store military hardware in the event NATO forces attacked."

"So, there's something in there we want to get?" Cubby asked.

"More accurately, there's something in there we want to prevent certain other people from getting."

The gathered pilots and SEALs remained silent.

"When the Soviet Union fell, more than 3,200 strategic nuclear warheads remained in Ukraine, Kazakhstan, and Belarus, most of them atop intercontinental ballistic missiles. But, most troubling, an estimated additional 22,000 tactical nuclear weapons with smaller yields and shorter ranges existed outside Russia."

Jug was the first to speak up. "Nukes?"

He nodded. "In the late nineties, the Nuclear Threat Initiative published a report quoting former Russian national security advisor Alexander Lebed, who claimed the Russian military lost track of more than one hundred nuclear suitcase bombs—"

"Oh, this just keeps getting better," Jug said.

"Our highest-ranking GRU defector described these 'suitcase bombs' in more detail. They weighed around fifty pounds and could last for many years if wired to an electric source. In the event of a power loss, a battery backup would activate. And if the battery ran low, the weapon would transmit a coded message by satellite to a GRU post at the nearest Russian embassy or consulate."

"I think you have our attention," Colt said. "Now, what's the mission?"

The stranger looked to Freaq. "Obviously, this information is highly classified—"

"All my boys are cleared at the highest levels, Mr. Smith," Freaq said, letting the spook know it was time to open his kimono and share some details.

"Very well. One of those devices began transmitting its coded message, alerting us to this particular site. While investigating the signal, we learned that a group of former Russian intelligence officers had targeted the site for exploitation, believing that as many as four of these devices were in storage there."

"Four?"

Mr. Smith nodded at Colt. "It was never intended to be a permanent storage facility, which is why a full accounting of them was not available following the collapse of the Soviet Union."

"So, why now?"

"With the Russian invasion plunging the country into chaos, our asset alleges that this group of intelligence officers intends to recover the weapons and transport them outside Ukraine for sale to terrorist organizations in the Middle East."

"Well, shit…" Cubby said.

"I expect that the president will soon authorize the task force to stage at Voznesensk Reserve Air Base, but we have asked him to approve an operation to secure the facility and prevent the suitcase bombs from falling into the wrong hands. We just don't have the green light yet."

"Well, why the hell not?" Jug asked. "This isn't something we want to mess around with."

If Mr. Smith had planned on answering, he didn't get the chance. A sailor working in the intelligence directorate suddenly ripped his headset off and spun to face him with a frantic look on his face. "Sir, we've got something."

The spook didn't seem rattled. "What?"

"A Rivet Joint over the Black Sea has detected Russian forces amassing in Perekop."

"Shit," Mr. Smith replied. "Get HQ on the horn. *Now.*"

10

Old Ebbitt Grill
Washington, DC

Punky sat alone at a table for two in the Corner Bar and studied its patrons' faces, looking for one that seemed even remotely familiar. Connor had told her the president's chief of staff was a notorious regular at the iconic tavern, but so far, she hadn't seen anybody who even remotely resembled the person she had seen in the photo.

"This is a waste of time," she muttered.

She drained the rest of her water and turned to look over her shoulder at the statue of a pointer hunting dog, sitting in the window as if keeping a vigilant watch. Sometimes, she felt like that dog, like she was the only one who seemed to care that there were people willing to sell out their country for a meager payday.

With a silent nod to the dog and a grunt of disappointment, Punky pushed back her chair and stood. With no other leads to follow, she was at an impasse. But that didn't mean she could sit around all day and wait for the answers to fall into her lap.

Maybe Camron's right.

She gave a little shake of her head to silence the subtle voice of doubt. She wasn't willing to believe that her intuition had led her astray. She had left San Diego and come to the capital for a reason. She had agreed to meet with Connor in Annapolis for a reason. And she had come to the Old Ebbitt Grill for a reason.

Even if those reasons all eluded her.

Punky turned away from the table and made her way around the room divider. It was crafted from solid wood like the rest of the bar but had several examples of waterfowl on display in glass cases, an obvious nod to the room's theme. A dozen barstools were arrayed along the drink rail that spanned the length of the partition, but each seat was vacant—a further reminder that she was only wasting her time.

Maybe I should just go home and forget this whole thing.

The voice was becoming more insistent and more difficult to ignore, but her daddy hadn't raised her to be a quitter. She walked up to the bar and leaned against its smooth surface while waiting for the bartender to make his way down to her. She felt dejected and lost, but her eyes never stopped moving.

Until she saw the two men sitting together halfway down the bar.

Samuel Chambers sat atop his usual stool and watched the dark-haired beauty in the mirror making her way to the bar. He had noticed her right away. Apart from the dark blue suit that made her look like every other public servant in the city, she carried herself with an arrogant confidence he found attractive. But she didn't seem to have come for conversation, so he turned back to his second Gin Balalajka and took a sip.

So far, Teddy Miller had been blessedly silent—except for the occasional slurp as he downed a Thatch Island oyster with classic mignonette—but Sam knew that wouldn't last long. If nothing else, Teddy was relentless when he suspected his friend was holding the key to a story. Teasing out the details was just the first step in making sure the reporter landed on his side.

"So, when are you gonna tell me what's going on?" Teddy asked when the last of his dozen eastern oysters disappeared.

That was quick.

Sam looked away from the woman's reflection and turned to his friend. "I told you—"

"Yeah, you don't really want to talk about it," Teddy said, cutting him off. "I know you left with the president yesterday and traveled to Camp David. But you came back, and he's still there. That's not normal."

Sam's eyes darted to the woman to see if she had overheard, then set his drink down and turned to look at Teddy. He shouldn't have been surprised by Teddy's intuitiveness—after all, he was a hell of a reporter with the natural instincts to sniff out a story. But it was unlike him to be so blunt.

"I can't really get into it," Sam replied, setting the hook.

Teddy returned the last of his empty half shells to the serving platter and took a moment to wipe his mouth with a linen napkin before responding. "Does it have anything to do with Aurora Holdings?"

It took considerable effort for Sam not to react to his question. He had only come to ensure Teddy's favorable reporting in the future, not to be blindsided with questions about the very thing he wanted to remain a secret. But nothing had changed since the first time Teddy had made a similar inquiry. He swallowed with some difficulty against the dryness in his mouth before replying. "The president still has no comment."

"I've been patient with this—"

Sam slammed his hand down on the bar top, earning a disgusted look from the woman in the dark blue suit. He locked eyes with her, openly challenging her to say something, then lowered his voice to respond. "Don't forget your direct access to the president is only because I allow it."

It sounded a lot like the threat he had used on Viktor.

But Teddy didn't back down. "I've been doing some digging into the company."

This is not how I wanted this to go.

Sam turned back to his drink and took another sip, trying to distract himself from the fact that he was being attacked from every angle. He already had enough to worry about with Jonathan's shortsighted stubbornness forcing Viktor into revealing their secret. The last thing he needed was also having to worry about Teddy penning a hit piece on the president. He kept his face impassive.

"Oh yeah?"

Teddy nodded, his expression resolute but sympathetic. "You know I can't sit on this much longer—"

"Teddy—"

But he was firm. "Sam, I can't. The only reason I haven't put out anything yet is because you asked me not to. But the more I learn, the more I can't keep this story quiet."

Despite himself, Sam felt defeated. "What *exactly* do you think you've learned?"

Teddy reached for his half-empty gin martini and took a sip before answering. "The president has been making regular payments to a company for twenty years—a company that, as far as I can tell, doesn't really do anything. I think he's paying someone off to remain silent."

Sam forced a chuckle. "Silent? About what?"

Teddy flexed his jaw muscles, and Sam could tell the dynamics of their friendship had suddenly changed.

"I don't know, Sam. But my readers might have a few ideas."

Sam felt his neck flush at the threat. He downed the rest of his drink and set the empty tumbler on the bar before pulling out several twenties from his wallet and placing them on the smooth wood surface. This wasn't how he had wanted things to go, but he should have expected it. In Washington, friendships were transactional and not based on mutual respect.

"Go fuck yourself, Teddy."

Sam pushed away from the bar and slipped off his stool, then made his way to the exit.

I'll figure this out myself.

Punky watched as Samuel Chambers seethed and stormed from the bar, obviously frustrated with the conversation she had just partially overheard. She hadn't been close enough to hear everything the two men had said to each other, but between her ability to read lips and the bits and pieces that were spoken in tones louder than hushed whispers, she knew her time hadn't been wasted after all.

She didn't know the man the president's chief of staff had just left sitting at the bar, but she watched him with growing curiosity as he casually finished his drink and prepared to leave. Seizing the opportunity, Punky walked to the seat Sam had just vacated and sat down.

The stranger slowly turned at her arrival, and his hard expression softened. "Can I help you?"

Punky held out her hand. "My name's Emmy."

"Teddy," he replied, taking her hand in his.

"This seat's not taken, is it, Teddy?"

He shook his head, and she did her best to appear relieved.

"I'm gonna play it straight with you, Teddy."

His eyes suddenly darkened. "Okay."

"I came here to find Samuel Chambers."

Teddy turned to look straight at the mirror behind the bar. "Well, you just missed him."

"I thought so," she said. "The thing is, I'm investigating a possible connection he might have with a former Marine who was just convicted of treason and sentenced to life in prison at Leavenworth."

Teddy twitched, resisting the urge to appear interested in what she had to say. "Oh yeah?"

She rolled the dice. "What can you tell me about Aurora Holdings?"

This time, Teddy didn't even bother trying to act like her words had no effect on him. He twisted in his seat and turned his entire body to confront her. "Who are you with?"

Punky turned and made a show of looking around the mostly empty bar. "Nobody. I'm alone."

"What outlet? TV? Newspaper?"

"No, I'm—"

"I've been working on this story since before the election. So, if you think you can just swoop in one day out of the blue and steal it from me, you're mistaken." Teddy wadded up his napkin and made a show of dropping it on the empty oyster platter.

"Wait, I think you have the wrong idea," she said, reaching inside her blazer for her credentials.

But Teddy held up his hand to stop her. "Save it. I'm not interested."

His indignation left her speechless, and Punky remained stock still as he left his seat at the bar and walked away. She could have stopped him or followed him outside to clear up the misunderstanding, but their brief conversation had left her with one concrete thought.

There's something to Aurora Holdings.

11

Samuel Chambers stood under the shade of a tree where Pennsylvania Avenue intersected with 15th Street, one block north from Old Ebbitt Grill. Before even leaving the tavern, he had come to accept that he was utterly alone when it came to dealing with this mess. His lifelong best friend refused to listen to reason, and his only other acquaintance in the capital was dead set on ruining his life.

He stared at the restaurant's entrance and ignored the constant flow of traffic as cars and trucks zipped by. It would have been so easy to saunter out into the busy street and let a distracted and overworked truck driver take care of the problem for him. But that just wasn't his style. He'd rather go down swinging than throw in the towel and let his opponents claim victory.

The tavern's front door opened, and Sam leaned forward when he saw Teddy walk out and turn north. The reporter had his head down and hands in his pockets, completely oblivious to his surroundings as he made his way back to his office across from Franklin Park on K Street. He didn't think it was likely Teddy would go to print on the story so soon, but he needed to intervene before that became a legitimate threat.

Sam stepped out from under the tree's shadow just as Teddy turned onto New York Avenue, following his predictable and regular route back to the *Washington Post* headquarters. But he stopped himself from crossing the street to follow when he saw the blue-suited dark-haired woman exit the tavern.

Unlike Teddy, the woman was far more observant, and she scanned the street in both directions before turning north. Granted, she'd had a fifty-fifty chance of turning in the same direction as the reporter, but Sam didn't think it was a mere coincidence. He prided himself on sweating the small stuff, because it was the small stuff that collapsed kingdoms and ended empires.

He narrowed his gaze and watched the woman practically strutting away from the tavern and turn on New York Avenue.

Is she following Teddy? Does he know?

Sam waited until she had gone several paces, then quickly crossed the street and fell in behind her. He hadn't even been sure why he hung around after leaving the bar, other than that he had the overwhelming sense that Teddy was getting dangerously close to revealing a secret that would, at best, end the Adams presidency.

At worst, it would put him in prison.

At the end of the block, Sam saw Teddy cross the street and continue north on 14th Street. The woman casually lifted her head and watched the reporter disappear around the corner, then picked up her pace to close the distance between them. Sam continued walking at the same speed, acutely aware that if she turned around, he would be caught in the open with nowhere to hide.

Just before reaching the intersection, the woman checked for traffic over her shoulder, then darted out into the street and crossed to the sidewalk on the other side. Sam cursed silently but continued to the corner where he would be forced to wait impatiently for the light to change.

As the woman disappeared around the corner, he again felt as if his carefully cultivated house of cards was on the verge of collapse. He understood why Jonathan couldn't allow Viktor's men to get their hands on the Ukrainian nuclear devices. But he also knew that defying the Russian would jeopardize Jonathan's presidency. And even if he somehow managed to navigate through that minefield, there was still Teddy's threat of revealing what he had learned about Aurora Holdings.

He suddenly stopped.

What if I can kill two birds with one stone?

Sam pulled out his phone and dialed Viktor's number for only the second time. The light turned green as he waited for the call to connect, and he stepped out into the crosswalk to follow Teddy and the mysterious woman.

"Have you made him heel yet?"

Sam gritted his teeth. "He won't change his mind—"

"Samuel—"

"But I might have a solution," he blurted, his eyes fixed on the back of Teddy's head as he continued north.

"I'm listening."

Sam's eyes darted between Teddy and the mysterious woman, unsure how she fit into the equation. There was a chance she knew nothing of Aurora Holdings, but the longer she followed Teddy, the less likely that seemed.

"What if I told you I could give you all the information you needed to ensure your operation overseas went according to plan?"

Viktor hesitated a moment before responding. "Go on."

"I can't convince the president to rescind his order," Sam said before pausing to swallow back the lump in his throat. "But I can give you all the details of the operation ahead of time to give your men the best chance at succeeding."

He knew what he was offering. To save Jonathan's political career, he was willing to go against the president's wishes and betray the men who had volunteered to go into harm's way to keep the world safe from nuclear holocaust. He was willing to sacrifice American lives so that the Russian would keep his secret.

"You would contravene the president's orders?" Viktor sounded surprised.

Sam saw Teddy cross 14th Street and enter Franklin Park. He had spent years cultivating a friendship with the reporter, but now he understood just how dangerous that relationship had become.

"Yes," Sam replied. "But I need you to do something for me first."

Punky first noticed Samuel Chambers following her when she jaywalked across New York Avenue. A few minutes later, she saw his reflection in a window on Washington Metro's Bus 54 when it came to a stop at the intersection with I Street. She couldn't fathom why the president's chief of staff would want to follow her, but she had long since stopped believing in coincidences.

Half a block ahead, she watched Teddy cross the street and enter Franklin Park. Punky hesitated for only a second before following, but her senses were on full alert. She knew that leaving the street and entering the park would make it a challenge for her to keep tabs on her shadow. But Sam's shoddy tradecraft made him seem almost harmless. Like a puppy following her home.

Punky took a curved walkway and followed it around to a fountain at the center of the park, but her eyes easily kept sight of Teddy as he continued to the north side of the park and crossed the street.

What's he doing?

She circled the fountain and caught a glimpse of Sam entering the park behind her, but her focus was on the man who had just disappeared inside the massive building on K Street. She thought about calling Connor to ask what businesses had offices there, but then she saw the sign over the door Teddy had gone through.

The *Washington Post.*

Punky stopped in front of one of the park benches lining the curved walkway and took a seat. His behavior at the iconic tavern suddenly made sense to her. The way he had grilled her about what outlet she was with and accused her of trying to steal the story could only be described as the protective actions of a reporter on the cusp of breaking something big.

Aurora Holdings?

Punky fished her phone out of her pocket and looked up the number for the *Washington Post.* Tapping on the number to dial, she brought the phone to her ear while scanning the park for the president's chief of staff. She had a brief moment of panic when she couldn't find him but relaxed when she caught a glimpse of him sitting on a bench on the park's western edge.

"The *Washington Post*, how may I direct your call?"

Punky narrowed her gaze on Samuel Chambers. "Can you connect me to the newsroom, please?"

"One moment," the operator responded.

The call went silent for a moment before an annoyingly generic music filled the empty space while the operator connected her with the newsroom. Punky looked over again at the president's chief of staff and noticed him looking in her direction. He quickly got up and exited the park to the south.

"Newsroom," a gruff voice said.

Punky watched Samuel Chambers hurry along the path and cross I Street.

"Hello?" the voice asked.

Punky cleared her throat. "Yes, I'm looking for someone named Teddy."

The voice sounded more than a little put out by her request. "Can you be more specific?"

She gave a soft laugh. "I'm sorry, but I just ran into him at Old Ebbitt Grill—"

"Oh, you must mean Miller. Hold on."

When the generic music returned, Punky ended the call.

Teddy Miller, she thought. *What kind of story are you running?*

12

Perekop, Crimea

Nikolai Voronov swung open the heavy door and climbed down from the back of the STS Tigr. The armored special vehicle's winged sheathed hull had an anti-splinter coating made of aramid fiber, but it was nothing compared to the vehicle he had come to see. He turned from the warehouse to the general officer who exited the vehicle on the other side.

"Where is it?"

Major General Yuri Morozov fired a hesitant glance in his direction, then spoke quickly into the mobile radio he held in a white-knuckled grip. Nikolai couldn't make out the words, but his tone was unmistakable.

Several seconds passed before a large door in the side of the warehouse slowly rolled open and exposed a darkened interior. Nikolai squinted and took several steps forward before hearing a turbocharged diesel engine rumble to life from within. Unlike the Tigr's four-stroke turbo diesel that produced roughly two hundred horsepower, the VPK-7829 Bumerang featured a BarnauTransMash engine that made over five hundred horsepower.

His eyes grew wide, but he remained stock still as the eight-wheeled armored personnel carrier surged forward and exited the pitch-black warehouse, exposing itself to the dull gray cloud-filtered sunlight. It was his first time seeing the Russian infantry fighting vehicle equipped with the laser weapon he had stolen from the Americans. And he fought to keep his face impassive against the pride swelling from within.

"What did the Americans call it?" Yuri asked.

The Bumerang came to a stop and Nikolai walked closer, admiring its lines the way a proud father admired his newborn son. If anything, it looked even better than the version the Americans had produced on the Stryker armored vehicle.

"They called it *DRAGON LINE*," he said.

The general grunted. "Stupid name."

Nikolai turned to face the general, who had a smug look on his face. He was the embodiment of the exact reason Russia had not yet defeated the inferior Ukrainian army. Their military was bloated with high-ranking officers who cared more for medals and the tsar's accolades than actual unit readiness. The same had been true in Chechnya, but it had only gotten worse.

"What should we call it? Morozov?"

The general's eyes widened at hearing his surname, but then he puffed out his chest with apparent pride. "I would be honored, comrade—"

"Then maybe you should get off your fat ass and win this war," Nikolai spat.

Morozov's face turned beet red, but Nikolai had already moved on. He circled the Bumerang and studied it from top to bottom the way a reviewing officer might on the parade field. It had been decades since he last wore the uniform in honorable service to the Rodina, but he could still admire when his fellow countrymen did something right.

And their fitment of the *DRAGON LINE* to the armored vehicle was even better than the original. It would be the perfect tool for what Viktor had asked him to do.

He finished his inspection of the Bumerang and returned to the Tigr where the general waited with his shoulders slumped. But Nikolai couldn't care less about the man's hurt feelings. The tsar had ordered him to secure a foothold north of the Dnieper River and retake ground they had lost upon their retreat from Kherson. But so far, his forces had been thwarted by little more than a ragtag group of peasant women and children. And now they would be forced to make a dangerous crossing to reach their objective.

"When do we leave?" Nikolai asked.

The general's face brightened as if pleased that he would soon be rid of an unwanted guest. "At nightfall, a convoy from the 247th Guards Air Assault Regiment will advance across the isthmus for the front lines."

"How many vehicles?"

"Twenty," the general said, obviously pleased that he had been able to secure a force more than twice the size of the one requested.

Nikolai's face darkened, and he glowered at the pompous officer. "That is not what I asked for."

Again, Morozov puffed out his chest as if to remind the intelligence operative of his importance. "It is more," he said, not recognizing that *more* was almost as bad as *less*. "I can assure you my men will see you safely to the objective."

I doubt that.

"You can take us as far as Nova Kakhovka. There, you will remain on the front lines and provide only five other vehicles to see us through to our objective," Nikolai said, reiterating the plan that had already been made clear to the general.

But Morozov's mouth fell open, and he gave a little shake of his head.

"Is there a problem, comrade?"

"I wasn't..." He hesitated before blurting the rest. "...planning on leaving Crimea."

Nikolai sighed and walked casually around the front of the Tigr to stand in front of the general. He wanted desperately to draw his PSS-2 silenced pistol and end the man's miserable existence. But killing one of the tsar's generals—no matter how inept—was a task he could not undertake without explicit permission. Instead, he shot out his hand and gripped the man's throat.

"You are as spineless as you are worthless," he hissed.

The general's hands clamped down on Nikolai's wrist, feebly attempting to pry his hand loose so he could breathe.

"You *will* accompany us to Nova Kakhovka," he said again. "Then you will wait there and keep forces in reserve until we have accomplished our objective. Am I clear?"

Morozov's eyes seemed to bulge wide, but he nodded.

Nikolai relaxed his grip, but kept his fingers wrapped around the fat man's neck. "If we call for help, I expect you to send gunships, air assault troopers, and every armored vehicle you have. And *you* will be in the first vehicle across the river."

The general nodded again.

"If you're not, you will wish the tsar had already recalled you to Moscow."

Nova Kakhovka
Kherson Oblast, Ukraine

Major General Morozov was silent as they crossed the five-kilometer-wide isthmus connecting the Crimean peninsula with mainland Ukraine. Were it not for the thin ribbon of land, the Syvash—or Putrid Sea—would have isolated Crimea from the rest of Ukraine. But with the red-hued wetlands on one side and the Black Sea on the other, the Russian armored convoy raced north for the front lines.

Nikolai Voronov sat in the backseat of Morozov's Tigr as his troops escorted the column into position. It had been as much to enjoy the comfort of the well-appointed staff vehicle as it had been to make sure the general followed his instructions to the letter.

When they arrived in the port city, the convoy halted well short of the river. Nikolai knew the general's engineers had been constructing a temporary bridge to span the section destroyed by the 205th Separate Motor Rifle Brigade. Their sabotage of the dam had been intended to prevent a Ukrainian counter-offensive when Russian forces consolidated on the southern shore, but now it only posed an obstacle to him reaching his objective. Nikolai's six-vehicle convoy would be the first across, following a relentless artillery barrage of Ukrainian defensive positions and a feint further downriver in Krynky.

"Are you sure six vehicles will be enough?" General Morozov asked, again stating his skepticism that Nikolai's plan would work.

"I need only one."

Morozov looked as if he was about to argue, but then reached up and massaged his throat where the intelligence operative had choked him. He fell silent and nodded once more to accept the terms. But Nikolai knew there was no way the general could understand what was at stake or that five of the six vehicles would engage the Ukrainian forces and provide a distraction for the Bumerang to slip away.

Nikolai stared into the darkness outside the Tigr and visualized his victory. If Viktor was right—and he usually was—it would be a short sprint from the river crossing to Yuzhnoukrainsk.

"Come," Morozov said. "Let's get you to your vehicle."

Nikolai nodded, then opened his door and climbed out of the Tigr. The convoy had halted several blocks from the hydroelectric power plant with each individual vehicle parked along tree-lined streets while waiting for the artillery barrage to begin. He walked around to the front of the Tigr and followed the general to the Bumerang.

Suddenly, a conscript raced forward and presented himself to the general. He had a worried look on his face and spoke in a rush, glancing over at Nikolai every few words as if to assess whether the stranger could overhear.

"What is it?" Nikolai asked.

Morozov issued orders to the conscript and sent him on his way before turning to Nikolai. "Our Mainstay in this sector has intercepted communications between a Ukrainian ground control station and an airborne Fulcrum."

Nikolai knew that several Beriev A-50 Mainstay surveillance aircraft had already been downed by Ukrainian forces. So he was pleased to hear that the military had committed another to keep an eye on the skies over Nova Kakhovka.

"Why is this concerning?"

"Because they mentioned our convoy and an attempted crossing," the general replied.

"*Pizdets!*"

Morozov gripped Nikolai by the elbow and pulled him onward. "Hurry. We must get you across now!"

13

Kherson Oblast, Ukraine

Starshyy Leytenant Polina Radchenko glanced underneath her night vision goggles at the blackness enveloping her cockpit. Unlike newer and more modern fighter aircraft that were designed with green NVG-compatible lighting, her aging MiG-29 Fulcrum was the product of a bygone era and came equipped with no such luxuries. To compensate for this, she had extinguished every light in the cockpit and purposely plunged herself into pitch black.

"Mech Five, control," the stern voice said.

"Go ahead for Mech Five," she replied.

"Vector south," the voice responded. "We received reports of Russian armor that recently moved north from Perekop attempting to cross at Nova Kakhovka."

Polina didn't need her instruments to know which direction was south. Even though the sun had set long ago, she could still see a glow on the western horizon through her night vision goggles. She pulled the stick against her right thigh to roll her fighter, then eased it back into her lap to pull the jet's nose smoothly across the horizon.

It was sluggish, but she might have expected that. In training, they had rarely flown with anything more than one or two R-73 short-range infrared homing air-to-air missiles—what the west called the AA-11 Archer. But ever since the Russians had invaded, she hadn't flown a sortie in the Fulcrum without also being laden with six 250 kg general-purpose unguided bombs.

"Mech Five is en route to the Dnieper River," she said, shoving the throttles forward to advance the Klimov RD-33 turbofan engines into afterburner. The glow surrounding the tail of her jet was visible even without the aid of her night vision goggles.

"Your target is a six-vehicle convoy on the southern shore."

"Don't the Russians control that side?"

Ukrainian forces had pretty well pushed the Russian invaders back across the Dnieper River, with the water acting as a natural barrier and preventing them from taking more ground at will. Even more so after the Russians had sabotaged the dam to destroy a section of the bridge and flood the lowlands downriver. Further to the east, where the river turned north, their forces were gripped in a never-ending battle to retake ground in the Donetsk and Luhansk regions.

Robotyne. Avdiivka. Bakhmut. Sometimes it felt to Polina as if they were but grains of sand, suffering the relentless onslaught of wave after wave of invading hordes. But the alternative was the end of Ukraine. And she was unwilling to accept that outcome.

Slava Ukraini!

"This appears to be in response to our push in Krynky," the controller said, displaying a surprising command of the tactical situation.

Though the Dnieper River had largely separated Russian and Ukrainian forces since Moscow's troops withdrew from Kherson, their push into Krynky appeared to be the foothold they needed to begin retaking Crimea—the peninsula illegally annexed by Russia over a decade earlier. But Polina didn't think in terms of strategic values for particular cities or pieces of land. It was her home, and she planned on fighting until every last Russian scum was dead or had fled back to Moscow.

"Roger," she replied, adjusting her course to aim for the hydroelectric power plant at Nova Kakhovka. Even at her distance, the glow of the city's lights was easy to see through her night vision.

Nearing the river, she reached for the SPO-15 Radar Warning System and moved the switch to select the "All" function mode, ensuring her greatest chance at detecting a threat before the sky was lit up by tracers or incoming missiles. As expected, the lamp above the "H" symbol illuminated, indicating that a Russian short-range radar was painting her aircraft.

"There you are," she muttered.

The direction light illuminated, showing the threat just right of her nose. She pushed forward on the stick and dropped to a lower altitude while bringing the Fulcrum out of afterburner. All her external lights were extinguished, and she raced into the fray at 650 kilometers per hour, her thirst for Russian blood almost overpowering.

"Mech Five, control, I've lost radar contact on you."

Polina grinned. "Good."

"Return to—"

"*Dermo!*"

Even at her low altitude, the MiG presented a juicy target for trigger-happy Russians. The sky in front of her lit up with tracers as the invaders responded to the sound of the approaching jet by firing blindly into the night sky and hoping for a direct hit. But she had something else in mind.

She abruptly banked left and pulled her nose up, rapidly trading her airspeed for altitude as she craned her neck to look down on the bridge the Russians were attempting to cross.

There!

Just as the controller had predicted, she saw the faint shapes of six evenly spaced armored vehicles beginning to edge onto the temporary bridge from the southern shore. Without even thinking about it, she increased her pull and adjusted the angle even further away to fine-tune her geometry. She had lost count of how many such missions she had flown against the Russian invaders, and her actions seemed almost rote—dispassionate and automatic.

A low-frequency tone sounded in her helmet, and she glanced down at the SPO-15 near her right knee where the light for an airborne radar secondary threat illuminated. The ground-based short-range radar was still the greatest threat—which was obvious from the growing web of tracer fire crisscrossing the sky—but that wouldn't last long. She needed to make quick work of this.

Reaching her desired altitude, Polina slapped the stick into her right thigh and rolled the Fulcrum onto its back, her eyes never leaving the lead vehicle in the convoy. She floated at the top for a beat longer, then stood up the throttles and pulled the stick into her lap to bring her nose back down to the earth.

"Mech Five attacking," she said, letting the ground-based controller know that her fangs were out and that he needed to keep her informed if the threat picture changed.

"A single Flanker has been vectored to your position."

She glanced back into the cockpit to ensure her Gardeniya jammer was active. "How far?"

"One hundred and twenty kilometers."

Not far, she thought.

But she couldn't worry about that now. In the lower left corner of her Heads Up Display, Polina saw that she was in "Visual Ground" mode and ready to unleash hell on her enemy. As she had done countless times before, she intended to make them pay for what they had done to her country, and she adjusted her pitch and angle of bank to steer the guidance cue onto the lead vehicle.

She watched the slant range rapidly decreasing in the HUD as her Fulcrum accelerated through five hundred kilometers per hour. She added a little forward pressure to the stick, countering the jet's natural inclination to pitch upward as the increase in airspeed resulted in an increase in lift. The unguided bombs required a precision she had perfected, and she ignored the tracers cutting through the sky on either side of her jet.

"*Yobtvoyumat'*," she said, pressing her thumb down on the pickle and holding it there until she felt her jet lurch as the first bomb fell away.

Polina smoothly pulled the stick into her lap and climbed back into the sky, banking hard to come up onto a wing as she craned her neck to look over her shoulder at the convoy racing across the bridge.

Three... two... one...

KA-BOOM!

A smile cracked her lips when her bomb impacted the lead vehicle, showering the bridge with debris as the Russian armored personnel carrier exploded. A split second later, another explosion rocked the bridge as the vehicle's ammunition detonated, forcing the remainder of the convoy to halt their advance across the river.

Just as she had wanted.

She rolled out heading northeast with the burning wreckage at her six o'clock and again dropped to a low altitude while putting distance between herself and the Russians. Her next attack wouldn't come as a surprise, and she knew they would put up everything they had to prevent her from wreaking havoc on the stalled convoy. But she was confident. Her victory was pre-ordained.

Polina banked right to cross the river east of the bridge and enter airspace the Russians claimed dominance over. But she refused to acknowledge it. This was *her* country. If she wanted to be successful in destroying the convoy, she needed to vary her direction of approach.

And they would never expect her to attack from behind their lines.

"Mech Five, control." The controller sounded almost frantic.

"Go ahead," she replied, just as she banked to the right and began to climb for her second attack.

The tone in her helmet sounded again, and she glanced down at the SPO-15 to see that the primary threat had shifted from the ground-based radar to the airborne radar. But the light strip had less than a half dozen lights illuminated, indicating that the Flanker's radar was still far enough away not to be a major concern.

"The Flanker has closed to seventy kilometers."

"Roger," she replied, then banked left to roll in on the convoy again.

14

Nova Kakhovka
Kherson Oblast, Ukraine

Nikolai stared in disbelief at the glowing wreckage of the BTR-80 blocking their way forward. He sat in the Bumerang's crew compartment with ringing ears as the scene unfolded on one of the console's two twenty-five-centimeter screens. But instead of using it to track a target for the laser weapon, the operator at the control station manipulated the Advanced Dual Optical Tracking System to give them a front row seat to ten of his countrymen being burned alive.

"We're sitting ducks!" he screamed, straining to be heard over the Bumerang's rumbling diesel. "Keep moving—"

KA-BOOM!

Nikolai flinched as a second explosion rocked the convoy. "Where'd that come from?"

"The trail vehicle," Yevgeny replied, his voice surprisingly calm despite the chaos surrounding them. "They've boxed us in."

Nikolai slammed his fist against the armored wall. "Keep moving, dammit!"

The diesel engine roared as the driver heeded his suggestion and surged backward, ramming into the nose of the BTR-80 behind them. They jolted to a stop.

"Not that way!" Nikolai screamed. "Move forward!"

The transmission shifted with a clunk and screech, and Nikolai lurched back as they again moved toward the Ukrainian side of the river. He kept his eyes glued to the monitor as the driver weaved around the stalled vehicle in front of them and the weapon operator scanned the opposite shore for obstacles that would prevent them from reaching safety.

He had no way of knowing if the three vehicles they left in their wake had followed their lead, but it was too late for that now. They had crossed the temporary bridge Morozov's engineers had erected and were on the original span. If they didn't reach cover on the opposite shore before the Ukrainian fighter came around for another pass, they would be easy pickings for the pilot.

"The artillery barrage is beginning," Yevgeny said, panning the camera to focus on a series of bright flashes lighting up the Ukrainian defensive positions. A split second later, Nikolai felt more than heard faint *thumps* as Morozov's mortar teams dropped round after round of 120 mm high-explosive projectiles on the opposite shore.

"Go faster," Nikolai urged.

The driver's voice echoed in his headset with a trace of fear edging his words. "Sir?"

"Faster," he repeated.

There was only a brief hesitation before the engine groaned louder and the Bumerang picked up speed. He understood why the driver was hesitant. The incoming mortar rounds were falling indiscriminately and would destroy them just as easily as a Ukrainian vehicle, and they were racing closer to the explosions.

But it was their only chance of reaching the other side before the pilot came around for another pass and picked off the rest of their column one by one.

"Sir, the Fulcrum is inbound for another attack," Yevgeny said.

Nikolai looked down at the monitor just as the jet rolled wings level with its nose pointed right at them.

"Driver, stop!"

The Bumerang came to a skidding halt.
This is going to be close.

Polina rolled wings level and ignored the artillery rounds exploding just left of her nose, cocking her head in surprise when she noticed the lead vehicle come to an abrupt stop in the middle of the bridge. But she quickly shrugged it off as just another poor tactical error the Russian conscripts were notorious for. Their mistake would be their undoing.

Though her eyes never stopped scanning or processing the incredible amount of data presented to her through the Heads Up Display, she relied on her "seat of the pants" feeling to time the release. Her instincts had made her one of the deadliest pilots in her squadron, and she placed her thumb on the pickle just as the deep humming of airflow around her canopy reverberated through the cockpit.

Now!

She pressed down hard on the pickle switch until she felt the familiar lurching of her jet upward as the bomb fell away. Then she snatched back on the stick to arrest her descent and banked right to pull her nose around to the Russian mortar positions. Without a second thought, she selected the GSh-30-1 30 mm auto cannon and overbanked her jet while moving her finger to the trigger.

Her eyes found the gun's aiming reticle in the HUD with ease, and she waited until it settled over the mortar positions in defilade before squeezing the trigger. The pitch black enveloping her cockpit was torn apart as balls of fire erupted just over her left shoulder and the jet vibrated with the sharp staccato of a two-second burst. Her eyes tracked the tracers as they snaked toward the earth, walking the sixty high-explosive projectiles—almost half her total load—into the Russian mortar positions.

Poshol na khuy!

Releasing the trigger, she snatched her nose up and reversed her pull while looking over her shoulder at the bomb detonating on the bridge. The flash illuminated the lead vehicle she had been targeting, but that brief glimpse was enough to see that she had missed. The armored vehicle must have moved during the bomb's free fall.

Yobtvoyumat'

"Mech Five, control."

"Go ahead," Polina said, putting aside her simmering anger at missing her target.

"Vector heading zero seven zero," the controller said.

She glanced down at the SPO-15 and saw the radar's strength reach near maximum with the yellow elevation hemisphere illuminated to indicate that the approaching Flanker was above her. She flipped the switch to put the radar warning receiver into "Lock" mode, giving her the best chance at detecting when the Russian fighter was preparing to fire.

When she didn't respond, the controller repeated his command. "Turn northeast immediately. Threat range fifty kilometers."

"Negative," Polina replied.

She had an advantage at being low altitude and knew that the Flanker's radar would struggle to retain a lock if she remained in the ground clutter. She might only get one shot at this, and it was her best chance at taking out the Russian jet.

"What?"

"I have a better idea."

Nikolai braced himself as the explosion rocked the Bumerang, the shock wave tilting it dangerously to one side. He had only guessed at how long it would take the bomb to fall when he screamed at the driver and told him to floor it. Even if he had timed it correctly, there had been no guarantee the lumbering armored personnel carrier would move fast enough to clear the blast radius.

But luck had favored him. Aside from the deafening concussion of the bomb's blast and the soft plinking of metal on metal as shrapnel impacted the Bumerang's armored walls, they were none the worse for wear. Nikolai muttered a hurried prayer of thanks but kept his eyes glued to the display screen as the operator struggled to maintain a visual track on the retreating fighter jet.

"The Fulcrum is fleeing," Yevgeny said, pointing at the screen that showed the twin-engine jet's glowing exhaust as it turned away from the bridge.

"Why?" Nikolai was unwilling to believe they were out of the woods yet.

"One of our Flankers is chasing it away."

"This is our chance," he said. "Make for the other side as fast as possible."

Through the thick armor, Nikolai heard the sound of machine guns firing and the distant thumps of mortar rounds pummeling the Ukrainian defenses. They just needed to make it to the other side and disappear into the countryside before the artillery let up. Or the Fulcrum spotted them making a run for it.

The operator panned the camera to their rear, showing the remaining three vehicles from the original six sitting idle in the middle of the bridge. But each of their turrets were spitting fire, their crews apparently satisfied with only using their 30 mm Shipunov autocannons to lay down covering fire while halting their advance.

"Bastards!" Nikolai muttered.

The Bumerang was the only vehicle continuing onward, making them an easy target for the Ukrainians if the artillery let up.

"Ready the laser," he said.

Yevgeny turned and cast a sideways glance but wisely remained silent. Instead, his fingers began flying across the controls to prepare the directed energy weapon for operation. Nikolai suspected the former soldier intuited that it was their only offensive capability since their own turret's autocannon had been replaced with the *DRAGON LINE*.

"Yes, sir."

A deep humming sound slowly grew louder and drowned out the turbodiesel's throaty exhaust. Nikolai could almost feel the electricity in the air. He knew the weapon's power supply needed several minutes to generate and store enough power for the laser to be effective. He just hoped they had enough time.

15

Polina knew she was playing an almost reverse game of chicken. She had no chance of outrunning the Flanker or even hoping to draw it deeper into Ukrainian airspace where their air defenses could bring it down. Her only chance was to pitch back into the enemy fighter and handle it herself.

Fortunately, she was accustomed to this.

"What's his range now?"

The controller's response was immediate. "I don't have you on radar—"

His excuse was drowned out by a high-pitched tone in her helmet, accompanied by a brilliant red flashing light in the middle of her SPO-15 radar warning receiver.

"Missile launch!" she shouted for the controller's benefit.

Without waiting for a response, she immediately slapped the stick into her left thigh, then yanked it back into her lap while craning her neck to look over her shoulder. Though it was pitch black outside, she knew Russian air-to-air missiles burned hot enough that she ought to be able to pick up the incoming missile using her night vision goggles.

Where are you?

She hazarded a glance back into her cockpit, assessing the array of lights and symbols on her radar warning receiver. Had the Flanker fired an active radar homing missile like the Vympel R-77—what the west called the

AA-12 Adder—the primary threat would have shifted when the missile's internal radar went active.

But it hadn't.

Her lips curled up in a hesitant smile, straining against the rising G-forces as she continued pulling her nose onto the attacking Russian fighter. Knowing that the missile wasn't actively homing on her aircraft was good news. It meant that the Flanker had likely fired some variant of the Vympel R-27, a semi-active radar-guided missile known as the AA-10 Alamo. And if the Flanker's radar was providing guidance, then she had two opportunities to avoid being swatted from the sky and becoming a smoking hole in the ground.

She could either defeat the missile itself—if she managed to gain a tally on it—or she could defeat the Flanker's radar. Either way, it was the best news she could hope for.

"Mech Five, status?" The controller sounded nervous.

"Stand by."

After 120 degrees of turn, she spotted the incoming missile's smoke trail. Polina eased her pull and placed her wingtip on the Flanker while keeping sight of the missile. If it remained in the same place on her canopy, it meant that the missile was continuing to guide on her jet. But if it started drifting aft, it meant that she had likely broken the Flanker's radar lock.

But the flashing red light and glowing yellow light strip on her radar warning receiver were enough to assure her that the four-meter-long missile was still the biggest threat.

"Come on," she muttered to herself, ignoring the sudden dryness in her mouth.

It wasn't her first time being fired on or even her first time tangling with a frontline Russian fighter. But it never got any easier. Everything came down to timing. And knowing when to shift her focus from the Flanker to the missile was the key to surviving this engagement.

From the corner of her eye, she noticed the red light stop flashing as the tone in her helmet changed in pitch. Filled with sudden hope, her eyes flashed down to the radar warning receiver and noticed one of the lights extinguish on the bar representing the strength of the threat's radar. Then a second light went out. Then a third.

Her eyes shot back up to the spot on her canopy where she had fixed the incoming missile and noticed that it had slid aft.

She instantly recognized the telltale signs that the Flanker's radar had lost its lock on her jet and was sending erroneous commands to the missile. So, she increased her angle of bank and pulled hard to bring her nose around on the pursuing Russian fighter. Her fangs were out, and she barely noticed as the missile sailed past her jet and detonated harmlessly in the night.

"Mech Five is engaging," she said, straining against the G-forces while angling her helmet to guide her Vympel R-73 missile's seeker onto the Flanker's hot exhaust.

She was thankful the intercept controller had remained silent. All her focus was on the descending Russian fighter and the tone in her helmet that represented her seeker's ability to guide on the targeted heat source. As the pitch rose and volume increased, she placed her finger on the trigger and squeezed.

"Mech Five firing," she announced.

But her missile launch hadn't gone unnoticed. Instantly, the Flanker banked into her and began jettisoning infrared countermeasure flares in an attempt to decoy her missile. But the missile known as the AA-11 Archer had a robust capability to ignore the decoy flares and continue homing on her target.

Come on, come on, come on.

A second salvo of flares fanned away from the Flanker, and she held her breath while waiting to see where her missile detonated. Less than a second later, the Archer impacted a decoy flare with a disappointing flash.

Now we're even.

They had each defeated an incoming missile, but she knew she still had the edge. While the ground clutter had been the likely culprit of the Russian losing its radar lock on her jet, she was still fortunate to have nothing but clear skies backdropping her target. It was the perfect environment for employing the Archer. She just needed to gain a more advantageous position to prevent her second shot from also being defeated.

"My first shot missed," Polina said.

"Copy. Vector north for—"

"No, I'm maneuvering for a second shot," she said, cutting off the controller's well-meaning guidance. "I'm not letting him get away."

When the last of the IRCM flares burned out, she caught a glimpse of the Flanker reversing direction as the pilot maneuvered to gain sight. But she had already positioned herself underneath the Russian fighter and was pulling to maneuver aft into his control zone. Though her Fulcrum didn't carry the most advanced version of the infrared homing missile, it still had an impressive off-boresight capability. And that meant she didn't need to point directly at the Russian fighter for the seeker to lock on to its exhaust.

Polina was patient. Another hasty engagement would almost certainly result in her second and final missile again being defeated by flares. Then she would be left only with the remaining ninety rounds of 30 mm in her Gryazev-Shipunov autocannon. That wouldn't be near enough to take on the advanced fighter.

"Mech Five, status."

She wanted to roll her eyes but didn't dare take them off the Flanker. Based on the way the pilot maneuvered, she was almost certain the Russian didn't know where she was.

"Stand by," she replied, again reminding the controller that she was busy.

The Flanker's wings waggled slightly from side to side, as if its pilot had reached an impasse and was unsure of which direction to turn. But then it suddenly banked right, and its exhaust glowed brighter as the pilot pushed up on the power to gain speed and retreat back to the safety of its base in Crimea.

Again, she angled her helmet to guide the missile's seeker onto the retreating Russian. Again, she listened for the tone rise indicating that her final Archer had locked onto the Flanker's exhaust. And, again, she placed her finger on the trigger and readied to fire.

"*Putinkhuylo!*"

Starshyy Leytenant Polina Radchenko squeezed the trigger and watched the heat-seeking missile streak forward from her wingline and arc up into the retreating Flanker. For a moment, she almost expected the Russian fighter to salvo another round of IRCM flares and defeat her last missile. But a second after that, she realized that her victory had been indeed pre-ordained.

She stared in fascination as the Archer streaked through the night sky like a comet and impacted the Flanker's tail. The detonation of the seven-kilogram warhead seemed almost pitiful, its flash brilliant but disappointingly small.

But then a second and larger flash followed half a second later as shrapnel pierced one of the Flanker's engines, causing it to tear itself apart and ultimately explode. Debris from that first disintegrated engine carried into the second and caused a third and even larger flash. Like an unstoppable chain reaction, the third explosion was followed by a fourth, then fifth, each one larger than its predecessor.

At last, the Flanker's remaining jet fuel ignited, and the frontline Russian fighter was engulfed in a massive fireball that glowed hot over the Ukrainian countryside. Polina stared with wide-eyed fascination until the fighter broke apart and tumbled to the earth in a shower of fiery debris.

But her growing smile faltered a little when one final flash caught her attention.

The Russian pilot had ejected.

16

The laser weapon was fully charged and ready to fire by the time the Bumerang reached the opposite shore. Nikolai sat next to Yevgeny with his eyes glued to the liquid-crystal display as he panned and tilted the sensor to look for a target. So far, it seemed as if Morozov's artillery had succeeded in keeping the *khokhlushka* at bay.

The driver accelerated and weaved between the large obstacles Ukrainian soldiers had placed in the road to slow advancing Russian vehicles. But the operator pivoted the sensor to scan the tree line on their left, unable to believe they could escape the gauntlet thrown in their way. "Is that..."

But he fell silent, and Nikolai's eyes grew wide at seeing the sharp nose of an armored personnel carrier emerge from the forest's shadows. He dug his fingers into the operator's shoulder, but the man had already seen the same thing and centered the crosshairs on a BTR-7, an improvement on the original Soviet BTR-70.

Nikolai reacted instinctively. "Target PC, front left, two thousand meters."

It was an unnecessary call, because Yevgeny had already engaged the target illuminator laser to provide engagement-quality tracking information to the *DRAGON LINE*. "Identified," he replied.

"Fire."

"On the way."

Unlike a traditional armor engagement that was followed by the concussive blast of a tank's main gun firing on the target, the only change in sound inside the Bumerang was an increase in pitch of the electric humming. A beam of light appeared on the screen as the Advanced Dual Optical Tracking System detected the high energy laser firing into the Ukrainian eight-wheeled armored vehicle.

The thick armor just beneath the turret glowed red hot as the laser punched a hole into the nose of the target.

"Cease fire," Nikolai said.

Instantly, the beam of light disappeared. The BTR-7 came to an abrupt stop as smoke billowed from the newly made hole. Then a split second later the vehicle shook with a series of explosions as its ammunition cooked off from the extreme heat.

"Out of action," Yevgeny said before pivoting the sensor right to continue scanning along the tree line. Again, the humming dropped to a lower octave as the energy source began building and storing power for a second shot.

"Driver, get us out of here," Nikolai shouted. He was thankful that the laser weapon had performed flawlessly but was uncomfortable with still being out in the open. The earsplitting roar of the diesel engine grew even louder as the Bumerang raced north.

Several seconds later, the wooded area left of the main road ended and they entered an open area that was exposed on all sides. Yevgeny seemed to feel the same unease, because he pivoted the sensor left and right, frantically searching for another enemy tank or armored personnel carrier that might maneuver to block them. They had another kilometer to travel before reaching the uninhabited countryside where they could vanish into the open fields.

"Anything?" Nikolai asked.

The operator shook his head, but beads of sweat ran down the sides of his face from the exertion of his search. "*Nyet.*"

Polina soared higher into the sky while straining to keep sight of the parachute floating down to earth. Part of her wished the winds would just carry the pilot into the Dnieper River and let fate have its way with the Russian invader. But another part of her wanted the aviator to land on the Ukrainian side of the river so her countrymen could capture him and make him pay for what he'd done to her country.

"Mech Five, control," the controller said. "The skies are clear."

She nodded but still glanced down at her radar warning receiver anyway. The SPO-15 showed only a weak signal emanating from a ground radar on the Russian side, confirming what the controller said was true. She was safe where she was, though she knew enough to avoid flying directly over the Russian positions where they could target her MiG-29 Fulcrum with shoulder-fired man-portable air defense systems and small arms.

"Copy," she replied. "The Flanker's pilot ejected and appears to be coming down on the north side of the river. Stand by for grid coordinates."

There was a slight delay before the controller answered. "Ready to copy."

Polina read off a set of grid coordinates to the controller, though she still hoped an errant gust of wind might carry the pilot into the water where he would drown under the weight of his survival gear. But that was probably too merciful for a man who had tried killing her only minutes earlier.

A rising tone in her helmet indicated a change to the threats targeting her jet, and she glanced down again to see yet another ground-based radar painting the night sky. The Russians were still looking for her.

"Looks like another radar just went active," Polina said.

"Affirm," the controller replied. "Might be a Shilka."

She had thought the same thing, and she took her eyes off the Russian's chute to scan the southern shore for massive balls of fire arcing up to swat her from the sky. The ZSU-23-4 Shilka was a lightly armored tracked vehicle with four 23 mm autocannons that used its own radar for guiding onto airborne threats. But as long as she remained outside its range, she should be okay.

She looked back to the northern shore just as the Russian pilot came down underneath an avalanche of silk. Suddenly worried he might disappear into the night and evade capture, she scanned the immediate surroundings and saw only darkness.

"Are forces being sent to the pilot's location?" Polina asked.

"Stand by," the controller replied.

She banked away and returned her focus to the southern shore once more to scan for muzzle flashes or blossoms of light warning her of an impending missile launch. But it was still dark.

Except for the faint glow of an object moving quickly across the ground. She squinted through her night vision goggles for several seconds before recognizing the unmistakable shape of a helicopter racing north at low altitude from behind the Russians' lines.

She cursed under her breath.

The Bumerang sprinted north on the two-lane blacktop for a thousand meters before reaching a stretch with nothing but open fields and narrow bands of trees stretching away in every direction. Yevgeny panned the sensor to the right, looking for a break in the crops they could exploit to disappear into the countryside.

"Drakon Six," the voice said over the command net.

Nikolai groaned at hearing Morozov's voice in his headset, but he keyed the microphone switch to respond to the general. "What do you want?"

"One of our pilots ejected and came down near your location."

Nikolai knew the general's open-ended statement was intended to elicit a voluntary offer to use the Bumerang to rescue the pilot. But that was the last thing he planned on doing. The specially configured armored vehicle wasn't intended to be a frontline weapon system and had been committed to an operation that was of greater importance than rescuing a single pilot.

"Please thank him for his sacrifice," Nikolai answered.

The radio remained silent for several seconds before Morozov's voice returned, full of bluster. "Drakon Six, I am ordering you to proceed directly to his position and ensure his rescue—"

Nikolai reached up and turned the radio off, ending the general's tirade.

Yevgeny looked over his shoulder and shot him a questioning glance. Nikolai shrugged.

"We will continue as planned," he said over the intercom, ending any doubt that they would continue with their mission.

"There!" the operator shouted suddenly, pointing at the display screen.

Nikolai saw what he was referring to, a break in the sprawling fields of loamy soil that played host to rows upon rows of tomatoes. "Driver, right two o'clock," he shouted, eager to be off the main road before the Ukrainian forces realized a Russian vehicle had made it behind their lines.

The driver acknowledged by steering the Bumerang right and dropping off the main road and into the soft gravel on the shoulder. The armored vehicle's suspension groaned as they careened into the field, clipping several stakes and smashing through tomato plants before finding the gap that would take them into the countryside.

Nikolai slapped Yevgeny on the back. "Well done."

The man had already returned his focus to the screen to continue scanning for threats. They still needed to travel almost two hundred kilometers behind enemy lines to reach their objective. There would be no room for complacency in the coming days.

17

The helicopter was operating lights-out, but Polina had been flying combat patrols on night vision goggles long enough to become adept at interpreting the shifting shadows and varying shades of green. The helicopter's rotor blades appeared to sparkle in the dim moonlight and gave her a clear target to track visually, even if she couldn't acquire a lock with her N019 pulse Doppler radar.

Not that it mattered. Her Fulcrum hadn't been loaded with semi-active radar-guided missiles like the Russian Flanker, and she had expended both of her heat-seeking missiles in bringing it down. Worst of all, thanks to her impulsive two-second burst on the Russian mortar positions, she had little more than that left in her GSh-30-1 30 mm auto cannon.

Two seconds, she thought with a little shake of her head.

Polina remained on the north side of the river and out of range from the Russian ZSU-23-4 Shilka that had begun painting her not long before she spotted the Mi-8 helicopter. At most, she would get only one shot at it, and her greatest chance would come when it was stationary. And that meant waiting until it had crossed the river and set down at the pilot's location.

"Control, Mech Five, I have a visual on a Russian helicopter nearing the river."

"Copy."

She looked away from the chopper and scanned the northern shore, hoping to see Ukrainian forces converging on the downed aviator. But still nothing.

"How much longer?"

The controller's response was almost predictable. "Stand by."

She cursed under her breath again, then reached for a penlight to illuminate her fuel quantity indicator adjacent to the SPO-15. The white vertical bar had dropped dangerously low and was nearing the red horizontal line indicating her minimum fuel quantity. If she waited much longer, she might not have enough to make it back to Voznesensk Reserve Air Base.

"Never mind. I'll take care of it myself."

She hadn't meant to key the microphone switch and transmit her frustration to the controller, but she wasn't upset that she had. After all, she was the one who had been dodging bullets and missiles all night to stop the Russians from gaining more ground.

But the controller understood and remained quiet.

Polina completed another orbit just as the rescue helicopter crossed the southern shore and pointed directly at the downed pilot in its race to beat the Ukrainian forces sent to capture him. But she still saw no sign of her countrymen and knew it was a race the helicopter would win.

Selecting the gun, Polina watched the sparkling rotor blades of the Russian helicopter cross the northern shore and hover over the pilot's position. It had obviously homed in on a radio beacon of some kind and was now stationary.

"Mech Five, attacking," she said.

Selecting the gun, Polina increased her pull to bring her nose around, then rolled the Fulcrum onto its back and pulled down until she was pointed directly at the helicopter. Rolling upright, she pulled her throttles to idle and eliminated almost fifty kilonewtons of thrust from her afterburning turbofan engines. Now, only her momentum and the Earth's gravity pulled her onward.

Unlike other strafing runs, she wanted to be as slow as possible to maximize her ability to control the gun's pipper and put as many of her ninety remaining rounds as possible into the rescue helicopter. But it only took one to hit a critical component.

Polina watched the slant range decrease in her Heads Up Display while caressing the trigger with her index finger. Normally, she would try to limit her strafing runs to one second, giving her multiple opportunities to hit her target. But between her rapidly disappearing fuel and the sense of urgency to take down the chopper before it could abscond with the Russian fighter pilot, she planned on one long three-second burst.

Her right hand made several twitching adjustments to the stick, and her eyes studied the pipper's corresponding movement before settling over the sparkling rotor blades. She took a deep breath, then squeezed the trigger.

Flames erupted over her left shoulder as her autocannon spit high-explosive rounds at the defenseless helicopter. Her Fulcrum vibrated with the onslaught, and she gritted her teeth while moving the stick to adjust her pitch and angle of bank and danced on the pedals to fan the fiery rope left and right.

One... two... thr—

The gun stopped firing, and Polina snatched back on the stick to arrest her descent before jinking right. When her nose was pointed safely away from the chopper, she reversed her turn to assess the damage. It was little more than a blur as she raced by, but she saw enough to know that it was still airborne and would make it safely back across the Russian lines.

"Mech Five is returning to base," she said, her disappointment dripping from each word.

Voznesensk Reserve Air Base
Voznesensk, Mykolaiv Oblast, Ukraine

Colt jerked awake when the MC-130J touched down and its propellers changed pitch to redirect thrust forward and slow the cargo plane. It wasn't the smoothest landing or rollout, but compared to slamming onto the flight deck of an aircraft carrier in the back of a COD, it felt almost luxurious.

He looked over at Dave and shook his head in amazement at seeing the SEAL still fast asleep. His head bobbed with the Herc's undulating movement as it taxied clear of the runway. A soft whine filled the cargo bay as the ramp lowered and exposed the pitch black of night, disappointing Colt yet again that they still had several hours before he could get some proper sleep.

In the end, the president's authorization to move the task force forward from Poland had come quicker than anyone expected. After tracking an armor convoy from Perekop to Nova Kakhovka, it quickly became apparent that it wasn't a large-scale offensive operation and was more than likely a decoy for something else. Unfortunately, they already knew what that something was.

The lumbering cargo plane came to a stop and the engines spooled down, indicating that they had arrived at their destination. Colt unstrapped and stood from the uncomfortable webbed seat, letting his personal defense weapon hang from its sling in front of his body. He turned and peered out into the darkness, scarcely able to believe they had just landed in the middle of a war zone.

"Whatcha thinking?" Dave asked, sidling up next to him.

On the horizon, Colt saw a muted glow in the clouds followed by the distant rumble of an explosion. Whether it was caused by inbound Russian artillery and bombs or Ukrainian air defenses, it didn't change the fact that Colt was about to experience war in a far more intimate manner than he ever had before. Combat looked different on the ground than from thirty thousand feet.

"Do you really think the president is going to give us the green light?"

Colt turned to look at the SEAL master chief, whose eyes were narrowed and studying the same glow on the horizon. He was silent for a moment, but then nodded. "Yeah, I do. He can't take the chance that terrorists will get their hands on these weapons. Russia having nukes is one thing. But can you imagine how much worse 9/11 would have been if Al-Qa'ida had used nukes?"

The SEAL had a point. It didn't seem the president had much of a choice.

Dave seemed to sense Colt's unease, and he placed his large hand on the back of his neck and gave it a squeeze. "Relax, flyboy. You've trained them well."

Another series of explosions rippled across the horizon and broke Colt free from his trance. He took a step forward to drop from the ramp and set foot on Ukrainian soil for the first time—just one more country added to his list. But this one felt different. Maybe it was because nobody knew they were there. Maybe it was because he knew what was at stake. Or maybe it was because he knew they would be facing off against Russians and had grown up under the specter of the Soviet bear.

Dave dropped down onto the tarmac next to him just as the unmistakable sound of an approaching fighter jet drew his eyes skyward. Colt tensed and stared into the darkness, trying to identify the single jet arcing across the sky.

"Is it Russian?" Dave asked.

Colt squinted, straining to make out features that might allow him to identify it, but he shook his head. "I don't know. I can't quite see it."

Cubby and Ron dropped down from the ramp and immediately turned to look at the jet that had rolled out and was pointed directly at them. "Who is that?" Cubby asked.

"Starshyy Leytenant Radchenko," the heavily accented voice said. "One of ours."

Colt turned back and watched the MiG-29 Fulcrum fly at high speed and low altitude down the length of the runway before pitching up and turning downwind. He had spent a career observing fighter jets, but this was his first time seeing the former Soviet fighter up close. It wasn't particularly sexy—rugged and utilitarian even—and was antiquated compared to the Super Hornet and Joint Strike Fighter.

But the pilot sure knew how to fly it.

"I am Polkovnyk Ivan Kovalenko," the officer said. "Welcome to Voznesensk Reserve Air Base. If you would please follow me, I will escort you to your temporary quarters."

Colt nodded respectfully to the senior officer. He was unfamiliar with the rank structure or insignia of the Ukrainian military, but he suspected Kovalenko was an air force colonel, or the equivalent of a navy captain.

"Thank you, sir. I'm Lieutenant Commander Colt Bancroft." He gestured to the others. "And we are grateful for your hospitality."

The colonel sighed, then turned and began shuffling back into the night. The airfield had a single eight-thousand-foot runway with more than two dozen hardened aircraft shelters, though task force analysts estimated that at least half of them were unusable. The base had been home to the 115th Guards Assault Aviation Division not long after Germany offered its unconditional surrender to the allies in the Second World War. But it later housed a Soviet fighter aviation regiment during the height of the Cold War.

And it looked like the base hadn't changed much since then.

"How many aircraft are based here?" Cubby asked, falling in alongside the colonel.

Kovalenko glanced over his shoulder at Cubby before answering. "We should have an entire squadron but are down to only four MiG-29s."

Colt turned back just as the Fulcrum they had seen approaching the airfield touched down and rolled out on the runway. He had flown combat missions in the skies over Iraq and Afghanistan, but he imagined what the Ukrainian pilots were experiencing was vastly different. Not only were they flying over their homeland, but they were facing off against numerically and technologically superior airborne threats while their own force dwindled to just a handful of combat-capable aircraft.

As if the colonel could read Colt's mind, he continued. "Our brigade is based at Lutsk Air Base, but we have been forced to disperse squadrons closer to the front lines." He waved his hand at the Fulcrum as it exited the runway and taxied to one of the hardened shelters on the northern end of the airfield. "And so, we're left with only a handful of capable pilots defending our country with outdated hardware."

"I can't imagine the toll the war has taken—"

Kovalenko wheeled on him. "*War?* This isn't a *war*. This is an invasion justified by a bully's weak claims of defending against fascist ideology and aggression from a *Western-armed* Ukraine." The colonel shook his head and held up four fingers. "I have only four fighters I can use to defend my country against this aggression. Four. And they are all former Soviet fighters." He spat. "*Western armed.*"

"I didn't mean…"

But Colt trailed off. He could tell just by looking at the senior officer that he was tired. Their forces were in a constant state of conflict. Unlike the American military that had grown accustomed to deploying for six months to a year before returning home for much needed rest and recovery, Ukrainian forces weren't given the luxury of a reprieve. They were literally scraping by with nothing but their fierce resolve to sustain them.

The colonel locked eyes with Colt for several seconds, then nodded. "I understand why your president wants to avoid provoking the tsar. I have seen the atrocities perpetrated by his army and believe he wouldn't hesitate to use nuclear weapons to avoid embarrassment."

"That's why we're here," Cubby said.

Kovalenko turned to the other pilot with an expressionless mask. "I have only been told to provide you with whatever assistance you require. But maybe you can tell me why you are in my country."

Colt suddenly wished Freaq had chosen to ride down on the MC-130 instead of him. He wasn't sure what information he was authorized to share with the Ukrainian colonel, but he figured it didn't matter much. If they were going to prevent the suitcase nukes from falling into the hands of Russians intent on selling them to terrorists in the Middle East, they were going to need the colonel's support.

Colt nodded. "After we get settled, I'd be happy to share with you what we know."

The colonel seemed to accept Colt's answer and turned to lead them up a narrow walkway to an isolated corrugated metal hangar surrounded by trees on three sides. The space wasn't much to look at. The walls were lined with a pale green tile that reminded Colt of Soviet interior design from every Cold War spy movie he had binged in his youth. At one time, it might have been possible to find beauty in its simplicity. But that was before decades of neglect had relegated the structure to nothing more than a glimpse into a less prosperous past.

Thick sheets of fabric covered the windows, blocking much of the single bulb's glow from reaching the outside. It was unlikely Russian forces would attack something as insignificant as a reserve air base with only four aircraft, but such discretion had allowed them to survive for as long as they had. The colonel sat on an uncomfortable-looking metal chair and gestured for the others to join him around the large table at the center of the room.

"Please tell me why you are in my country."

Colt glanced at Dave, who gave him a subtle nod, then took a seat opposite the colonel. "We have received intelligence regarding a former KGB cache site near Yuzhnoukrainsk that might contain up to four RA-115 tactical nuclear weapons—"

"So-called suitcase nukes," the colonel said, his tone somewhat skeptical.

Colt nodded. "And that same intelligence suggests that former Russian intelligence operatives are moving to retrieve the weapons with intent to sell them on the black market."

Kovalenko reached into his pocket and removed a crumpled cellophane-wrapped pack of Parliament cigarettes. He shook one free from the end and perched it between his lips while digging around in his other pocket for his lighter. The unlit cigarette jostled as he spoke. "Did you know Philip Morris donated half a million packs to our military?"

The idea of lighting up indoors was completely foreign to Colt, and he watched as the colonel sparked a flame and held it to the end of the cigarette. With a snap, he closed the lighter and slid it back into his pocket.

"And they have committed $30 million to launching a new production facility in Lviv." Kovalenko pursed his lips and drew the smoke into his lungs. He closed his eyes as nicotine bonded to his dopamine receptors and triggered a pleasure response, then exhaled the blue-tinged smoke into the air above the table. "But one in five packs of cigarettes sold in Ukraine is counterfeit. Who's to say these suitcase nukes aren't also counterfeit?"

The Americans watched silently as the Ukrainian colonel smoked his cigarette, knowing it was probably one of the rare pleasures he allowed himself.

Colt could understand his reluctance to take the intelligence at face value, but he couldn't fathom sitting idle when there was even a chance that a weapon with such capacity for destruction could wind up in the wrong hands. "So, you propose we do nothing?"

His eyes twitched up and met Colt's gaze, and he shrugged. "As I said, I have been instructed to provide you with whatever you need. But I don't believe there is a cache of RA-115 nuclear devices—if they even existed—in a former KGB storage facility that has gone undetected for over three decades. I'm sorry, but your president is being made to look the fool."

Colt felt his face flush, and he stiffened his back as if good posture was the only way of defending his commander in chief's honor. But he kept his fingers interlaced on the table in front of him and struggled to keep his composure. "I'm sure your country suffers the same malady. Politicians make decisions that put the military in harm's way, and we are left with adapting to a poor tactical situation."

Kovalenko took another drag from his cigarette, its cherry burning hot as the colonel's eyes narrowed. He exhaled the smoke with a chuckle. "Yes, this is true. We suffer the same."

Sensing an easing of tensions, Dave leaned forward and addressed the colonel. "We were deployed here from Poland because one of our ISR assets detected a small column of Russian armored vehicles gathering along the Dnieper River."

The colonel nodded. "Yes, yes. Starshyy Leytenant Radchenko has just returned from there."

Colt breathed a sigh of relief that maybe there was no longer a threat. But before his body completely relaxed, the door flew open and a Ukrainian fighter pilot walked in from the darkness, still fully dressed in bulky helmet and cumbersome survival gear.

"Just in time," the colonel said.

Colt's mouth fell open when the pilot removed her flight helmet and revealed long blonde hair that fell halfway down her back. "Who's that?"

The colonel ignored his question. "Polina, how was your mission to stop the Russians from breaking through our defenses."

She held Colt's gaze for several seconds before turning back to Kovalenko. "A disaster," she said.

18

US Naval Academy
Annapolis, Maryland

Punky walked along the redbrick path with her eyes fixed firmly on the massive granite building in front of her. It loomed over a courtyard whose entrance was guarded by cannons on either side, and whose space seemed overly imposing for its intended purpose. But she suspected the structure known as Bancroft Hall had been built like the early American Navy to withstand the test of time.

She walked around to the front of a statue and read the inscription there.

FIGUREHEAD
OF THE
USS
DELAWARE

BRONZE REPLICA
GIFT OF THE
CLASS OF 1891

Punky had heard others refer to the statue as "Tecumseh," a great warrior that made it both heroic and appropriate for the midshipmen who lived in Bancroft Hall. But she knew the figurehead that had been salvaged from the USS *Delaware* had been intended to portray Tamanend, the great chief of the Delawares, a lover of peace, and friend of William Penn. The statue was a case of mistaken identity that had persisted even after forty years of wind, sun, and rain took its toll on the original wooden form.

She wheeled away from the patinated statue and walked across an equally weathered bronze compass rose emblazoned with the Academy crest. Redbrick. Granite. Bronze. Everywhere Punky looked, she sensed a uniformity and symmetry that was appealing to her investigative mind.

The sun was just beginning to set, and the sky was painted in crimson and orange with wisps of clouds breaking up the pastel colors. And it was eerily quiet.

Lights winked on and lit up the facade, illuminating the towering granite columns on either side of the massive doors. Another set of opposing cannons were mounted on fixed carriages near the stairs leading up to the entrance. But everywhere she looked, Punky saw ornately carved ships, tridents, torches, and waves. Even the building's decorations were made to pay respect to the sea service and those who studied it.

Taking her time, Punky walked up the steps and through the large center door into what was known as the rotunda. A painting high over the main entrance depicted a sea battle of some kind with a majestic battleship plowing through a turbulent ocean. But up another, narrower set of stairs was an entrance to another room boasting a framed flag whose message could be seen from where she stood.

DON'T GIVE UP THE SHIP.

She started up the steps but stopped when a voice spoke from the shadows.

"Did you find him?"

She turned just as Connor stepped out from behind a column and leaned against it. He made a show of taking in the craftsmanship of the building, though he had only come for one reason.

"I saw him at least," she said.

"Did you learn anything?"

"No."

He shoved off from the column and ambled closer. "No? What happened?"

"He got into an argument with someone at the bar."

"The bartender?"

Punky shook her head. "Another patron. Does the name Teddy Miller ring any bells?"

Connor surveyed the spacious room as if to look for eavesdropping midshipmen, then lightly gripped Punky's elbow and steered her back toward the main entrance. She was getting tired of all the cloak and dagger nonsense and suddenly wished she had just listened to Camron. Even with what she'd been through, things seemed so much simpler in San Diego than they did in the capital's orbit.

Once outside, Connor released his hold on her arm. "Teddy Miller's a reporter with the *Washington Post*."

"Yeah, I sort of gathered that. I followed him from Old Ebbitt Grill back to the *Post*'s headquarters on K Street."

"You followed him?"

She nodded. "And I wasn't the only one."

Connor's forehead wrinkled with concern. "What's that supposed to mean?"

"It means that I spotted Samuel Chambers tailing me from the bar to the *Washington Post*. And that's nothing to brag about—he's got shitty tradecraft."

"So, was he following Miller or you?"

Instead of answering, Punky decided to play the other card she'd been holding on to. "What about Aurora Holdings? Does that mean anything?"

The wrinkles in Connor's forehead disappeared. "Aurora…"

"Holdings," she repeated.

"No. Why? What is that?"

"I don't know," Punky said. "But that's what they were discussing when Chambers stormed out. And when I confronted Teddy Miller about it, he accused me of trying to steal a story."

A bell in the distance began chiming, and Connor looked out across the grounds. "Punky, I think you're barking up the wrong tree—"

"Connor—"

He cut her off. "But I'll do some digging into it for you. In the meantime, I want you to consider that he could have been following you and that you could be in danger."

"From the president's chief of staff?" Even the notion was preposterous.

"You don't understand DC."

"And I don't want to," she said. "But you don't have to worry about me. I know how to take care of myself."

Connor eyed her up and down. But he wasn't appraising her physical attributes in a lecherous manner in the way some men did. He was evaluating whether she was competent enough to withstand whatever trials awaited her. "I believe you," he said.

She gave him a curt nod to acknowledge his faith in her. But she didn't need it. She had been ambushed twice by gunmen and walked away mostly unscathed. She had gone toe-to-toe with a Chinese assassin in the shallows off Santa Cruz Island and bested her. And she had taken down Russian convicts during a brazen daylight attack at a casino in Reno. Surely, she could handle herself against an arrogant politico.

"Let me know what you find out about Aurora Holdings?"

Connor hesitated for a beat, then nodded.

"Don't worry," she said. "I'll be safe."

The Washington Post
Washington, DC

Teddy's use of his thumb and middle finger on the "Command" and "S" keys was almost second nature. He used the shortcut after writing each paragraph on most stories, but one with this much potential required more frequent saving. And not just on his local hard drive. He had also made copies on his personal Dropbox account as well as on a flash drive that he kept hidden inside a picture frame on his desk.

He couldn't risk losing months of research and interviews that had led to this moment.

Leaning back in his chair, Teddy pushed his glasses up onto his forehead and rubbed his eyes. The story would have been much more compelling if Samuel had come through with a quote from the president, but he still thought it was a worthy article—not a slanderous hit piece that would land him in hot water. He let the glasses fall back onto the bridge of his nose and folded his arms across his chest with a satisfied smile.

Maybe not Pulitzer-worthy, but at least a contender for another Aldo Beckman Award.

With a contented sigh, Teddy leaned forward and lifted his desk phone from its cradle and stabbed at the button that connected him with the investigations editor, Maxwell Finch. As usual, Max picked up on the first ring.

"Is it done?"

"Just finished," Teddy replied.

"And you're sure you want to go through with this?"

Teddy appreciated that Max understood what was at stake. Even if he had thoroughly vetted each of his sources and accumulated a library's worth of research to substantiate his claims, it was going to cost him. Samuel might play nice and even allow him to remain in the press pool, but their personal friendship would be over.

"I don't see how I have much of a choice," he replied.

Max grunted on the other end. "You've waited this long. Sleep on it one more night."

"But—"

"It's too late for tomorrow's edition anyway," Max said, cutting him off.

But Teddy knew that wasn't true. In a world where headlines broke on the social media platform X, there was no such thing as being too late. But Max was giving him one last chance before they published a story that would topple the balance of power in the capital.

Teddy opened his mouth to reply but stopped himself when his phone lit up on the desk next to his MacBook. The name on the CallerID was the last one he expected to see. "I'll send it in the morning," he blurted, then hung up.

He reached for his cell phone and stared at the name "Samuel Chambers" at the top of the screen for several seconds before swiping to answer.

"Hey, Sam."

"You still want that quote?"

Teddy glanced at the article he had just finished, knowing that a quote from the president was the only thing that would make it more compelling. He licked his lips as he thought about the possibility.

"Is the president willing to give me one?"

"Meet me at the Corner Bar in thirty minutes, and you'll have it."

Sam's last words to him before storming out of Old Ebbitt Grill rang in his head, but he couldn't pass up the opportunity. "You're buying," he said, then hung up.

Teddy ejected the thumb drive and removed it from his MacBook, then slipped it into its hiding place along the bottom of a framed picture of him flying on Air Force One for the first time. But with a quote from the president, he could replace the picture with one of him receiving the Pulitzer Prize. His smile grew.

Teddy slammed the lid closed on his MacBook, then scooped it up and thrust it into his shoulder bag. He pushed away from the desk in his cubicle and stood, already picturing his confrontation with a contrite Samuel Chambers.

19

Teddy wasn't surprised it was almost dark when he walked outside. Time had a tendency to slip away from him when he was working on a story. Especially one with the potential of Aurora Holdings. But he was surprised it had taken Samuel so long to come around and see the wisdom in providing a quote from the president. The last thing the administration needed was a scandal to derail the traction they were just now gaining.

He slung his bag's strap over his shoulder, then turned right and strode along the sidewalk with his eyes fixed on the ground a half dozen paces in front of him. He had made the trek to Old Ebbitt Grill so often that he was on autopilot, barely paying attention to the normal buzz of the capital surrounding him. Pedestrians and bikers whisked by on all sides, and the occasional box truck lumbered past on its way to another delivery.

But all he could think about was seeing the look on Sam's face when Teddy told him he wasn't sure he needed the president's quote.

That'll teach him.

Teddy picked up his pace just shy of skipping and came to a stop at the crosswalk in front of Via Sophia. He waited for the light to turn green, then headed south on 14th Street and passed Franklin Park where fewer people were sitting on benches than there had been earlier in the day. Teddy turned and gave a mocking salute to the statue of Commodore John Barry—a man who shared the moniker of "Father of the American Navy" with one who was interred thirty miles east in Annapolis.

"Spare change?"

Teddy lowered his salute and shifted his bag to the other shoulder while doing his best to avoid looking at the beggar in rags. His lip curled up in a sneer as if he could smell the gutter on his clothes and cheap alcohol on his breath.

The city really needs to clean this up!

He waved off the man but said nothing. It was better not to even engage with the trash.

"Hey, mister."

"No," Teddy replied, annoyed at the rattling of loose coins in the beggar's plastic cup.

"How about a light?"

Teddy shook his head and picked up his pace, proud that he had resisted even the slightest temptation to feel pity for the man. If he had enough money for cigarettes, then he sure as shit had enough money to buy a hot meal.

"What about a laptop?" the homeless man hollered.

The request caused Teddy to falter for half a step. *A laptop?*

But he kept his eyes fixed ahead of him, not wanting to give the impression that the man's words had any effect. He was certain it had only been a lucky guess based on the size and shape of his shoulder bag, but he still tucked it against his side with his elbow. At least he had saved the story to the cloud and on the flash drive hidden in the picture frame on his desk.

Up ahead, a biker was stooped over and affixing a chain to secure his bike to the rack set just off the main sidewalk. He glanced over his shoulder just as the beggar began hurtling curse words in Teddy's direction. The two locked eyes, and the biker shook his head as a show of solidarity with the harassed pedestrian.

At least there are still good people in the world, Teddy thought.

He nodded in thanks at the biker as he walked past, then fixed his gaze on the sidewalk, crossing I Street. The crowds had thinned considerably but the lack of traffic at the intersection caused the hairs on the back of his neck to stand on end.

"Hey, buddy," the biker called out.

Teddy stopped and turned, only just beginning to realize the oddity of being hailed twice on the same block. He walked the same route several times a week without speaking to another soul. This was unusual.

"Yeah?"

"Can I have that bag?"

Teddy furrowed his brow in disbelief, and he pinched it even tighter against his side. "What?"

"It'd be easier if you just handed it over."

The man's shape had been obscured by the fading daylight, but Teddy suddenly realized the biker held a handgun pointed at him. But it wasn't a handgun he expected a common criminal looking for an opportunistic score might use. This one had a long, cylindrical-shaped object on the end.

A silencer?

Teddy had always wondered how he might act in a situation like this. Would he wet his pants and fall to his knees to beg for his life? Would he turn and run, hoping to outpace a supersonic bullet? Or would he confront the specter of physical violence head on and fight for his life.

In the end, Teddy did none of those.

"I'm not going to do that," he said in a calm and almost detached voice.

The gunman cocked his head to the side as if he hadn't heard him correctly. Then he shrugged, and the pistol in his hand coughed twice. Teddy staggered backward as the bullets slammed into his midsection, barely noticing that his shoulder bag had lost its perch and slipped to the sidewalk. He gripped his abdomen with both hands as the pain took hold and stared incredulously at the biker.

Teddy pulled his hands away and stared at the blood. He was losing far more than he thought he could withstand and already felt lightheaded and on the verge of passing out. The biker casually walked closer and bent to retrieve the shoulder bag, then placed a comforting hand on Teddy's back as if he was merely a Good Samaritan offering assistance to another pedestrian in need.

"Did you get it?" a second voice asked.

Teddy looked over and saw the homeless man walk up. He also held a silenced pistol in his hand.

"This one had some balls," the biker replied. "Didn't want to hand it over."

Teddy's knees gave out, and he started to collapse to the sidewalk. But the biker quickly hooked his arm underneath Teddy's armpit to steady him.

"Help me move him."

The homeless man shrugged off his raggedy blanket and gripped Teddy underneath his other armpit, helping the biker drag him to the bike rack. They set him onto a piece of cardboard on the ground, positioning him on his side in the fetal position.

"Did you get his phone?" the beggar asked.

Teddy's eyes rolled lazily from one man to the other, fighting off the overpowering urge to close them and sleep. Even the sharp stabs of pain radiating from his midsection did little to keep him alert. He didn't even move as the biker rifled through his pockets and removed his phone.

"Got it."

"Good. Let's get out of here." The beggar returned to the discarded blanket, then picked it up and tossed it across Teddy's limp body. He dropped the plastic cup with coins at Teddy's feet, then poured some cheap whiskey on the blanket and set the half-empty bottle within arm's reach.

The biker squatted down near Teddy's head and surveyed their handiwork. He nodded with apparent satisfaction. "You know, you were never going to survive this. You pissed off the wrong people, my friend."

The last thing Teddy saw was the silencer pointed at his head.

Old Ebbitt Grill
Washington, DC

Samuel Chambers sat atop his usual stool and glanced in the mirror behind the bar every time another patron walked into the room. Viktor hadn't shared his plan to resolve the problem of the overly inquisitive reporter, but he could guess what it involved. He just hoped it took place before Teddy came to confront him at their usual haunt with the details of what he had learned about Aurora Holdings.

His phone rang, and he picked it up without looking at the CallerID. "Yeah?"

"It is done," Viktor said with an emotionless voice.

"Did you get his computer?"

"*Da.*"

"And his phone?"

"*Da. Da.* And we erased the file from his cloud storage as well."

Sam's shoulders slumped with relief, but his stomach knotted up with a sudden and intense pain. The immediate threat of being exposed had been dealt with. But betraying his friend to the Russian had only bought him some time. And at what cost? Now, he needed to deliver on his promise to provide details of the task force's operation in Ukraine.

What have I done?

"It's your turn, Samuel," Viktor said.

"I know. As soon as I hear—"

"Tomorrow," the Russian said, then hung up.

Sam dropped the phone back onto the lacquered wood and stared at himself in the mirror. Two decades had passed since he and Jonathan had launched their first political campaign and set out to change the world. But he seemed far older than he should. His eyes had a sunken look that belied how little sleep he actually managed each night.

"Another?" the bartender asked, pointing at the empty Gin Balalajka in front of him.

Sam cleared his throat and shook his head. "No, thanks."

"Waiting on Miller?"

The question caused his stomach to knot up again as his mouth filled with sour spit. All he could manage was a weak shake of his head before pushing back from the bar and dropping off his stool. He stood there for a moment and battled against a sudden wave of vertigo, making him question how he would ever be able to survive seeing through Jonathan's first term.

Then Sam took a long and slow breath in through his nose and slowly exhaled through pursed lips. He straightened his back to once again assume the persona he had worn since their early days at Berkeley, then spun and headed for the door.

Viktor had only given him one day.

Just one.

20

White House Situation Room
Washington, DC

The uneasy feeling in the pit of Sam's stomach was still there by the time he reached the Situation Room—the most famous SCIF, or Sensitive Compartmented Information Facility—located directly beneath his office in the West Wing of the White House. Unlike most Hollywood depictions of the space as a single conference room, it was actually a highly sophisticated five-thousand-square-foot complex that was manned twenty-four-hours a day by a team of professionals from the military and intelligence communities.

Sam walked onto the watch floor and looked at the wall at the front of the room. Made from twelve individual monitors, it looked like one giant screen that had been segmented to play feeds from various intelligence-gathering sources. But he found it ironic that the two screens on the far left showed muted live feeds from the leading cable news networks.

Not seeing what he was looking for, Sam walked into Olivia Manning's office at the back of the watch floor. As the director of the Situation Room, she was responsible for managing a staff of professionals that included audiovisual specialists, communications technicians, and intelligence analysts. If there was anybody who knew what was happening in Ukraine, it was her.

"Mr. Chambers," she said in greeting, not bothering to get up from behind her desk but reaching underneath to activate a switch that frosted the surrounding glass and prevented anyone from looking inside.

Sam closed the door and took a seat in one of the two chairs opposite her. "What's the latest in Ukraine, Olivia?"

It was an open-ended question, but he knew she would grasp what he was really asking. Ever since they had first received intelligence surrounding former Russian intelligence officers recovering suitcase nukes to sell on the black market, it had been their top priority. She leaned back in her chair and studied him for a moment before answering.

"An Air Force Rivet Joint over the Black Sea detected a column of Russian armored vehicles moving from Perekop to Nova Kakhovka on the front lines. Based on our assessment that it was likely linked to this plot, the president ordered the task force to move forward and stage at Voznesensk Reserve Air Base."

Sam's stomach twisted into knots again with an overwhelming fear that events were spiraling faster than he could control. But he reined in his emotions and focused on the solution instead of the problem. "Where's the president now?"

"On his way back from Camp David," she said, glancing at her watch. "Marine One should be arriving shortly, and he has instructed the National Security Council to convene in the Kennedy Conference Room."

"Can I see the Sit Room Note?" Sam asked, referring to the summary accounting of the event that precipitated the president's order.

Olivia nodded and reached for a folder sitting atop her desk and slid it across to him. Sam snatched the folder and opened it, reviewing the written summary of the column's movement from Perekop to Nova Kakhovka and its attempted crossing of the partially destroyed bridge.

"This says that a Ukrainian Air Force MiG-29 engaged the column and destroyed several of the vehicles," Sam said, hoping that maybe he wouldn't have to betray his fellow countrymen after all.

"Look at photos one and two," she said.

Both pictures appeared to have been taken from high altitude, likely from one of the Air Force's remotely piloted vehicles that maintained constant vigilance over the battlefield. In the first picture, six vehicles appeared to have crossed onto the bridge from the southern shore in a narrowly spaced column. In the second, two vehicles were burning, and three others appeared stationary.

Sam looked up at Olivia. "Where's the other one?"

Her mouth curled into a frown. "We don't know."

"What do you mean *we don't know*?"

A phone on her desk buzzed, and she immediately scooped it up. "Yes?"

Sam's heart pounded in his chest as he stared at the photos, hoping to spot what other more capable individuals had failed to find. Because if one of the vehicles *did* make it through, then he knew he was operating on borrowed time before the president authorized a mission to secure the storage facility.

"We'll be right there," Olivia said and hung up. She hit the switch under her desk to turn the glass panes clear again, then stood. "The president just landed and will be here in five minutes. The council is already starting to file in."

Sam dropped the folder on her desk and stood, but she had already opened the door and was making for the Kennedy Conference Room. As director, it was her responsibility to ensure the space was ready for the president's briefing, and she had already dismissed Sam without so much as an apology. But Sam followed hot on her heels and ignored the oppressive guilt as he prepared to do what he never thought he would.

Maybe they found the sixth vehicle, and the president can stand down before this gets out of hand.

Halfway to the conference room, Sam nearly bumped into Frank Short, the stocky secretary of defense, who was walking at a faster than normal pace. "What's going on, Frank?"

The former Army four-star general saw Sam and scowled. "Just got word we have a Reaper overhead, tracking the target vehicle."

Sam's stomach turned over. "How far is it?"

Frank's already ample eyebrows kneaded together to form a single large one as his scowl deepened. "From what?"

"The storage facility," Sam said, thinking his question obvious.

They reached the door to the Kennedy Conference Room, and Sam opened it while gesturing for the secretary to enter first. "We'll get an update once the president arrives, but at last reporting they still had over a hundred and fifty kilometers."

Sam did the math in his head and knew they were running out of time. He took a seat at the table next to Frank, who eyed him suspiciously. Normally, he would greet the president and walk in alongside the commander in chief, but today he needed the information sooner. "What are you going to propose?"

Frank glanced up and nodded as General Tilley, the chairman of the Joint Chiefs of Staff, entered the room. The four-star general and former Army Ranger had commanded both the Joint Special Operations Command and the United States Special Operations Command before being tapped for the Joint Chiefs. He saw the SECDEF's gesture and walked around the table to sit at his other shoulder.

"Mr. Secretary." His tone was subdued but reverent.

"Bart, Mr. Chambers here wants to know what we're going to propose to the president. Can you give him a quick synopsis of the plan our boys in Virginia Beach have come up with?"

Bart Tilley turned to the side and leaned over slightly to fix Sam with an iron stare. "We have an assault force from the Navy's JSOC task force aboard two AFSOC CV-22 Ospreys en route to Voznesensk Reserve Air Base. They are being escorted by two A-29 Super Tucanos from Light Attack Squadron Four."

Sam already knew most of this because he had been present when the president authorized Frank to deploy the assets to Poland. But knowing that they had already moved from Lask Air Base into Ukraine meant that he would need to move quick. He swallowed. "Do you intend to hit the target vehicle before it reaches the storage facility?"

Bart nodded. "There are really just two options, but that's what we're going to ask for. The longer we let these lone wolves go unchecked, the greater the risk of them succeeding. The Reaper crew will let us know once the target vehicle has crossed inside fifty kilometers. That will be our trigger to insert the assault force."

"If the president authorizes it," Sam said.

Bart didn't flinch. "Yes, sir. If the president authorizes it."

"Do we know who's behind this?"

Of course, Sam already knew. He just didn't want to let the others know that.

"We don't know exactly who, but intelligence suggests a group of former SVR operatives might be trying to fill the void that was created when Wagner's leader died in a plane crash over Tver Oblast."

"So, you don't believe this was sanctioned by the Russian government." Sam knew the Wagner Group had been a thorn in their side in places like Syria, Sudan, and the Central African Republic, and he wasn't naive enough to believe that taking out their leader would eliminate the need for an unacknowledged organization that could do the Russian president's dirty work. He just wanted to know if Viktor had the Kremlin's blessing.

Before Bart could answer, Olivia's voice carried over the hushed murmurs from those seated around the conference room table. "We have video from the Reaper overhead."

All eyes turned to the large central screen on the far wall.

21

Voznesensk Reserve Air Base
Voznesensk, Mykolaiv Oblast, Ukraine

"Put it on the screen," Colonel Kovalenko said.

Colt and the others gathered around the senior Ukrainian officer as the thirty-inch monitor flickered to life with a grainy black-and-white image of a dense forest. His mind instantly interpreted the infrared video, but the colonel grunted with frustration as the crosshairs shifted several more times and danced across the screen.

"Why is it not steady? Where is the target?"

Colt pointed to what looked like a vehicle moving slowly across the uneven terrain and picking its way through the trees. Almost as if he had directed the drone's sensor operator, the crosshairs slewed one final time and centered on what appeared to be an armored personnel carrier.

"Is that a BMP?" Cubby asked.

Dave shook his head. "I think it's a BTR."

Colt couldn't help but think it looked eerily similar to the Stryker armored vehicle he had destroyed in the Fallon Range Training Complex after it shot down Cubby's F-35C Joint Strike Fighter. But they were far from the Nevada high desert and facing consequences that were far graver than the destruction of a multimillion-dollar fighter jet.

"That's it," Polina said.

Kovalenko turned and looked at her. "Are you certain?"

She nodded, and Colt noticed the intensity in her eyes. He knew she saw the white-hot image of the armored vehicle as more than just another target. She saw it as the manifestation of her failure—as the one that got away. "I'm certain."

"Where is this?" the colonel asked.

But Dave had already pulled out an Android tablet connected to his AN/PRC-161 to enter the Reaper-derived coordinates displayed in the monitor's upper right corner. The map on his tablet centered on a forest in Mykolaiv Oblast, and he held it out for the colonel. "Recognize this location?"

Kovalenko reached for the tablet and turned it over in his hands. "What is this?"

"This is a BATS-D," Dave said. "A Battlefield Awareness and Targeting System, Dismounted. We use it as a portable blue force tracker and situational awareness display."

"Fancy," the colonel replied.

"Does this location look familiar to you?"

He shook his head. "That could be anywhere." Dave zoomed out on the map to give the senior officer a better perspective. "Wait. Yes—"

Suddenly, the monitor with the Reaper video went black.

"What happened?" Colt asked. "Where'd the video go?"

The Ukrainian airman sitting behind the computer console scrambled frantically to recover the video feed. But no matter what he tried, the monitor remained frustratingly blank.

"*Molodshyi!*" Kovalenko spat.

"I'm sorry, Colonel. The feed was lost."

Colt turned and locked eyes with Cubby. He could see the same thought reflecting back at him, and his stomach turned.

I've got a bad feeling about this.

White House Situation Room
Washington, DC

"What happened?"

Sam looked from Bart to Olivia, whose ashen face said it all. The video that had only just begun streaming on the large central screen abruptly stopped and was replaced with the White House logo. She picked up a phone and spoke in hushed tones, and Sam wondered what poor technician on the watch floor was getting an earful.

Frank's voice was calm. "Miss Manning?"

She cursed under her breath and slammed the phone down a little harder than she likely intended to, then looked up at the secretary of defense as worry creased her forehead. "I'm afraid we've lost the feed from Ghost Three Two."

"I can see that," he replied. "Can we get it back before the president gets here?"

Almost as if on cue, Jonathan Adams strode confidently into the room and took his place at the head of the table. He glanced at each of the others, who had quickly stood upon his entrance, then lowered himself into his chair. "From the looks on each of your faces, I get the feeling I'm about to get some bad news?"

Sam saw the silent plea in Olivia's brown eyes, and he cleared his throat to come to her rescue. "Mr. President…"

"Sam?"

He knew that his lifelong best friend was probably questioning whether he had spoken with Viktor. But the less he knew, the better. "We were just watching live video feed from an MQ-9 Reaper orbiting over the target vehicle in Mykolaiv Oblast."

Jonathan looked up at the White House logo on the large monitor at the end of the room, then proceeded to look at the same logo on each of the other screens around the conference room. "Okay? Where is it?"

Olivia's shoulders rose and fell with a deep breath, and she turned to face the president. "Sir, this is my responsibility. We lost the feed just before you arrived, but our technicians are already in comms with the Air Force to figure out what happened and correct it."

Jonathan nodded. "You and your people do a fine job, Olivia. I know the problem will get resolved. Let's go ahead and continue with our discussion while we wait for the video feed to return."

Frank sensed it was his turn to take the floor, and he leaned forward to address Jonathan. "Mr. President, the convoy our Rivet Joint spotted moving on Nova Kakhovka reached the bridge where it was engaged by a Ukrainian MiG-29 Fulcrum. Several vehicles were destroyed in the attack, but one made it across and disappeared into the countryside. The Ukrainian government gave us permission to fly an MQ-9 Reaper into their airspace to locate and track the vehicle."

The president gestured to the screen. "Which you were apparently able to do."

"Yes, Mr. President."

"And where is it?"

A map of Ukraine replaced the White House logo on the screen at the end of the room. Frank lifted a laser pointer and fixed it on an area between two locations labeled Nova Kakhovka and Yuzhnoukrainsk. "At this time, we believe it is approximately one hundred kilometers from the facility where we believe the nuclear weapons are being stored."

Sam saw Jonathan's expression harden, and he knew the president had made up his mind.

Mykolaiv Oblast, Ukraine

Nikolai Voronov leaned away from the screen with a satisfied smile. Although the VPK-7829 Bumerang was more cramped than the American Stryker, it was far more suited for this weapon than any of the previous BTR models. Even the newest model of the venerable Russian armored personnel carrier would have been unable to carry the requisite power supply and controls needed to operate the *DRAGON LINE*.

"Target negated," Yevgeny said, though that was apparent.

On the screen, the crosshairs were centered on what remained of an American MQ-9 Reaper as it tumbled through the sky. Even after the laser stopped firing, the remotely piloted vehicle's bulbous nose glowed hot where they had burned through its control systems.

"Very well," Voronov said. But the specter of another Ukrainian fighter jet rolling in on them loomed large at the front of his mind. "Any additional airborne contacts?"

The sensor operator shook his head. "Negative. The radar picture is clear."

Voronov swiped the back of his hand across his forehead and lamented the poor air flow compared to the American fighting vehicle. He keyed the microphone switch. "Driver, continue to the target."

"Yes, sir."

The Bumerang lurched, and Voronov closed his eyes as the eight-wheeled armored vehicle continued traversing the dense forest toward their destination. He jostled from side to side in the aft compartment, where there was normally room enough for seven soldiers. But after installing the power supply and controls needed to operate the laser weapon, there was barely room enough for two. But two was all they needed.

"Keep an eye out for more aircraft," he cautioned, knowing that his men were more than capable of doing that without being told. They all knew what was at stake. They all knew their future depended on the success of this operation.

"Yes, sir."

Voronov's knee bounced nervously, and he keyed the microphone switch on the intercom. "How far are we from the target?"

"One hundred kilometers," the driver replied.

"Very well." He leaned back in the uncomfortable seat as Yevgeny looked over his shoulder with a trace of fear hidden in his expression.

"Do you think the *Molniya* really exists?"

"I don't know," Voronov said. "But that's why we have the DRAGON LINE."

The operator swallowed, then turned back to his workstation as if to avoid thinking about it.

22

White House Situation Room
Washington, DC

The president stood. "Thank you, everybody."

Sam slowly rose to his feet with an odd sense of detachment. As Jonathan strode from the room, Sam's mind swam with the details of the operation they had just discussed for over an hour. Each member of the National Security Council was given an opportunity to weigh in on the proposed military action. But, in the end, it was the president's call.

And he had given Frank the green light.

"So, what happens now?" Sam asked.

The secretary of defense gathered the papers spread out on the table in front of him and tucked them back into the yellow-bordered folder with the words "TOP SECRET//SCI" in red across the top. Sam's eyes fell to the folder, and he casually wondered if it was even possible for him to make copies and remove them from the SCIF.

But, of course, he knew it wasn't.

"Now, I call General McCloskey at Fort Bragg and tell him the president has given them the green light."

Sam thought it seemed like such a casual thing. With one phone call, Frank would put the wheels in motion to launch two Ospreys filled with Navy SEALs that would fly through the dead of night to a facility filled with nuclear weapons. With a conversation that might only last a minute or two, orders would be issued, and American servicemen would put themselves into harm's way to prevent evil men from getting their hands on those weapons.

And Sam was going to give Viktor everything he needed to stop them.

"When?"

Frank looked at his watch. "I'll call when I get back to my office. It's almost morning there, so we'll have to wait for the next period of darkness to execute."

Less than twenty-four hours, Sam thought.

"Do me a favor and let me know when you've spoken to the CG."

Frank nodded, then picked up the folder and turned for the door. Sam knew he needed to speak with Viktor while the details were still fresh in his mind, but for the first time in as long as he could remember, he felt like he was torn between competing allegiances.

Olivia Manning stuck her head in through the door. "Sam?"

"Yeah?"

"The president asked you to meet him in the Executive Residence."

He nodded, having expected as much. "Thank you."

As the rest of the National Security Council slowly filed from the room and returned to the tasks that composed their daily routines, Sam felt as if he was being swept out to sea. He was unaccustomed to not being in complete control of his environment and didn't like that he was being summoned to the president's private living apartment on the second floor of the White House.

Because that was the one place he could be certain they wouldn't be overheard.

JW Marriott
Washington, DC

Punky sat at the bar in the lobby and sipped on a Hazy IPA while letting herself unwind. It was late, and she felt the cumulative fatigue of each of the day's previous hours. But the beer's mango, orange, tangerine, and cannabis flower flavors carried her to a place of comfortable stillness that she knew would lead to a dreamless sleep.

She was accustomed to living in a world of treachery and deception. But the level of corruption that surrounded her in the nation's capital seemed overwhelming. A traitorous Marine who had conspired with the Chinese to sink an American aircraft carrier. A Russian plot that involved the same Marine and the president of the United States. And a shadowy corporation that seemed to be at the root of it all.

What the fuck is going on?

Punky took another sip of her beer, then felt her pocket vibrating with an incoming call. She glanced at her watch, not wanting to disturb the hops-induced tranquility she was just beginning to feel with a conversation that would likely elevate her heart rate.

But she knew there were things she couldn't ignore. If there was a conspiracy involving the Russians and the president, she couldn't simply bury her head in the sand and wish it would go away. She set the pint glass on the table and pulled her phone from her pocket, staring at the name on the CallerID for several seconds before swiping across the bottom to answer it.

"Hey, Connor."

"Where are you?"

She was about to take another sip of her beer, but the tone in the case officer's voice stayed her hand. "I'm in my hotel—"

"Meet me at Franklin Park."

"What? Now?"

"Yes. Now."

Connor ended the call, and Punky stared at the blank screen while the competing requirements of getting adequate sleep and fulfilling her duty wrestled in her mind. But after several seconds, she tossed a crumpled twenty on the wood bar top and pushed herself back. There was something in Connor's voice she didn't like.

Punky's hotel was only four blocks away from the park that fronted the *Washington Post* headquarters, so she exited the hotel and turned right on 14th Street. Though she was exhausted and wanted nothing more than to go up to her room, strip out of her clothes, and climb into her king-size bed, she knew Connor wouldn't have called if it wasn't important.

She kept her eyes fixed on the ground ahead of her. But as she drew closer to Franklin Park, she saw the flashing red-and-blue lights of several Washington Metro Police cruisers, and her heart sank. With rising anxiety, Punky's fatigue seemed to evaporate into the capital evening, and she increased her pace almost to a jog.

Crossing I Street, a uniformed police officer stepped in front of her. "Ma'am, you need to stay back."

Punky gripped the break point in her blazer and pulled it back to reveal the badge clipped to her belt. "Special Agent King with NCIS."

"Punky," a voice called out.

She saw Connor standing outside the cordoned-off area with a worried look on his face, and she broke away from the Metro cop to confront the Agency man. "What's going on?"

"It's Miller," he said.

"What?"

Connor nodded at a gaggle of police officers and crime scene investigators gathered around what looked like a bike rack at the southwest corner of the park. "I was digging into Aurora Holdings like you asked when I got word that Teddy Miller had been murdered."

"What are you talking about?" Punky shook her head in disbelief. "I just saw him."

"I don't know anything. I don't have a badge, so they won't let me get near."

Punky knew what that meant, and she wheeled away and ducked underneath the crime scene tape that had been put up to keep looky-loos at bay. She saw several police officers turn in her direction, but she unclipped the badge from her belt and held it up for them to see as she walked around the corner and peered down at Teddy Miller's slain body.

He was lying on top of a flattened cardboard box with a filthy blanket pulled to the side to reveal his blood-soaked shirt and a small-caliber entry wound in his temple. His forehead was swollen and disfigured from where the bullet had rattled around inside his head and permanently turned out the lights on a talented reporter.

"What happened?" Punky asked one of the officers.

It was pretty apparent that somebody had shot him in the stomach and head—at point-blank range—and positioned him to appear like he was just another homeless man occupying space on the capital's sidewalks. But things like this didn't normally happen so close to the White House in a more upscale part of town.

"One of our regulars found him here."

"Regulars?"

The officer nodded at a middle-aged white man with an unkempt appearance speaking with a plainclothes detective. "We've had run-ins with him in the past, but nothing violent. This doesn't fit with his normal behavior."

"Murder weapon?"

He eyed her up and down as if to evaluate whether she belonged there. "I'm sorry, who are you?"

"Special Agent King." Again, she held up her badge. But she purposely omitted her agency since she knew the Naval Criminal Investigative Service had no jurisdiction over a homicide in the capital.

Fortunately, the officer didn't press her for more. He was probably used to having others from any number of federal agencies crowding in on his turf. "No murder weapon, and nobody reported hearing gunshots either."

"So, he was either killed somewhere else and dumped here—"

"Which wouldn't make sense unless somebody was trying to send a message," the officer said.

"Or this was a professional hit with suppressed weapons."

Punky could tell her assessment made the officer uneasy, and she looked over her shoulder at the large building bordering the north end of the park. The *Washington Post* reporter had just been murdered right outside their headquarters, and there was no way she could believe it was merely a coincidence or random act of violence.

"Who did you say you were with?" he asked.

She ignored the question. "Did you find anything on him? Like a computer or cell phone?"

He hesitated for a second, but then shook his head. "Nothing."

23

Punky knew she had worn out her welcome when the officer stopped answering her questions. But by then she had learned enough to get an idea of what had taken place. They were still gathering footage from the neighboring businesses' security cameras, but she already knew what they would find.

Teddy Miller had been gunned down less than a block from the *Washington Post* headquarters by men who clearly knew what they were doing. They were brazen enough to ambush the reporter only blocks from the White House but skilled enough to do so without attracting attention. The *what* was clear to her. It was the *why* that had her troubled.

Deep in thought, she walked back over to where Connor stood beyond the crime scene tape.

"Well? What did you find out?"

Punky looked up and studied the faces of the people standing nearby. She gestured for him to follow her, then started walking east along the southern perimeter of the park. She wanted to get away from the police and anybody who might be watching to see who came to investigate. Her anonymity was a weapon only as long as she remained hidden.

When they were a safe distance away, she began telling him what she had pieced together based on what little evidence they had given her access to. "He left his office on his own, either as part of his normal routine or because somebody drew him outside. My suspicion is the latter. His assailants had already set an ambush for him and waited until he walked into the kill zone before springing the trap."

"What makes you think it was pre-planned?"

She looked over her shoulder at the intersection where police cruisers blocked traffic in either direction. "This place is too public with too many witnesses and security cameras. If it wasn't planned ahead of time, they wouldn't have been able to control all the variables. At the very least, his body would have been discovered within minutes of the shooting. Not hours."

Connor was silent for a moment as he let her words sink in. "So, what do you think happened?"

"I think there was a team of at least two but no more than five. There were two vehicles—possibly public works maintenance trucks to give an air of credibility—that blocked the road in either direction or prevented traffic from passing at the time of the ambush. He was approached by two assailants on foot, one who let him pass so that he couldn't retreat once confronted."

"You sound like you've thought this through."

Punky couldn't help but think of all the times she had been on the receiving end of an ambush. "It's what I would do. Besides, the lack of physical evidence at the scene suggests it wasn't a robbery gone wrong or a random act of violence."

"Like what?"

She stopped walking and turned to face the *Washington Post* headquarters on the opposite side of the park. "You've probably met a reporter a time or two, right?"

Connor nodded.

"And when was the last time you saw one without a phone to record interviews and take notes or a laptop to work on their stories?"

"Never. But maybe it *was* just a robbery."

She shook her head. "If that was true, he wouldn't have been shot in the gut *and* the head. If that was true, his body wouldn't have been staged to make him appear as if he was just another vagrant sleeping off a hangover. And if that was true, there would still be shell casings on the sidewalk."

"Okay. So, why then?"

The corner of her mouth turned upward in a smile. The *why* was the reason she had become a special agent with the Naval Criminal Investigative Service. It wasn't enough for her to put bad guys behind bars. She wanted to understand what made American men and women forsake their sworn oaths to support and defend the Constitution of the United States. The *why* was where she excelled.

"Let's make some assumptions," she said. "Let's assume that Teddy was working on a story about Aurora Holdings."

Based on her interaction with Teddy at the Old Ebbitt Grill and the altercation she observed between the reporter and the president's chief of staff, it was an easy assumption to make. "Okay…"

"Let's also assume that somebody with power didn't want the story to get out."

"There are plenty of people with power in DC. But we don't even know what Aurora Holdings is, let alone if anybody would want to keep it quiet."

She waved his objection away. "We'll get to that. But for now, if we assume those things, how might somebody try to keep him from running the story?"

"They might try convincing him to shelf the story on his own," Connor said, playing along.

"Like what I saw at Old Ebbitt Grill," Punky suggested. "And maybe Teddy refused, which is why Samuel Chambers stormed out."

"Maybe."

"Let's say that appealing to reason failed. Then what?"

"Blackmail."

Punky nodded. "We can dig into Teddy's past and see if we come up with anything that could have been used in an attempted blackmail, but let's skip that for now. It's a moot point now that he's dead. What next?"

"A warning? Maybe they try to scare him into keeping the story hidden?"

She agreed with him. That seemed like the most logical next step but would require some amount of leverage over him. Like blackmail, they would need to circle back on that one. "And if that failed?"

"Violence is the obvious answer," Connor said.

"Obviously."

"But even if you silence the reporter, you still have to contend with all the research and written notes he's likely collected. The story itself is only a concise reporting of his investigation, but the facts themselves can be harmful even without a conclusion."

Punky nodded at the *Washington Post* headquarters. "I agree. And even if his assailants took his laptop and phone, I'd be surprised if he didn't keep some sort of backup. Either in the cloud or on a dedicated server at the newspaper."

"Or both," Connor agreed. "But even if we find it, what will that tell us?"

"I think *not* finding it will tell us more. It will tell us that he was murdered because of a story he was working on. And this person of power went to great lengths to cover his tracks and bury all the research on the matter."

"Aurora Holdings," Connor said.

Punky agreed. "It all leads back to that."

"So, what now?"

She started walking into the park. "Now we go see if Teddy left any breadcrumbs for us to follow."

Yellow Oval Room
The White House
Washington, DC

Sam climbed the stairs to the second floor, where the president's private living apartment was located. It was hard to imagine that before the Theodore Roosevelt renovation of 1902, the public had full and free access to this area. The government that had been founded by the people for the people had slowly eroded into what their forefathers had warned them against.

But Jonathan would change that if he managed to get out of his own way and allow Sam to do what he had always done. As undergraduate students, they had dreamed of making a difference in American politics. Now, they were in a position to do something about it.

"Mr. President," Sam said when he walked into the oval room.

Jonathan looked over the top of his reading glasses at his longtime friend, then leaned back in the armchair and gestured for Sam to join him. "You think I'm making a mistake, don't you?"

He had been formulating his response to that question ever since Olivia told him the president had summoned him to the executive residence. "I've always believed you make your decisions with the good of the people in mind."

Jonathan cocked his head to the side, as if looking for a trap that his best friend had hidden in his line of reasoning. "I take it your conversation with Viktor didn't go as expected?"

Sam took a seat in a chair opposite the president. "I think it went just as expected but not as I'd hoped."

Jonathan plucked his glasses from his face and rubbed his eyes with thumb and forefinger, a clear sign that this entire ordeal was wearing on him. Like most who had been in his shoes, even his brief time as president thus far had aged him. "Do you really think he will follow through on his threat to expose our secret?"

Sam sighed heavily. "I'm not really sure. If he does, he will have lost his bargaining chip as well as his access to you. But if he doesn't, he's lost his credibility, which makes his leverage useless."

Jonathan stopped massaging his eyes. "Bargaining chip. Leverage. Just who the fuck does he think he is?"

"Jonathan—"

The president slammed the stack of papers down on the coffee table, visibly seething. "I will *not* be controlled by this Russki thug!"

Sam motioned for Jonathan to calm down. "I know. You're doing the right thing."

Like a spring thunderstorm, the president's anger vanished as quickly as it had appeared. He rose from the armchair and stretched to his full height, looking down on his lifelong friend. "Do whatever damage control you have to do, but the operation is going as scheduled. I will not allow anyone to think they have enough leverage to stop me from preventing nuclear weapons from falling into the wrong hands. Do you understand me?"

"Yes, sir."

With that, Jonathan turned and walked from the oval room into his bedroom and slammed the door behind him.

24

The Washington Post
Washington, DC

Punky and Connor sat in the lobby while the receptionist contacted somebody from the newsroom to escort them upstairs. But she was beginning to have her doubts they were going to be as helpful as she'd hoped.

"You'd think they'd be a little more interested in helping us find whoever killed him."

Connor shot her a sideways glance. "Journalists are notoriously suspicious of law enforcement."

"Maybe you should have shown them your credentials then."

He chuckled. "They're even worse when it comes to people like me."

Punky should have expected that. Journalists ranging from Pulitzer Prize winners to aspiring true-crime writers spent time in jail for refusing to give up their notes and sources. It was naive for her to think they could just waltz into the *Post*'s headquarters and be granted unfettered access to Teddy Miller's possessions. Still, she had hope.

She jumped to her feet and walked over to the receptionist. "Can you tell me when we might expect—"

"Special Agent King?"

Punky turned and stared at a thick-necked man sporting a high-and-tight and wearing a sport coat. He wasn't what she expected when the receptionist had forwarded her request upstairs. "Yes?"

"My name's Roland Brown," he said, holding out his hand. "I'm with the *Post*'s physical security department. I understand you have some concerns about one of our reporters, Teddy Miller?"

Security guard, she thought. *That explains it.*

"I guess you could say that," she replied, shaking his hand. "He's dead."

Roland didn't appear shocked, though Punky was almost certain she was the one who had broken the news. Instead, he released his grip on her hand and gestured for her to join him at the large bank of elevators. "I've been asked to escort you upstairs while we determine how the *Washington Post* can help the Naval Criminal Investigative Service."

Punky glanced at Connor, who rose and joined them. "Connor Sullivan," he said, shaking Roland's hand.

"This is my partner," Punky said, hoping to forestall Roland's naturally suspicious nature from requesting credentials or another form of identification. "We really do appreciate your help in figuring out who might have wanted to harm Mr. Miller."

Roland swiped his access card in front of a reader, then punched the button to request a car. The doors opened almost immediately, and he gestured for them to enter the elevator. "Like I said, I'm only here to escort you upstairs to Ms. Frost. She'll be able to answer your questions."

As the doors closed, Punky studied Roland's behavior and recognized a few key markers that betrayed his past. "Where did you serve?"

Roland glanced over his shoulder and eyed her up and down. "North Carolina."

"Army or Marines?"

The elevator emitted a soft ding as the car ascended past the second floor.

"Army."

She smiled. "Fort Bragg then?"

"I think it's called Fort Liberty now," he replied.

Punky waved off the comment. "Yeah, well, that doesn't really change anything, does it?"

She saw his lip curl up in a smile as if she had just voiced an opinion that was too unpopular for him to utter in a place like the *Washington Post*. That changing the name of a military post didn't erase its history or how the men and women who served there referred to it.

"No, ma'am," he said. "Guess not."

Another ding, then the elevator came to a stop, and the doors opened. Roland gestured for Punky and Connor to step out before guiding them down a narrow hall to a large, open room filled with cubicles. He guided them to a quad of cubes and offered them stylishly ergonomic chairs to sit in while they waited for Ms. Frost to come collect them.

"Any idea when we might expect her?"

Roland looked over both shoulders to make sure they were alone before answering. "Just between us, she's meeting with legal right now to make sure she crosses her t's and dots her i's before she stonewalls you."

Punky pursed her lips.

"But you didn't hear that from me," he said with a playful wink.

"Of course not," she replied, then quickly added, "All the way."

He grinned. "Airborne, ma'am."

As Roland walked away, leaving Connor and Punky alone in the vacant cubicles, she couldn't help but feel frustrated that they would probably walk away empty-handed because their fellow Americans cared more for the sanctity of a journalist's privacy than they did for his life. Whoever had ordered his execution would get away scot-free.

And that pissed her off.

"You okay?" Connor asked.

She took several breaths and nodded, but she knew she wasn't fooling him. "We need to get into his damn files."

"I know, I know. But you heard the man. They're not going to just hand them over."

She banged her fist on the cubicle's desk, knocking over a framed picture that sat next to a laptop's docking station. It was an uncharacteristic outburst, but she was beginning to wonder if she was the only one who cared that their nation's enemies were already at the gates. She took a deep breath to calm herself, then leaned over to pick up the picture she had knocked over.

Propping it back up on its easel, Punky turned back to Connor. "Yeah, but..."

She froze.

Something tickled at the back of her mind, and she suddenly felt light-headed. Turning back to the picture in the frame, she leaned in close and studied the face of the photo's subject.

"What is it?"

"Who does that look like to you?"

Before Connor could get a closer look, a woman's voice broke the uneasy silence between them. "Ms. King?"

Startled, Punky jumped to her feet and turned to see a woman with short-cropped silver hair in a powder blue pantsuit approaching. "I'm Special Agent King," she replied, emphasizing her role to make it clear that she was there on official business. For what little good that would do her.

"I'm sorry to have kept you waiting." The woman held out her hand, almost as if expecting Punky to kiss it. "Diana Frost. I'm one of the newsroom managing editors."

Punky shook her hand with slightly more pressure than she normally would but didn't let it linger. She was afraid that her building anger over Roland's confession that Diana intended to stonewall her might spill over into physical violence, so she pulled her hand back and shoved it into her pocket. But still, it balled into a fist.

Connor seemed to sense it, because he stepped forward and took the lead. "We're sorry for the loss of your colleague."

Diana studied him for a moment as if to assess whether his comment was genuine, then nodded slowly. "Yes, Teddy was one of the good ones. He had a real gift for journalism that was apparent when he won the Aldo Beckman Award for his coverage of the last administration's handling of the Afghanistan withdrawal. We'll feel his loss for some time."

"I'm sure he's not somebody you can easily replace," Punky said, trying to regain control of the situation. She remembered the way Teddy had become defensive when he thought she was trying to steal the story about Aurora Holdings. "I'd hate to be the person who has to step in and finish whatever stories he was working on."

Diana's eyes narrowed. "I'm not aware of anything he was working on."

"Who might have that information?" Connor asked.

"I'm sorry, but I can't really say."

"Can't or won't?"

Diana gave a forced smile. "I do appreciate you coming to let us know about this tragedy—"

"But you don't intend to help us, do you?" Punky asked, forcing her to admit what Roland had already told her.

Her smile turned genuine. "I've been advised by our legal counsel to answer no further questions. You may return with a subpoena, but I'm sure you're aware that the issue of a reporter's privilege is protected by the First Amendment."

Despite expecting the response, Punky felt her cheeks flush hot with anger. "I don't give a damn—"

But Connor interrupted her. "And I'm sure you're aware the Supreme Court rejected constitutional privilege for reporters in Branzburg v. Hayes."

Punky's momentary shock of the Agency case officer's grasp of constitutional law was only surpassed by Diana's indignation. "I've been advised by our legal counsel—"

"Enough," Punky said. "We can go back and forth and keep playing these games if you want to, but it's not going to help us track down Teddy Miller's murderers. We really don't care what stories he was working on beyond how they might help us bring those responsible to justice."

Diana folded her arms across her chest and pursed her lips. "Be that as it may, it is our official position not to share any information with you at this time." She stepped forward and handed Punky a business card. "Any further inquiries can be directed to our legal department."

Punky was about to shred the card into pieces when she felt Connor's hand on the small of her back.

"Thank you for taking the time to speak with us," he said.

"If you'll wait here, I'll have one of our security guards return and escort you out."

Again, Punky was about to protest, but Connor's hand pressed harder into her back to keep her quiet. Together, they watched Diana Frost pivot on her sensible shoes and saunter away from the cubicles as if she had just scored a major victory for the sanctity of journalists everywhere.

When she was out of earshot, Punky wheeled on Connor. "What's gotten into you?"

Instead of answering, he held his hand out in front of him and revealed a thumb drive. "This fell out of the picture frame when you knocked it over."

25

Thomas Jefferson Memorial
Washington, DC

After leaving the White House, Sam had hurried to send Viktor a message and implored with him to meet at their usual location. It left a bad taste in his mouth to bend to the will of others, but he didn't really have a choice.

If they were going to survive this, Sam needed to see it through. For better or worse, their future was tied to the Russian, and that meant meeting with Viktor at the memorial. The first time they had met there, the Russian had recited several lines from the Declaration of Independence and insinuated that it was the duty of the American people to alter or abolish their government to protect against despotism.

But as he roamed the grounds and stared out across the placid tidal basin, he couldn't help but think that despotism was exactly what Viktor had in mind. As long as Russia was in control of the despot.

"Do you have what I require?"

As always, the voice of the older Russian surprised him. Sam stopped walking and bowed his head slightly with a sense of resignation that for all his political maneuvering, he had failed. He nodded. "It's going to happen tomorrow night."

"Details, Samuel."

Sam looked across the water again and stared at the White House in the distance. Despite the late hour, he doubted the president was already in bed. For all his faults, Jonathan was a dedicated public servant who gave every ounce of himself to uphold the oath he swore. It almost made Sam feel guilty that he was barely a mile away and meeting in secret with a Russian intelligence operative.

Almost.

"The president authorized a plan that calls for two CV-22 Ospreys to insert a team of Navy SEALs directly onto the objective and secure the facility while your armored vehicle is destroyed by their dedicated light attack aircraft."

Viktor didn't flinch at the news. "What is their route of flight?"

Sam reached into his pocket and pulled out a sketch of the route he had made from memory after leaving the Situation Room. Each waypoint was identified by a code name with latitude and longitude and included an estimated time of arrival. "There's always a chance the operation will be delayed—"

Viktor ignored him. "How many SEALs?"

Providing the Russian with a sketch of the assault team's route of flight was one thing. But divulging the number of Americans he was betraying was another. Though he had never met the men who had volunteered to go into harm's way, there was no way he could continue to view his treason in the abstract. But he was already in too deep to stop now. "Sixteen," he replied. "Two squads of eight. One on each Osprey."

"And the attack planes?"

"Two A-29 Super Tucanos," Sam replied. He was hesitant to remind Viktor that the A-29 had been the plane used to destroy a Stryker armored vehicle in the Fallon Range Training Complex during Jonathan's visit to launch his bid for the presidency. "They are single-engine turboprops with a crew of two each."

"Turboprops? Not sophisticated jets like the Joint Strike Fighter?"

Sam shook his head. "These planes are part of a new squadron designed to operate exclusively with the Navy SEALs."

But Viktor didn't seem to dwell on it. "Will there be surveillance assets in the skies overhead?"

Sam thought back to the drone footage that had abruptly gone blank and decided to leave out their plans for additional ISR coverage. "The A-29s both have sensor pods that will stream live video back to the Situation Room, but other than that, no. We had an MQ-9 Reaper assigned to find and track the vehicle inside Ukraine, but we lost contact with it."

Viktor didn't take the bait to confirm what Sam suspected. "Is that everything?"

Sam swallowed, wanting desperately to regain control of the situation. "Are we good?"

"I took care of your reporter friend like I promised, didn't I?"

He felt squeamish that it had come to that, but he didn't dare say anything to break the tepid truce, like mention the woman he had followed from Old Ebbitt Grill. The sooner they could be out from underneath Viktor's thumb, the better.

"Yes, Samuel. We're good."

Mykolaiv Oblast, Ukraine

Voronov's head bobbed from side to side with the gentle swaying of the armored vehicle. Beads of sweat trickled down the sides of his face, but he ignored them as just another nuisance that came with riding in the Bumerang's crowded troop compartment. It was hot and noisy, and the stench of motor oil intermixed with body odor did little to quell his nausea.

The armored vehicle wasn't moving particularly fast, but they were still making good time traversing the Ukrainian countryside en route to the Yuzhnoukrainsk storage facility. Of course, it helped that they hadn't been slowed by *khokhol* forces or harassed by fighter jets. Despite his discomfort, Voronov was beginning to believe that the worst was behind them.

"We just crossed inside fifty kilometers," the driver said over the intercom.

The words were accompanied by a sudden surge of adrenaline that jolted him awake. Voronov's eyes snapped open, and he swiped at the sweat coating his face when he realized how far they had come. They had spent years preparing for this moment. And now that the nuclear devices were within reach, he suddenly feared that defeat would be snatched from the jaws of victory.

"Anything on radar?" he asked.

Yevgeny manipulated the vehicle's sensors before shaking his head. "The skies are still clear."

Voronov nodded. After narrowly escaping the attack on the bridge, he had been skeptical that shooting down the drone would eliminate surveillance entirely. The Ukrainians must have known the Bumerang had made it through their defenses and was now operating with impunity behind their lines, even if they didn't know why. Voronov could imagine no scenario in which they would be allowed to reach their destination without encountering resistance.

But in spite of his fears, all the evidence seemed to support that they had been successful in losing themselves in the forest.

We might reach the facility after all, he thought.

Then he felt his phone vibrating.

He had just begun to believe the tides had shifted in their favor, but the incoming phone call seemed an ill omen. He fished it from his pocket and felt his stomach drop when he saw Viktor's name appear on the CallerID.

"Viktor. What is it?"

"The Americans are launching an operation to stop you," Viktor said, his voice surprisingly calm given the news he had just delivered.

"What?" Voronov's stomach suddenly bottomed out worse than the overtaxed suspension of the off-roading armored vehicle.

"I have just learned they are inserting a team of commandos at the facility and have directed attack aircraft to destroy you before you reach it."

"What about your leverage?"

"The president seems to have a spine after all."

"Driver, stop!" Voronov shouted.

The Bumerang lurched to a halt, and he quickly unstrapped from the jumpseat and turned for the rear exit. Learning that the Americans were violating their long-standing policy of not directly intervening in Ukraine suddenly made him feel trapped. He felt an overwhelming need to escape the constricting steel walls, and he opened the hatch to stumble out into the darkness.

"Did you hear what I said?"

Voronov gulped in a lungful of fresh air and listened to the panicked beating of his heart over the soft puttering of the vehicle's diesel engine. "How are we supposed to complete our mission now?"

"By doing exactly what I say."

He hated how quickly his fear had taken root and overcome him. He focused on how the breeze cooled him and took several deep breaths through his nose until his heart slowed to a more normal rhythm. He had always trusted Viktor without question, and the older operative had never disappointed him. If Viktor wasn't worried about the Americans, then he shouldn't be either. "Okay. What do you want me to do?"

Without preamble, Viktor told him everything he needed to know to shift the tide back in their favor and disrupt the American ambush. He listened intently and absorbed the information as his heart again started beating faster inside his chest.

Only this time it was from eager anticipation instead of fear.

26

Voznesensk Reserve Air Base
Voznesensk, Mykolaiv Oblast, Ukraine

The hangar was set apart from the rest of the base, making Colt feel even more isolated than he really was. He took several paces into the darkness, then stopped and tilted his head up toward the heavens to stare at the broad expanse of stars. It was so peaceful and serene, he could have almost convinced himself he hadn't been plopped down in the middle of a war zone.

But he knew better.

The hangar door behind him opened with a groan, then slammed shut. "We never found that laser weapon, did we?" Cubby asked.

Colt sighed and dropped his chin to his chest, listening to Cubby's footsteps erasing his momentary tranquility as they made their way across the cracked and uneven concrete. "Nope."

"You don't think..."

Colt shook his head, refusing to give credence to his fears. "These things just happen, Cubby."

"Bullshit."

Colt turned to look at the other pilot. "Come on. You know as well as I do that things just break sometimes."

"Yeah, but you don't really believe it. I can see it in your eyes." When Colt didn't defend against the accusation, Cubby continued. "How long has the Air Force been operating drones? You don't think they've ironed out the wrinkles by now?"

"Yeah, but—"

"Shit happens. Yeah, I know. But I think it's awfully coincidental that an experimental laser weapon went missing in Fallon around the same time the Russians were there doing some shady shit. Or did you forget that part?"

"I didn't forget," Colt said, remembering with vivid detail the morning when a van full of Russian gunmen kidnapped a Marine corporal in front of the Nugget Casino Resort. "But are you sure this doesn't have anything to do with you being shot down?"

Cubby's face hardened. "Maybe it does. Maybe it means I have an appreciation for what this weapon is capable of, and I think you're downplaying the potential risks. Drones aren't designed to just disappear like that. Even if the mission crew lost their ability to control it, the drone should have flown on its own back to the airfield where the launch-and-recovery element could use line-of-sight commands to land it safely."

"What makes you think that's not what's happening now?"

"Because if that were the case, we'd at least still be receiving telemetry data and would know where it was." Cubby shook his head. "No, I think you know as well as I do that *something* brought it down. I just don't want you burying your head in the sand and pretending like there's no risk. If we launch on this mission, we need to be prepared for every eventuality."

"Like laser weapons?" Colt asked.

Cubby threw his hands up in the air. "Cut the crap, Colt. I'm not crazy. At least tell me you think it's possible."

He had resisted letting his fears take root but couldn't ignore it any longer. "Fine. Yes, I think it's possible."

Cubby exhaled with apparent relief. "Okay. So, what are we gonna do about it?"

"What can we do? We still have a mission to accomplish. If the president gives us the green light—"

"That's a big if."

"Maybe so, but we still need to be ready to provide air support for the assault force, so the Russians don't use this weapon to knock the Ospreys out of the sky."

Cubby champed his mouth shut, obviously struggling to avoid stating the obvious.

What if they knock us out of the sky first?

But Colt knew what the Black Ponies crews were capable of. He had trained them relentlessly in Fallon and had developed their tactics to keep them safe from a multitude of surface-to-air threats. True, they hadn't specifically trained to defeat a directed energy weapon like the *DRAGON LINE*, but that didn't negate their tactics.

Colt placed a hand on Cubby's shoulder. "The Super Tucano is a tougher target to hit than a slow-moving Reaper loitering at high altitude."

"Tougher than a Joint Strike Fighter?"

Colt frowned. "You know what I mean."

"Yeah, but we still don't know where the laser is. That's a big question mark."

And that was the rub. Once the Reaper had been taken out, they were left blind to the potential danger. They knew that encountering the directed energy weapon was no riskier than coming across small-arms fire or man-portable air defense systems. But the difference was that the laser weapon was invisible. No tracer rounds. No smoke trails to see and avoid. No radar providing guidance they could detect and defeat.

Colt understood what had Cubby shaken, but there wasn't anything they could do about it. "In that case, let's just hope the task force puts up another drone and can locate the armored vehicle before we launch."

Before Cubby could protest further, the hangar door squeaked open again. Both pilots turned at the offending sound and saw Dave walking out to join them. "What are you two girls chattering about?"

Instead of answering, Cubby asked, "Any luck getting the drone feed back yet?"

Dave shook his head. "Looks like it was a hard kill."

"We still have some time," Colt offered.

"Probably not as much as you think."

Colt cocked his head to the side. "What's that supposed to mean?"

"It means that we just heard from the Beach. The president gave us the green light."

Colt's stomach dropped, and he turned to look at the faint glow on the eastern horizon portending the coming dawn. He swallowed. "When?"

"Tomorrow night," Dave replied. "Or, well, tonight. The others should be here soon, so we might want to get some rest."

Just then, Colt's ears perked up at the deep rumble of distant prop rotors approaching, and he knew the master chief was right. There wasn't much else they could do other than get some shut-eye to be rested for the mission. It didn't matter if they knew where the laser weapon was located or not. They had a mission to execute and an objective to complete.

"Roger that," Colt replied.

Hours later, Colt tossed back his poncho liner and stared up at the ceiling. For as exhausted as he had been on the flight down from Poland, he would have expected to simply collapse on the canvas cot and effortlessly slip into a deep slumber.

But sleep eluded him like a riddle without an answer, and he tossed and turned in frustration.

He stared at the narrow band of daylight that had found its way into the darkened room and traced its movement across the ceiling. Like the inverse of a sundial, he used it to calculate how much longer he had to sleep before waking to prepare for the mission. Or, more accurately, how much longer he had to brood over not being able to.

"Well, dammit..."

Colt sat up and swung his legs over the side of his cot and propped his elbows up on his knees. He was no stranger to the pre-mission jitters, but he wasn't a wet-eared lieutenant junior grade on his nugget cruise anymore either. It had been years since he lost sleep over it, and he had more than enough experience under his belt not to feel this way.

"Can't sleep?" Dave asked.

Colt looked over his shoulder at the bearded frogman lying flat on his back with his hands folded across his chest. He looked like a mortician had placed him *just so* for an open casket viewing, but his eyes were open and staring straight back at Colt.

"What gave it away?"

"Oh, just the moaning and groaning coming from your cot every few seconds."

"Sorry 'bout that."

Dave dismissed the apology. "Don't sweat it. We all get nervous before an operation."

Colt turned and surveyed the other cots in the room. Each one was occupied with the sleeping form of a man who had voluntarily shouldered the burden of risking his life to keep the world safe from the threat of nuclear Armageddon. "Yeah? So, why are they all sleeping like they don't have a care in the world?"

Dave lifted his head off the cot and looked around. "Maybe because they believe that good will always triumph over evil?"

Colt shook his head. "If only it were that simple."

Dave propped himself on an elbow and turned to face Colt. "Maybe it really is. Every man in this room volunteered to don the cloth of his nation. We're not a group of ragtag conscripts forced to do our master's bidding."

"Yeah, but war—"

"Is hell. Yeah, I know. But we're like the San Francisco 49ers the night before taking on the Charlotte 49ers."

Colt shook his head.

"And not the Niners team with Jimmy Garoppolo under center. The one with Steve Young."

"Are you saying I'm like Steve Young?"

"No, you're more like Trey Lance." Dave plopped back down onto his cot. "But we're still gonna crack some skulls tomorrow."

Colt stared at the SEAL in disbelief.

"Get some shut-eye, flyboy."

27

Colt bolted awake with his heart racing at a full gallop and took several labored breaths while struggling to orient himself. But then he remembered he had set his alarm to rouse him before the operational briefing. That didn't do much to calm his nerves. But it at least gave him something to focus his nervous energy on.

It was a short walk to the hangar where they had reconstituted the TOC after moving forward from Poland, and Colt was surprised to find it already crammed full of people when he walked inside. He made eye contact with the blonde MiG-29 pilot and gave her a respectful nod.

"Listen up!"

Colt looked over at Freaq, who stood on a plywood dais and waited for every head in the room to turn in his direction.

"It is now H minus three, and I need each person in here to tell me if it's going to happen tonight. If you have any reason to believe we should delay for twenty-four hours, speak up."

The room was silent, and all eyes were on him.

"Let's start with Two," he said, referring to the intelligence directorate.

A Navy lieutenant stood up. "There have been no significant changes in the threat picture. The Russians continue to be the largest opposition to our operation, but the bulk of their forces have remained south of the front lines along the Dnieper River. Potential threats to air include small arms, heavy machine guns, and man-portable air defense systems, but we assess that threat to be negligible in our area of operation. Threat to ground forces also includes small arms and a very low probability of rocket-propelled grenades or improvised explosive devices."

The lieutenant was confident and continued without consulting notes, aiming a laser pointer at the magnified aerial imagery on the screen at the front of the room. "The target location is in a remote heavily wooded area that should be accessible with minimal opposition via ingress from any direction."

He tapped on a button to advance the slide, showing a picture of an eight-wheeled armored personnel carrier. "We assess that the only enemy opposition will come from this vehicle, a VPK-7829 Bumerang—an improvement of the BTR-80 infantry fighting vehicle—armed with a 30 mm or 57 mm autocannon."

Or laser weapon, Colt thought.

The slide changed and the intelligence officer concluded his brief. "There has been zero chatter on social media or through SIGINT that our presence has been detected in Ukraine, and the Russian forces south of the river remain at a decreased defensive posture. I recommend go."

"Thanks," Freaq said, then nodded to the task force's operations officer. "Three?"

A Navy lieutenant commander stepped forward and advanced the slide to show a list of aircraft supporting the operation with several colored circles to the right of each one indicating their readiness status. "All aircraft are currently Fully Mission Capable, fully fueled, and armed in preparation for the mission. We will have two Super Tucanos from the Black Ponies orbiting overhead during the duration to provide overwatch for the insertion, actions on the objective, and exfiltration. In addition, we expect to have overlapping ISR coverage supported by armed MQ-9s."

Colt cringed when he thought about the previous Reaper that had simply vanished.

The lieutenant commander advanced the slide to the sync matrix. "Our current state will remain the same until H hour when the Super Tucanos will takeoff and provide overwatch. Once the Ospreys lift for troop movement, Ukrainian Air Force MiG-29s will enter into an Alert Five posture and on call for close air support until all assets have returned here."

Colt glanced at the MiG pilot, whose eyes were narrowed with intense focus.

"Based on intel's threat assessment, we are green across the board. I recommend go."

"Thank you," Freaq said. He turned to his communications folks. "Six?"

A young petty officer stepped forward and advanced the presentation one slide. "Primary communications will be via SATCOM with UHF relayed through the MQ-9 as secondary. Since we assess the enemy can monitor unsecure communications and use the transmissions to geo-locate, the team on the ground will communicate via secure VHF. The overwatch aircraft will monitor all three and can support a nine-line from any. We don't anticipate satellite degradation at all during this period of darkness and recommend go." Given the range, SATCOM, or Satellite Communications, was the preferred method, but standard ultra-high frequency and very-high frequency radios could be used as backups.

"Will we be able to monitor all three here in the TOC?"

The communications expert shook his head. "We'll have SATCOM and a delayed datalink reception from the UHF relay, but secure VHF will be strictly line of sight."

Freaq turned to Todd Lawson, the Black Ponies WSO who had drawn the short stick to remain behind in the TOC during the operation. "Todd, can you work with that?"

In the event things went to hell, he could direct close air support from the TOC—a small consolation for being left behind while his friends got to have all the fun downrange. He nodded. "Yeah, no problem, boss. If I need to get ahold of the Super Ts, I'll reach them on SAT. But my primary CAS platform will be the Fulcrums, and that comm's wired tight."

Satisfied, Freaq moved on to the other functions that fell within his operations staff. "Weather."

An Air Force staff sergeant stood at the front of the room. "Moonrise was at zero four forty local time at zero five five degrees and will set at twenty thirty-nine local time at three zero one degrees with a maximum illumination of zero point one percent. The moon will remain below the horizon during the entirety of the operation and will rise again at zero five fifty-four local."

He advanced a slide. "Astronomical twilight ends at twenty-two thirty local time and begins at zero three zero one. Wind will be negligible at H hour and will increase to seven knots from the west-southwest during exfil. Temperature will be sixty-nine degrees at H hour and increase to seventy-one at exfil, making thermal distinction ideal. Humidity is stable at fifty-two percent."

He advanced the slide again, showing satellite imagery of the entire country. "There are scattered clouds in the region; however, they appear largely stationary over the Black Sea and aren't expected to impede ISR coverage. Conditions are ideal. I recommend go."

Freaq nodded again. "Thank you. Personnel Recovery."

As the Air Force meteorologist sat, a trained SERE—Survival, Evasion, Resistance, and Escape—specialist stood. Colt knew it was his responsibility to ensure the larger global response network was prepared to act in the event one of their team found themselves isolated and behind enemy lines. He leaned forward to listen intently.

"EUCOM has set up a Guardian Angel team on alert with a Personnel Recovery Task Force and has the ISOPREPs for all aircrew and assaulters involved in the operation." Colt's ISOPREP, or Isolated Personnel Report, had been filled out years before and contained two color photos—a headshot and profile—and detailed each of his identifying tattoos and scars. "If we end up with downed aircrew, their E and E plan calls for them to clear the crash site by at least one klick before activating their beacons. The Ospreys will be the primary rescue platforms with the PRTF alert HC-130J and HH-60G Pave Hawks as backup. We have all Personnel Recovery assets in place. I recommend go."

Freaq nodded, then turned to survey the crowd of people assembled there. Colt had been impressed with the skipper from day one and knew he took his responsibility as squadron commander seriously. Freaq attributed his success to the efforts of his people, but he owned his failures.

His eyes found Colt's, and he quickly glanced at his watch before speaking. "Colt, do you have any concerns you want to address?"

Where do I begin?

He cleared his throat and put aside his reservations. "We all know what's at stake here. I'm confident we will be successful in our mission because of your hard work and dedication, and I couldn't be prouder to be a part of this team."

Freaq cracked a smile and nodded at Colt's sentiment, but his booming voice drowned out the excited murmurs. "Alright, folks, the operation is a go."

28

Colt watched the coalition of American and Ukrainian service members return to their assigned duties, completely in awe of the coordination required for an operation of this magnitude. While most of the men and women gathered there would remain in the TOC for the duration of the mission, he knew each of them played a vital role in its success.

"Wish I was going up with you boys," Todd said.

Colt turned to the SEAL and saw the earnestness etched on his face. "Me too, brother."

"Give 'em hell."

"Always."

They clasped hands, then Colt broke away and headed for the door as his stomach turned somersaults. But he knew that Dave had assembled the rest of the team in the hangar by now, and they would be waiting on him for the coordination brief. In the words of Kris "Tanto" Paronto before his favorite podcast, *The switch is on.*

There was no more room for nerves.

Colt pushed through the door and walked out into the darkness, absorbed by thoughts of the upcoming operation. He took two steps and came to an abrupt stop when he almost ran into the blonde MiG pilot who was silently staring up into the night sky.

"Oh, I'm sorry."

She turned to look at him, and he could see the worry marking her face even in the darkness.

"Colt Bancroft," she said, her voice confident but thick with a heavy accent.

He held his hand out to her. "I'm sorry we haven't been formally introduced."

"Polina Radchenko," she replied, giving his hand a firm squeeze.

He smiled at her in the darkness, impressed more by her toughness than her actual physical strength. Polina was hardly the first woman he had met to don a flightsuit and strap into a fighter jet. But she was the first one to have done so while enduring sustained combat operations over her homeland.

"Pleased to meet you, Polina."

She released his hand and turned to resume her contemplative observation of the night sky. The stars stretched from one end of the airfield to the other and reminded Colt that even though Ukraine was on the other side of the world, they were inextricably connected. It also reminded him that for as peaceful as things might appear at a distance, death and destruction loomed large over the horizon.

"You are a fighter pilot, yes?"

Colt nodded. "I am."

"Have you ever shot down another?"

Again, Colt nodded. "I have."

She turned with a surprised expression on her face. "Where?"

The details of his mission over the South China Sea were still highly classified. But somehow, he didn't think those rules applied when he was standing on the darkened ramp of a Ukrainian reserve air base, talking to a Ukrainian fighter pilot on the cusp of a high-stakes mission to prevent nuclear weapons from falling into the wrong hands.

"China," he replied.

"When?"

"I was on deployment in the South China Sea when I was launched to defend an American helicopter that was being attacked by Chinese fighters." Colt left out the part about the helicopter being used for an incursion into Chinese airspace to rescue an Agency case officer.

"So, you took a life to defend a life."

"That's our job, isn't it?"

Polina glanced up into the sky once more as if bidding the stars farewell, then turned and started walking for the hangar. Colt kept pace alongside her, content with the comfortable silence between them. He hadn't lost a wink of sleep over what he'd done to protect Dave and his fellow SEALs, and he suspected she felt the same about what she'd done to defend her country.

But he had seen enough to know better than to ask.

Halfway to the hangar, Polina abruptly stopped and gripped Colt's arm, turning him to face her. "I want you to know that I will take a life to defend yours."

Colt swallowed. "Thank you."

"I've got your six."

When Colt and Polina walked into the hangar, he was pleased to see that everyone was already present and waiting for them. He took his place in front of those gathered and waited until Polina had taken her seat at the rear of the room.

"Conditions are ideal for tonight's H hour," he said.

An excited murmur rose from the crowd and was accompanied by subdued fist-bumping and back-slapping. Colt was nervous, but that was nothing new. And he was scared too, but he'd been scared leading up to missions before. But it just felt different this time. The one thing that didn't feel different was standing in front of a group of dedicated professionals to detail the plans for a complex operation with little to no room for error.

"You all know why we're here, so I won't bother giving you a pep talk. At H minus thirty, the Super Tucanos will start engines while the assaulters load up on the Ospreys. At H minus ten, I'll initiate a roll call and wait for confirmation from the TOC—callsign Advocate—that we're still a go. At H minus five, the Super Tucanos will launch into a climbing orbit overhead to provide overwatch for the Osprey lift."

Colt glanced down at the Black Ponies crews assembled in the front row. "Dave and I will be the lead in Pony One One. Cubby and Ron will be in Pony One Two. Standard section procedures, yeah?"

Cubby nodded.

"At H hour, the Ospreys will lift and begin their transit to the target with the Super Tucanos maintaining a figure-eight orbit above them." Colt gestured to the lead CV-22 pilot. "I will now turn it over to Major Steve Urszenyi, the Osprey mission commander."

As the bald-headed Air Force special operations pilot stood and made his way to the front of the room, Ron leaned over to Dave and asked, "What kind of name is Urszenyi?"

Steve didn't bat an eye. "It's Hungarian. But there are only two or three families with this name worldwide." Without skipping a beat, he quickly shifted the focus back onto the mission. "I'll be the lead in Knife Two One, and Wedge will be the aircraft commander in Knife Two Two. We had our own intel folks select five suitable LZs based on proximity to the target and surrounding vegetation and have picked this one here as the primary." He pointed to the one closest to the storage facility's northwest corner. "The secondary will be half a klick north. To minimize detection of the ground force, we'll break off to the south at twenty klicks and execute two spoof insertions."

Everybody in the room knew the idea behind setting down multiple times during an insertion was to confuse the enemy and make them guess where the assault force was coming from. But it already looked like the SEALs were going to have an almost five-mile ruck to reach the target area from the primary LZ and even more from the backup.

Steve continued. "Following that, we will transit north and insert at the primary one bird at a time while the other loiters and provides cover. Once the entire assault force has offloaded, we will lift off and retrograde back to the twenty-klick mark, where we will wait until the assault force has given us the signal for extraction. Check?"

The bearded troop chief nodded once at the major. "Check."

Colt noticed the intensity in the SEAL's eyes and felt his nerves begin to dissolve as he took his place back at the front of the room. "The Ospreys will be the primary CASEVAC but a PRTF and Guardian Angel from EUCOM will be on Alert Five in Poland as a backup. Both Super Tucanos will remain airborne during the operation to provide close air support, but Starshyy Leytenant Polina Radchenko will also be on Alert Five in a MiG-29 here at Voznesensk in case shit hits the fan."

Colt nodded in thanks to the blonde fighter pilot. "Polina, anything to add?"

"*Slava Ukraini*," she said.

Her response elicited another round of fist bumps.

"Okay, we've got one hour until H minus thirty. Let's get it done."

As the crowd broke up to begin making their final preparations for the mission, Dave walked up to Colt and slapped him on the back. "Steve *motherfucking* Young."

29

JW Marriott
Washington, DC

After being turned away by the wicked witch of the *Washington Post*, Punky and Connor returned to the JW Marriott where she went upstairs to retrieve her laptop. Both were eager to see the thumb drive's contents and were mentally prepared for a long night of sifting through its secrets to find the one morsel of information tasty enough to kill for.

"I ordered you a beer," Connor said when she returned to their table.

"You can leave now if you ordered me a Bud Light."

He chuckled and shook his head. "Figured you'd want something a little bit stronger than that."

Just then, the waitress arrived and set two tall pilsner glasses on the table in front of them. She was pleased to see he had ordered her what looked like a Hazy IPA—possibly a double—but knew that she would need to nurse her drink to keep her wits about her.

After the waitress left, Punky opened her laptop and inserted the thumb drive. She scanned it for viruses, then double-clicked on the icon to open it. A second smaller window opened in its place with the words "Enter Password."

"Should have expected that," Connor said.

Punky grunted and scooped up her glass to take a large gulp of the mental lubricant.

"What are we going to do now?"

Truthfully, she didn't know. But she wasn't about to let Connor sniff out her indecisiveness. She had always prided herself on taking bold action when others faltered, and she wasn't about to confront this challenge any differently. She set her beer down and reached for the laptop, resting her fingers on its keys.

"I'm going to crack this code," she said.

"Okay." Connor didn't seem to share her confidence. "Where do we start?"

She chewed on her lip for several seconds, then typed *WAPO* into the window.

"*Washington Post?*"

"No, water polo," she said, then huffed. "Yes, *Washington Post*."

But the small window shook and returned the message "Incorrect Password. Four tries remaining."

"Well, shit," Connor said. "Maybe we should hand this off to somebody who knows what they're doing."

She glowered at him but reached for her phone and Googled Teddy Miller. Several articles he had written popped up, but instead of picking a random article and hoping for a minor miracle, she tapped on the Wikipedia link and opted for a major one. Connor took a sip of his beer and leaned in to read over her shoulder.

"Forty years old. Grew up in Sheffield, Massachusetts. Single. Never married. No kids."

Punky's eyes scanned the page and she ignored Connor's running commentary.

"Undergraduate degree in journalism from George Washington University." Connor paused. "What's their mascot?"

She stopped scrolling and opened another browser window to start a different search. "Looks like... Revolutionaries?"

Connor shook his head. "Doesn't sound right."

She continued scrolling through the results until she found a new answer. "Here. The school changed their mascot's name from 'Colonials' to 'Revolutionaries' after receiving criticism that their mascot represented colonizers who stole land and resources from indigenous groups."

"Seriously?"

She typed *Colonials* into the password window. Again, the window shook.

"Three more guesses," Connor lamented.

Punky closed the browser window and returned to the Wikipedia article. "We can't pick his birthday or hometown. Those are too obvious. He didn't have a wife or kids, so we can't use their birthdays or names. Those would be obvious guesses too."

"Try 'Password' or a number string?"

Punky shook her head. An award-winning journalist with the *Washington Post* wouldn't pick something so banal. "No, he probably thought he was smarter than everybody else. It has to be something overly clever."

"We're going to be here all night," Connor said.

Punky took a sip of her beer. "No, we won't."

"We won't?"

She shrugged. "We only have three more guesses."

"Then what?"

That was a good question. She doubted the thumb drive had some sort of *Mission Impossible* self-destruct feature that would cause it to start smoking and melt its components. But there had to be some sort of consequence for entering the wrong password five times. "I don't really want to find out," she replied.

The two leaned back in their seats and stared at the laptop screen as if trying to divine the answer to the riddle among the pixels on the screen. But instead of some revelation, they were left staring at a frustratingly blank box underneath the phrase "Enter Password."

"What about 'Atlantic' for the magazine that printed his first byline?"

Punky chewed on the inside of her cheek. It was a good suggestion, but it didn't feel right. "I don't know. Somehow, I don't think we'll find the answer on his Wikipedia page."

Connor grunted and fell silent as Punky listened to the sound of her laptop's fan kicking on as if mirroring their level of mental exertion to come up with an answer. But after several seconds, Connor snapped his fingers.

"I've got it. What was the name of the award that woman from the *Washington Post* said he won?"

"The Aldo something-or-other?"

"Try 'Aldo.'"

She tapped the name into the window and said a silent prayer before hitting the enter key.

The window shook.

"Dammit!"

But Punky still thought they were on the right track. She opened another browser window on her phone and Googled the award. "Here it is. Aldo *Beckman*."

Without waiting, she typed "Beckman" into the window.

It shook.

"Wait," Connor said. "We only have one more guess. We don't know what happens if we get it wrong, but it can't be good. Are you sure you want to try again and risk finding out?"

"We're onto something. I can feel it."

"Okay, so what is it?"

She clicked on the Wikipedia link for the award and scrolled down through the list of past awardees to find the entry on Teddy Miller. It showed that he won the award while working for the *Washington Post*, but it didn't say what the article was about.

This time, it was Punky who felt like she had stumbled on an *Aha!* moment. "What did she say the article was about?"

"Afghanistan?"

She shook her head. "No, she said it was on the withdrawal from Afghanistan."

Connor leaned back in his chair and rubbed his eyes. "That could mean anything. It could be '083121' for the official conclusion to the war. Or maybe it's the name of the last American to leave. Or maybe—"

"Maybe it's a reference to the suicide bombing?"

"Abbey Gate?"

She typed "Abbey" into the window and paused before hitting enter. "What was the date of that attack?"

Connor picked up his own phone and started tapping on the screen. Punky waited patiently for him to come up with the answer while she agonized over her decision to use their last attempt on what amounted to nothing more than a wild-ass guess.

"August 26th, 2021," Connor finally said.

She added the date to her entry. *Abbey082621.*

"Are you sure about this?"

Punky shook her head and took a deep breath. "Here goes nothing."

She hit the Enter key and waited for the window to shake like it had done the previous four times. But instead, it disappeared and was replaced by a much larger window that contained several folders with seemingly innocuous names.

"Holy shit," Connor said. "I can't believe that worked."

Me either, she thought.

"Where do we go from here?" Punky asked, scrolling through what seemed like hundreds of folders, each one presumably with some piece of research or writing that Teddy wanted to safeguard.

"Stop. Wait. Go back."

Punky reversed her scrolling until Connor stabbed his finger at the screen.

"That's it. Start there."

She double-clicked on the folder labeled "AuroraHoldings_SourceX."

But instead of being rewarded with a trove of word documents or PDFs detailing the minutiae of a corporation with secrets powerful enough to kill for, a dozen icons for audio files greeted them. Each audio file appeared to be labeled with a six-digit number corresponding with dates. The oldest appeared to have been just before Jonathan Adams announced his intent to run for president. She hovered the cursor over its icon and hesitated before tapping on the track pad.

Connor looked over at her and nodded.

She double-tapped the track pad to play the audio file, and they both leaned in close to the laptop's miniature speakers. The recording was of relatively good quality without the *hiss* and *pop* of a defective microphone or electromagnetic interference. The voice of Teddy's "Source X" came through loud and clear and sent a chill down her spine.

"Recognize the voice?" she asked in a whisper.

Connor shook his head. But it was clear he was having a similar reaction to hearing the voice of a woman with a thick Russian accent.

30

Both of their beers were left forgotten as they listened to one recording after another with an increasing sense of foreboding. It seemed that Teddy Miller had gone down a rabbit hole after receiving an anonymous call from a Russian woman he referred to as *Source X*.

"So, what do we do now?" Connor asked.

Punky chewed on the inside of her lip. "Go back to the beginning."

"The beginning of what?"

She shifted in her chair to face him. "This all started because a Marine corporal who had been abducted by Russians ended up in the same room as the man who is now the president of the United States. I had always believed there was a purpose to that meeting, but..."

When she trailed off, Connor took over. "But Garett never told you what it was."

Punky shook her head. "I honestly believe he didn't know. I pressed him hard and came at him from every angle I could think of, but he insisted he had only been instructed to present Jonathan Adams with a cigar box."

"A gift?" Connor asked.

"Or a message," Punky replied.

Connor pointed at the laptop. "If any of what we just heard from *Source*

X is true, then maybe Garett was telling the truth. Maybe his abduction was all part of an elaborate plan to deliver a message."

And that's what bothered Punky the most. In an era of modern communications like cell phones, email, and social media, it was a relatively easy thing to pass along a message. So why the effort? Why go through the trouble of kidnapping a Marine and then arranging for him to have a private meeting with the man who would become president?

"Why him?" she asked.

"What do you mean?"

"The last time I questioned Adam Garett, a Marine guard asked me what was so special about him." She paused as she thought about her response. "I told him he was the key."

"The key to what?"

"I don't know. But I had been trying to unmask him for years and still believe he is part of some bigger scheme." She chuckled when she thought about what the Marine guard had said to her in response. "And you know what the guard said to me?"

"What?"

"He said, 'maybe you should just turn him.'"

Connor's eyes narrowed. "What if somebody already did?"

Punky felt a chill run down her spine. She knew Garett had been the adopted son of a woman who ran the West Coast network for China's Ministry of State Security. She knew he had been involved in revealing secrets to the Chinese that resulted in the development of a weapon capable of hacking into the stealthy F-35 Joint Strike Fighter. And she had always assumed that his abduction by the Russians had been intended to secure leverage over the woman known as *Mantis*.

"Keep going with that," she said.

Connor licked his lips as he tried compiling his thoughts into words. "You said he spied for the Chinese, right?"

She nodded. "He was convicted of espionage at a court-martial."

"And he was abducted by the Russians, who released him days later to hand-deliver a cigar box to the president, right?"

Again, she nodded. But she was beginning to feel her frustration boiling to the surface. She knew all of this already, which was why she had been relentlessly questioning the corporal at the Pendleton brig. "Yes, but what do you mean somebody turned him?"

"I mean, what if the Russians had kidnapped him to turn him into an asset?"

"An asset they allowed us to arrest? Doesn't seem like a good use of resources."

"Unless that was their plan all along," Connor said. He seemed excited, as if the mystery was beginning to reveal itself to him, and the words continued flowing. "Unless their plan was to put him someplace safe and keep him safe until they needed him."

"For what?"

"For leverage," he said, then shook his head in disbelief. "But not leverage over the Chinese. Leverage over…"

It hit Punky like a lightning bolt. "Over the president."

"Jesus, Mary, and Joseph," Connor said. "What was it that *Source X* said on that first recording?"

Punky leaned forward and clicked on the first audio file they had listened to, then tapped up on the volume keys so they wouldn't need to crowd over the small speakers to hear.

"*Jonathan Adams has a secret,*" the woman's voice said.

Punky hit the track pad to pause the playback. "How on earth could a disgruntled Marine corporal convicted of espionage be used as leverage over the president?"

"Depends on his secret, don't you think?"

Punky exited the folder labeled "AuroraHoldings_SourceX" and opened another labeled "AuroraHoldings_FormationDocs."

"What are you looking for?" Connor asked.

"I don't know." And that was the most frustrating part. She thought he might be onto something, but still didn't know where to look to find the smoking gun. "But we need to know more about this company, Aurora Holdings."

"It's probably just a shell."

"Exactly. But even shells need to at least appear legitimate. That means they need to have articles of incorporation filed with the Secretary of State, operating agreements, licenses, and an employer ID number used by the

Internal Revenue Service. They need to have annual reports and tax returns."

Punky scrolled the list of documents and clicked on one labeled "AuroraHoldings_ARTS-CL."

When the document opened, they saw that it was a scanned copy of articles of incorporation for a close corporation that had been filed with California's Secretary of State.

"What's a close corporation?" Connor asked.

"It means it's held by a limited number of shareholders and isn't publicly traded."

He pointed to the first line, which listed "Aurora Holdings" as the name of the corporation. "Looks like we might be getting somewhere—the corporation's address is in Berkeley, California."

"Didn't the president go to school there?" Punky asked.

Connor nodded. "So did Samuel Chambers. They were roommates, I think."

Punky pulled up the address on her phone and groaned.

"What?"

She turned it to show him the map zoomed in on an empty lot at the end of Grayson Street, adjacent to a mile-long lagoon that was the centerpiece for Aquatic Park. "If there was a physical location, it's not here anymore."

"What about the California registered corporate agent?" he asked.

She scrolled down to see that a woman named Lana Roman was listed as the registered agent in the block for service of process. She entered the associated street address—also in Berkeley—into her phone's map application and zoomed in on a simple cottage across the street from San Pablo Park. "What is the chance Lana Roman still lives here?"

"Probably not very good," he replied, echoing her pessimistic mood.

"This says that two thousand shares can be issued but held by no more than two persons," Punky said.

"Two people who probably know what the company's purpose is," Connor added. "Too bad it's a close corporation and the shareholder's identities are confidential."

Punky exited the articles of incorporation document and double-tapped on the icon for one labeled "AuroraHoldings_OA."

"What's that?"

"The operating agreement," Punky replied. "Even if the shareholder information isn't public, the operating agreement filed with the Secretary of State should list the shareholders."

She scrolled through the document and scanned the titles for each section, looking for the one that would unlock the secrets of Aurora Holdings. Though she imagined Teddy Miller had already exhausted the same sources during his investigation, she couldn't help but follow the breadcrumbs as she saw them.

Introduction, Formation, Purpose, Management and Governance. She continued scrolling until she came to the section titled "Shareholder's Rights and Responsibilities." Connor leaned in close, and they read the names together.

"Mila Smith? Who's that?"

Punky shook her head. "No clue, but she owns ninety percent of the two thousand shares."

"Who owns the other ten percent?"

Punky continued scrolling until reaching the second named shareholder. "Is it just me, or does that look like a Russian name to you?"

"Oh shit." He jumped up from the table and backed away several paces before bringing his phone up and dialing a number.

"Who are you calling?"

"Langley."

Punky felt her blood run cold. "What? Why?"

Connor stared at her as he waited for his call to connect. "Because Viktor Drakov is a known Russian intelligence operative. I don't know what Aurora Holdings is, but if there's any connection between Viktor and the president, we need to run this up the flagpole. ASAP."

31

White House Situation Room
Washington, DC

There were fewer people in the Kennedy Conference Room than there had been earlier when they briefed the president on the situation in Ukraine. Sam sat in his usual chair over the president's right shoulder and stared at the White House logo on the large flat-screen monitor at the other end of the room, waiting for it to blink on and come to life with images from the other side of the world.

"How much longer, Bart?" Jonathan asked.

General Tilley, the chairman of the Joint Chiefs of Staff, spoke quietly into the handset, then placed it back on the cradle in front of him. "Our forces are preparing to spin up now, Mr. President. All conditions are ideal to launch at the planned H hour."

Sam glanced over at the digital clock on the wall and saw that they were only minutes from reaching the appointed time to commence the operation.

Jonathan casually glanced over his shoulder and did a double take. "Everything okay, Sam?"

He nodded quickly and was about to reply when the conference room door opened, and Olivia Manning walked in. His heart bolted, renewed with the sudden hope that the operation had been scrubbed or that unforeseen technical difficulties might prevent them from watching Americans dying in high definition. He glanced in her direction, then narrowed his eyes with concern when he realized she had come to speak with him.

Olivia crossed the room quickly and bent to speak quietly into his ear. "Sam, you have a phone call."

He waved her off. "Not now."

"It sounds urgent."

Again, his heart bolted. "From who?"

"Lana Roman?"

JW Marriott
Washington, DC

Punky thought about leaving another message but instead dropped her cell phone on the table in disgust. Connor had been busy filling in several of his co-workers at Langley about their discovery that Viktor Drakov was a shareholder in a company of dubious origins. And while they were following up on the leads they had uncovered, she still felt a twinge of guilt that she was just sitting there and waiting for the answers to fall into their lap.

Connor returned to the table and sat down without saying a word.

"Well?" Punky asked, waiting for him to share with her what he had learned.

He replied with a subtle shake of his head. "Nobody has heard anything about Aurora Holdings."

"So, that's it? It's just another dead end?"

Connor rubbed his eyes. They were both tired and had been through so much already, but she couldn't stomach the thought of pressing pause on her investigation just to get some sleep. "No, that's not it. People are looking into it, and we just need to be patient."

Punky sighed loudly. "Be patient."

The Agency man pulled his fists away from his face and glowered at her. "We're looking into it. What have you come up with?"

It sounded far more accusatory than he probably intended. "Nothing."

Connor gave a little shake of his head, almost as if saying, *See? I told you so.*

"I tried the number for the registered agent, Lana Roman, but only got a messaging service."

"Did you leave a message?"

Punky nodded. "I don't even know if the number is still accurate or if anybody even checks the messages anymore. But I left my contact information and asked Lana to call me back at her earliest convenience."

They fell into an uneasy quiet as their fatigue and the weight of the situation fell over them. A reporter had lost his life because he was investigating the president's connection to Aurora Holdings, and Punky couldn't help but feel like they were barreling down the same path.

"Maybe we need to take a break and reattack this with fresh eyes," Connor suggested.

She was loath to admit it, but she had been thinking the same thing. She was exhausted—physically, mentally, emotionally—and knew she wasn't seeing things clearly. She nodded.

Connor stood. "Let's meet for breakfast in the morning."

"Where?"

"Chick and Ruth's," he replied. "I'll send you the address."

"Okay."

Punky stared through the center of the table while Connor hovered over her. "Punky..."

She glanced up. "Yeah?"

"We'll get to the bottom of this."

She swallowed and nodded, though she was beginning to feel like this investigation was one big roadblock after another—a one step forward, two steps back kind of thing. But despite her overwhelming exhaustion, she was unwilling to mail it in. She wasn't built to give up or accept defeat.

"You'll call me if you hear anything," she said, more as a statement than a question.

Connor nodded. "I will."

"And I'll let you know if I hear back from Lana Roman."

"I know."

"Okay then," she said. "We'll regroup tomorrow with fresh eyes."

"Bring an appetite," Connor said, then spun for the exit.

White House Situation Room
Washington, DC

"Everything okay, Sam?" Jonathan asked.

It was the same question the president had asked before Sam left to take the call, but this time he struggled to put on a brave face and smile for his boss. The two had been together for so long that he was certain Jonathan would see right through his facade and sense that something was amiss. He cleared his throat as he lowered himself into his chair. "Everything's fine."

The president nodded, then turned back to General Tilley, who was again on the phone with somebody from his staff. The general pulled the phone away from his ear and covered the handset as he leaned forward and fixed his gaze on Jonathan.

"Mr. President, the assault force is spinning up now, and we will be patching into the task force operations center in Virginia Beach momentarily."

"Very well," Jonathan replied.

Bart pulled his hand away from the handset and resumed speaking with whoever was on the other end, but Sam was so absorbed by his own thoughts that he couldn't have cared less what was being said. Before Olivia had walked in the conference room to tell him he had a phone call, the idea of watching Americans die on the large screen in front of him had been the worst thing he could imagine.

But now...

The screen at the front of the room flickered as the White House logo disappeared and was replaced with a view of what looked like a command center full of men and women in green camouflage uniforms. A tall, silver-haired man at the center of the room with a subdued Navy SEAL trident on his chest turned and looked directly into the camera.

"Mr. President, can you hear me?"

Jonathan appeared to relax at seeing the senior SEAL on the screen. "Loud and clear, Captain."

"Very good, sir. With your prior approval, I gave the assault force the green light to commence the operation."

Sam could sense the task force commander's anxiety as he addressed his commander in chief. And with good reason. The senior SEAL knew what was at stake and understood that the ramifications for failure extended far beyond the impact on his own career. Sam knew it was more than hyperbole to say that the fate of the free world rested squarely on the shoulders of the men who were preparing to launch a daring mission in Ukraine.

A daring mission that was about to fail because of Sam.

He swallowed.

And now I need to figure out what to do about Emmy King.

32

All remnants of his anxiety had completely vanished by the time Colt flashed his light at Cubby to let him know it was time to start their engines. He completed the startup sequence just as he had done on every training mission in Fallon. To him, it didn't matter whether he was sitting on the paved tarmac in front of their hangar back home or at a reserve air base in the middle of Mykolaiv Oblast in Ukraine. The procedures were the same, and he completed each step from memory with practiced hands.

Within minutes, the Super Tucano's engine turned the large propeller, and the airplane bucked and pranced in place. Dave was quiet in the back, working to align the inertial navigation system while using the global positioning system to tighten their location and ensure they maintained radio contact with the rest of the assault force.

"Pony check-in," Colt said over SAT. "Pony One One."

"Pony One Two," Cubby replied, his transmission sounding hollow.

"Pony One One, this is Advocate," Todd said from the TOC. "Envy Three Three and Envy Four Two are both on station. No change to picture. We are green."

"Pony One One."

Colt looked up at the stars through the canopy, imagining the MQ-9 Reapers orbiting his position while they scanned for threats, but he couldn't see them. Just as he couldn't see the laser that would bring them down if the Russians knew they were there. He just had to trust they were going to take the enemy by surprise.

We are green.

He flipped down his NVGs and turned them on, almost surprised by the alien scene surrounding him. The airfield lights were turned off, but they had marked the runway boundaries with IR chem lights that lit up like brilliant orbs in a straight line stretching from left to right. Farther down the flight line, the Ospreys glowed under their covert lighting configuration, turning what had once been pitch black into an instant Christmas tree of lights.

"You ready?" he asked Dave over the ICS.

"Let's do it."

He advanced his throttle and released his brakes, using his peripheral vision to sense his forward movement as the plane crept forward across the ground. He stepped on the right pedal to swing the nose in that direction, trusting that Cubby was following him.

As the two planes crept onto the departure end of the runway, Colt allowed his momentum to build and pressed hard on the right brake to swing his nose around and line up on the far side. He glanced over his shoulder and saw Cubby taking his position.

"Pony One Two set."

Without waiting, Colt advanced to full power and began rolling down the blacked-out runway. He danced on the rudder pedals to keep his nose pointed straight, sensing his speed build more than looking for a specific number in his Heads Up Display. But after several seconds, he gently pulled back on the stick and coaxed it into the air.

"Pony One One airborne," Dave said.

Colt kept the plane's nose five degrees above the horizon and allowed the speed to continue building before reaching forward to raise the landing gear and flaps. He felt an almost instantaneous decrease in drag and countered it by lifting his nose even higher.

"Pony One Two airborne."

Colt craned his neck to the left and spotted Cubby's plane lifting off the runway and beginning a shallow turn to join on him.

"Deploying turret," Dave said over the intercom.

"Roger."

They leveled off at ten thousand feet in a left-hand orbit over the reserve air base with the two planes opposite each other. Though intelligence had assessed there to be a low probability of a surface-to-air threat at Voznesensk, they adhered to tactics that were designed to mitigate risks that were inherent had they been operating from a remote FARP, or Forward Arming and Refueling Point, behind enemy lines. As such, they cleared the area surrounding the airfield before giving the tiltrotors clearance to launch.

"Looks good to me, boss," Dave said.

"Roger. Knife Two One, you are green for launch."

Major Urszenyi breaking squelch twice was his only response. Colt glanced down at the right display and saw the two tiltrotor aircraft turn to parallel the runway and begin a short takeoff roll in quick succession. The dust cloud was enormous, but within seconds, they cleared the runway and turned to the east.

Colt looked up from watching the Ospreys and glanced across the circle at Cubby. "Pony One Two, take one zero thousand."

"Copy, one zero thousand."

Colt added power and lifted his nose to climb another two thousand feet, ensuring deconfliction from Cubby's plane. Dave had retracted the turret once the Ospreys turned east, and they increased their speed to just under three hundred miles per hour. Though the Super Tucanos could slow to match the troop transports, their tactics called for them to fly at close to their normal cruise speed of three hundred and twenty miles per hour while flying in a figure-eight pattern above the tiltrotors.

Leveling off at twelve thousand feet, he reversed to the right and began a turn back to the east above the northernmost Osprey. Jim was on the opposite end of the formation, in a left turn toward east above the southernmost Osprey. They would pass over each other in the middle of the eight.

"How's it look?" Colt asked Dave over the ICS.

"Lookin' good, boss." He knew Dave would let him know if he saw anything, or if one of their radar warning receivers indicated that a surface-to-air weapon system's radar was painting them. But based on intel's assessment, he didn't expect that this far from the front lines.

He let Dave focus on their displays while he kept his eyes outside, scanning the darkness for muzzle flashes or smoke trails like he'd seen in the skies over Syria. But it was still the invisible threat from a directed energy weapon that occupied most of his thoughts.

Remain vigilant.

It was a silent mantra, but one that kept his head in the game. Colt knew carelessness was the leading cause of aviation mishaps, and the complexities of combat only increased the risk.

Eighteen minutes after the Ospreys began their transit east, Steve keyed the SAT channel. "Knife and Pony passes phase line Ducati."

The response from the TOC was immediate. "Advocate copies Ducati. You are green."

Every operation hinged on timed coordination of assets. The leadership team in the TOC ensured each asset was in place at the specified time, which meant they needed to know whether the assault force was ahead of or behind timeline. Though they were tracking the air movement by their transponder beacons, they had identified pre-determined locations known as phase lines where the Ospreys would check in to give the TOC an opportunity to verify conditions were still acceptable to continue.

The operation had been broken up into an aerial movement and a ground movement. The air movement had two phase lines, Ducati and Harley, that corresponded with one hundred klicks and fifty klicks from the target. They could delay at either phase line if conditions had worsened, but after passing Harley they would be committed, and their final go/no-go decision would be made at time of insertion.

"Copy, green," replied Steve.

Colt took a deep breath and exhaled into his mask. At the rate they were traveling, they would reach Harley in just over six minutes and would receive the last update before the Ospreys broke off to execute their spoof infils. At that point, he and Cubby would climb above twenty thousand feet to orbit the storage facility and cover the SEALs' insertion and ground movement.

"Still looking good," Dave said. "They won't even know we were here."

Colt nodded, then forced himself to do an inventory of their status. He checked the fuel and compared it against their mission planning numbers. The wind was lighter than what they had expected, and they were well above the fuel state they had planned to be at when they crossed Ducati. More gas meant more loiter time and a greater chance of completing the mission.

Looking good.

The Super Tucano carried an internal fuel load of 695 liters, or just over 180 gallons. But Colt referred to his fuel load in terms of pounds, which meant that he had taken off with just over twelve hundred pounds of fuel—a number that made him cringe, given that the Hornet had an internal capacity eight times greater.

But even with less gas, the light attack planes could loiter over the objective for one and a half hours before they needed to return to Voznesensk to refuel. Based on the contingencies they had briefed, if they hadn't secured the nuclear weapons within thirty minutes of arriving at the facility, Colt would depart while Cubby provided overwatch as a single ship.

"Knife and Pony passes phase line Harley."

Steve's transmission broke Colt from his trance.

"Advocate copies Harley. You are green."

It's go time.

"Pony moving to high cover," Colt said.

Both light attack aircraft rolled out heading east and began a climb to twenty thousand feet. Cubby leveled off below Colt as both pilots pulled power to slow to their most efficient loiter speed.

"Deploying turret," Dave said from the backseat.

"Roger."

Below them, the Ospreys broke away to begin spoofing the insertion. The butterflies that had been dormant in Colt's stomach returned, flittering gently as a reminder of what was at stake.

33

25 km west of Yuzhnoukrainsk

Voronov scanned the dark horizon, more for something to do while ignoring Yevgeny's incessant prattle as he gave a running commentary of what contacts had been detected on radar so far. But none had fit the flight profile Viktor had described, and he was quickly running out of patience.

"My brother left..."

Then he heard it.

"Shhh!"

But the younger man ignored him and continued telling the story of his childhood.

"...when I found..."

Voronov wheeled on him. "Shut your mouth!"

Through the darkness, he saw his rage reflected off Yevgeny's startled expression as the sudden violence scared him into silence. Voronov raised his hand, holding a single finger outstretched, and pointed at his ear in the universal hand signal to listen.

There was nothing.

"What is it?" the operator asked, his body taut under Voronov's gaze.

"There was something..."

His voice trailed off as he turned his head and pointed his ear to the sky to listen for the sound that had broken through the quiet of the night. It had been faint. So faint it barely registered over the whisper of wind and tickled at the back of his mind.

Yevgeny rose from his console and scrambled from the rear of the Bumerang to stand next to Voronov. Together, they turned their heads to scan the horizon where the sea of stars met with the dark canvas of earth.

"I hear nothing."

"If you don't stop talking," Voronov growled, "I'll silence you myself."

It sounded like a threat, which it was. He was certain he had heard something. And if his half-witted companion could keep his mouth shut long enough, he knew he could hear it again.

There!

"What..." But the younger man bit off his question, afraid to upset their precarious peace.

Voronov felt a chill down his spine, but his lips curled into a wicked smile.

They are coming. Just like Viktor had predicted.

In between brief gusts of wind that rustled through the bushes surrounding them, he had heard two, maybe three, beats of a large blade thumping the air. It sounded different from the helicopters he'd heard in the past, but he knew without a shadow of a doubt it was the Americans.

"They're coming," he said.

The operator stood motionless.

"Ready the weapon."

Voronov kept his voice low and calm compared to how he had spoken to the younger man earlier. He had been hard on him but knew that rattling him now would not achieve the desired reaction. But the operator remained motionless.

"Yevgeny," he said.

The operator turned back to him, mouth agape.

"Ready the weapon. Right. Now."

As if broken free from his paralysis, Yevgeny scrambled back into the Bumerang and rushed to prepare the *DRAGON LINE* for engagement. But

Voronov took his time. He sat down in his seat next to the operator and stared at the screen as Yevgeny acquired a lock on the first aircraft.

Thump thump thump thump.

The droning of the American helicopters was unmistakable by the time the weapon's power supply had stored up enough energy to complete a single engagement.

"How far are they?" Yevgeny asked.

He ignored the question. "Engage the TILL."

"Engaging," he responded.

Voronov stared at the monitor displaying images from the Advanced Dual Optical Tracking System and saw a military aircraft centered on the screen. A beam of light instantly appeared as the target-illuminator laser focused on the target and fed information back to the weapon's computer.

"Developing solution," Yevgeny said.

Voronov knew that a second laser measured the beam's distortion caused by atmospherics and generated a correction to the main laser for engagement. It was all very high-tech and scientific, but all he cared about were the results. Viktor had trusted him to prevent the Americans from meddling in their operation, and he intended to do just that.

"Solution complete," the operator said only seconds later.

"Engage target."

It was already too late for the Americans.

PONY 11
Navy A-29 Super Tucano

After passing phase line Harley, Colt reined in his nerves and focused intently on the darkened landscape beneath them through his night vision goggles. He trusted that Dave was using their multi-spectral targeting pod to acquire potential targets while he kept his eyes peeled for threats.

"Sure is quiet up—"

"Holy shit!" Dave yelled, cutting him off.

Acting on instinct, Colt reversed his angle of bank and craned his neck over his shoulder to look for whatever had startled his WSO. "Talk to me."

"Just caught a flash off one of the Ospreys," he replied.

"A flash?"

Dave was no stranger to coming under fire, and it was unlike him to react so strongly without a good reason. But as he glanced down at the Ospreys that appeared all but invisible in the darkness, he couldn't see anything to corroborate the SEAL's claim.

Then a thought occurred to him. "Aim the pod at the Ospreys."

"What?" Dave asked, his confusion apparent. "Why?"

"Humor me."

Colt felt his heart thudding in his chest as he glanced down at the screen and waited for Dave to center the crosshairs on the first of two Ospreys. He hoped he wasn't right, but maybe Dave had accidentally detected the first volley.

"Knife Two Two... We're losing oil pressure on the starboard engine." The fear in the Osprey pilot's voice was unmistakable.

The first Osprey appeared on the screen. "What are we looking for, boss?"

Colt studied the image but didn't see anything out of the ordinary. Especially something that might indicate enemy action that could have caused an issue with Knife Two Two's engine. "Shift to the second Osprey."

"Knife Two Two's losing power..."

The transmission was broken and chaotic, the sound of alarms and vibration carrying across the airwaves to all who were listening.

"Abort," Steve said over the radio. "Get out of there."

As their sensor pod's image centered on the second Osprey, Colt's heart suddenly stopped as a feeling of cold dread settled over him. Smoke was trailing the right engine, and it was apparent they had suffered a major failure that could still turn out to be catastrophic.

"Get out of there, Knife," Colt urged.

But beyond the smoke visible on his display, it was the narrow beam of light boring into the stricken Osprey that had shaken him. Cubby was right, and now the enemy had struck the first blow.

It was time to hit back.

"Find that fucker for me!"

"On it," Dave replied.

He pulled power and dropped the nose, descending to a lower altitude to set up for an attack run. The most obvious weapon of choice was the one Dave had selected on the stores page. The GBU-12 Paveway II five-hundred-pound laser-guided bomb might have been overkill for personnel operating MANPADS, but it wasn't half as big as he wished he could shove down the Russians' throats.

"There!" Dave exclaimed, slewing the sensor pod to a shallow wash approximately twenty-five klicks west of the storage facility. It was one of the few open patches of ground without trees in the forest surrounding Yuzhnoukrainsk.

"I see 'em," he replied. He marveled at the skill with which the SEAL manipulated the targeting pod—arguably better than most of the Super Hornet WSOs he'd seen while an instructor at TOPGUN. But something else bothered him.

How did they know we were here?

"Pony One One has eyes on," he said over the command SAT channel. "Setting up for an attack run from the north."

"ROE?" Todd queried. He knew they had heard Knife's call but wanted him to spell out the rules of engagement for recorded posterity in case the lawyers came knocking after the dust settled.

"Collective self-defense," he replied. Though his aircraft wasn't in imminent danger, his right to self-defense extended to other friendly forces in the vicinity. But he couldn't have cared less. He was going to extinguish the bastards, regardless. "Launch the Alert Five."

"Working it," Todd replied.

"Heading one five zero," Dave said.

He steered onto the vertical line in his Heads Up Display, indicating the attack heading. Like the Hornet weapons delivery cuing, as they approached the cone of release over the target, a horizontal line dropped from the top of the HUD along the vertical line. When it intersected his flight path vector, the bomb would release and fall to the target.

"Going hot," he said, reaching up to move the Master Arm switch from Safe to Arm. Then, as the horizontal line came into view, he mashed down on the pickle button on top of his stick and waited for it to intersect with his flight path vector.

When it did, his plane lurched upward, suddenly five hundred pounds lighter. "One away," he said.

He banked to the right, steering the plane in a shallow turn away from the target while he focused on the target under the crosshairs on his right multi-function display. Dave slewed the crosshairs to keep them centered on the armored vehicle, ignoring the brilliant beam of light that continued shining on the wounded Osprey.

"Ten seconds," Dave said. "Firing laser."

The crosshairs shifted into a diamond and began flashing as the SEAL sent laser energy to the ground to guide the Paveway bomb to its target. But less than a second later, Colt knew they were in trouble.

"He's moving."

"Stay on him," Colt urged. But he knew once the armored vehicle disappeared into the cover of the trees, the laser wouldn't be able to penetrate the canopy and continue to guide the bomb onto the target. After that, it was a crap shoot whether the bomb found its target.

But Dave was steady. He continued firing the laser until the Bumerang had disappeared.

"Dammit!" Dave shouted.

When the timer reached zero, a blur entered the field of view and detonated well short of where the armored vehicle had escaped. The screen flashed white, and he zoomed out to capture the entire fireball on the screen. Colt reversed his angle of bank and watched the inferno over his shoulder.

"That's a miss," he said.

A second explosion drew his attention away from the forest clearing, and he glanced over in time to see the crippled Osprey's right engine burst into flames. He keyed the microphone switch, but Dave beat him to the punch.

"Knife, you're on fire!"

34

KNIFE 22
Air Force CV-22 Osprey

The impact knocked Brian off his feet, but he rebounded and scrambled forward to the gunner's station. The violent hull vibration blurred his vision, but he ignored it and set his sights on the one thing he could do to help them in their predicament.

"Get on the gun!" the pilot yelled over the intercom.

What does he think I'm doing?

He didn't reply. He couldn't. Technical Sergeant Brian Billeaud of Lafayette, Louisiana, was busy screaming at the SEALs to prepare for an emergency evacuation. If the pilots couldn't keep them in the air, they were going to have to ride it in and get off the crippled Osprey as quick as possible to prepare for contact.

He stumbled over their feet as unseen hands gripped him and propelled him forward to the gunner's chair. Regaining his balance, he moved in a low crouch with his hands held out to steady himself as the pilots fought to keep them in the air.

He collapsed into his seat and flipped on the power for the GAU-17 minigun recessed in the tiltrotor aircraft's belly. The small screen in front of him flashed as it powered up and cycled through its modes in preparation to fire. He picked up the remote—about the size and shape of an Xbox controller—and pressed the button to lower the minigun.

The gun swung forward, extended on its mount into the slipstream as the camera blinked to life and broadcast images back to the screen in front of him. He toggled through its various modes, switching between electro-optical, thermal, and infrared before finally settling on the white-hot thermal setting.

He jammed the joystick to the right, and the gun responded with a mechanical whir as it spun clockwise.

Come on... where are you?

"Where's the gun?" the pilot yelled again.

"I'm on it! Where's the shooter?"

As the gun completed a full 360-degree traverse, Brian grew dismayed he hadn't seen a single heat signature. Of course, if he had, he probably would have just gone hammer down until firing each of his 7.62 mm armor-piercing rounds into a wild boar or roe deer. At 3,000 rounds per minute.

"Seven o'clock! Seven o'clock!"

The fear in the pilot's voice was palpable, and Brian spun the turret to scan the darkness in that direction. Although configured to allow the co-pilot the ability to operate the Defensive Weapon System from the cockpit, Brian knew they had their hands full trying to stay in the air. It was up to him to find the threat and eliminate it before it hit them again.

He jammed the joystick to the side and spun the turret counterclockwise, looking for a smoke trail or blossom of light that might help him find the target. Instead, all he saw was the remains of a distant explosion.

What the hell?

"Knife, you're on fire!"

The voice sounded like it came from one of their escorts. He responded by centering the crosshairs on an opening in the forest where he had seen the explosion, then depressed the trigger in a short two-second burst. The satisfying zipper-like sound of the minigun spitting rounds at the target ended as the pilot banked away to make for the reserve air base.

Staring at the screen, the tilting world disoriented him. He lifted his eyes from the screen and looked aft toward the open ramp to re-cage his internal gyro. He caught sight of the stoic SEALs staring at him from the back of the tilting and shaking aircraft, waiting for him to give them the signal to brace.

But they were still in the fight.

The violent shaking only grew worse, but Brian kept his eyes glued to the screen while frantically searching for a target to shoot.

"Pony One One is tally target and setting up to suppress," their escort's voice said. "Get outta there, Knife!"

Voznesensk Reserve Air Base
Voznesensk, Mykolaiv Oblast, Ukraine

"Get outta there, Knife!"

Polina gritted her teeth as she listened to the one-sided fight unfolding over the radio. She recognized Colt Bancroft's voice, though it sounded far more stressed than it had when they spoke in private before the coordination brief. But that wasn't surprising. He and the other Americans were engaged in battle, and she was stuck sitting on the sidelines.

"Advocate, Mech Five requests clearance to launch."

Her heart pounded an angry cadence as she waited for the powers that be to debate the merits of launching their alert close air support platform. She had already heard Colt requesting as much, but they had still kept her grounded.

"Stand by."

Pizdets!

Her MiG-29 already had electric power, giving her the ability to monitor the operation over the radio while she sat on her hands on the sidelines. But Polina didn't intend to remain on the ground any longer. She pushed her throttles forward into the idle detents, then simultaneously engaged each engine's BK-100 turbine starter.

Matching left and right "Engine Start" red lamps illuminated on the panel to Polina's right, giving her a visual indication of the start sequence that matched the whine of her spooling turbofan engines. She watched the needles on her Interstage Turbine Temperature gauges fluctuate for several seconds before finally stabilizing at ground idle. The "Damper Disabled" warning light illuminated as the AFCS, or Automatic Flight Control System, began its three-minute built-in test.

"Mech Five, Advocate."

"Go ahead," she replied.

"Ummm... are you starting your engines?"

"*Nemaye.* They're already started."

The next transmission was garbled and distorted by rustling in the background, but soon she heard the voice of Polkovnyk Ivan Kovalenko. "Starshyy Leytenant Radchenko, you do *not* have permission to take off."

The Damper push light began flashing on the AFCS panel, indicating that the system had moved into the second half of its test. Once it was complete, she would be free to advance her throttles and taxi to the runway.

"You can ground me when I return," Polina said.

His voice softened. "Polina—"

"I'm going, Ivan."

And that was that. The "Damper Disabled" light extinguished, and she immediately pushed both throttles forward to spool up her RD-33 engines. Once she had attained breakaway thrust and the MiG-29 began rolling across the cracked concrete apron, she backed off the throttles and allowed her momentum to carry forward as she steered toward the end of the runway.

"Check in with Pony One One when you get on station. They are the airborne forward air controller," Kovalenko said.

"Mech Five," she replied.

Going against the orders of her superiors would not bode well for her future in the Air Force. But thankfully she didn't give two fucks about her future in the Air Force. All she cared about was taking on every last Russian who had dared set foot on Ukrainian soil and eradicate them or send them back to Moscow with their tails tucked between their legs. And if the Americans had come to stop the Russians from getting their hands on man-portable nuclear devices, then she cared very much about seeing them succeed.

Polina reached up and clipped her oxygen mask into place as she steered onto the runway. Her eyes were well adjusted to the dark, but the runway edge lighting was nothing more than a dim glow in the thin ground fog blanketing much of the airfield. Satisfied that her Fulcrum would carry her faithfully into the fray, she pushed the throttles to the stops and waited for the afterburners to ignite.

She felt herself sink back into her ejection seat when all 36,000 pounds of thrust engaged. There had been a time when that feeling alone would have put a smile on her face. But that time had long since passed. Now, the joy of flying was blunted by the fact that her 1970s technology Mikoyan multirole fighter was nothing more than a weapon for her to wield against hordes of Russian invaders.

A third of the way down the runway, she felt her nose start to creep upward and pulled back on the stick to leave the earth once again. It was without fanfare or celebration, and Polina simply commemorated the occasion by nosing over to fly just above the runway while reaching forward and lifting a lever to retract her landing gear into the fuselage. The numbers representing her airspeed ticked upward quickly as the fighter jet accelerated with ease in the cool air.

By the time she reached the end of the runway, Polina was flying at well over three hundred knots. The air hummed around her canopy as she raced into the pitch black before snatching back on the stick and popping the nose up to climb into the star-filled sky.

"Control, Mech Five is airborne."

The familiar voice of the sector's air intercept controller filled her helmet, putting her instantly at ease. No matter what was taking place in the skies over Yuzhnoukrainsk, she was right where she was meant to be.

"Mech Five, Control. The skies are clear. Vector north."

Polina slapped the stick against her left leg, then pulled it back into her lap to bring her nose around. With as close as the reserve base was to the storage facility and as fast as her Fulcrum could fly, she would be on top of the fight in minutes.

35

PONY 11
Navy A-29 Super Tucano

Dave was good. Colt watched his right display as the SEAL master chief manipulated the controls to center the crosshairs on the armored vehicle. It was largely hidden from the sky, but its thermal signature was almost impossible to ignore.

"Fuck!" Dave shouted.

Colt jerked the stick and craned his neck to look for another threat, when the caution on his left display caught his attention.

LASER MALFN.

Laser malfunction.

"Reset the system," he prodded.

"That's what I'm doing!"

He could tell by the muted cursing and loud banging coming from the backseat that the normally levelheaded SEAL was frustrated. The Super Tucano's sensors weren't exactly delicate, but he didn't think beating them into submission was going to work.

"Switch to rockets," Colt said over the intercom before keying the microphone to transmit over the tactical frequency. "Pony One One is switching to rockets and dropping to a lower altitude."

Cubby replied without hesitation. "Pony One Two is tally target and can engage."

"Don't you let him have it," Dave said.

He smelled blood in the water, and his thirst for it overpowered his good judgment. They should have called it off and cleared in Cubby to employ from the higher altitude. But Dave smelled it too. It was *their* target. And he wanted the pleasure of stopping the Russians before they could close on the storage facility and recover the nuclear weapons.

"Negative. Pony One One is in from the north."

Dave clapped his hands in the backseat. But Colt ignored the impromptu celebration and focused through his NVG's two narrow tubes at the dim symbology in his HUD as he rolled the Super Tucano on its back.

He lowered the nose twenty degrees below the horizon, pushed forward on the stick to unload his wings, then rolled upright and lifted his nose to the fifteen-degree watermark in his HUD. The world tumbled around the diamond centered in the middle, but his eyes took in the data needed to verify he was within parameters, almost without thought. Altitude, airspeed, and angle of bank all affected where the rockets went. And he wanted them dead on the money.

If they can make it through the trees.

Like a gun run, the plane's forward movement caused rocket impacts to "walk" along a line following their flight path. To counter that, he pushed the stick forward and bunted the nose to keep it fixed on a point on the ground—a point that was nothing but pitch black beyond his HUD.

Without the laser to provide accurate ranging to the target, Colt relied on his altitude to know when to depress the pickle switch. Fortunately, his steadfast WSO backed him up with callouts.

"Ninety-five hundred... Nine thousand... Eighty-five hundred..."

If he had been in an older airplane that relied on steam gauges, the white altimeter needle would have spun counterclockwise in a blur as they raced toward the earth. But only the digital numbers in his HUD decreased, and it felt like an eternity as he waited for the numbers to count down to the release altitude. Nose low on the dive wire, Colt knew he was vulnerable to fixating on the target and ignoring everything else to their detriment. So, he forced his eyes to move.

"Six thousand... Fifty-five hundred... Five thousand..."

He reached up and again moved the Master Arm switch to Arm, then glanced down at his stores page to verify Dave had selected the high-explosive-tipped rockets and programmed them to fire in a three-round salvo.

"Three thousand..."

Before Dave called out the next altitude, he mashed down on the pickle switch and saw three 2.75-inch folding-fin aerial rockets streak forward from the right side of his plane. When the third one had cleared, he pulled back on the stick and lifted the nose above the horizon before banking to the right to fly away from the target.

"Pony One One, off safe."

Though the sensor pod's laser designator had malfunctioned, it still provided thermal imagery to their displays in the cockpit. And while he was tempted to overbank and look over his shoulder at the rockets impacting the target, his gaze dropped to the display and saw that they had missed their mark.

Shit!

"Pony One One is circling for an immediate reattack from the north," Dave said, leaving little doubt they intended to finish off the armored vehicle before Cubby directed them into high cover.

"Let's switch to guns," Colt said. He couldn't be sure, but it looked like the rockets had all hit well past his aim point, and he doubted a subsequent salvo would do the job unless he applied Kentucky windage. He wasn't about to mess around with guessing when lives were at stake.

"You got it, boss," Dave replied.

He craned his neck to the right, looking through his NVGs at the dim glow that was all that remained from their rocket attack. They raced north to the west of the target, and he kept his eyes glued to the smoldering fire, forgoing his instruments for his Mark one, Mod zero eyeball. It had served him well in the past.

"Five thousand feet," Dave said, a gentle reminder he had allowed the Super Tucano to dip below the delivery's roll-in altitude. He bumped the stick back and climbed above the mark while adjusting his angle of bank to ensure he had enough spacing on the target before beginning his ten-degree dive.

Reaching the roll-in point, he pulled until they were pointed at the target, then eased his back-stick pressure and rolled the Super Tucano onto its back once more. Unlike the rocket attack, they would do the strafing run at ten degrees, meaning the pull below the horizon was short-lived.

Colt floated in his seat, held in place only by his lap belt, as he shoved the stick forward to unload his wings before rolling upright. Having begun the dive from a lower altitude, they were much closer to the target.

"Pony One One in from the north."

"Forty-five hundred... Four thousand... Thirty-five hundred..."

He listened to Dave's callouts while again forcing his eyes to keep moving, avoiding the temptation to stare at the target until it was too late to recover. In the Hornet, he used to program altitude alerts to cue him into releasing his ordnance, with the final annoyingly loud alert set to shake him free from fixation and recover his jet before plowing into the ground.

He had the same alerts programmed in the Super Tucano, but he had something even better—a heavily muscled and bearded frogman who would kick his ass if he got them both killed.

"Three thousand... *Yippee ki-yay*, motherfucker!"

Colt lifted the Master Arm switch for a third time and squeezed the trigger. Bunting the nose, he held the pipper centered on the diamond in his HUD and counted to two as the plane shuddered with the machine guns spitting bullets at 1,100 rounds per minute.

One potato... Two potato...

He released the trigger and pulled his nose up to the horizon, stopping their climb at fifteen hundred feet, then banking hard to the right. He reached up and flipped the Master Arm switch down. "Pony One One, off safe."

"Direct hit, Pony One One," Cubby said.

But Colt knew his strafing run probably had little effect on the Russian armored vehicle. It would take a lot more than .50-cal high-explosive rounds to stop the Bumerang from breaking contact and reaching the storage facility.

As if reading his mind, Dave chimed in. "What do you say, boss? Think we let the other boys have some fun?"

"Good call," Colt replied, then keyed the microphone switch. "Pony One One is breaking off to the northwest."

As he flew away from the chewed-up ground, Colt took a deep breath and exhaled. His heart still raced in his chest, amped up on the adrenaline that came with raining down fire and hate on the bad guys. But with Cubby and Ron descending to take on the attack role, he eased back on the stick to begin a climb to high cover and allowed himself to come down from his emotional high.

"Five miles," Dave said, letting the other crew know they had vacated the cone around the target and were clear to descend and engage.

"Pony One Two is dropping down to five thousand," Cubby said.

"You're clear."

With the excitement behind them, Colt turned his attention to the more mundane task of checking on his aircraft systems. Starting with fuel, he compared their current state with the mission planning guide they had built to ensure they had enough to remain on station for the duration of the mission. Despite their low-altitude attacks, they still had over twenty minutes of fuel remaining before reaching a Bingo fuel quantity that would force them to leave for home plate.

Next, he checked the engine instruments to make sure the venerable Pratt & Whitney was operating within parameters. Aside from an elevated Exhaust Gas Temperature, every needle was in the middle of the green arc on the digitized displays. Their pony was running hot, but still ready to trot.

"Keep an eye on the EGT for me," he said to Dave, bringing him into the loop on his thought process. Unlike in a single-seat aircraft, he wanted to make sure he let his backseater in on every concern, no matter how big or small.

"Rog," Dave replied. "It's been a little high the whole flight."

"It's probably nothing then."

"Pony One One, Knife flight is clear to the west."

He heard the relief in Steve's voice, though Knife One Two probably wasn't even aware they had survived being targeted by a directed energy weapon. But with the Black Ponies keeping the pressure on the Bumerang, Colt felt confident they could escape and return to base.

"Pony One One copies. We'll catch up."

"Guess that about does it—"

The sudden explosion in front of Colt's canopy drowned out whatever Dave had been about to say. But the immediate loss of power and violent shaking caused his heart to bolt.

36

Colt reacted to the explosion on instinct and slammed the stick against his right leg before pulling it back into his lap. He craned his neck to try gaining sight of whatever had hit them while working the flare dispenser switch as fast as he could move it—a reaction that had been ingrained in him over years spent in the Fallon Range Training Complex.

"Do you see it?" he shouted.

In the moment, he couldn't recall whether they had programmed a sequence of chaff and flares designed to defeat the most common passive infrared homing missiles. But in the back of his mind, something told him it didn't really matter.

"Dave!"

He continued trying to gain sight of the threat, even as he came to accept that it was a futile effort. Even if he had been looking in the right piece of sky, he knew the laser weapon that was the likely culprit had used directed energy that was invisible to the naked eye. But all he could do was fall back on habits that had been drilled into him over hundreds of hours of training.

A second explosion rocked the turboprop. The concussion was so violent that he lost his grip on the stick and slammed his head against the canopy, knocking his NVGs clean off his helmet.

"We're hit! We're hit!"

He grasped the stick with both hands in a death grip as the displays flickered and filled up with caution messages. Red warning lights illuminated, and horns blared, but it was sensory overload. He couldn't process which systems had recognized faults in the circuitry and restarted, and which had shit the bed.

"You with me, Dave?"

His ears were ringing. But next to keeping them in the air, his only other thought was on the SEAL in his backseat. He hadn't heard a peep from him since the explosion interrupted whatever he had been about to say. Aside from the sheer terror he felt at being hit by the laser weapon, the unnerving silence from the backseat inched him closer to panic.

"Dave!"

Again, his call went unanswered. The plane shuddered violently, and the engine coughed, killing what little thrust remained and pushing him forward in his shoulder harness. His left hand found the throttle and slammed it as far as it would go. He couldn't remember if that was a habit from his time flying the Hornet or if it was the correct procedure for the turboprop. All he knew was that he needed to gain speed.

Speed is life.

It was a simple saying that one of his primary flight instructors had repeated often, reminding him that when the shit hit the fan, he only needed to think of two things: airspeed and altitude.

And the shit had certainly hit the fan.

He could either trade airspeed for altitude, or altitude for airspeed, but he needed to get as far away from the ground as he could and distance himself from the impending smoking hole if he failed.

With the throttle firewalled and the engine still sputtering, he reefed back on the stick and felt only a sluggish response from the nose as it lifted only five then ten degrees above the horizon. Sweat poured down his face and his muscles ached from the strain, but he needed to trade airspeed for altitude and get the hell away from whoever had shot him.

"...turn... two... sev..."

As the ringing subsided, he noticed another voice talking to him. But it wasn't Dave, so he tuned it out. His subconscious picked up on the word "turn" which caused his eyes to drift to his navigation display, where he saw they were flying northeast and farther away from the safety of the reserve airfield.

Shit!

He tried moving the stick to the left, to nudge the crippled plane back to the west, but the controls fought him even harder in that axis. He gave up and focused on his flight instructor's lifesaving advice, using what little power he had to climb to a safer altitude. He would worry about trying to turn the plane later.

Altitude is life insurance.

Two more red lights illuminated, and a faint buzzing sound faded in and out as he watched his airspeed drop close to stall speed. He relaxed his back-stick pressure and allowed the nose to fall, hoping to keep it level with the horizon and limp his plane home at seven thousand feet.

But the numbers in his airspeed box continued to dip lower and the stall warning horn grew louder. If he didn't drop the nose, the wings would lose lift and he would fall out of the sky.

His flight instructor's final caveat came to mind: When you're out of airspeed and out of altitude, you're out of options.

Shit! Shit! Shit!

As the nose dropped below the horizon, he pressed the transmit button and said something he thought he'd never say again, "Mayday! Mayday! Mayday! Pony One One is punching out." Then, over the intercom, "Eject! Eject! Eject!"

He gripped the black-and-yellow loop between his legs with both hands, put his heels on the floor, pushed his shoulders back into the seat, put a slight tilt in his chin, and pulled with as much force as he could muster.

When he pulled the handle, the Martin-Baker Mk10 operating sequence began by firing the canopy miniature detonation cord. The explosive propelled the canopy away from the plane and ensured the ejection seat had a clear path before the next step in the sequence. He barely had time to recognize that his light attack plane had become a convertible, because once the canopy was clear, the main gun, a telescopic tube with two pairs of explosive charges, fired in sequence and moved his seat up its guide rails.

Emergency oxygen actuated as his connection to the stricken bird was severed, and the rocket pack fired by a telescopic static rod fixed to the plane. The rapid acceleration pushed him clear of the Super Tucano and subjected him to fourteen Gs—close to double the maximum g-forces of the Hornet.

That's when Colt blacked out.

The acceleration ended when the rocket motor burned out, and his thumping heart began pushing blood back up into his brain. He had been unconscious for less than five seconds but was still in a fog when the drogue gun fired and deployed two small parachutes to keep the seat from tumbling as it began its downward trajectory. His head snapped back with a start when the main chute deployed and jerked him free from the seat.

It took him less than a second to recognize his predicament. But more than twice that to suspend his disbelief that it could have happened to him again. The last time, his parachute fall had ended with him plunging into the frigid waters of the South China Sea. But this time, he was preparing to come down in the middle of a war zone.

The thought injected a shot of adrenaline into his blood stream as he quickly recalled the acronym IROK from his aviation physiology and water survival training. But he was having difficulty focusing.

IROK... IROK... IROK?

He kept repeating the acronym but couldn't recall what each letter represented. He thought the I stood for "inflate," which made sense if he had ejected over water like the last time. But he hadn't, so he brushed past it. Then he remembered the virtual reality trainer where he had worn goggles while suspended from the ceiling.

Inspect!

He tilted his head back to look up at his parachute and cursed.

Instead of one large round canopy above his head, he saw the faint outline of two. One was larger than the other, a malfunction he diagnosed as a partial line over. Unlike a full line over—what aviators often referred to as a "Mae West"—he knew his condition was unstable and would increase his rate of descent. But they had taught him what to do.

As the stars spun around the parachute over his head, he closed his eyes to keep his vertigo in check and reached up with both hands to grasp the riser on the side with the smaller canopy. He pulled himself up until his chin was level with his hands, then released his grip and dropped back down into his harness. The snap of the riser traveled up the lines and popped the errant line closer to the edge of the canopy.

The small circle became smaller, so he tried again. He knew he was running out of time before the earth came up to meet him, and he performed one more pull-up and dropped into his harness. He looked up but saw that the small circle had stopped shrinking.

Move, Colt!

He pushed the malfunction from his mind and moved on to the next steps.

Raft.

Again, useful if he had ejected over water and needed to deploy his survival raft. But over Ukraine he had different needs.

Rifle.

Instead of a survival raft, his ejection seat carried his combat kit containing the PDW and spare magazines. He reached down under his right thigh and gripped the handle, yanking it clear to allow the combat kit to fall free from the seat pan and dangle below him on a tether. Aside from eliminating the bulk on his person as he prepared for a parachute landing fall, having the combat kit dangling below him gave him advance notice of the ground's approach. When the taut line became slack, he knew he'd have less than two seconds until impact.

He looked down but couldn't see anything that gave him a clue how high he was. Given the altitude he'd ejected from, he knew he didn't have much time, so he returned his focus to the acronym and moved on to the next step.

Options.

The only options he could recall involved his visor, gloves, and mask. Since he didn't wear a visor when using NVGs, and never wore gloves, the first two were meaningless. He reached up for the bayonet fittings to remove his mask when he felt the line under him go slack.

"Well, shit..."

He lifted his eyes to the invisible horizon and brought his legs together with a slight bend in his knees. He'd jumped off boxes into sand pits before, but he had a feeling this was going to be a completely unique experience.

When he hit, he knew he was right.

The pain hit like a freight train when the bones shattered in his right ankle. Instead of falling to the side and allowing each part of his body to absorb the impact, he had come straight down, and his knees buckled and toppled him forward onto his face. The impact knocked the breath from his lungs, but his face flushed with the onslaught of agony.

Welcome to earth.

37

White House Situation Room
Washington, DC

Sam's mouth fell open in stunned silence as those gathered in the conference room watched the video feed from the lead Super Tucano tumble erratically before going blank. They had been listening in on the task force's communications and knew things had gone sideways. But this...

"What the hell just happened?"

Sam turned to look at Jonathan, whose complexion had paled and shoulders were slumped in defeat.

"Mr. President," Bart Tilley began. "It appears that one of the A-29 Super Tucanos has been shot down—"

Jonathan cut him off. "I can see that, Bart. By what?"

Sam knew Bart didn't have the answers. Everyone in the room had just seen the exact same thing as the president and were privy to the exact same information. But the question had been largely rhetorical. Jonathan really didn't care what had brought down the turboprop, but it was his attempt to regain some semblance of control over a situation that had spiraled very quickly in the wrong direction.

"I'll find out, sir."

As the chairman of the Joint Chiefs picked up the phone on the table in front of him, Sam recognized an opportunity and rose to his feet. He inched closer to his boss and leaned down to speak quietly in his ear. "Mr. President, maybe we should recall the rest of the assault team and focus on recovering the downed crew."

Jonathan gave no outward sign that he had even heard Sam's suggestion, but his jaw muscles flexed in time with the flaring of his nostrils as he tried to rein in his emotions. After several seconds of silence, he turned slowly and locked eyes with Sam.

"No."

Sam flinched, as much from Jonathan's resolute determination to continue with the mission as from the silent accusation hidden behind his gaze.

"Sir, I think—"

Jonathan cut him off in a quiet but firm tone. "I am not willing to back down at the first sign of adversity." He pointed at the screen that had just begun broadcasting images from the Super Tucano that was still airborne. "Those men haven't given up, and I won't give up on them as long as they're in the fight."

Bart pulled the phone away from his ear and covered the handset again before turning to address the president. "Sir, one of the two Ospreys has suffered critical damage, and we have lost one of the two light attack planes supporting them. I recommend we pull our forces back and regroup. At least until we understand what we're up against."

Jonathan slammed his hand down on the table, causing those seated there to startle. "Are you people forgetting what's at stake here? Did you forget that if we fail, *nuclear weapons* will end up in the hands of terrorists who won't hesitate to detonate them in Times Square or on the National Mall? Giving up and abandoning this mission is not an option I am willing to entertain. Do I make myself clear?"

Bart's expression didn't change. He only nodded once and replied with a curt, "Yes, Mr. President."

"That goes for all of you. If you're not sure of our reason for being here, you can see yourself out. I only want people willing to give me solutions, not excuses. Now, help me figure out how we can accomplish this mission and bring all our men home."

The room remained silent for several more seconds before everybody seated around the conference table began speaking at once in hushed but animated tones. Sam retreated to his chair against the wall and watched the chaos unfold as the best and brightest their country had to offer put their collective minds together to come up with a solution the president could accept.

But in the back of his mind, all he could think about was that his betrayal had brought down an American light attack plane and that he had given Viktor everything he needed to ensure that the best and brightest failed.

He felt sick to his stomach.

---

25 km west of Yuzhnoukrainsk

Colt's first thought was, *Thank God I'm alive*. But a new set of problems quickly replaced that gratitude. He had survived what had to be a directed energy weapon shooting him out of the sky and the subsequent ejection, but now needed to figure out where he was, find Dave, and get to safety.

As if that wasn't enough, the agony of his ankle gave him something else to worry about.

He pushed himself onto his hands and knees and flexed his foot. The stabs of pain made him nauseous, but he had no choice but to roll with it. He released his Koch fittings, letting the straps fall away, thankful that the wind was calm and the parachute had collapsed on landing instead of dragging him across the rough ground.

Rolling onto his back, he brought his knee to his chest and reached for the boot holding his broken ankle. He felt it swelling and did the only thing he could think to do in the circumstances—untie his boot and yank on the laces as hard as possible. Again, the agony was overpowering, but it would help keep the ankle immobile.

He wouldn't win any footraces, but he only needed to hobble far enough to find Dave.

With the boot retied, he released his lap belt harness that kept the seat pan attached to him and fumbled for the tether affixed to his combat pack. When his shaking fingers found it, he reeled the satchel across the ground to him, then unzipped it and removed the PDW. He extended the butt stock, inserted a magazine, and chambered a round as an afterthought.

Taking a few moments to collect his thoughts, he turned his head and peered into the night, looking for movement that might alert him to an approaching threat. He was armed, but that didn't mean he wanted to end up in a firefight. All the better if he made it back to Voznesensk Reserve Air Base without even pulling his trigger.

Then, when he noticed the surrounding sounds muffled by his flight helmet, he thought of the MBITR. He reached down on his survival vest and opened the pouch holding the boom microphone on a bayonet fitting, then slid it into his helmet and connected the pigtail to the AN/PRC-148. He found the switch to turn the radio on, knowing they had preset it to their primary E&E, or Escape and Evasion, channel.

Nothing.

Instead of the warm static he had expected, he heard silence. Their E&E plan called for them to evade clear of the crash site before activating the beacon, but the silence unnerved him.

"Pony One Two, Pony One One," he whispered.

Still nothing.

He retraced his cords, beginning with the boom mic down to the MBITR to ensure he had seated them correctly.

"Pony One Two, this is Pony One One. How do you read?"

Silence.

He retraced his cords a second time, unplugging and plugging them back in, before accepting what he had already guessed. His radio had shit the bed. He removed it from his vest and found the problem right away. His less-than-graceful parachute landing fall had dented the front and smashed the LCD screen to pieces. By looking at it, he thought it might still work, but the silence in his ear cups was proof enough it didn't.

Well, shit. Maybe the beacon will.

He had a broken ankle, a broken radio, and no way of reaching Cubby, who was orbiting overhead. But at least he was alive and had a gun. Like the motto of his former Hornet squadron went, *Have gun... will travel.*

He pushed himself to his feet, favoring his left ankle in a crouch. He draped the PDW's sling over his shoulder and turned to scan the horizon. The world looked different without the aid of night vision goggles. The absence of discernible landmarks made it impossible for him to tell which way was which.

He reached into his survival vest again and pulled out the standard-issue lensatic compass with glowing tritium markings. Their E&E plan called for them to move almost due west at a distance of at least one klick before activating the beacon. He spun the bezel ring to place the west cardinal heading on the fixed black index line, then rotated his body until the luminous arrow aligned with the short luminous line, showing the compass was oriented to north.

Then, looking through the sighting wire on the flipped-up lid, he searched for something to use as a visual guide to point him in the right direction. But the surrounding forest was dense, and it was difficult to distinguish the shadow of one tree from the next. He'd have to do it the old-school way, like he did back in Matador, Texas, as a Tenderfoot Boy Scout. He'd have to hold the compass in front of him as he walked.

With one more look over his shoulder, he lifted his injured foot and placed it gingerly on the ground in front of him. It held his weight, but just barely. The familiar stabs of pain and wave of nausea hit him as he set his weight down on the foot, but he gritted his teeth and took another step anyway.

"Don't you *fucking* shoot me, flyboy."

He wheeled his head to the side and saw the SEAL materialize out of thin air. First, he wasn't there. Then he was. "Dave?"

"Who else would it be?"

He relaxed, despite the pain and shitty situation. "My radio's busted."

"So, you were gonna just lounge around and wait for me?"

"No—"

But Dave cut him off. "Typical officer. Let's get the fuck outta here."

He took a limping step toward the SEAL, relieved not to be alone in the wilderness any longer but knowing they still had a long way to go before he could feel good about their situation.

Dave watched him hobble with skepticism. "You okay?"

"Peachy."

He slapped Colt on the back. "Let's get clear of the crash site and then hunker down. They're probably out looking for us now, and we don't need to make it any easier for them."

He said nothing but nodded. His throbbing ankle left a coppery taste in his mouth that he tried to swallow away. He wasn't sure how far he could walk on it, but he didn't have a choice.

"You good?"

"You gonna stop talking?"

Dave wheeled away and led them deeper into the night.

38

25 km west of Yuzhnoukrainsk

Voronov stared at the distant explosion on the screen with detached wonder. The *DRAGON LINE* had damaged one of the Ospreys Viktor told him would be carrying Navy SEALs to the storage facility. But the laser weapon's effect on the single-engine turboprop was nothing short of astonishing. Within seconds of engaging the light attack plane, its engine exploded and both crew members ejected.

They watched the stricken plane corkscrew through the sky in a downward trajectory until disappearing behind trees, where it exploded on impact. The glow on the screen was clearly visible, but they heard little more than a muted *ka-thump* through the armor.

"Should we go after them?" Yevgeny asked.

Voronov knew who he meant. They had lost sight of the ejection seats shortly after they left the stricken plane but knew their parachutes had probably come down somewhere nearby. Normally, that might be cause for concern, but he didn't think either the pilot or backseater had the potential to pose a threat to him completing his mission. He shook his head. "*Nyet.* What of the other plane?"

Yevgeny shifted his focus to a second monitor depicting the air contacts surrounding them and studied it. "It's circling overhead. Probably searching for survivors of the one we shot down."

"And the transports?"

"They moved back to a safe distance after we damaged the first one."

He scowled. They should have brought that one down as well. The SEALs on board the Ospreys were the real threat. Viktor had told him their mission was to reach the storage facility and secure the nuclear weapons inside. And if that happened, then all his preparation and sacrifice would have been for nothing.

"But for how long?" Voronov wondered aloud.

"Sir?"

He shook his head. "Never mind. We need to move on the storage facility immediately."

Before Yevgeny could question him, Voronov jumped to his feet and pushed his way forward to the driver's seat and slapped him on the shoulder to get his attention. He didn't appear startled in the least and only ducked down to look back at the Russian intelligence officer.

"Proceed directly to the storage facility," Voronov shouted over the din of the Bumerang's diesel engine. "We cannot allow the Americans to reach it before we do."

The driver appeared unfazed. "But what of the attack planes?"

"We shot one down and—"

"Not that one," the driver said, cutting him off. "*That* one."

Just then, the Bumerang shook as a fighter jet passed low overhead, and Voronov froze. Even through the thick armor plating, he could hear the deep rumble of the jet's afterburners as it zoomed past. His heart sank with fear, and there was only one thought that echoed in his mind.

Viktor didn't warn me about this.

MECH 5
Ukrainian MiG-29 Fulcrum

Polina yanked back on the throttles and came out of afterburner, then simultaneously pitched up and thumbed the switch on her throttle to actuate the jet's flare dispenser. Brilliant flashes of light blossomed at the edge of her narrow field of view through the night vision goggles, but that didn't distract her. She had seen what she needed to—a Russian armored personnel carrier tucked underneath a stand of trees.

"Advocate, Mech Five," she said, rolling inverted and pulling back on the stick to arrest her climb. She craned her neck to keep sight of the dark patch of earth where she had seen the vehicle. It was almost invisible in the darkness. Almost, but not quite.

"Go ahead."

"I have a visual on the target," she said, her voice carrying a touch of pride.

There was a pause on the other end of the radio before the disembodied voice of the joint terminal attack controller in the TOC returned. "Confirm you are tally the target?"

"Affirm." She brought her nose down to the horizon, then rolled back upright and banked the Fulcrum to begin an orbit around the Bumerang. This vehicle had gotten away from her once before, and she didn't intend to let it get away a second time. She intended to make up for her failure at the bridge.

"Stand by."

Polina clenched her jaw muscles as she seethed inwardly at the sense of urgency she found lacking by those far removed from the fight. Of course, she knew the Russian armored vehicle had already shot down one of the two single-engine turboprop attack planes. And she knew the Americans were still unaccounted for. But neither reason was a valid excuse for not authorizing her to attack the Bumerang immediately.

She completed one full lap around the infantry fighting vehicle before her frustration got the better of her, and she keyed the microphone to let the decision makers in the TOC know. "Advocate, what are you waiting for?"

She heard somebody key the microphone on the other end, followed by what sounded like voices raised in anger and a commotion she couldn't quite make out. She caught bits and pieces of harsh words in English and her native tongue, but none were clear enough for her to get a feel for what was being said. At last, she heard a familiar voice come on over the radio.

"This is Polkovnyk Kovalenko—"

"I know who you are," she spat.

"Then you know I don't say this lightly…"

Polina felt her shoulders sag with defeat. Once again, politicians and senior officers with more concern for their careers had stepped in to prevent the actual warfighters from doing what they have been trained to do. They had intervened in the battle to curry favor from a strong ally like the United States and now risked losing the war.

"That vehicle is declared hostile," Kovalenko said. "Destroy it at all costs."

The commotion resumed on the other end of the radio before the colonel released the transmit switch. But she had heard all she needed to.

Declared Hostile.

"*Slava Ukraini!*"

---

25 km west of Yuzhnoukrainsk

Each step was agony on Colt's destroyed ankle, but it was nothing compared to the pain he knew they'd endure if they were captured by the Russians who had shot them down. That was all the motivation he needed to keep moving.

Dave had taken the lead in guiding them away from the crash site, and Colt hobbled to keep up. He didn't mind that the SEAL had taken point. Colt was more of a liability than an asset on the ground and agreed that it made sense for somebody with Dave's skill set to be at the front of their two-man column. Colt belonged in the sky. Not the mud.

Dave slowly turned and appraised Colt with a questioning look. He gave the SEAL a thumbs-up.

As a newly winged pilot, Colt had attended SERE school in Maine the summer before beginning Super Hornet training in Virginia Beach, Virginia. He had partnered with a SEAL then too and relied on the frogman's experience in ground combat and patrolling to keep them hidden from the role-playing enemy forces until the bitter end when the training scenario mandated their capture.

Colt remembered listening to the diesel truck blaring its horn to signal an end to the evasion phase. Their instructor cadre had been clear—when the horn sounded, they needed to proceed directly to the truck and surrender. He could still hear the deep knocking sound of the deuce and a half as they descended the hillside to…

Colt froze.

The sound of the rumbling diesel engine wasn't only in his mind.

Before he could warn Dave, the SEAL stopped and crouched low while lifting the short-barreled rifle and scanning the darkness in front of them. Colt mimicked the master chief but hobbled closer.

"You hear it too?" Dave asked in a low whisper.

Colt nodded. "That has to be the Bumerang."

Both men scanned the shadows for dismounts that were probably scouring the forest for them. Even though they were less than thirty klicks from Voznesensk Reserve Air Base, they knew they were isolated and in a precarious position so close to Russian forces. It didn't matter that a second Super Tucano was orbiting overhead to provide overwatch or that two Ospreys filled with elite Navy SEALs were in a holding pattern nearby. They were on their own.

Before Dave could reply, the sky was split open by an earsplitting thunderclap as a jet raced overhead in full grunt. A blast of air hit them only seconds later when the jet pitched up for the heavens and dispensed flares as a precaution.

A smile cracked Dave's face. "She knows we're here."

But it didn't feel right to Colt, and he shook his head.

"What are you shaking your head for, flyboy?"

Even though the Fulcrum was flying without lights, Colt traced its path through the night sky as it blotted out the stars overhead. He could almost picture the pilot craning her neck to look down on the piece of ground she had just flown over. He could feel the G-forces on her body and the strain as she maneuvered her fighter through the sky.

Then it dawned on him.

"We need to move."

"What? Why?"

As the Fulcrum completed one full orbit overhead, he heard the drone of the distant jet engines change in pitch. Colt glanced up in time to see the fighter jet pulling its nose across the horizon, then roll onto its back to begin a dive.

Just then, the Bumerang's diesel engine roared to life.

"Because she doesn't see us," Colt said. "She sees *them!*"

39

MECH 5
Ukrainian MiG-29 Fulcrum

Polina leveled her wings and aimed at the spot on the ground where she had seen the Bumerang hidden beneath the trees. It wasn't the first time she had rolled in on a target she couldn't see, but it always unnerved her to have her thumb resting on the pickle switch without positive hostile identification.

"Mech Five, attacking," she said, letting others on the command net know she had rolled in on a bombing run.

"Mech Five, Pony One Two, are you tally target?"

The voice had come from the second Super Tucano, who she knew technically owned the airspace as the airborne forward air controller. But Kovalenko had already blessed her attack, and she wasn't about to let an American tell her how to repel the Russians who had invaded her country.

She didn't reply.

In her Heads Up Display, she watched the aiming pipper dance across the ground as minor variations in her pitch, roll, and yaw caused the computed impact point to shift. She poured every ounce of concentration into guiding the pipper onto the patch of dark earth where she had seen the Russian armored vehicle.

"Mech Five, there are friendlies in the vicinity," the JTAC in the other plane said. "Confirm you are tally target."

Her thumb lifted slightly from the pickle switch as she was gripped by momentary hesitation. She understood what was at stake and what the Russians had come to Yuzhnoukrainsk to do. She shouldn't have let the risk of collateral damage sway her commitment in stopping them, but she couldn't help it. If she sacrificed friendly lives in the process, was she any better than the men who had invaded her country and raped and murdered innocents?

"Mech Five," the voice said again, more insistent.

"*Pizdets!*" Polina shouted.

She lifted her thumb completely off the pickle switch and snatched on the stick to climb back into the sky. She grunted under the strain of G-forces but craned her neck to look down on the patch of dark earth where she had been certain the Russian armored personnel carrier had been hiding.

But it was gone.

"Mech Five is off target," she said. "No drop."

When the voice returned to the radio, it sounded confident yet relieved. "Mech Five, take angels fifteen."

Polina would have been justified in dropping a pair of 250-kilogram bombs since her immediate superior had declared the armored vehicle hostile and given her permission to destroy it. But the airborne forward air controller was right—she couldn't risk bombing friendlies. Especially without being able to see it.

"Mech Five, climbing to fifteen thousand feet," Polina said.

Disappointment dripped off every word as the Russians again slipped through her fingers.

---

25 km west of Yuzhnoukrainsk

Colt ignored the throbbing in his ankle and stabbing pain that radiated up his entire body with each step. Even propelled by the specter of being consumed by a massive fireball when the Fulcrum's bombs detonated, Colt knew he wasn't running fast enough. Dave could have easily left him in the dust, but instead the frogman only gripped the back of his survival vest and propelled him onward.

But as the seconds ticked by, Colt began to accept his fate. It was his fault he hadn't taken Cubby's warning about the laser weapon seriously enough. It was his fault he had overestimated his capabilities against the Russian armored vehicle and allowed them to be swatted out of the sky. And it was his fault they weren't running fast enough to avoid being incinerated by a Ukrainian bomb.

Then Dave's grip on his vest tightened and jerked him to a halt.

He's given up too.

Colt heard the roar of the fighter jet as it pitched up and climbed away from the ground. He could almost picture the bomb falling through the sky while a silent timer counted down the seconds until it impacted the forest and detonated. Surprisingly, he felt an odd sense of acceptance that this was how it would end.

Eight... Nine... Ten.

Before Colt could wonder what had happened to the bomb hurtling through the sky toward them, Dave tugged on his vest and pulled him down to the ground. The SEAL brought his mouth close to Colt's ear and whispered.

"Enemy patrol."

Still no explosion. Colt nodded.

"They're moving toward the crash site," Dave whispered.

The attacking jet retreated again into the sky, and Colt accepted that they were still alive. They were still in the fight. He turned to look at the SEAL. "Can we let them pass?"

Dave nodded and gave him a thumbs-up to show he agreed with the plan. With his free hand, the SEAL flattened his palm and gestured for Colt to drop onto his belly. He got the hint and pressed himself flat against the earth beneath a bush next to their path. Dave made some minor adjustments to his camouflage, then scampered away to crawl under a shrub of his own.

The ground reminded Colt of home. Brittle, coarse dirt with an astringent and medicinal aroma that triggered memories of desert shrubs like creosote flats and cholla. The ground wasn't as dry as West Texas, but the soil had absorbed every ounce of moisture to provide sustenance for its flora. He burrowed himself further into the dirt and peered over the barrel of his rifle to gain sight of the men hunting them.

But he heard them first.

They chattered with excitement, unworried about the noise carrying across the landscape as if believing they were still too far from their quarry to spook. Colt took a deep breath and controlled his exhalation to remain as silent as possible as his finger caressed the short-barreled rifle's Geissele trigger.

There!

He was straining to discern human shapes among the shifting shadows but saw only one strolling in his direction fifteen yards away. Within seconds, another form materialized out of the night and matched pace with the first soldier. Then he saw a third and fourth man within arm's reach of one another, cradling their rifles as they sidestepped larger bushes and flattened dry clumps of dirt under their worn combat boots.

When the soldiers had moved within ten yards, Colt felt his heart racing with the sudden realization that they hadn't drifted to the left or right of his position. They were walking straight at him.

CBDR, he thought.

At the Naval Academy, he had learned about Constant Bearing and Decreasing Range as an early warning to prevent a collision at sea. If a radar contact continued to close the distance while remaining on the same line of bearing, the ship would eventually hit yours unless you took evasive action. He'd applied the same principles to his career in aviation and refused to ascribe to the *big sky, little plane* theory.

But he never expected he would need to apply CBDR to Russian soldiers hunting him in the middle of the night in Ukraine. They were just outside five yards when he slowly turned his head to look in Dave's direction. Even though he knew where the SEAL was hiding, he couldn't see him and turned back to the approaching men while praying that he was just as sheltered from view.

Static broke through the silence, and an excited voice crackled over the radio. The men stopped, and Colt held his breath while listening to the lead soldier unclip the Motorola from his belt and raise it to his mouth.

"*My yikh ne znayshly,*" the soldier said.

The man clipped the radio back onto his belt and took another step toward Colt, scuffing the ground and kicking tiny pebbles into his face. Colt closed his eyes and fought the urge to brush the dirt and grime away, when the voice on the other end of the Motorola spoke again.

The lead soldier groaned. "*Ya yikh ne bachu.*"

The others laughed, and he silenced them with a sharp command, then walked away from the group to respond in privacy. Colt tracked his movement as he neared Dave's position and placed his thumb on the rifle's safety selector. Though he wanted to avoid direct contact if at all possible, he wasn't about to let him take Dave down without a fight.

But the man finished his conversation, unbuttoned his fatigue pants, and urinated into the bushes. After two shakes, he buttoned up and walked back between the Americans. Colt traced his movement, careful not to disturb his surroundings and give himself away.

"Colt Bancroft!" the soldier shouted. "Dave White!"

Colt froze at hearing their names, but his heart raced with an immediate surge of adrenaline. He wasn't about to expose himself but wondered how the Russians had discovered who had been piloting the Super Tucano they shot down.

But the soldier continued. "We are with the Svyatyi Mykolai Battalion and are here to rescue you."

Colt exhaled but remained still.

"The Russians have left. You may come out."

After several more seconds, the soldier gave an exaggerated sigh, then unclipped his radio and brought it up to his mouth. After issuing a lengthy command, he lifted the radio above his head. Colt watched in silent fascination and wondered what kind of trick the man held up his sleeve.

But then he heard a voice he recognized.

"Colt, these guys are legit," Freaq said over the radio. "They're here to bring you home."

He was still hesitant to expose himself. But after several more seconds, Dave materialized from the shadows and walked over to where Colt was still hidden. His hair was wet, and he had a scowl on his face as he looked down at Colt.

"Wait. Did he just…" Colt couldn't finish his thought.

"I don't want to talk about it," Dave growled.

40

PONY 12
Navy A-29 Super Tucano

Cubby focused on keeping his voice calm and reassuring, despite his racing heart. He hadn't bothered to check the Garmin Fenix 6 on his wrist, because he already knew his heart rate was well over ninety beats per minute. He wasn't a stranger to combat, but seeing his wingman shot down by the same weapon that had shot him down in Nevada had put him under some serious stress.

But Cubby knew that if he sounded scared on the radio, others would lose confidence—his backseater, wingman, troops on the ground, whoever. And when they lost confidence, their performance suffered, and bad things happened. It was a slippery slope Cubby didn't want to go down.

"Advocate, Knife Two One is approaching the target from the northwest."

"Wait one."

That made him nervous. After calling off the MiG-29 from making a bombing run on the Russian APC and confirming that the Ukrainian militia in the area had found Colt and Dave, the TOC had given instructions for the Ospreys to continue with the insertion at the storage facility.

"Say delay," Major Urszenyi fired back.

"They're debating recovering the downed crew and scrubbing the mission—"

The Osprey mission commander cut him off. "Who's debating it?"

Cubby cursed inside his mask. He knew that sort of talk wasn't coming from the Tactical Operations Center at Voznesensk Reserve Air Base or even from the command back in Virginia Beach. He had once wrongly believed that the Greatest Generation had ended with his grandfather and that his generation would never dare undertake something as dangerous as an invasion of occupied Europe. But the man in his backseat, the two on the ground, and the pissed off Air Force major were proof positive that they would.

"Washington."

Bingo.

The men and women of his generation wouldn't even hesitate to storm the beaches of Normandy if called on to do so. But their senior leaders—both military and civilian—were averse to the idea that lives might be lost.

"This is bullshit," Steve said, just in case there was some question where he stood on the topic.

Cubby had to hand it to the AFSOC pilot. Steve had known full well that his radio transmission was being broadcast in real time at the White House Situation Room and that the president had heard his proclamation. But guys like him didn't care about medals or accolades. They cared about the mission and making the world a safer place, not promotions and career advancement.

"Copy," the voice said from the other end of the radio.

Cubby glanced down at his fuel and knew it was about time they either shit or get off the pot. "Advocate, Pony One Two is Joker fuel."

Not quite as precarious as being Bingo fuel that required an immediate return to base, Joker fuel implied that he was getting close. Again, they couldn't just loiter in the skies over Yuzhnoukrainsk indefinitely. It was now or never.

White House Situation Room
Washington, DC

"This is bullshit."

The proclamation echoed in the conference room, and Sam felt his face flush with embarrassment for Jonathan. The president had wavered on his previous stance of not scrubbing the mission in favor of recovering the downed aircrew, but nearly every other person in the room had heeded his earlier admonishment and panned the idea.

"What did he just say?" Bart said, voicing his indignation on behalf of the commander in chief.

But Jonathan didn't appear fazed. "He said, 'This is bullshit.'"

General Tilley's face flushed. "I'll have him—"

"I agree with him," Jonathan said with his hand raised. "Proceed as planned."

General Tilley nodded in acknowledgment of the order, then spoke into the handset that had been in his grip since the operation commenced. Sam couldn't hear his words, but he was almost certain the general was making it clear he wanted the Air Force pilot reprimanded for his lack of decorum on the radio. But given the circumstances, Sam couldn't fault him for it.

Bart lowered the handset again. "Knife Two One is approaching the insertion point, Mr. President."

On the large flat-screen display, they watched video broadcast from the orbiting Super Tucano as the lone CV-22 Osprey approached the primary landing zone with its massive proprotors turned skyward. Scintillating light from the spinning blades made the black-and-white imagery appear almost ethereal, and nearly every man and woman in the room leaned forward in their chairs as it descended closer to the earth.

Sam was no exception. He squinted at the screen as clouds of dust billowed around the tiltrotor aircraft moments before it set down. Within seconds, eight figures emerged from the back and fanned out in a half circle, infrared strobes blinking on top of their helmets to make them visible from the air.

"Advocate, Templar Six is at point Alpha."

The voice was little more than a whisper, but Sam could hear the bass drum of the Osprey lifting off in the background. On the screen, he watched the tiltrotor pivot and nose over before racing clear of the landing zone and returning to a holding point away from the target. Sam glanced at the clock on the wall and knew it was a race against time.

"Templar Six, Advocate, continue to point Bravo."

"Where's point Bravo?" Jonathan asked.

This time, it was the voice of Captain Cross, the senior SEAL officer in Virginia Beach who commanded the task force. "Mr. President, if you'll look at your screen, you'll notice the points along the ingress route labeled on an overlay. Point Bravo is the first of two checkpoints before reaching the storage facility."

Sam glanced down at the screen showing an aerial image of the target area with a grid reference system and each of the checkpoints from the landing zone en route to the target location. Each SEAL on the ground was outfitted with a Blue Force Tracker beacon that allowed their position to be annotated in real time.

"How long will it take them to get there?"

Captain Cross didn't hesitate. "The terrain is relatively flat and easily navigable. In the absence of opposition—which we do not expect—they should be able to reach point Bravo in twenty minutes."

Again, Sam glanced at the clock. Hardly any time had passed at all, and he knew that each checkpoint was spaced approximately two miles apart. It would be close to an hour before the SEALs were able to get anywhere near the storage facility and secure the nuclear weapons.

"How much fuel does Pony One Two have on board?" Jonathan asked.

Captain Cross muted the microphone and turned to speak with an officer in green camouflage with a set of embroidered Naval Aviator wings on his chest. The two spoke animatedly for several seconds before the senior SEAL officer unmuted himself and faced the camera.

"Mr. President, we assess that they only have twenty minutes of loiter time before they need to return to base and fuel up."

"Twenty..."

Sam saw Jonathan's neck flush from his vantage point against the wall and knew that his friend was growing frustrated.

"Stand by for one moment, Captain," Jonathan said, then leaned forward and fixed his gaze on the chairman of the Joint Chiefs of Staff. "Bart, what do you suggest?"

The general turned from the president to the image of Captain Cross on the screen, waiting patiently for further instructions, then back to the president. "Sir, I recommend that we let those on the ground dictate how best to proceed. They understand what's at stake and what the risks are better than we do."

"Are you comfortable letting the ground force proceed to the target without air cover?"

"Respectfully, they're not without air cover, Mr. President." General Tilley lifted his laser pointer and shone it on the icon of an aircraft circling the target area. "There is a Ukrainian MiG-29, callsign Mech Five, with a full air-to-ground load."

"But didn't you say they needed to have a joint terminal controller?"

"A joint terminal *attack* controller," General Tilley corrected. "But, yes, sir. Under normal circumstances, a qualified JTAC is required to authorize the release of ordnance in close proximity to friendly ground forces."

"What do you mean, 'under normal circumstances'?"

"In extremis, any military member can call in an air strike if needed. But there are obvious risks to doing so."

On the screen, Captain Cross lifted his hand. "If I may, Mr. President."

Jonathan nodded his head. "Go ahead."

"It's true that the Templar JTAC was aboard the damaged Osprey and not inserted with the ground force." He paused and looked back at the Naval Aviator who was speaking to him in hushed tones. He nodded his head and returned his focus to the camera. "But there is a qualified JTAC on the ground right now."

"Who?"

"Pony One One's backseater is a Navy SEAL master chief and qualified JTAC. If we can link him up with Templar en route to the storage facility, we will have everything we need to complete our mission."

Sam swallowed as Jonathan surveyed the faces of those gathered in the room and was met only with subtle nods of agreement. Any hope that

Jonathan might end the mission and allow Viktor's men to recover the nuclear weapons vanished.

"Okay, Captain Cross. You may proceed."

41

Yuzhnoukrainsk
Mykolaiv Oblast, Ukraine

The Bumerang came to a stop and the driver shut off the diesel engine. Voronov's ears rang in the silence as he stared at the unassuming structure centered under the crosshairs on the screen. It had been constructed from reinforced concrete and built into the hillside with earth and grass covering the roof to keep it hidden from the prying eyes of foreign satellites.

"This is it?" Yevgeny asked.

Voronov squinted as he studied the screen for signs of the boobytraps Viktor told him had been placed there to protect the facility from intrusion. Even after three decades, he had been warned to respect the *Molniya* and not rush his approach. "This is it," he confirmed.

"What now?"

Voronov reached over to open the rear hatch and felt immediate relief as the cool air washed over him. He had been trapped inside the armored personnel carrier for so long that he was beginning to forget what it felt like to walk on his own two legs and hear the peaceful sounds of nature enveloping him instead of the constant drone of machinery.

He carefully extricated himself from his seat and ducked through the hatch. They were still hours away from sunrise, but he knew they couldn't delay making entry into the facility. The Americans had surely noticed their disappearance and would rightfully assume they were making for the storage facility.

Yevgeny exited the Bumerang behind Voronov and followed him around to the front of the vehicle. "And the *Molniya*?"

Voronov understood his concern. Everybody on the mission had been rightfully leery of breaching the facility when they knew to expect explosive boobytraps. Though normally used for smaller caches and containers, the potential for a much larger device existed at a facility of this size and importance. In the late 1990s, a smaller device had exploded when Swiss authorities used a water cannon to neutralize it after a KGB defector identified a site near Belfaux.

Voronov pointed at the main entry door recessed into an alcove. "Do you see those two columns on either side of the door?"

"Yes."

"We will remain at a safe distance and use the *DRAGON LINE* to burn through the concrete along those posts. If the *Molniya* exists on the exterior of the building, it will be there."

Yevgeny nodded in understanding, but Voronov could tell he was still tense and on edge. "And the Americans?"

"Are surely on their way here now," Voronov said. "So, we have no time to waste."

Instead of replying, the weapon operator turned for the rear hatch and ducked inside once more. Voronov remained in place where he stood next to the eight-wheeled vehicle and lifted his head to stare up into the sky above. Only a few thin wisps of clouds blotted out the stars, and he felt as if they were destined to achieve their mission and flee Ukraine with the weapons safely in their possession.

But then he saw a larger shadow pass in front of the stars.

"Fire up the weapon," he shouted. "We have no time to waste!"

Colt knew the injury to his ankle was holding the group back, but he tried his best to just grit his teeth and keep up with the militiamen. Dave, on the other hand, seemed like their trek through the woods was nothing more than a Sunday morning stroll through the park.

"You okay there, flyboy?"

Colt wanted to smile and fire back something witty in reply, but the pain made even faking it difficult. "I'll manage."

The squad of soldiers split into two groups, with four men leading the column and four behind them. Even though they were well inside Ukrainian-controlled territory, they were all acutely aware that a Russian armored personnel carrier was lurking somewhere nearby. And none of them wanted to be caught with their pants down.

After close to a half hour of trudging through the forest, their column came to an abrupt halt. Colt's heart bolted with a sudden surge of adrenaline, and he dropped to the ground as if expecting enemy soldiers to materialize from the darkness and spray them with gunfire.

But as the seconds ticked by, Colt realized that none of the Ukrainian soldiers appeared concerned. He pushed himself to his feet and brushed dirt off the front of his body, feeling almost silly that he let his fear get the better of him. Dave walked over and leaned in close.

"Nice reaction time."

"Shut up," Colt said, though he knew the SEAL was only giving him a hard time.

From the front of the column, the soldier carrying the Motorola walked back and thrust the handheld radio at Dave. "It's for you."

"You mean him," Dave said, nodding in Colt's direction. "He's the officer."

Colt grabbed the radio and keyed the push-to-talk. "This is Colt."

"Colt, it's Freaq. How you holding up?"

On the surface, it sounded like the Black Ponies' commanding officer only wanted to check on the welfare of his crew that had been shot down. But Colt knew better. "We're making it. Not sure I can hike all the way to Voznesensk Reserve Air Base on this ankle, so hopefully they have a truck stashed somewhere."

When Colt released the push-to-talk switch, his comment was met with silence.

"How copy?"

"I heard you, Colt." Freaq paused for a moment. "Command wants you and Dave to link up with the Templar ground force."

Dave heard this and stepped forward to speak into the radio as Colt held the button down. "You mean they still went ahead with the insertion after all this?"

"Half of them. The other half returned to base on the wounded bird."

"I need to be in the air, Skipper. Not down here on the ground," Colt said.

"Actually, Command needs Dave to be there on the ground. We need a JTAC."

Dave nudged Colt. "Where I go, you go."

Colt looked up into the sky. It was beginning to grow brighter with the coming dawn, but he saw no sign of Cubby and the other Super Tucano. "What about Pony One Two?"

"They returned to base to gas up."

"Then why do we need a JTAC?"

Before Freaq could answer, a MiG-29 raced overhead and pitched up into the sky.

MECH 5
Ukrainian MiG-29 Fulcrum

Polina was moving far too fast to make out any details, but she saw the column of personnel on the ground and knew the Americans were in that group. Whether the same could be said if she had dropped her bombs on the Bumerang was the kind of thing that kept her up at night. It wasn't the countless Russian soldiers she had killed or fighters and attack helicopters she had knocked from the sky. It was the fear that she might fuck up and kill a friendly.

"Mech Five has eyes on," Polina said, banking away from the column to return to her orbit high above the battlefield.

"Advocate copies," the American voice said. "We need you to escort them until they link up with the Templar ground force outside the storage facility."

"Copy," Polina replied.

As she climbed higher into the sky, the air around her fighter jet became smoother and less turbulent. She cracked back on the throttles, reducing the amount of fuel she was dumping into the afterburning turbofan engines. Until somebody else came to relieve her, she was it. She was the only support the people on the ground would have.

The radio crackled, and a new voice replaced the controller in the TOC. "Mech Five, this is Pony One One."

"Go ahead," she replied.

"Thanks for the airshow," the JTAC replied. "We're making our way toward point Charlie to link up with Templar at this time."

Polina referenced the miniature chart she had clipped to her kneeboard, showing the ground force's intended route of travel from the insertion point. Each point was identified by a latitude and longitude, and she quickly entered the coordinates for point Charlie into her navigation computer.

"Mech Five copies."

"If you can scan along our intended route to make sure we're not walking into an ambush, we can make better time."

"Copy."

But Polina knew they weren't walking into an ambush. The Russian Bumerang armored vehicle was long gone and probably already at the target location. She wasn't sure why the powers that be hadn't just flattened the hidden storage facility and saved them all the trouble. But she assumed it was probably due to an infinitesimal chance that a kinetic strike on the building might cause a radioactive leak, irreparably harming the environment and poisoning the groundwater for generations.

"Control, Mech Five is proceeding to point Charlie," she said, addressing the Ukrainian air intercept controller for her sector.

"Mech Five, Control. Picture clean."

Polina selected the waypoint for point Charlie and glanced at the steering cue in her Heads Up Display, rolling out until it was pointed directly ahead of her.

42

Yuzhnoukrainsk
Mykolaiv Oblast, Ukraine

Voronov sat inside the back of the Bumerang and leaned over Yevgeny's shoulder as he used the joystick to manually aim the directed energy weapon at the column on the left—the side he suspected contained the hinges for the massive steel door.

"The weapon is ready, sir," Yevgeny said.

Voronov didn't hesitate. "Fire."

The weapon operator squeezed the trigger, and Voronov watched on the screen as an invisible beam of light stretched across the open ground to the concrete next to the door. In less than a second, the solid surface began glowing a bright white. Without design details, they could only estimate the thickness of the concrete. But Yevgeny agreed it would take less than five seconds to burn through the pillar.

Voronov had been trained in sabotage and countering insurgencies, not complex mathematics. But even he understood that the laser beam's diameter grew over distance using an equation that involved variables like laser quality, wavelength, and a collimated distance where the rays of light were parallel. It was well above his head, but the conclusion was that at a distance of one hundred meters, the laser beam's diameter would be roughly seventy-five millimeters.

"Shifting," Yevgeny said, five seconds after squeezing the trigger.

On the screen, the beam of light moved down along the pillar. Voronov estimated they had shifted the laser's energy approximately fifty millimeters, overlapping with the hole created from the initial salvo. They guessed that the door was roughly 2,400 millimeters tall, requiring Yevgeny to adjust his aim point just under fifty times.

"Shifting," he repeated after another five seconds had elapsed.

"This is going to take forever," Voronov muttered.

"Shifting," Yevgeny responded.

Feeling his patience waning, Voronov stood from the bench seat and ducked through the rear hatch and stepped out into the pale gray of dawn. Even the vibrant greens and browns of the forest seemed muted in comparison to the humming coming from the Bumerang's cabin.

"Shifting."

Yevgeny's voice was quieter, but carried a tension through the air that Voronov couldn't ignore. He stepped around the corner of the armored vehicle and looked at the distant storage facility where a narrow crack was glowing hot along the left side of the door. He knew the *DRAGON LINE* had an unprecedented power supply that could sustain an unbroken laser beam for nearly five minutes. But that would only be enough for one column.

"Shifting."

It would take close to an hour for the weapon to generate and store enough power for another sustained beam to cut through the column on the right. But assuming the first column didn't contain a *Molniya* boobytrap that destroyed the facility, they could inspect the first column to confirm the laser had penetrated the concrete and adjust their beam duration per spot accordingly.

"Shifting."

Voronov turned his back on the storage facility and studied the surrounding woods. For as powerful as the weapon was, he knew they were vulnerable to attack. And there wasn't a damn thing he could do about it.

"Shifting."
Pizdec!

After being told they weren't being repatriated to the reserve air base, Colt couldn't help but feel a sense of urgency to reach the squad of SEALs who were making haste for the storage facility. Everybody knew they were racing to reach the nuclear weapons before the Russians, and the blistering pace the Ukrainian militiamen kept up was the clearest sign of that.

"You hanging in there, Colt?"

He grunted in reply, though he could still recognize Dave's sincerity through the fog of pain that had blanketed his entire body. Normally, the frogman would have cracked a wiseass comment about Colt being a useless officer or something equally irreverent. That he hadn't meant that he was either genuinely concerned about Colt's injury or genuinely impressed by his toughness.

"Or do you need me to drop my rifle and carry you?"

There he is.

Colt turned and fixed Dave with a mirthless grin. "I'm good."

Up ahead, the lead militiaman held a fist in the air to signal that they were stopping. Despite the pain radiating up his leg, Colt wasn't sure that was a good idea. He hobbled a few more steps, then stopped and felt a deep throbbing in his ankle as it swelled against the tightly laced leather boot. He swallowed back a metallic taste in his mouth and waited for the Ukrainian soldier to approach.

"Sir, command wants talk." The soldier spoke in hushed tones and addressed Colt, still clearly under the impression that he was in charge as the ranking member of the group.

But despite Colt's best efforts to comprehend the man's broken English, he could barely think straight and only shook his head in response.

"Please talk," he urged, handing the radio to Colt.

"I got it," Dave said, reaching out for the Motorola.

Colt felt beads of sweat breaking out across his brow, but he clenched his jaw and gave another shake of his head to clear the cobwebs. Dave was clearly the better choice to take command of their ragtag group, but he couldn't simply hand over his responsibilities.

"Go for Dave," the SEAL said.

"Dave, it's Todd. Envy Three Three and Envy Four Two both have eyes on the target complex, but there is no sign of the Bumerang APC."

Colt heard the words but couldn't quite process what he was hearing. The armored personnel carrier had broken contact long before they even linked up with the Ukrainian militia and should have reached the target location by now. "That doesn't make sense," he muttered.

"Copy all, Todd. What's your assessment?"

"Freaq is talking it over with Colonel Kovalenko, but so far there's no change to our mission. Templar is continuing to the facility, and it looks like they will beat you there. Just keep trucking along your current route and link up with them there."

Dave pressed the push-to-talk to reply but quickly released it. He turned and made eye contact with Colt. "What are you thinking, boss?"

Another wave of pain washed over Colt, but he swallowed back the bitter taste and focused on their situation. "The Russians should have been there by now."

"I agree."

"And if the Reapers orbiting the storage facility can't see them, then we have to assume they're either out hunting us, or…" Colt trailed off as a sickening thought crossed his mind.

"Or what?"

Colt turned to the young Ukrainian fighter. "Did you grow up around here?"

The man scrunched up his face as he processed Colt's question, then he shook his head.

"Did any of you?"

Again, the soldier's face remained passive, as if he didn't understand what Colt was asking. But then his eyes widened, and his face brightened as he turned to one of the other men in the group. He said something in Ukrainian that Colt couldn't understand, but he assumed he was relaying his request to the others.

"What are you thinking, boss?" Dave asked again.

"I don't think the Russians are out hunting for us. If they were, they would have already found us by now. I think they're exactly where we think they are."

"Then why can't the drones see them?"

"Because maybe the storage facility we've been targeting isn't the right one."

Again, Dave keyed the push-to-talk to relay their concerns to the TOC, but he released it when a second soldier approached and spoke with the one who Colt had been speaking with. They had a rushed and brief conversation in Ukrainian, then knelt and started drawing in the dirt.

"What are they doing?" Colt asked.

But Dave knelt and looked on as they continued their discussion while animatedly pointing at various spots in the dirt, then gesturing to the surrounding woods. "It's a sand table. I think they're talking about locations around us, but I can't make out what they're saying."

Just then, the first Ukrainian soldier looked up at Colt. "He say another Soviet bunker nearby."

Dave didn't wait and keyed the Motorola. "Todd, we think there might be another facility."

"Copy."

The SEAL manning the desk in the TOC didn't sound dejected, just matter of fact.

"Can you show me where this other bunker is?" Colt asked, pulling out his Escape and Evasion chart.

He placed the chart on the ground, and Dave knelt next to it, pointing out their current location as well as the storage facility where they had been steadily marching before learning that the Russians had disappeared. The Ukrainian soldiers nodded their heads and gestured at the same spots on the map, then the soldier who had grown up nearby pointed to an unmarked spot on the map and tapped on it several times.

"He say bunker here."

Colt was more recently familiar with aviation charts than topographic maps, but once a Boy Scout always a Boy Scout. His shoulders slumped when he realized that they were closer to the new location than the ground force that had inserted north of the storage facility. "We've been going in the wrong direction."

"Looks like it," Dave said.

43

White House Situation Room
Washington, DC

When it became apparent that the task force had potentially been monitoring the wrong facility, the composure of those gathered in the conference room fractured. Sam leaned back against the wall and watched as the various members of the National Security Council pointed fingers at one another for what could only be described as a failure of epic proportions.

"How did this happen?" Jonathan asked.

Eleanor Sinclair, his director of national intelligence, turned to face him with a look of pure shame on her face. She had been instrumental in dismantling the fiefdoms and silos that defined the intelligence community as a whole prior to terrorist attacks on September 11th, and she prided herself in not passing the blame onto others.

"This is my fault," she began. "I take full responsibility, Mr. President. You'll have my letter of resignation on your—"

He held up a hand to cut her off. "Not now, Eleanor. There will be time after this is all over to figure out what went wrong. But I'm not interested in placing the blame anywhere. Right now, I'm only interested in stopping the Russians from getting ahold of these nuclear weapons."

She looked down at the wide oak desk and appeared sufficiently chastened. "Yes, Mr. President."

General Tilley leaned forward in his chair and faced Jonathan. "We have approximate grid coordinates for the new facility based on the intelligence we received from the Ukrainian militia escorting our downed aviators."

"Great, then let's push the SEALs there and secure the building before the Russians get there."

"I'm afraid it's not that easy, Mr. President." The chairman of the Joint Chiefs of Staff turned toward the monitor at the far end of the room that was broken into four quadrants. In the upper left was the live video teleconference with Captain Cross, the SEAL task force commander in charge of the operation. The upper right and bottom left showed real time video feeds from the two MQ-9 Reapers that had been orbiting the wrong storage facility. But he aimed his laser pointer at the bottom right.

"Our ground force inserted northwest of the storage facility identified by intelligence as the probable target." The red dot danced at a location in the upper left corner of the map.

Sam thought the general's words were wisely chosen to forestall further infighting between the military and intelligence representatives gathered in the room.

"Our downed aviators were recovered south of the storage facility in this vicinity." He shifted the dot to a location toward the bottom of the map. "They have been expeditiously moving north to point Charlie to link up with the SEALs.

"But if our new intelligence proves accurate, then the SEALs are even farther away than we thought." He moved the laser spot once more to the far-right side of the map. "But I must stress that this location hasn't been corroborated yet."

Jonathan nodded, accepting the general's alibi.

"If accurate, it will likely take them hours to reach the new location."

"What about the aircrew?" Jonathan asked.

General Tilley shook his head. "Sir, they're not equipped for this kind of mission."

The president looked up at Captain Cross, who was listening intently to the discussion from Virginia Beach. "What do you think, Captain?"

"Sir, the general is right. They are *not* equipped for this kind of mission..."

General Tilley leaned back with a pleased look on his face.

"...but I'm afraid we don't have much of a choice. It's not the force I would choose to put into play, but we still have eight seasoned Ukrainian fighters and a Navy SEAL JTAC who can reach the new location before it's too late."

"And a pilot who is untrained for this type of mission," General Tilley shot back.

Sam could tell the room's mood was beginning to shift again. But before Jonathan could corral them, Admiral Andy Peterson, the chief of naval operations, spoke in a clear and commanding voice. "Lieutenant Commander Colt Bancroft is not your average fighter pilot."

"He's not a SEAL—"

Jonathan cut off General Tilley. "Wasn't Colt Bancroft on the NAWDC staff in Fallon?"

Admiral Peterson responded. "Yes, Mr. President. He intervened during a kidnapping at the Nugget Casino Resort when I was at Hook two years ago."

"Intervened? How?" General Tilley seemed surprised by the revelation.

"He drew his personal weapon and killed one of the kidnappers, who turned out to be Russian."

Sam swallowed.

"I remember him," Jonathan said. "He took me for a flight in a Super Hornet during my visit to Fallon."

But the chairman of the Joint Chiefs of Staff wasn't impressed. "Be that as it may, Mr. President, I still believe he would be a hindrance to the operation."

Sam waited with bated breath as Jonathan evaluated the evolving situation. Like always, he was a patient leader who considered each argument before making a decision. But once he made his decision, he could not be swayed.

"General, I appreciate your perspective. But, in this case, I am going to side with Admiral Peterson and Captain Cross." He looked up at the screen and addressed the camera. "Captain, you have my permission to push this element directly to the new location and use them to secure the weapons. If you run into any resistance, let me know, and I will call the Ukrainian president and personally request that those soldiers be placed under your command."

"Yes, Mr. President."

Sam exhaled quietly as he watched his plan to derail the operation unravel at the seams. Despite his best efforts, it appeared that the military —and its commander in chief—seemed particularly adept at evolving to the changing scenario. He knew it would be pointless to continue trying to disrupt the operation, so he leaned back in his chair and could only hope for the fickle finger of fate to intervene.

One way or another, he would have to face Viktor and answer for his failure.

Distracted by his thoughts, he didn't notice Olivia Manning sneaking into the conference room and crossing to where he sat against the wall. He looked up as she bent down to whisper in his ear.

"What is it?"

"Lana Roman is on the phone for you again."

Sam followed Olivia to her office on the watch floor and took a seat behind her desk. She remained outside but closed the door to give him privacy as he took the call. Lana had already told him that a woman named Emmy King was looking into Aurora Holdings and dredging up the past, so he couldn't imagine what was so pressing that would make her reach out to him a second time in the same night.

"What is it?" Sam asked when he picked up the phone.

"I've been looking into Emmy King," Lana said, almost breathless with anxiety.

Sam pinched his eyes shut and kneaded the tension from his forehead. "Why would you do that? I told you to let it go."

"That's easy for you to say. You're sitting in the White House with the president. I'm out here hanging it all on the line for you."

Sam knew the woman was rattled, but he was beginning to feel like he was being attacked from all angles. The Russians had already killed the closest thing he had to a friend beyond Jonathan, and he had enough to worry about with the operation in Ukraine going sideways on him. The last thing he needed was the woman whose job it was to keep Jonathan's secrets buried unraveling on him.

"Fine," he said. "What have you learned?"

"She's a special agent with the Naval Criminal Investigative Service."

This surprised him. "Why would somebody from NCIS be interested in Aurora Holdings?"

"It gets worse," Lana said.

Sam remained quiet, waiting for her to reveal the reason she had felt the need to call him when he was ensconced in the White House Situation Room. But he grew impatient when she said nothing. "What could be worse?"

"In the last year, she's visited the Camp Pendleton Base Brig several times."

Sam wasn't seeing the connection. "Okay?"

"Don't you know who's there?"

He was tiring of these games. "Who?"

"Adam Garett."

Sam's stomach dropped. If Emmy King had spent time with Adam Garett and was looking into Aurora Holdings, it was only a matter of time before she uncovered the truth. Then, no matter what happened in Ukraine, he wouldn't be able to stop the wheels of justice from steamrolling Jonathan.

"Shit."

"Yeah," Lana said. "She's assigned to the NCIS Southwest Field Office in San Diego, but she's not in California."

Sam thought that was good news, since Lana and the legitimate side of Aurora Holdings were in the San Francisco Bay Area. "Where is she?"

"She's in DC."

"You're kidding me."

"I'm afraid not."

The flickering feeling of hope vanished, and Sam hung up the phone. There was no way to avoid it. Emmy King needed to be dealt with before she started peeling back the same layers that Teddy had. And the only way Sam could think of dealing with her was in the same way he had handled Teddy.

I need to speak to Viktor.

44

Yuzhnoukrainsk
Mykolaiv Oblast, Ukraine

Voronov had inspected the results after five minutes of sustained cutting and was pleased to discover that the *DRAGON LINE* had penetrated completely through the concrete and weakened the steel door. But after forty minutes of waiting for the weapon to store up enough power for a second cut, he had grown anxious and was ready to break into the vault and retrieve the weapons.

"Is it almost ready?" he asked, for the third time in as many minutes.

"Almost," came Yevgeny's predictable reply.

Voronov spun away from the Bumerang's open hatch and studied the surrounding woods again. It looked different now that daylight had happened upon the forest. It felt different too. He couldn't put his finger on it, but he had spent enough time in the outdoors to know when something was off.

"Enough," he mumbled, then turned back to the armored vehicle. All they needed to do was weaken the door's frame so the Bumerang could yank it from the concrete bunker. The cut didn't need to be clean. It just needed to work.

"It's ready," Yevgeny blurted with a tone of triumph.

"Fire," Voronov commanded.

The tenor of the electric humming changed as the weapon went from storing power to expending it. Again, he couldn't see the invisible beam of light crossing the open ground to the storage facility. But he felt the energy in the air.

He ducked back into the back of the armored vehicle and stared at the screen as Yevgeny patiently shifted the beam of light every few seconds to make overlapping cuts on the second column. Unlike the first, however, he didn't announce when he was shifting the laser beam. Both men sat in silence and waited for the directed energy weapon to chew through the concrete and bring them just one step closer to achieving their goal.

After almost five minutes, the laser stopped firing.

"Is that it?" Voronov asked.

Yevgeny nodded, almost breathless with the exertion of manually keeping the beam of light focused on a spot only millimeters wide. But Voronov could sense the pride in the younger man at having completed such a difficult task under stressful conditions. Though they hadn't spoken of it, both had been acutely aware that a *Molniya* boobytrap could have been embedded in the concrete pillars and been triggered by the laser weapon.

"Do you think it's safe?" Yevgeny asked, turning to look over at Voronov.

"Let's find out," he replied, then banged on the vehicle's bulkhead and shouted forward to the driver. "Move us into position to attach the cables."

The diesel engine rumbled to life, and both men braced themselves as they rolled across the uneven ground and drew nearer to the hidden building. If they were successful in pulling the door down, they could secure the weapons and be clear within minutes. If not, then they might have to wait another forty minutes to store up enough power to weaken the top frame of the structure.

"Will it work?" Yevgeny asked, giving voice to Voronov's own hidden fears.

I hope so, he thought.

Colt had thought the Ukrainian militiamen were moving at a fast clip to link up with the Navy SEAL ground force. But after receiving orders to change directions and proceed to the new location, they moved even faster. It would have been a punishing pace even if Colt hadn't been injured, but it was pure agony on his wrecked ankle.

But unlike before, nobody seemed overly concerned with Colt's condition. Even Dave had fallen mostly silent, except for the occasional barb thrown in his direction to challenge him. Colt knew what was at stake and refused to throw in the towel. He wouldn't be the reason they failed to prevent the Russians from getting ahold of the hidden nuclear weapons.

The column came to a sudden stop, and the soldiers at the front dropped to the ground just before cresting another hill. The two in the lead conferred for several seconds before sending a third scampering back to relay the situation to the rest of the squad.

"He say bunker over this hill," the soldier whispered before continuing to the rear of the column.

Dave traded glances with Colt. "Let's have a look."

Colt nodded, and together they lowered themselves to the ground and low-crawled to the crest of the hill. Peering over the edge, Colt didn't see anything that immediately stood out to him as a man-made structure. There wasn't a road or trail cut into the forest that would have given credence to the young soldier's assertion that a former Soviet weapons cache was hidden there.

"There you are," Dave whispered.

Colt squinted but could only make out what looked like a straight line cut into the clearing. "Is that—"

Before he could finish, the unmistakable sound of a diesel engine straining cut him off.

"Shit, they're already here," Dave said, pushing himself up onto a knee.

Colt remained frozen with indecision. But when the SEAL rose into a crouch and darted over the hill, he pushed himself off the ground and followed. He might not have had the same combat training or real-world experience that the master chief had, but he wasn't about to allow his backseater to charge the enemy without backup.

Colt looked back at the Ukrainian soldiers. "Let's go!"

As one, the eight men rose from their positions and followed the fearless Navy SEAL and wounded pilot into battle.

With each step, Colt realized that the straight line he had seen was the edge of a roof someone had disguised with dirt and foliage to blend in with the rest of the forest from the sky. They were approaching the bunker from the rear, where it had been built into the hillside, and he couldn't make out the Russian armored personnel carrier at the front.

He held his short-barreled rifle up in front of him, hoping and praying they still had the element of surprise in their favor and could stop the Russians without a firefight.

But as Dave stepped up onto the hidden roof, Colt finally caught a glimpse of the Bumerang armored personnel carrier racing away in the opposite direction.

We're too late.

Voronov leaned his head back against the bulkhead and closed his eyes, allowing himself a moment to savor the victory they had just achieved. Against all odds and deep inside Ukrainian-controlled territory, they had just pulled off one of the greatest heists and were about to become very rich men.

"We did it," Yevgeny said, his voice tinged with excitement.

"Yes, we did," Voronov agreed.

Surpassing even his wildest hopes, the heavy steel door had toppled without much resistance following the second cut. There had been no *Molniya* boobytraps; no additional barriers to prevent them from collecting the RA-115 devices to secure inside the Bumerang for transportation back to Crimea. They were heavier and bulkier than Voronov had expected but not enough to give them any trouble.

Within seconds of securing the suitcase nukes and closing the rear hatch, the driver had quickly put the armored vehicle into gear and sped east away from the bunker. Even if nobody said it, they all knew that they needed to get as far from Yuzhnoukrainsk as possible before the Americans showed up to stop them. And they needed to remain hidden from the prying eyes in the sky.

Ting!

Voronov's eyes shot open. "What was that?"

Yevgeny wasted no time and leaned into the computer workstation and took control of the sensor mounted on the turret. He scanned the forest directly ahead and to either side, looking for any sign that they were being engaged by Ukrainian armor.

Ting! Ting!

"I don't see anything," the weapon operator replied.

Voronov couldn't be sure, but it sounded like the rounds were impacting the thick armor plating at the rear of the vehicle. "Driver, do you see anything?"

"We're being fired on," he shouted back.

"From where?"

"I think it's coming from—"

Ting! Ting! Ting!

This time, there was no question. Voronov was certain they were taking fire from the bunker they had just raided. But that made no sense. They had just cleared the facility and taken the nukes without resistance.

"Do we stop?" the driver asked.

"No!" Voronov shouted. "Keep driving. Get us out of here!"

The Bumerang weaved suddenly to the right, and for a moment Voronov feared they had suffered some mechanical failure that would bring their hasty retreat to an abrupt halt. But then it veered left, and he quickly realized that the driver was doing his best to avoid rocks and trees that were keeping them hemmed in.

Yevgeny pivoted the sensor around to their six o'clock and studied the bunker at the center of the screen, looking for any clue as to where the gunfire was coming from. "I don't see them!"

Ting! Ting!

Just then, Voronov spotted two distinct muzzle flashes from on top of the bunker and breathed a sigh of relief. It appeared to be just one man.

One gun. Not a sizable enemy force with enough firepower to stop them from getting away.

"Keep driving!" he shouted again. "It's nothing. Just a—"

Then he heard the jet.

45

Thomas Jefferson Memorial
Washington, DC

After leaving the White House, Samuel Chambers had sent Viktor a message to meet at their usual place, then drove his Rivian back across the National Mall to the landmark south of the White House. The Russian hadn't responded yet, but Sam's message had made it clear that it was all going to come crashing down around them if they didn't take care of this new problem.

Special Agent Emmy King.

Normally, Sam would have taken his time to look for other visitors who might observe him meeting clandestinely with a Russian intelligence operative. But it was still the middle of the night, and he didn't think that was likely.

"This is becoming tiresome," the voice said from the shadows to his right.

Sam hadn't even reached the memorial's rotunda before he came to a stop and wheeled on Viktor. "A special agent with the Naval Criminal Investigative Service has been digging into the same things as the reporter."

Viktor gave a soft grunt to show his displeasure. "Weren't you just in a room with military leadership?"

Sam knew what he was hinting at. In a country like Russia, it would have been a simple and acceptable thing to strong-arm a defense minister into stopping an internal investigation. But in the United States, doing something like that brought unwanted attention. "It's not that easy," he replied. "Besides, I think it's just one woman."

"One reporter. One woman." Viktor stepped out of the shadows, shaking his head. "Where does it end?"

Sam swallowed. "It ends with her."

"How goes the operation in Ukraine?"

Sam wasn't sure if Viktor had changed the subject and asked the question to throw him off-balance or if he really didn't know. He had always assumed he was in direct communication with his people on the ground in Ukraine, but maybe he was waiting like everybody else to see if they could pull off the heist. Still, Sam couldn't risk lying to the Russian when he needed him to take care of the woman.

"Better than expected."

Viktor cocked his head and stared at him with his one good eye as if trying to discern Sam's meaning. "What does that mean?"

Again, Sam wondered what information Viktor was privy to but decided to play him straight. "It means that our forces were watching the wrong location and lost tabs on the armored vehicle."

"How did you manage that?"

Sam shook his head. "I didn't. Now, what are you going to do about this woman?"

"Me?"

"Yes, you."

"I'm not sure how this is my problem, Samuel."

"If you don't—"

Viktor cut him off. "Samuel, have you forgotten that you just helped a foreign intelligence officer recover tactical nuclear weapons by sabotaging an American military operation? No matter what happens with Aurora Holdings, I have all the leverage I need to ruin you."

The knot in the pit of Sam's stomach suddenly loosened, and he feared his bowels would let loose too.

"I own you now," Viktor said.

Sam was unaccustomed to negotiating from a position of weakness, but he couldn't walk away. For all the political power he had amassed over the years, he didn't have access to the kind of power he needed to deal with a federal law enforcement officer.

In a rare sign of weakness, Sam dropped his gaze to the ground and sheepishly asked, "What do I do?"

Before Sam could register what was happening, Viktor's right hand had darted inside his suit jacket, drawn a subcompact pistol, and aimed it at him. Sam's eyes grew wide with shock, but he didn't bother raising his hands in surrender. He already knew it would do no good.

But just as quickly as Viktor had drawn the gun, he spun it around and held it out grip-first to Sam. "Take care of the problem yourself."

Sam briefly entertained the fantasy of taking Viktor's gun and shooting him with it. But instead, he took the pistol and held it carefully between thumb and forefinger as if even touching it would bring certain death. He had fired a gun before but was hardly proficient.

"Me?" Sam asked.

"What's her name?"

"Emmy King."

Viktor gave him a look of open disdain. "Keep your phone on, and I will send you her location."

Sam knew the Russian wasn't joking.

Viktor waited until Sam had tucked the pistol into his pants and left to return to his vehicle. He stood on the steps of the Jefferson Memorial and looked north across the tidal basin at the White House. It was lit up and stood out like a beacon of freedom in the darkened city, but all Viktor saw was a trophy for his prowess.

Things were turning out even better than he could have hoped for. By the time Samuel Chambers realized he had never been Viktor's partner, it would be too late. The Russian had taken a chance on a young California politician two decades earlier, and now he would reap the benefits of having control over the president of the United States.

No other intelligence operative had achieved such a coup.

He steadily marched down the steps while removing his cell phone and placed a call to the same team that had cleaned up that mess with the reporter. He found it remarkable that somebody with the kind of power Samuel claimed to possess was unable to find the location for a low-level law enforcement officer. But no matter. *He* had that kind of power.

"Yes, sir?"

"I need you to work up a target package on a special agent with the Naval Criminal Investigative Service," Viktor said.

"Name?"

"Emmy King."

"It's going to take some time," the man said.

Viktor acknowledged, then ended the call before turning away from the tidal basin to begin a slow walk back to his car on the other side of the Washington Channel. He was going to miss his time living in the capital, but once the operation in Ukraine concluded, he would have no choice. He was a relic of the Cold War anyway and deserved to live out his retirement in peace.

It didn't even bother him that he would be handing over to his successor the keys to the kingdom. With a compromised president in the White House, his legacy in Yasenevo would be cemented. Nobody in Moscow would care when he dropped off the face of the earth and chose to live out the rest of his life in obscurity.

And with the money he would make selling the nuclear weapons, his obscurity was all but assured.

Viktor turned right onto Maine Avenue and walked underneath the overpasses that carried cars and trains across the channel and Potomac River to Crystal City on the other side. The city wasn't as beautiful as Moscow or Prague or even Paris or London, but it had been his home for over a decade. He knew every nook and cranny and had met with his agents in many of them—some even there along the waterfront—and he felt completely at ease walking the darkened streets.

He turned off Maine onto 12th Street and spotted his luxury sedan parked along the side of the road. It wasn't lost on him that he had parked within two blocks of the International Spy Museum and wondered how many others in his profession had often picked a location for its irony.

Halfway up the street, his phone vibrated, and Viktor swiped to answer and brought it to his ear. "Do you have it?"

"Yes sir, she is staying at the JW Marriott on Pennsylvania Avenue."

"What did you find out?"

Viktor continued walking as the man on the other end briefed him on the woman who had shaken Samuel Chambers. "She's assigned to the Southwest Field Office in San Diego, California, but took a leave of absence to fly out here."

This revelation surprised Viktor. "She's not here on official business?"

"Not that we were able to uncover. But she was seen with another man near the *Washington Post* after we took care of that reporter."

Viktor pursed his lips. Samuel was right to be concerned.

"Do we know who the other man is?"

"We do. He's known to us."

Viktor knew what that meant. There was an unspoken rule among Russian and American intelligence officers that their people were off limits, so it was in their best interests to know who worked at Langley.

"Is he going to be a problem?"

"*Nyet*. We can handle this easily."

Viktor approached his car and reached into his pocket for the key fob to unlock it. The lights flashed twice, and he opened the driver's door and climbed inside. It seemed like the president's chief of staff had created quite the mess for himself.

"Keep tabs on the woman, but do not engage. I have an idea."

"Yes, sir."

Viktor ended the call, then pressed on the button to start the car before pulling away from the curb. His time as the top Russian spy in Washington, DC, might be coming to an end, but he wasn't above getting his hands dirty.

46

JW Marriott
Washington, DC

Punky woke far earlier than she wanted to and tossed and turned for several minutes before reluctantly climbing out of bed. She remembered a time when she could have stayed in bed well after the sun came up, but those days were in the past. Now, it seemed like her brain kicked into gear the moment her eyes opened, and sleep instantly became an elusive dream just beyond her reach.

Most mornings, it was thoughts of her active investigations that took root in her brain. And this morning was no different. Before her eyes had fully adjusted to the room's darkness, she was already replaying her conversation with Lana Roman. Something about it seemed off, but Punky couldn't quite put her finger on it.

Still puzzled by the phone call, she walked into the bathroom and ran hot water in the shower to let it steam while she brushed the morning fuzz from her teeth. She hadn't gotten near the amount of sleep she needed to operate at peak performance, but there was no use in trying now. She was in full-on investigator mode and resolved not to let the sun go down again without getting the answers she needed.

Reaching around the curtain, she felt to make sure the water had reached an acceptable temperature, then slipped off her shorts and USC T-shirt and stepped into the shower. The water was a shade below scalding, but it felt good. Her long, dark hair fell down her back as she gently rolled her head from side to side and worked out the kinks.

But still her brain never stopped working.

Lana Roman had seemed nice enough on the phone. She hadn't been overtly obstructive in answering Punky's questions. But over the years, Punky had questioned enough people who had something to hide that she managed to catch several cleverly hidden clues that Lana was being evasive. She wasn't telling Punky the full story.

Maybe it was the way she seemed *too* transparent. Nobody gets a call from a stranger who claims to be a law enforcement officer and answers questions fully without first trying to verify their bona fides. Or maybe it was the way her answers seemed readily on the tip of her tongue, despite her involvement having been fleeting and over two decades earlier. Punky could still remember her first job as a lifeguard, but that didn't mean she could remember the names of every other guard she had shared the whistle with. Lana didn't seem to have that problem. She had recited names and dates almost as if she was holding an open ledger in front of her.

Punky shook off her unease and washed her hair with shampoo from the wall-mounted dispenser, then ran the miniature bar of soap over her body as thoughts of Lana turned over in her mind. By the time she had finished, she was more certain than ever that Lana's involvement in Aurora Holdings was larger than she had made it seem over the phone.

After deciding to cut short the rest of her trip and return early to California, Punky turned off the water, stepped out of the shower, and grabbed a towel from underneath the sink to dry off. She left the bathroom and walked to the large bedroom windows, where she threw open the drapes to see a city still ensconced in darkness.

The view through her window was of a bustling city that had fallen still. But she could remain still no longer.

Resolved to confront Lana Roman and get to the bottom of things, Punky quickly packed her things before reaching for her cell phone to book an earlier return flight to San Diego. But just as she picked it up, the screen lit up with an incoming text message.

Unknown Caller: WE NEED TO MEET.

She almost dropped the phone in surprise but quickly composed herself.

EK: WHO IS THIS?

Unknown Caller: THE PERSON WITH ANSWERS.

EK: TO WHAT?

Unknown Caller: AURORA HOLDINGS.

Punky inhaled sharply through pursed lips. She knew that she was onto something big if somebody had taken the time to find her number and reach out to schedule a meeting. Of course, she wasn't naive enough to believe that the unknown caller's intentions were noble. But she wasn't without means of protecting herself.

EK: WHEN AND WHERE?

Unknown Caller: NEW CARROLLTON METRO STATION. ONE HOUR.

New Carrollton Metro Station
New Carrollton, Maryland

Forty-five minutes later, Punky stepped out of the Uber in front of the New Carrollton Federal Building and scanned the quiet streets. She had no idea who she was supposed to meet with, but her past experiences had taught her to be ready for anything. At this point, a car full of gunmen wasn't out of the question. In fact, it was probably likely.

As the driver pulled away and left her alone on the sidewalk, she turned and began walking through a plaza adorned with a fountain and two flagpoles. The hour could have been classified as late at night or early in the morning, but all it meant to Punky was that she was alone. Over the clacking of the halyard's stainless-steel clasps against the metal flagpoles, she heard the whir of sparse traffic on nearby Route 50. But the metro cars at the station were silent. They wouldn't begin running for another hour.

Punky climbed a wide set of steps to exit the plaza and turned left for the arcing pedestrian bridge that would take her to the station. She kept her head on a swivel, looking left and right for any signs of the person who had sent her the text message. But so far, the soft plodding of her boots was the only sound.

She was halfway across the pedestrian bridge when twin beams of light swept across the street beneath her as a car turned the corner and approached from the southwest. She paused and watched the electric vehicle turn into the train station's lot and park in a spot near the entrance. Punky remained still and waited to see who emerged from the vehicle. But when nobody exited, she continued across the bridge.

It would have been easy for her to succumb to tunnel vision and focus only on the new arrival. So, she took slow breaths in through her nose to activate her parasympathetic nervous system and quell the natural desire to rush down the steps to the parking lot.

The pedestrian bridge was lit, but she moved casually, as if she wasn't in a hurry to make a clandestine meeting. She reached back with her elbow and felt for her pistol tucked tight against her body in a Kydex holster above her right hip. She hoped she wouldn't have need to draw it, but hope was never a good plan to rely on.

Punky reached the far end of the bridge and descended the stairs next to the escalator. Though the electric vehicle was the only other movement she had seen, she scanned the rest of the parking lot through the glass on her left and the train platforms to her right.

As she reached the street level, the Rivian's lights turned off and the driver's door opened. Acting on instinct, she swept the hem of her blazer back and rested her hand on the butt of her pistol, blading her body away to shield the pistol from the driver's view. But he hadn't seemed to notice. The driver had his cell phone pressed against his ear, and he was looking toward the federal building on the other side of the street.

Maybe that's not him, she thought, despite the adrenaline coursing through her veins.

Punky continued walking toward the escalators leading down into the metro station but paused when the driver turned, and a streetlamp illuminated his profile.

In one fluid motion, she drew her pistol and darted behind a low sign standing next to a covered bus stop. She knew the sign only afforded her marginal concealment and would do nothing to stop bullets if they began flying in her direction, but it was the best she could come up with. She just hoped like hell that the president's chief of staff hadn't brought her here to kill her.

Peering out from behind the sign, she watched Samuel Chambers standing next to the Rivian and shifting his weight from one foot to the other. He appeared nervous. Even more so after slipping his cell phone back into his pocket.

Punky watched with curiosity as an idea came to her. She reached into her pocket to remove her own phone and brought up the text thread that had summoned her there in the dead of night. She thought for a moment, then tapped out a brief and simple message before hitting send.

EK: HERE.

Once the blue status bar at the top of the screen disappeared and was replaced by the word "Delivered" underneath her message, she looked up and waited for the president's right-hand man to respond. It was the only way she could think of to verify that he was the man she had come to meet.

Her phone vibrated in her hand, and she looked down in shock at the return message.

Unknown Caller: PARKING LOT. NORTH SIDE.

Samuel Chambers hadn't moved.

Then she heard the squeal of tires.

47

Punky knew what was about to happen, and she stood up from behind the sign to shout a warning at Samuel Chambers. The president's chief of staff turned away from the approaching SUV, and she briefly saw the confusion on his face before she returned her focus to the imminent threat.

"Get down!"

Samuel hesitated for a split second, then dropped to the ground just as gunfire erupted and split apart the early morning silence. Punky heard the rapid staccato of a small-caliber machine pistol and the whistling cracks of rounds breaking the sound barrier as they tore across the vacant parking lot. But neither was a foreign experience for her, and she lifted her pistol and returned fire while sprinting toward the Rivian.

The SUV screeched to a halt next to Chambers, and the shooter leaned out from the rear seat, unloading on the prone politico. But to Punky's surprise and delight, he rolled underneath the electric vehicle to escape the onslaught.

She worked the trigger on her SIG Sauer pistol as fast as she could and only stopped when the slide locked to the rear. But she continued on at a dead sprint and thumbed the magazine release to drop the empty onto the concrete with a clatter while reaching back with her free hand to draw one of her two spare magazines on her left hip. In one fluid motion, she indexed the magazine into the pistol and sent the slide forward to chamber a round and resume laying down covering fire.

Punky was halfway across the parking lot when she noticed her cell phone vibrating in her pocket. But she ignored the incoming call and raced toward the rear of the Rivian where she could take cover behind the SUV, hoping its internal components were dense enough to stop a bullet from reaching her.

Halfway through her second magazine, she began walking her shots toward the shooter in the rear seat. But as the first round plinked off the idling SUV, the driver gunned it and took off down the street. Punky slid across the ground and came to a stop behind the Rivian's rear wheel, panting from her exertion and sudden adrenaline dump.

"Mr. Chambers, are you okay?"

Her question was met with silence that stretched long enough that she feared he had been killed. But then she heard a weak voice cry out. "I'm hit."

Punky pushed herself into a squat and peered around the quarter panel at the SUV's retreating taillights, then scampered forward to peer underneath the Rivian. "Hurry. We need to get out of here."

Sam looked over at her with a frightened expression on his face, but he began inching his way across the ground to crawl out from underneath the electric vehicle. When he was within reach, Punky holstered her pistol and grabbed a fistful of his shirt to help pull him clear before the shooters could return to finish the job.

Bright red splotches dotted the front of his linen shirt and were spreading fast enough that she knew he needed medical treatment. "Do you have a first aid kit?"

His eyes pinched shut as his body gave a little shudder. "A what?"

Punky hooked her arms underneath his armpits and pulled him upright, struggling to get him to his feet so she could open the rear door open and lay him down on the Rivian's rear bench seat. "A first aid kit," she repeated. "Do you have one?"

He shook his head. "No."

She leaned into him and braced him against the side of the electric vehicle while reaching around his limp body to open the rear door.

Droplets of blood rained down on the concrete from the loose shirt that was beginning to cling to his chest. Without even examining the wounds, she could tell the president's chief of staff was gravely wounded. But the first priority was getting off the X.

With the door open, she hobbled forward and tipped him over onto the rear seat. "Come on, we need to get out of here."

Sam stared at her with confusion for several seconds but then started elbowing his way back across the seat so she could close the door. Once his feet were tucked inside, Punky slammed the door and ran around the SUV to the driver's door and climbed in. She ignored his groaning from the backseat as she turned on the electric vehicle and backed out of the parking spot.

Unlike the cars she favored, the Rivian only made a quiet whirring sound as she put it into drive and sped from the parking lot. She was unfamiliar with the area and didn't know where the nearest hospital was, but her first priority was getting clear of the ambush site before the gunmen returned to make sure they had completed their task of silencing Samuel Chambers.

"Who wants you dead?" she blurted, unable to stop the investigative side of her brain from trying to piece together what had just happened.

He mumbled an incoherent reply, but her brain was already analyzing what had taken place from a detached perspective—almost as if a text message from an unknown number hadn't summoned her to the scene of the crime in the dead of night. Her face flushed as she recalled the phone vibrating during the ambush, and she fumbled in her pocket to retrieve it.

"What are you after?" Sam asked from the backseat.

She glanced in the rearview mirror but couldn't see his supine form. He groaned again, and she brought her phone to her face to see that she had missed two incoming calls from the same "Unknown Caller" during the ambush. It was clear Sam hadn't been the one making those calls, which meant he hadn't been the one asking her to meet.

"Why were you at the train station?"

His groaning stopped. "I came to meet with you."

"Me? Why?"

His voice was weak, but she heard a soft chuckle. "To kill you."

Punky felt a chill down her spine as she heard the sincerity in his words. Somebody had arranged for her and Sam to be there at the same time, but it was clear whoever that person was had something different in mind. There was still a good chance they wanted her dead as well. But based on what had happened in the parking lot, it seemed like Sam was the real target.

"Why?"

He coughed, and Punky heard the wet splatter of blood consistent with a chest wound that had compromised his lungs. Sam was in rough shape and needed immediate medical attention. But she knew they were still in danger, and she scanned her mirrors for signs of the SUV that had ambushed them.

"It doesn't matter now," he said weakly after catching his breath. "It's too late. Viktor already has what he wants."

Her foot came off the accelerator briefly. "Viktor Drakov?"

"Yes."

"What does he want?"

Another cough. Another splatter of blood. His voice sounded wet and strained. "To steal nuclear weapons… in Ukraine… and sell them to jihadis."

Punky was no stranger to complex international plots with far-reaching consequences. But this one surpassed them all. She had been a young girl when terrorists flew commercial planes into the twin towers of the World Trade Center and crashed another into the Pentagon, but she clearly remembered its impact on her. She couldn't fathom how that day might have been different had nuclear weapons been used.

Sam's admission gave her more questions than answers, but she didn't have time to satisfy her curiosity. Not when she was looking at the potential of a nuclear attack on the horizon. As she pressed the Rivian hard through the maze of streets to get to the freeway, she unlocked her phone and dialed the number for the only person she could think who might be able to help.

Sam coughed again, followed by a guttural moan of intense pain. Punky ignored him.

"Punky—"

"Connor, I need your help."

"Do you know what time—"

She cut him off again. "I've got Samuel Chambers in the backseat. He's been shot."

"What? Where are you?"

Her eyes flashed up to the street sign as she turned right. "I just turned onto Annapolis Road."

If Connor had been sleeping, she couldn't tell from his voice. "From where?"

"I don't know! We were at the New Carrollton train station."

"Okay. Okay. Leave your phone on, and I'll get help to you. Are you still in danger?"

Punky's eyes flashed at each of her mirrors, again looking for the SUV that had sped off after gunning down the president's chief of staff. "I don't know. But, Connor, there's something going on in Ukraine—"

The sound of rounds impacting the electric vehicle cut her off, and she felt the Rivian's back end let loose. Punky dropped her phone and gripped the steering wheel with both hands, fighting against the fishtailing SUV as she ignored the brilliant headlights that had just appeared behind her.

48

MECH 5
Ukrainian MiG-29 Fulcrum

Polina had been monitoring the radio communications between her fellow countrymen from the Svyatyi Mykolai Battalion and the Americans in the TOC at Voznesensk. When she learned that the SEAL ground force had been inserted north of the wrong storage facility, she abruptly pulled off and raced for the new location. She was running low on fuel and knew she wouldn't be able to remain in the fight much longer.

Feeling as if time was running out, she orbited the new location for several minutes before spotting isolated gunfire coming from a clearing in the trees. Without hesitation, she rolled in on the dense forest to get a closer look at what was taking place beneath her.

"Mech Five, status?"

With the sun now up, she had already stowed her night vision goggles and squinted against a daylight that seemed almost foreign to her. She ignored the intercept controller's query and continued in her dive until pulling off at the last possible moment after catching a fleeting glimpse of a Russian armored vehicle.

"Over the target now," she replied, pulling her turbofan engines out of afterburner and dispensing flares as she raced back into the sky.

"Copy, push channel thirty-three for Pony control."

Polina glanced at her remaining fuel and knew she would likely only get one chance at this. She craned her neck to look over her shoulder at the Bumerang armored personnel carrier as it zigzagged through the trees and raced away from the camouflaged storage facility. There was no question it was the same one that had escaped her at the bridge and again after the American turboprop was shot down.

It would not get away again.

"Mech Five, Pony One."

She grinned at hearing the American's voice as she switched her radio to the new frequency. "Pony One, Mech Five is overhead your position with four two-hundred-and-fifty-kilogram general-purpose bombs." She released the transmit switch briefly before quickly adding, "Tally target."

Polina knew that joint terminal attack controllers were trained to relay information in a scripted exchange that culminated in a nine-line close air support brief. Normally, the intensive back-and-forth was necessary to ensure the attack pilot knew where the friendlies were in relation to the target on the ground. But she had already seen the single shooter unloading on the armored vehicle.

And she knew he was still within the blast radius.

"Make your attack from south to north," the JTAC replied.

"South to north," Polina echoed. "Confirm you are Danger Close?"

"Danger Close. My initials are Delta Whiskey."

She swallowed. "Copy."

Polina held the control stick in a loose grip as her MiG-29 Fulcrum arced across the sky to prepare for her attack run. She had dropped hundreds of bombs on Russian troops and killed countless invaders, but she had never felt as nervous as she did in that moment. She was one with the machine wrapped around her, and all her focus was on the armored personnel carrier hiding in the forest below.

Reaching the roll-in point, Polina smoothly pulled the stick into her lap and pointed her nose at the earth. She rolled wings level, placed her thumb on the pickle switch, and keyed the microphone. "Mech Five, in from the south."

"Cleared hot."

**Yuzhnoukrainsk
Mykolaiv Oblast, Ukraine**

Voronov wiped the sweat from his eyes and reached up to adjust the vent over his head. The vehicle was air-conditioned, but apparently passenger comfort had come in dead last in design requirements. He should have been thankful for the thick steel body that was deflecting the incoming gunfire away from its occupants, but he would have appreciated even a marginally more effective air-conditioner.

"What now?" Yevgeny asked.

"We keep going. Losing ourselves in the forest is the best chance of surviving."

The weapons operator shook his head, obviously wishing he could employ the *DRAGON LINE* to take care of the jet circling overhead. They had already knocked down one attack aircraft and could easily swat this one from the sky as well. But they had expended all the stored energy and needed to generate more before employing the laser again.

Suddenly the Bumerang lurched, and Voronov's stomach dropped as they were flung sideways. A deafening explosion rocked the cabin, followed quickly by a second, compressing the air and painfully squeezing his head before slamming it against the thinly padded headrest. His vision went dark.

Smoke filled the cramped space and they crashed to the ground, rocking violently before coming to rest, listing to the left side. He hung limp in his seat, thankful he had remembered to attach the shoulder harnesses that were cutting into his collarbones while his arms and legs twitched, and his vision cleared to fade in the horrific scene.

"Yevgeny," he croaked.

But he couldn't hear himself. He lifted a hand to his ear and felt the slick trickle of blood leaking down the side of his face.

Voronov released his buckle and reached for the unconscious weapons operator. He fumbled with the man's harness and struggled to release him but was distracted by a tinny popping sound that filtered through the ringing in his ears and reminded him they weren't alone in the forest. The hollow sound of bullets plinking against the armored hull intensified, and he knew he couldn't just sit there and wait.

Wiping the sweat from his eyes, he released his grip on Yevgeny's harness and scrambled away from his unconscious body. He fumbled over the suitcase nukes that had been flung across the rear of the Bumerang as it rolled onto its side, grunting and pulling them out of the way to search for the AKS-74U he had stashed in a duffel bag before leaving Perekop.

He hadn't planned on needing it but was left with no choice.

The *ukorochenny*, or shortened, version of the venerable AK-74 assault rifle had been his weapon of choice on the front lines in Chechnya. But it had proven an ideal weapon to carry inside the armored vehicle.

Finding the duffel bag under a crumpled seat frame, he yanked it open to reveal a low-visibility soft armor vest designed to stop smaller caliber pistol rounds. It would do little against the powerful rifles firing at him, but it was better than nothing. He slipped it over his head and cinched the Velcro straps down on each side, then reached back inside for the short-barreled rifle and slipped the sling over his head.

Voronov knew he was outmanned and outgunned. But if he survived the initial assault, there was a good chance he could evade the remaining attackers and escape into the Ukrainian countryside. He just needed to hold on.

BOOM!

The detonation of breaching charges on the rear door knocked him to the floor. He felt more than heard the smaller explosion and knew his time was up. Before the smoke cleared, he swung the AKS up and squeezed the trigger, sending rounds through the open door into the throng of Ukrainian soldiers swarming the overturned armored vehicle.

Most ducked to either side of the gaping hole, but he hit one in the back and sent him sprawling to the forest floor. Voronov scooted backward, toward the front of the Bumerang, while tugging on Yevgeny's limp body to stack him on top of the debris to build a gruesome barricade of sorts.

Some version of a Kalashnikov appeared around the corner, but its owner remained hidden behind the armor as he sprayed blindly into the cramped space. The rounds sizzled and cracked through the air over his head and impacted the weapons operator's body with a loud *thwap thwap thwap!*

Had he been better equipped, he would have returned fire to keep the shooter at bay. But with only two spare thirty-round magazines and what remained of the one in his AKS, he couldn't afford to be indiscriminate.

He had to wait. Bide his time. Look for the perfect opportunity.

The stubby barrel of his rifle moved in a subtle figure-eight pattern as he waited for another target to appear. When it did, he quickly shifted his point of aim and squeezed the trigger, satisfied when the militiaman collapsed to the ground under a cloud of pink mist.

Two down.

Keeping his eyes on the open door, Voronov used his non-firing hand to reach for the Iridium SAT phone in his left pocket. He pulled it out, extended the antenna with his teeth, and dialed Viktor's number. He wasn't sure what the old spymaster would be able to do for him, but if he had any hope of surviving and making it out of Ukraine alive, then he needed help. And he needed it now.

But instead of the steady beeping tone indicating the call was bouncing from satellite to satellite to the Russian over eight thousand kilometers away, he heard only the ringing in his ears and the muted shouts of men closing in on him. He hazarded a glance at the screen.

Searching for Iridium.

"*Pizdec!*" he shouted.

Voronov dropped the useless SAT phone and refocused his attention on the open door, wincing when he caught sight of a blurred object flying into the rear of the Bumerang. Instinctively, he rolled away and tucked his chin to his chest, closing his eyes and opening his mouth to prepare for the concussive blast.

Boom!

Even through his clenched eyelids, the flash of light was blinding. And the minimal amount of hearing he had regained was once more replaced by a renewed, relentless ringing. He rolled onto his chest to get back into the fight.

Without aiming, Voronov pointed the AKS in the opening's direction and squeezed the trigger. He glanced down at the Iridium SAT phone resting next to Yevgeny's corpse and noticed that a timer was counting up as if his call had finally connected. He shifted fire toward what seemed like movement approaching through the smoke, then scooped up the phone and held it to his ear.

"I'm being overrun," he shouted, though he couldn't hear anything on the other end. He choked on the thick smoke and felt lightheaded but thought back to their contingency plan. "Send Morozov, or we'll lose everything!"

49

Washington, DC

Viktor held his breath while pressing the phone to his ear. Calls made from SAT phones were notorious for lengthy delays, but they generally rivaled most domestic cellular carriers in quality. But the background noise made it almost impossible to hear what his man in Ukraine was saying from the other end.

"Nikolai, repeat your last."

There was a loud boom followed by the unmistakable report of a Kalashnikov on full automatic in an enclosed space. Viktor leaned forward and closed his eyes, trying to imagine the scene unfolding on the other side of the Atlantic. He heard a scuffling noise as if somebody had moved the phone, rapid breathing, followed by Nikolai's voice that carried an unmistakable tone of urgency.

"I'm being overrun."

Viktor's heart bolted with sudden fear. Samuel had told him the operation was going in their favor, and he had expected nothing but good news from his men downrange. But this proclamation was far from good.

"What? By who?"

Nikolai coughed and choked, and Viktor imagined the former Spetsnaz soldier straining to breathe through a thick cloud of smoke.

"Send Morozov, or we'll lose everything!"

Viktor ended the call without replying, knowing that his men were fighting for their lives and there was nothing he could say to change that. The only thing he could do was send help, just like Nikolai had asked. He cursed under his breath, then placed a call to Major General Yuri Morozov—a pompous asshole that was the epitome of what had gone wrong with the Russian military, but the only person in a position to affect the outcome.

"Morozov."

"General, this is Viktor Drakov."

There was a pause on the other end, and for a moment Viktor thought the imbecile was going to hang up on him. "Yes, sir?"

"You are aware of your role in this operation, are you not?"

Another pause. "Yes, sir."

"Then why have you not mobilized your forces across the Dnieper River and supported my assets?" Viktor knew the best way of getting the general to spring into action was by making him believe he had somehow failed in his duties and would soon be recalled to Moscow to answer for his crimes against the Fatherland.

"My forces have been waiting—"

"Waiting for what?" Viktor boomed, cutting the general off. "Move your asses now!"

He ended the call before Morozov could bluster some more, then turned his attention to the other matter at hand. As if the potential of losing the nuclear weapons in Ukraine wasn't bad enough, his men in New Carrollton had informed him that they had only succeeded in taking down Samuel. The woman NCIS special agent was still alive and threatened to expose them.

He dialed the number for his team in the field and waited with growing impatience for the call to connect. When it did, he didn't wait for them to speak or give them a chance to make excuses. "Keep her there," he said. "I'll handle her myself."

Lanham, Maryland

Punky relaxed her grip while trying to turn into the skid, but it was too late. The loss of traction was too much for her to overcome, and the Rivian's back end spun around before slamming into the concrete median dividing the eight-lane road. She braced herself for the impact, but her head still slammed into the side window and caused her vision to swim.

Not another one, she thought.

Unlike each of her previous vehicular mishaps, the Rivian didn't have an internal combustion engine or a fuel tank that threatened to explode. But just like the others, men with guns were waiting in the wings to finish her off. She needed to move, and she needed to move soon.

"Are you okay?" she asked, turning to look at Samuel Chambers in the backseat.

Before he could answer, the windshield in front of her splintered with incoming rounds, and she threw herself across the center console onto the floorboard in front of her seat. But it took only a second for her to recognize the folly of the move. The Rivian wasn't a normal SUV with an engine under the hood that could be used for cover. At best, she was only shielding herself with aluminum and plastic.

"Samuel, can you move?" she shouted over the maelstrom.

"I think so."

"When I tell you to, open the door and make for the other side of the median." The concrete barrier was sufficient cover, but she knew it would be fleeting. "Ready?"

"No."

"Now!"

Without waiting to see if the president's chief of staff had followed her instructions, she pushed herself off the floorboard, drew her pistol, and thrust it through one of the holes in the windshield. She didn't really care if she hit one of their attackers and was only trying to keep their heads down long enough to give Samuel a chance to escape.

The slide locked to the rear on her SIG Sauer, and she withdrew it from the windshield while turning to climb over the front seats into the back. As she thumbed the magazine release to begin her emergency reload, she caught sight of Samuel Chambers flopping onto the ground through the open rear door.

At least he listened.

Punky tumbled onto the floorboards in the rear of the Rivian and twisted her body to gain access to the last spare magazine on her hip. She had eleven more rounds before they were up a creek but couldn't waste energy worrying about something she couldn't change. Indexing the final magazine into the pistol, Punky sent the slide forward, then followed Samuel through the open door.

Instantly, the darkened street turned into day as a blindingly brilliant light shone down on her.

Punky flopped down onto the concrete street and glanced up just as the helicopter's spotlight shifted to the shooters standing one hundred yards away on either side of a blacked-out SUV. They shielded their eyes from the light but kept their focus on the stricken Rivian and continued unloading on it with their machine pistols.

Rounds plinked into the ruined electric vehicle and surrounding pavement, sending fragments of the road up into her face. She looked away but felt the shards cutting into her exposed skin while holding her pistol out and blindly working the trigger. Her gunshots were barely audible over the deafening sound of the helicopter's rotor wash, but she continued firing while working her way around the Rivian to the cement barrier on the other side.

"This is the Maryland State Police. Drop your weapons."

She couldn't be sure if the police chopper was addressing her or the men shooting at her, but it didn't matter anymore. Her slide had locked to the rear once again, and she was out of ammunition. Punky dropped the pistol and let it clatter to the pavement just as she reached the cement barrier and heaved herself to the other side.

But her attackers didn't seem to have the same problem, and their gunfire continued pouring into the Rivian and the concrete barrier she and Samuel were sheltering behind.

"Drop your weapons now!"

Punky glanced over at the president's chief of staff long enough to see that he was moving and still alive, then pushed herself up to peer over the barrier at the attackers. They had closed the distance between their SUV and the wrecked Rivian, apparently still disregarding the commands from above as they alternated dumping rounds in her direction.

Suddenly, one of the men spun his machine pistol upward and began spraying rounds at the police helicopter. Sparks flew as bullets hit its aluminum skin and the spotlight went dark, but the helicopter only pivoted right and nosed over to race away from the gunfire. Once more blanketed in darkness, the gunmen resumed their advance.

Punky dropped behind the barrier again and scrambled over to Samuel Chambers. "We need to get across the street."

"I can't," he moaned.

She didn't know if he had any new holes, but his once white shirt was now a dark shade of red. He had lost a lot of blood and was weak. But Punky knew that if the gunmen reached them, it would be game over. They only had one chance of making it out alive, and that meant she needed to get them across the street where they could hide in the trees or get lost in the parking lot.

Punky pulled one of Samuel's limp arms across her shoulders and wrapped her other around his waist to grab his belt on his left hip. Fueled by adrenaline and fear, she hoisted him onto his feet and turned for the parking lot four lanes away. He was limp and lethargic, but she wasn't about to give up on him. No matter what he had done, they were in this together and needed to make it to safety.

But safety seemed so far away. Especially when she heard bullets sizzling through the air.

And felt Samuel's body jerk.

50

Almost immediately, Samuel's legs stopped moving, and he became dead weight in her arms. Her momentum carried her forward several more steps, but the burden became too much for her, and she toppled over on top of him. Bullets continued peppering the ground around them, splintering the pavement and cracking the air like a whip.

"Get up," she urged, trying like hell to pull him back to his feet.

But he wouldn't budge. A strained whistling sound escaped his mouth as he opened and closed it while trying to take a breath. His eyes were wide with fear, and he had a panicked expression that screamed at her.

I don't want to die!

"You're not going to die," she said, though she knew her words sounded hollow.

She pushed herself to her feet, then bent over and tugged and pulled, ignoring the incoming rounds while using all her strength to lift him from the pavement. But he barely moved. He was too heavy, and his body had already given up.

"Samuel, you need to—"

A round slammed into his head, spraying blood across the road. But she barely had time to notice the moment his lights went out, because another bullet clipped her shoulder and spun her around. She tried taking a step to steady herself, but her legs failed to gain purchase, and she fell onto her back.

Punky's head slammed into the pavement, again filling her vision with stars. But she focused through the dancing, twinkling lights at the real stars above, wondering if that would be the last thing she saw. Her shoulder burned like it had been branded, and ice filled her veins as she teetered on the precipice of blacking out. She knew she wasn't mortally wounded—not yet—but she couldn't see her way out.

She had been shot. She was unarmed. And the men hunting her had killed her companion and shown no hesitation in the face of law enforcement. A red light blinked high above her as a jet crossed the sky, and she found herself wishing she was miles above the earth instead of on the ground only miles from the nation's capital.

You're not out of the fight.

It wasn't her father's voice. It wasn't her coach's voice. It wasn't her Uncle Rick or Camron Knowles. And it wasn't Jax Woods, Connor Sullivan, or Colt Bancroft.

It was her.

You're not done. Get up, Punky.

Wincing, she pushed herself off the road and looked at Samuel's still body. His jacket had fallen open, and she spied a pistol tucked into his waistband. Still woozy, she reached over and removed the pistol and studied it carefully. It wasn't one she had ever seen before, with Cyrillic writing along the slide, but she was certain it worked just like any other.

She gripped the slide and yanked it back to chamber a round. The gunmen might still finish her off, but she wasn't about to lie down and give them a better chance of winning. She had been in tough spots before, and this was no different. As long as she had breath in her lungs, she would continue fighting. She rose to her feet and aimed the pistol across the cement barrier, waiting for a target to materialize.

Suddenly, a gust of wind blasted her weakened body, and it took a moment for her to realize that the police helicopter had returned. She looked up as the Leonardo AW139 descended from the dark sky and hovered between her and the shooters.

Yuzhnoukrainsk
Mykolaiv Oblast, Ukraine

Colt hadn't expected to be left behind when Dave and the Ukrainian militiamen descended off the roof to assault the armored personnel carrier. But they hadn't left him much choice. The MiG-29's air strike had been on the money—just shy of a direct hit—and enough to immobilize the Bumerang and knock it onto its side. Colt understood why they immediately leaped into action and left him behind, but it didn't mean he wasn't frustrated that his injury prevented him from doing the same thing.

As Colt retreated back up the hill to circle around the hidden structure, he listened to the squad firing at the stricken vehicle. The sound of Dave's suppressed personal defense weapon was unmistakable against the cacophony of AKs on full automatic, but he suspected he wouldn't have the same luxury when trying to differentiate the Ukrainian Kalashnikovs from the Russian.

But the one thing Colt knew he could distinguish with certainty were the sounds coming from the sky. It had been silent after Polina left in the Fulcrum to return to base. But he was beginning to pick up a faint thumping that sounded like it was growing louder.

Colt froze in his tracks and braced himself against a tree as he looked up into the sky. The sound was getting louder, but he couldn't quite make it out. "Must be the Ospreys," he mumbled.

It made sense. They had probably only gone back to Voznesensk to consolidate before returning to recover the SEAL ground element they had inserted at the wrong location. He reached for the MBITR radio secured in the pouch on his chest and paused before bringing it to his mouth.

"Shit!"

In the heat of the moment, Colt had forgotten he busted the radio in the ejection. Or, more accurately, in the clumsy crashing that happened after. But if the noises he had heard were coming from one of the CV-22 Ospreys, then it was likely Dave and the others—the ones with the working radios—already knew about it.

But what if it's not?

And that's what troubled him most. He hadn't seen any Ukrainian helicopters since arriving, but that didn't mean they didn't exist. He knew they did. But his mind listened to the *whomp whomp whomp* of the approaching rotors and could only picture a Mil Mi-24 Hind attack helicopter chasing down the American resistance fighters on horseback in the iconic eighties movie *Red Dawn*.

Of course, it hadn't mattered to a younger Colt that the helicopters were actually French SA 330 Pumas disguised to look like the real deal. To him, they were Soviet attack helicopters through and through. And the sound he heard now gave him the same feeling of dread.

"I have to warn them."

The door covering the Bumerang's rear hatch had been blown off, and whoever was still alive inside was doing a good job of making a final stand. Even after one of the militiamen had tossed in a flash-bang grenade, the resistance didn't seem to let up. Already, two Ukrainian soldiers had been dropped by gunfire coming from the enclosed space, and Dave had pulled the others back behind cover to regroup.

If he could just get down to where they were, he could warn them of the approaching helicopter before it was too late to mount a defense—not that they were equipped to fend off an attack from the air. Still, it was better than being caught in a crossfire.

Colt focused on the gaggle of men Dave had corralled at the bottom of the hill and saw one of the militiamen give up on trying to revive one of his squadmates who had been shot. They hadn't even bothered trying to revive the other. Their original squad of eight was down to six, plus a Navy SEAL master chief. And a busted up Naval Aviator too far away to do any good.

But like his wrestling coach used to say, *It's not the size of the dog in the fight; it's the size of the fight in the dog.*

Of course, that was easy to say when you were wrestling somebody who was at most only seven or eight pounds heavier than you.

Colt waved his arms over his head to get their attention, but it was clear they were more focused on figuring out how to smoke out the burrowed Russian fighters than in the pilot hobbling down the hillside behind them. He glanced up into the sky again just as a dark shadow passed overhead.

And he froze.

Unlike the make-believe attack helicopters featured in 1980s action films, the one that flew overhead was very real. The rocket launchers mounted under its stubby wings were real. The gatling gun mounted under its bulbous chin was real. And the red star of the Russian army was very real.

Just when Colt thought Dave and his ragtag group of militiamen would hear the helicopter and recognize the looming danger, a Russian soldier opened a hatch on what was once the top of the armored vehicle and fell out onto the forest floor. Several of the Ukrainian soldiers spun in his direction, but he was already firing at them with a short-barreled Kalashnikov on full automatic.

With another glance at the helicopter that looked like it was preparing to loop around for another pass, Colt gritted his teeth and started running down the hill. Instantly, a metallic taste filled his mouth as his vision swam from the excruciating pain. But he pushed aside his agony and focused on the importance of what they were doing.

There were nuclear weapons inside that armored vehicle. If they didn't stop the Russians here and now, then who knows where they might end up. Atlanta? Baltimore? Chicago? Dallas? This little patch of dirt and trees in Mykolaiv Oblast was their last stand, and Colt wasn't about to let a Russian attack helicopter rain on their parade.

As the Mi-24 Hind completed its loop and approached the clearing, Colt stopped and brought the butt stock of his personal defense weapon up into his shoulder. Though designed for close-in engagements, Colt knew the kinematics of its 5.56 NATO round were enough to still carry a wallop at range. He placed the red dot in his holographic sight on the helicopter's forward canopy—the one he reasoned protected the attack helicopter's gunner—and thumbed his weapon selector off safe.

I hope this works...

Colt pressed back on the trigger and felt the short-barreled rifle jerk in his hands with each round that he walked back along the Russian attack helicopter's fuselage. Sparks flew amid the faint *tings*, but otherwise his fire seemed largely ineffective against the flying tank. Not even a flinch as it continued its descent into the clearing while pivoting away from Colt and pointing its gatling gun and rocket launchers at Dave and the Ukrainian soldiers.

From his vantage point, he couldn't see if the undersized squad of militiamen was even aware that a Russian helicopter had flanked them and descended into the clearing bordering the hidden bunker. He would have thought they could feel the downwash from its massive rotor blades or hear the thumping over the clatter of their gunfight. But he wasn't willing to rely on that.

Lowering his rifle, Colt pushed off the tree he had been bracing himself against and resumed his downhill sprint. This time, however, his focus was on the helicopter and not the overturned armored vehicle. He was certain Dave and the others could handle whoever had exited the Bumerang to confront them. But he was less than certain they would be able to fend off a rocket attack from the attack helicopter.

He reached the bottom of the hill just as the side door on the helicopter opened. If there had been any doubt that the helicopter was Russian, that evaporated the moment Russian troops poured out and immediately turned toward Dave and the militiamen with their Kalashnikovs pointed in their direction. Colt flung himself to the ground and brought his rifle up to sight in on the nearest soldier.

Just as the first Russian opened fire—dropping a third Ukrainian soldier—Colt placed his reticle on his target and squeezed the trigger. He had been aiming for between the shoulder blades but immediately saw that he hadn't accounted for the range and watched the round drop at the Russian's feet and kick up a cloud of dirt. He immediately corrected his aim and sent a second round downrange, just as the Russian spun in his direction. The 5.56 NATO round caught the trooper in his face and knocked him backward off his feet.

More troops poured out from the Hind, splitting their forces in two. Half turned to join their compatriots in facing down Dave and the Ukrainian soldiers, while the others turned and began firing in Colt's direction.

Colt shifted his aim to one of the newcomers dumping rounds into the forest around him, and squeezed the trigger again, catching him high in his chest and spinning him to the ground like a dervish. He shifted to a third

Russian and continued squeezing the trigger but failed to find his mark before the bolt locked to the rear.

As he took his finger off the trigger and moved it to release the empty magazine, incoming AK rounds impacted the ground in front of him and showered him with dirt. As the incoming fire snapped and cracked at the air around him, he turned away and reached back into his survival harness for his only spare magazine.

Still in the fight!

Voronov was surprised at how quickly Viktor had been able to mobilize Morozov's forces. He hadn't expected help to come for hours, but he could see the proof right there through the open rear hatch—an air assault Mi-24 Hind descending to insert its payload of troops behind his attackers. All he needed to do was remain behind the armored walls of the Bumerang and wait for his countrymen to liberate him.

But his feeling of hopefulness began to wane when the driver's gunfire slowed, then stopped. Voronov knew it had been folly to let him try to make a run for it through the top hatch, but it had served its purpose. In the end, the man's sacrifice meant that Voronov and the nuclear weapons were safe from being overrun for at least a few minutes more.

A few minutes that would be all the time his rescuers needed to mop up the Ukrainian forces surrounding him and escort him to the waiting helicopter.

But when the gunfight beyond the armored vehicle's steel walls intensified, he began to doubt things were going as smoothly as Morozov's men expected. He pushed himself up and peered over Yevgeny's corpse and saw that half the Russian troopers were engaging somebody up the hill while the others were trading fire with the Ukrainian forces who had swarmed the Bumerang.

"This is madness," he grumbled, glancing over at the pile of nuclear weapons they had risked everything to recover. If he couldn't get them to the cargo ship waiting in Sevastopol, then it would have all been for nothing. The men they had sacrificed infiltrating Ukraine. The assets they had burned acquiring the *DRAGON LINE*. The decades of deception, waiting for the moment to capitalize on the American president's compromise.

And it all meant nothing if they couldn't sell the weapons.

Nothing.

The gunfire intensified again, and Voronov recognized it for what it was. It wasn't much of a chance, but if the Russian and Ukrainian soldiers were shooting each other, he might be able to sneak away from the overturned armored vehicle and get to where he could have the helicopter return and pick him up.

With the AKS in one hand, he pushed himself to his feet and crept toward the rear. He hazarded a glance outside again and once more saw that the soldiers were too busy fighting with each other to notice him. Without hesitating, he grasped the handles on one of the duffel bags containing an RA-115 nuclear device and hefted it off the Bumerang's floor. It was heavier than expected, but still manageable.

He took a deep breath, then scrambled through the open hatch and turned left away from where he had last seen the Ukrainian forces. The hairs on the back of his neck stood on end as he waited for a bullet to slam into him from behind, but he scampered around the Bumerang and took cover behind its bulky tires.

So far, it seemed as if his escape from the armored vehicle had gone undetected, and he was left with a choice. He could either cut his losses and try to make it to safety with one of the devices, or he could risk returning through the gun battle to retrieve another. Selling one was better than nothing. But two was even better than that.

Even as Voronov recognized that his decision was based purely on greed and not on the tactics required for the evolving situation, he felt good about his chances. Leaving the first duffel pressed up against the mangled wreckage of the Bumerang's drivetrain, he darted out from behind cover and sprinted for the rear hatch. With less than half a meter from the opening, he launched himself off the ground and dove through just as the Hind lifted off and flew away.

After crashing into Yevgeny's dead body, he quickly scampered to his feet, pulled his AKS around from where it was slung across his back, and prepared to engage. But miraculously, his return to the Bumerang seemed to have gone unnoticed. He moved the stubby AK around to his back again and gripped the handles on the remaining two duffel bags, lifting them from the deck to test his balance with such a cumbersome load.

Either they were lighter than the first or the symmetry of having one in each hand made them seem less unwieldy. For whatever reason, he felt a sense of elation that rivaled that of pulling down the bunker's door and retrieving the weapons from where they had been in storage for decades. Feeling almost invincible—as if his victory was pre-ordained—Voronov didn't bother looking outside before tossing the duffels through the hatch and crawling out after them.

But almost immediately he knew something was different. Instead of advancing on his position and cutting through the Ukrainian defenses like butter, the Russian soldiers were retreating toward the bunker. Through the clatter of sustained automatic gunfire, he heard the unmistakable sound of the Russian Mil Mi-24 Hind approaching the clearing at high speed from the north.

He looked up into the sky at the attack helicopter, then down at the clearing where the Russian soldiers were bounding backward, then back into the sky. Almost immediately, he understood what was happening and praised the brilliance of whoever Morozov had put in charge of the rescue operation.

"They're drawing them in..."

With a little shake of his head, Voronov retrieved the duffels from the ground and turned to duck back around the belly of the Bumerang where he had stashed the first. Even if the helicopter's attack run didn't finish them off, it meant they would be too busy to worry about one man sneaking off into the forest with tactical nuclear weapons.

Viktor would be proud.

51

It was obvious from Colt's vantage point what was happening. He had counted eight Russian soldiers exiting the helicopter before it took off again, and he didn't think there were any more in reserve. But despite both sides seeming to have lost an equal number of soldiers, the Russians were far better equipped to take on the Ukrainians.

But still they were retreating.

At least, that's how it had looked initially. But as Colt used the momentary lull in gunfire aimed in his direction to hobble to safety on the southern flank of the bunker's clearing, he realized it for what it was. Just like the Russians had perfected the technique of using technologically inferior fighter aircraft to lure more capable adversaries into the weapon engagement zone for surface-to-air missiles, it looked like the dismounted Russian soldiers were drawing Dave and the militiamen toward the bunker.

But why?

Then he saw it. The Mi-24 attack helicopter hadn't fled from the battlefield but only repositioned itself for an attack run. Maybe the pilots hadn't wanted to risk injuring anybody still alive inside the Bumerang. But most likely, they had assumed that it would be too dangerous to fire on the Ukrainians when they were so close to the armored vehicle and the nuclear weapons inside. What they needed was a way of drawing the Ukrainians away from the overturned personnel carrier so they could engage without risk of damaging a nuclear weapon.

Of course, all Colt cared about was preventing the Russians from slaughtering Dave and the ragtag group of militiamen who believed they had routed the superior Russian force.

Colt pushed off another tree and steered once more for the clearing, hoping to get Dave's attention and stop him before it was too late. But as he gritted his teeth and winced with the pain radiating up his leg, he noticed movement near the Bumerang and saw what looked like two duffel bags flying out through the rear hatch.

The nukes!

He froze just as a lone figure emerged and retrieved the duffel bags from the forest floor. If he thought he had any chance of dropping the man, he wouldn't have hesitated to raise his weapon and take the low-probability shot. But his chances were close to zero.

Colt followed the man's gaze up into the sky at the approaching helicopter, then down into the clearing where the Russian troops were laying their trap. But when the man turned and spun from sight around the Bumerang's destroyed undercarriage, he knew he had to make a choice.

He could either continue on into the clearing to try warning Dave before it was too late, or he could break off and intercept the man trying to sneak away with the nukes. He couldn't do both. And he cursed when he knew he really didn't have a choice at all.

No matter how Voronov tried arranging the load, it was impossible for him to carry all three RA-115 nuclear weapons. Each package weighed roughly twenty-five kilos but could only be carried by their handles. Maybe it would have been possible if they had been outfitted with slings or straps, but then they probably would have been given the moniker "backpack nukes."

"But *nyet*. Stupid suitcase nukes."

He entertained the notion of returning for the third package after the Hind made easy work of the Ukrainian resistance, but he had resigned himself to only escaping with two. Still, two was better than one.

Hefting one duffel in each hand, he descended down the hill sloping away from the Bumerang to the south. He couldn't recall where the nearest road was and knew it would be a hike. But he was more concerned with escaping the battle and disappearing into the forest before somebody noticed there was nobody left inside the armored vehicle to put up a fight.

Worse, he needed to be long gone before they realized the nuclear weapons were missing.

Except the one you left behind.

Voronov froze in his tracks as he considered the implications. If anybody survived the helicopter's attack run and searched the Bumerang's wreckage, they would discover an RA-115 nuclear weapon tucked underneath one of the vehicle's massive tires. Not inside where it should have been, but in the dirt where somebody had placed it.

That meant they would know somebody had survived long enough to move it.

Pizdec!

Voronov lowered the heavy duffel bags to the ground and turned back to look up at the armored vehicle through the trees. Maybe it would be best to retrieve the third duffel and bring it down into the forest where it wouldn't easily be discovered. They might still find it after a thorough search, but at least it wouldn't be a clue as obvious as a neon sign that somebody had escaped.

Grunting in frustration, Voronov lamented his old injury and dug his boots into the loamy soil to begin trudging up the hill in his trademark limping gait. All he needed to do was get his hands on that last weapon and drag it with him back down the hill before the Hind turned in on its attack run. Because once that happened, anybody still alive would recognize the trap for what it was and return to the Bumerang to finish what they had set out to do.

He was halfway up the hill when the rhythmic beating of the helicopter's rotor blades changed in pitch. He froze and stared up into the sky but caught only glimpses of the Hind streaking toward the clearing through the trees. Then he saw a series of bright flashes followed by the *whooshing* of rockets streaking through the air toward the bunker.

He cursed again, then resumed his frantic sprint up the hill to recover the last weapon.

Colt had descended the hill south of the bunker while trying to look through the dense forest in the direction of the Russian armored personnel carrier. He wasn't sure if the man he had seen was only taking refuge behind the thick steel of the wreckage or if he was attempting to escape. All he knew was that he needed to make sure those nuclear weapons never left the forest of Yuzhnoukrainsk.

Over his shoulder, Colt heard a loud *whooshing* sound that was unmistakable. He turned and saw several puffs of smoke and white streaks as rockets left the pods mounted under the Hind's stubby wings and raced for the clearing. He shook away the thought of the rockets finding Dave and the militiamen in the open and turned back for the one outcome he could control.

Whump! Whump!

Colt felt the rockets detonating through the earth under his feet but continued racing down the hill. By now, the agony in his ankle had become so normal that he barely noticed the ever-present metallic taste on his tongue or the tears ringing his eyes. There would be time later to worry about any permanent damage he had incurred by continuing to put weight on his injured ankle, but that would have to wait.

Whoosh! Whoosh! Whump! Whump!

The second salvo of rockets hit closer this time, and Colt almost lost his balance in the blast. He didn't know what kind of warheads were on the rockets employed by the Russian Mi-24 Hind, but they didn't sound as powerful as the four-kilogram warheads on the Mk 4 Folding-Fin Aerial Rockets he had fired at the Bumerang from his Super Tucano. Still, he knew they were powerful enough to make him stop worrying about his ruined ankle. Permanently.

The ground leveled out beneath him, and he stepped around a tree just as the attack helicopter flew overhead at the completion of its first pass. He swallowed back the taste of sour spit in his mouth and suppressed any thoughts that Dave might have been caught in the barrage. Like the damage to his ankle, there would be time to worry about that later.

Colt crested a small rise, then descended again once more, keeping his eyes level with the horizon as he scanned for any sign of the man he had seen fleeing the Bumerang. But before he found his footing, the steel toe of his flight boot caught on something hard and sent him sprawling. His arms flew out in front of him, and he lost his grip on his personal defense weapon as he braced himself for the fall.

As Colt came down, he tucked his shoulder and rolled into the bushes only slightly more gracefully than he had under his parachute after ejecting. He tumbled end over end for several seconds but had the presence of mind to arrest his descent and turn back for his short-barreled rifle before he had gone too far.

That was when he noticed what he had tripped over.

And when he noticed the Russian pointing a stubby Kalashnikov at him.

52

Colt stared at the short-barreled AK, fully expecting to see its muzzle flash with the gunshot that ended his life. But the surprise on the Russian's face seemed to rival his own, and Colt seized on the fleeting opportunity. He pushed off the ground with both legs and launched himself at the Russian with his arms outstretched, praying he had reacted fast enough.

The rifle barked, and Colt flinched. But his decisiveness had paid off. His left hand knocked aside the barrel and sent the round sailing harmlessly into the trees behind him. He tried clamping down on the rifle to control it but couldn't get a grip before he slammed into the Russian's chest and knocked them both to the ground.

The Russian grunted as all of Colt's 190 pounds came down on top of him, but he responded like someone who was accustomed to the martial arts. Colt's experience was limited to the judo, boxing, and wrestling classes he had been forced to take as a midshipman at the Naval Academy. But what the fighter pilot lacked in skill, he made up for in fervor and determination.

As the Russian muscled Colt onto his back, he swung up with the Kalashnikov and caught Colt in his chin with the butt stock. His head snapped back, and an intense pain exploded in his skull that temporarily overshadowed the agony of his ankle. When stars filled his vision, he reacted on instinct and strained to force blood up into his brain to keep from blacking out.

Lose sight, lose the fight.

Colt's focus was naturally drawn to the danger of the compact rifle. But as the Russian swung the barrel down to aim at Colt, he reached up to block it while bridging and twisting his body to the side. The Russian lost his balance, and Colt once more pressed his advantage by rolling on top of the Kalashnikov and pinning it harmlessly to the earth.

Though temporarily not in danger, he was hardly in a good position. Both men were on their sides, facing each other, and Colt's eyes moved up to the Russian's snarling face. He saw an intense anger and hatred plastered there, but he also saw something he hadn't expected. Doubt.

Colt's experience in combat had been in the skies far above the battlefield. His instincts had been honed to analyze the strengths and weaknesses of his opponents during fleeting glimpses at the merge across hundreds of feet. He knew when to go high. He knew when to go low. He knew when to feint left and go right, or feint right and go left. And he knew when each engagement had shifted from defensive to neutral, and from neutral to offensive.

In that one expression, Colt knew hand-to-hand combat was no different.

He swung his right fist in a wide arc aimed for the Russian's head. When his opponent's eyes flicked upward at the threat, he capitalized on the feint and fired his knee straight into the man's groin. There was no skill in the simple West Texas brawling, but it connected solidly. The Russian gasped in shocked pain, but the strike seemed to have done little to dull his anger. He reached up to parry Colt's arcing fist and wrapped his arm around it, pinning it to his side.

With his free arm trapped, Colt drew his knee back and prepared to fire another offensive blow, but the Russian released his grip on the rifle and hooked his hand around the base of Colt's neck and violently pulled him into a hasty headbutt. Recognizing the threat at the last second, Colt tucked his chin, and their skulls collided with a *thud* that caused stars to swarm his vision with a vengeance.

But even as his vision narrowed once more, he recognized that the

Russian had temporarily relinquished control of the short-barreled rifle. He felt it pinned under his left side and digging into his ribs. So, instead of trying for another knee to the groin, he shifted his hips and scrambled to gain purchase on the ground with his steel-toed boots. His ankle protested the maneuver, but he ignored the agony and pushed himself into the Russian while reaching back to blindly feel for the AK.

Colt didn't know where his personal defense weapon had fallen when he tripped and stumbled over the nuclear weapons, so the Russian's rifle was his only chance of gaining an advantage and ending this fight. But the Russian seemed to sense what Colt was trying to do, and he kept his grip on Colt's neck while using his momentum to continue their roll away from the Kalashnikov. The entangled duo completed several revolutions before coming to a stop with the Russian again on top with a clear offensive advantage.

Once more, Colt's attacker demonstrated his proficiency in physical violence and rained ferocious punches into him. Colt's head snapped left and right as the Russian's fists connected solidly with his cheekbones, chin, and neck. The stars Colt had managed to keep at bay returned, and he felt his vision closing in once more. Even as he tried bringing his hands up to defend himself, he felt his energy flagging and knew the tide had shifted back in the Russian's favor.

Colt dropped his hands and let them fall to the dirt at his sides, but his left hand struck something that felt man-made. He was losing the strength to defend himself against the Russian's relentless punches. But his attacker only grunted and cursed while wearing himself out. Colt's fingers twitched and swept across the forest floor for anything he could use as a weapon. Again, he felt something solid near his left leg and reached for the familiar object.

He coughed and spat a mouthful of blood across his face, staring up at the man on top of him. As the punches stopped, the Russian slowly lowered his hands and wrapped his fingers around Colt's neck. He made no move to stop him, but his left hand finally gained purchase on the foreign object at his side, and he recognized the familiar feel of his personal defense weapon's cold steel tubular handguard.

"Who... are... you?" the Russian asked.

Colt's entire body felt weak, fatigued from the cumulative exertion of being shot down, forced to eject, and hobbling across the Ukrainian countryside to stop Russians from stealing nuclear weapons. His brain was fogged over with unrelenting exhaustion that made even answering that simple question seem as impossible as escaping the melee.

"St..." He coughed and spat another mouthful of blood that spilled over the Russian's hands.

Colt's eyes closed, and he felt an overwhelming desire to keep them closed. Even as his attacker's fingers tightened around his neck and began cutting off the supply of blood to his brain, he felt a detached calmness settle over him. He had accepted his fate.

"Who are you?" the Russian repeated.

No.

Colt's fatigue evaporated with a sudden burst of adrenaline, and his eyes shot open. Through the fogginess enveloping him, Colt recognized the rhythmic thumping of the Russian attack helicopter circling around for another pass. For another opportunity to kill his friends.

"Steve," Colt croaked.

"Who?"

Using every ounce of strength he possessed, Colt swung the personal defense weapon up and caught the Russian in the side of the face with its extended butt stock. His swing wasn't powerful enough to dislodge his attacker from the mount, but it forced him to weaken his grip around Colt's neck and allowed oxygen-rich blood to flood his brain. Like dumping fuel into a hot exhaust, it gave the defensive fighter pilot an immediate burst of energy.

With a flick of his wrist, Colt twisted the short-barreled rifle to loop the slack sling over the Russian's neck, then yanked downward with a violent jerk. The nylon webbing dug into his attacker's neck and pulled him onto the ground at his side.

Suddenly free from the Russian's oppressive weight on top of him, Colt reached over with his right hand and gripped the butt stock to keep tension on the sling. Then he twisted the rifle in his hands to close off the loop, preventing the Russian from being able to free himself.

The man fought like an ensnared badger, thrashing and twisting, but

Colt lifted a leg and planted his boot between the Russian's shoulder blades, pressing out as hard as he could. His arms burned with the strain of retaining his grip on the PDW, and his ankle thrummed with agony from the tension of using every ounce of strength to try separating the Russian's head from his neck.

The sound of the approaching attack helicopter grew louder but was quickly replaced with the deafening report of a .50-caliber machine gun ripping through the forest like a chainsaw. Colt barely noticed as he waited for the Russian's flailing hands to finally fall still.

"Steve *motherfucking* Young," Colt said.

As the Russian went limp, Colt released his grip on the personal defense weapon and collapsed onto his back. But his momentary relief was replaced with terror as an earth-rending explosion tore across the Ukrainian sky.

53

After the explosion's concussive blast had rolled across his supine frame, Colt turned and looked up the hill to bear witness to the carnage the Mil Mi-24 Hind had brought upon Dave and the remaining Ukrainian soldiers. Even his elation at defeating the Russian and preventing him from sneaking away with the nuclear weapons wasn't enough to dampen the soul-crushing sadness. He was alone and isolated in the forest.

Through the trees at the top of the hill, dark smoke billowed upward from where the Russian attack helicopter's machine gun had delivered death and destruction on the Ukrainian resistance. But even through his fatigue and sadness, Colt knew something didn't seem right.

A heavy machine gun caused that?

Suddenly, a dark gray object raced through the air over the clearing at the top of the hill, and the unmistakable roar of its Pratt & Whitney Canada PT6A-68C turboprop engine drowned out the memory of the explosion. Colt pushed himself into a seated position and turned to watch in surprise as the A-29 Super Tucano banked away and returned to its protective perch in the sky.

"Let's go, Cubby!"

Colt leaned to the side and struggled to his knees, feeling new aches and pains spreading across his battered body. His head and neck throbbed with the memory of the Russian's heavy fists. His ribs and chest ached from the brief life-or-death grappling match. But seeing his wingman soaring in the sky above him filled his fatigued body with a renewed hopeful energy.

Maybe Dave is still alive...

He leaned over the still Russian to remove the sling from around his neck and feel for a pulse. But after several seconds of searching, it became clear that his victory had been permanent. He draped the sling over his neck and let the PDW fall to his side, then pushed himself to unsteady feet and looked down on the body of the man he had just killed. He felt no guilt or remorse, but it was the last thing he had expected when strapping into his ejection seat at Voznesensk Reserve Air Base the night before.

Colt gritted his teeth and braced himself to begin the painful climb up the hill to inspect the aftermath of the battle. But something flashed and caught his eye. With some effort, he squatted back down and tugged up on the Russian's sleeve, revealing a watch unlike any he had ever seen before. He let his PDW hang from his sling while he released the watch's clasp and slid it from the dead man's wrist.

Colt didn't recognize the watch's maker but saw Cyrillic writing on its face. Elegant stones encircled the steel case, and he turned it over to see the double-headed eagle of the Russian coat of arms on the back. He didn't know if the watch was worth anything, but he knew is previous owner wouldn't miss it. He slipped the watch into his pocket just as he heard a voice call out.

"Hey, flyboy, you okay?"

Colt looked up and saw Dave's trademark grin as the SEAL stood at the crest of the hill and looked down at him.

With some effort, Dave helped Colt up to the top of the hill where he saw the charred remains of the Russian attack helicopter smoldering in the clearing in front of the hidden bunker. The surviving Russian troops who had lured Dave and the Ukrainian soldiers into the open for the helicopter's rocket attack were on their knees with their hands on their heads, looking up at the militiamen with fear in their eyes.

"I thought you were done for," Colt said.

Dave leaned Colt against a tree and gave his shoulder a gentle squeeze. "Come on, you know it's not that easy to kill a frogman."

"Yeah, but..." Colt trailed off and gestured at the Hind's wreckage.

Dave nodded. "Yeah, we got lucky in that rocket attack. But we probably would have been smoked on that last run if not for Cubby."

Almost as if the other pilot had heard his name spoken in vain, the miniature speaker in Dave's MBITR radio squawked to life. "Pony One One, Pony One Two. Dave, you got your ears on?"

The SEAL master chief kept one hand on Colt's shoulder to steady him, then reached down for the push-to-talk affixed to his survival vest. "Yeah, Dave's up. Go ahead."

"Any luck?"

Dave winked at Colt. "He's asking about you."

Colt gestured for the radio, and Dave removed it from the pouch on his chest and handed it over. Colt surveyed the scene in front of him and wondered if the people back home would ever learn what heroics had taken place here to keep nuclear weapons from falling into the hands of terrorists. If not for guys like Cubby and Dave or the Ukrainian citizen soldiers who fought like lions to repel the Russians, things would have turned out much differently.

Colt squeezed the button on the side of the radio. "Hey, Cubby, thanks for showing up, brother."

There was a momentary pause, and Colt looked up into the sky just as the dark gray Super Tucano made another pass over the clearing while waggling its wings. "Man, it's good to hear your voice, Colt!"

"Not sure we would've made it if you hadn't shown up," Colt said, remembering the sobering fear he had felt when he heard the Russian helicopter returning for a second attack. "How'd you take down the Hind?"

"Discipline and precision," Cubby said. "Isn't that what you said sets us apart? What keeps us alive?"

Colt glanced over at Dave and saw the SEAL shake his head. "Looks like all your training back in Fallon paid off after all," he said.

"Always knew you were the best," Colt said into the radio.

"Yeah, well, hang tight and we can hash all that out over a few cold ones."

As the Super Tucano retreated once more into its low-altitude orbit, Colt lowered himself to the ground and leaned back against the tree. He was tired again, but not from the kind of exhaustion that felt overwhelming and hopeless. He was awash with relief that they had succeeded in stopping the Russians from stealing nuclear weapons and selling them on the black market.

Dave squatted down next to him. "You okay?"

Colt nodded. "I just want to go home."

The SEAL squeezed his shoulder again, then looked up into the sky where he had just begun to make out the deep bass drumming of approaching prop rotors. "Sounds like our boys will be here soon."

Colt nodded and stared blankly at his boots. His ankle still throbbed, but even its persistent pain seemed to have dulled under the weight of his exhaustion. He felt content just sitting there and waiting for the Osprey to land and take them home.

Out of the corner of his eye, he saw the dark gray Osprey come into view with its massive prop rotors turned skyward as it slowed and began its descent into the clearing. Dave squeezed his shoulder once more, then stood and watched the AFSOC tiltrotor aircraft touch down. Almost immediately, SEALs from the Templar ground force poured from the ramp and raced in their direction.

"Time to go, flyboy."

The sudden flurry of activity gave him a moment of clarity, and he looked over his shoulder at the forest where he had left the Russian's body at the bottom of the hill. "What about the nukes?"

Dave didn't answer right away but stepped forward to greet the two SEALs who had run up to him. Colt couldn't hear their exchange, but he saw Dave gesturing down the hill and suspected he had told them where to find the suitcase nukes. After the two disappeared into the forest, Colt turned back to the clearing and saw several other SEALs zip-tying the Russian conscripts who had surrendered to the Ukrainian soldiers after the Hind was destroyed.

"Dave?"

The SEAL leaned down and helped Colt to his feet. "We've got it all covered. Let's get you on that bird."

Colt draped an arm over Dave's shoulder and let the master chief guide him across the clearing toward the waiting Osprey. He nodded at the Ukrainian militiamen who had sacrificed everything to rescue him and intervened when it seemed as if the Russians would succeed in stealing the nukes.

"What about them?" Colt asked.

"This battlefield is their home," the SEAL replied. "We get to go back to America, but they have to stand their ground and fight until every last Russian is gone."

As Colt stepped up onto the ramp, he looked over at the Russian conscripts on their knees and knew exactly what Dave had meant. For a brief time, he had seen the ugliness of war up close and personal. But the Ukrainian citizens were forced to live their lives under the constant fear of losing their homes and their loved ones because of the tsar's ego and greed.

"Maybe we should stay too," Colt muttered.

"Not our war, flyboy."

The Air Force crew chief took ahold of Colt and guided him onto a stretcher as the team's medic moved in close to administer a dose of morphine and check him over for injuries. Within seconds of feeling the sharp prick in his thigh, a feeling of warmth settled over Colt. His eyelids grew heavy, and he succumbed to the siren's call as the world around him faded to black.

54

Joint Base Andrews
Camp Springs, Maryland

Punky leaned back in the forward-facing seat in the Leonardo AW-139 helicopter and stared through the port window at the ground far beneath them. She was still recovering from the shootout in New Carrollton and avoided looking at the body of Samuel Chambers on the stretcher next to her.

His corpse was just another reminder of the fear that had coursed through her veins when she thought she was finished. Even after taking the Russian pistol from the president's chief of staff, she knew she couldn't stand a chance against her armed pursuers. If the Maryland State Police helicopter hadn't returned and placed itself in between her and the gunmen, she would have been on an identical stretcher next to the slain politico.

"Where are we going?" she asked the trooper sitting across from her in one of the rear-facing seats.

"Joint Base Andrews," he said. "Our instructions were to deliver you there."

Punky nodded. She hadn't asked, but she suspected Connor had been the one to sound the alarm and vector the police helicopter onto her position. So, it made sense they would take her to the Washington Section. Given what Samuel Chambers had told her before being gunned down in the streets, she assumed Connor would want her to debrief his superiors at Langley as soon as possible.

As the helicopter started its descent to the airfield that was home to Air Force One, Punky turned and studied the president's man. He had admitted that he had come to the train station to kill her, and she knew it was because of her investigation into Aurora Holdings. But she still hadn't discovered the secret that was powerful enough to kill for.

Her eyes searched his still form as if his secrets might be written there, but she paused when she saw an odd-looking crown peeking out from under his sleeve. She quickly glanced up at the trooper seated in front of her, and when she saw that he was distracted looking through the window, she reached down and snatched back the sleeve to expose the watch Garett had seen in the picture.

The watch that had started it all.

Without thinking, she removed the watch from Samuel's wrist and slipped it into her pocket. There was something special about that watch. It had drawn her to Maryland and placed her in danger, but it had taken Samuel's life. It represented the secret she still needed to unmask, and she wouldn't stop until she did.

"Ma'am?"

Punky looked up at the trooper. "I'm sorry?"

"I said, there's a car waiting for you when we land."

Punky nodded in thanks and turned to look at the darkness through her window as the helicopter settled onto the vacant tarmac. She knew she needed to call Camron and fill him in, but the more pressing need was to get to Langley where she could brief the Agency on what Samuel had told her about the nukes in Ukraine.

Punky waited until they had slid the helicopter's door open before climbing down from her seat and ducking under the spinning rotor blades to make her way across the tarmac to the waiting Agency car. She waved at the driver who stood solemnly next to the dark sedan, but he only acknowledged by opening the rear door and waiting for her to climb inside.

He closed it behind her and took his seat behind the wheel. "We should have you there in about twenty minutes," he said.

Punky closed her eyes and leaned back into the seat. After everything she had been through that night, she felt her lack of sleep catching up with her. "Is Connor meeting us there?"

"Yes, ma'am," the driver replied.

She settled in as the driver backed the sedan out of its spot, then reversed directions to pull out of the parking lot and head for the base's exit. Twenty minutes seemed like such an insignificant time to wait. But given what she had just experienced, it felt like an eternity. She reached into her pocket and pulled out her cell phone, then scrolled to Connor's number and tapped on it.

Punky brought the phone up to her ear and waited for it to ring but grew frustrated when she heard nothing but silence. She pulled it away to see "Call Failed" on the screen and tapped on the button to try again. But she was rewarded with the same disappointing result.

"Dammit!"

"Something wrong, ma'am?"

She groaned. "I can't seem to get a signal."

"I'm sure it's just a dead spot," the driver replied.

Punky glanced up at the back of the driver's head, then down at her useless phone. Normally, if she was outside her carrier's cellular coverage area, she would see "SOS" in the upper right-hand corner, showing that she could at least make an emergency call. But even that was missing. Next to the icon representing her cell phone's battery level, the screen was blank.

That's odd.

As they left the base and turned onto Allentown Road, Punky turned and looked through her window at the motel and gas station.

I should definitely have service, she thought.

It's not like they were in the middle of rural Maryland. They weren't even fifteen miles from the nation's capital.

She looked at her phone again, then held the action and volume down buttons until a slider appeared at the top of the screen to power off her phone. She quickly swiped across the top of the screen until her phone turned off, hoping that when she turned it back on, she would have service.

While she waited for the phone to finish shutting down, she glanced up at the rearview mirror and noticed the digital compass displaying "NE." She wasn't as familiar with the area as she was with San Diego, but she thought Joint Base Andrews was southeast of the capital and on the opposite side of the Potomac from Langley.

"Excuse me, where are we going?"

"Cutting over to Pennsylvania Avenue and taking that into the city." The driver reached up and adjusted the rearview mirror to get a better look at her. "Is everything okay?"

Punky felt ice flood her veins.

No, everything was not okay. But she forced a smile onto her face and nodded. "I just thought we were going to Langley."

Again, the driver flashed a look at her in the rearview mirror, which is when she noticed something odd about his eyes. In the darkness, it was difficult to tell exactly what it was that had set off alarms in the back of her head. But it wasn't just the driver's eyes that had filled her with dread.

She reached into her pocket and pulled out the watch she had removed from Samuel's wrist. Elegant stones wrapped around the steel case and a two-headed eagle adorned the black dial at the twelve o'clock position. Turning it over, she saw the same coat of arms centered on the back with Cyrillic writing along the edge. It was a unique timepiece.

Too unique to also be on the wrist of an Agency driver.

"We're not going to Langley, are we?"

The driver looked up into the mirror again, and his eyes narrowed. "I'm afraid not, Miss King." Without the need for pretense, his accent slipped back into his native Russian. "You've created quite the problem for me."

"Viktor Drakov, I presume?"

The older man smiled at her in the mirror. "I can see why Samuel was worried about you."

She couldn't imagine how he had managed to gain access to the base or arranged to be there when the helicopter delivered her there. But that was the least of her concerns. She needed to brief Langley about the nuclear weapons in Ukraine before it was too late.

"You're too late, you know."

Her stomach dropped as he echoed her fears, but she needed him to keep talking. "Too late for what?"

"My people in Ukraine have already recovered the nuclear weapons."

It was as if the Russian spymaster could read her mind. "Was that why you had Samuel Chambers killed? You didn't need him anymore?"

Viktor laughed but turned onto Pennsylvania Avenue as if they were only taking a casual drive. "Samuel was making too many mistakes and letting people get too close to the truth."

"Like Teddy Miller?"

"And you."

Punky reached back for the pistol she had retrieved from Samuel. "And what truth is that?"

The two locked eyes in the mirror for several seconds. She didn't believe Viktor planned on letting her live after this, but she also knew she couldn't kill him until she got the information she needed. She slid the pistol from the holster and held it tight against her leg.

"That the president's illegitimate son spied for the Chinese."

55

Viktor's words hit Punky like body blows, knocking the wind from her lungs as she struggled to come up with an argument to counter his accusation. "Do you mean Adam Garett?"

"That's right, you were there when they arrested him."

Her mind swam as the missing pieces of the puzzle finally fell into place and revealed the whole picture to her. From what she had already learned about Aurora Holdings, she surmised that the shell company had been created to filter funds intended to keep Adam's mother quiet.

"What happened to Mila? Where is she?"

"I was right to think you were dangerous," Viktor said. "You seem to have discovered quite a bit on your own already."

"Where is she, Viktor?"

He shrugged. "We sent her back to Russia once Jonathan Adams entered the national spotlight. The last thing we needed was a mother who regretted giving up her child for the good of the State coming forward to make wild accusations."

"Is she alive?"

"Alive. Dead. It doesn't matter."

His answer was so casual that Punky understood Garett never stood a chance. An evil puppet master had pulled on his strings and made him dance even before his birth—ripping him from the arms of a Russian spy and delivering him into the arms of a Chinese one. He had been born only to give Russia leverage over Jonathan Adams, and he had ended up in prison because of his birthright.

Punky felt dizzy as the reality of her situation swelled and crashed over her, and she struggled to find her way to the surface. "What was in the cigar box?"

He laughed. "A cigar."

Punky's finger stroked the pistol's trigger, tempted to erase his condescending attitude. "Just a cigar?"

Viktor waved his hand in the air as if to swat away her question like a meddlesome fly. "Only one of the most expensive and sought after cigars in the world. I thought it was a touching gesture and an appropriate way of introducing Jonathan Adams to his son."

Then she understood.

Connor had been right that the Russians had arranged for Garett to be arrested in order to keep him safe. They wanted him to rot in a military prison as a constant reminder to the president that his secret was vulnerable to being exposed. And she had been complicit in that.

"And you thought you could keep the president under your thumb by killing Samuel Chambers."

Viktor bobbed his head from side to side. "More or less."

Punky moved her thumb to the pistol's bobbed hammer and slid it back until it clicked. "First you got rid of Mila Smith—"

"Popov," Viktor said, cutting her off. "Her name was Mila Popov."

"First you got rid of Garett's real mother. Then you killed his adopted one—"

"Mantis got in the way."

"Then you had Samuel Chambers killed. Who's next? Lana Roman?"

"Actually, Miss King... it's you."

For an older man, Viktor moved with surprising speed. It was little more than a blur as he reached inside his jacket to retrieve a weapon and make good on his promise. But she had the advantage. Her weapon was already drawn.

Without hesitation, Punky lifted the PSS-2 silenced pistol and aimed it at the base of Viktor's skull. She knew shooting the driver of a moving car would put her at risk. But she pulled the trigger anyway and heard little more than a faint *pop* as the gun fired a wedge-shaped bullet into the back of the Russian spy's head. His body went limp as blood sprayed across the windshield.

Instantly, the car surged forward when his dead foot came down hard on the accelerator pedal. She fell backward but quickly shoved off her seat and lurched across the sedan's cab for the steering wheel. She couldn't do anything about slowing the car just yet, but she could at least keep it going in a safe direction.

Reaching over Viktor's limp body, she glanced to her right and saw a device that looked like a wireless router sitting on the passenger seat. It was the size of a paperback novel and adorned with stubby antennas and lights that twinkled across the front. She couldn't help but wonder if the device was the reason her cell phone didn't have service, and she added it to the list of things that had gone wrong that night.

With one hand on the wheel, Punky reached over and felt for a switch of some kind to turn it off. But she lost her chance when they hit a dip in the intersection with Southern Avenue, and the device skittered to the floor. Looking back up, she saw brownstones whipping by on both sides of the road as they crossed into the District of Columbia. And the red-and-blue lights of a police car patrolling the residential neighborhood's tree-lined streets.

"Dammit!"

Punky hazarded a glance at the speedometer and saw that the sedan had crept north of seventy miles per hour. She didn't have her seatbelt on and knew she wasn't in a position to survive a crash. She needed to get the hurtling car to slow before another errant bump sent her careening into a parked car or thick oak tree.

Forgoing her attempt at retrieving the cellular jammer, Punky reached down and tugged up on Viktor's leg. At first, it felt wedged in place, but then his foot slipped off the gas pedal, and the sedan began to slow. As the flashing police lights reflected off the car's bespoke interior, she breathed a sigh of relief when another glance at the speedometer needle showed that it had dipped back below seventy.

Sixty-five miles per hour...

But that momentary distraction was all it took. The sedan's front left tire clipped the raised curb of the median dividing Pennsylvania Avenue, and she jerked on the steering wheel to keep the car from jumping across into oncoming traffic. But her correction had been too drastic. She sideswiped a parked car on the opposite shoulder and flinched when the side-view mirror was ripped off and sparks flew with metal screeching against metal. Once more, she corrected and ping-ponged the sedan back into the road.

Sixty miles per hour...

The car's speed continued to drop, but she hit the median again with such force that no amount of steering could correct back into her lane.

Fifty... forty-five... forty...

The Russian's sedan veered across the single lane of oncoming traffic and aimed for the opposite curb like a missile that was guiding on a parked car. Punky recognized the impending collision and released her grip on the steering wheel, hoping like hell she had done enough to keep from being ejected. She flung herself back into the rear seat and braced herself.

Less than a second later, the mobile missile she had been trapped inside came to an abrupt stop. She slammed into the back of Viktor's seat and felt the car's rear wheels lift off the ground as Newton's First Law tried transporting them through the parked car. Glass shattered and sprayed across the car's interior, but she closed her eyes and champed her teeth together while she waited for the nightmare to end.

Over the ensuing silence, Punky heard the engine ticking as it cooled in the sudden stillness. Her nose wrinkled at the pungent scent of something burning and a faint aroma of gasoline, spurring her into action. She pushed herself off the crumpled floorboards to open the rear door. But the handle was stuck.

Whoosh!

The gasoline ignited under the front of the car with a sudden flash and sent a surge of adrenaline coursing through her. She tugged on the handle again and pushed on the door, but it refused to budge. The car began filling with smoke, and Punky turned to mule kick the opposite rear window. It took several tries before the tempered safety glass shattered and gave her a way out.

Her aches and pains forgotten, Punky lunged for the opening and pulled herself through. She collapsed onto the pavement, beaten and bruised, but thankful to be alive. Her vision was blurred from the hits she had taken to her head, but the flashing police lights pierced through the surrounding darkness and blanketed the scene with an eerie alternating blue and red.

The officer rushed to help her up and guided her away from the burning car. "Are you okay, miss?"

Punky coughed and shook her head. "I need…"

The officer misunderstood her plea and looked back at the car where Viktor's limp form was still trapped inside. Without care for his own safety, he tried pushing Punky aside so he could return to the inferno and rescue another victim.

"Wait!" she shouted.

"There's someone still there!"

Punky clamped her hand down on the officer's wrist and held him in place. "He's dead."

"You don't know that," he countered.

"Yes, I do. I killed him."

The officer stopped trying to pry himself free from her grip and stared at her with open-mouth amazement. "You *what*?"

Before she could answer, the car exploded and rained fiery debris down on the street. The officer spun her away and covered her with his body, but her eyes remained fixed on the car and the Russian spy she had shot in the back of the head.

"Who are you?" the officer asked.

She unclipped her badge and held it up to him. "Special Agent Emmy King."

"What the hell is going on?"

"I need you to take me to the White House."

56

The White House
Washington, DC

Punky sat in the backseat of the Metropolitan Police cruiser and calmly stared out the window as they rolled up to the closed gate off Pennsylvania Avenue. After convincing the officer that she wasn't dangerous and hadn't lost her mind, she reached out to Connor and arranged for him to meet them at the White House.

"You sure they're expecting you?"

Punky shifted in her seat to look out at a uniformed officer of the Secret Service's Uniformed Division walking from the guard shack and turning for the police cruiser. "I sure hope so."

He shot her a dirty look in the rearview mirror, obviously hoping that she wasn't wasting his time. He unrolled his window as the Secret Service officer approached. "I have Special Agent Emmy King," he said. "I believe she's expected."

The officer leaned over and gave Punky a cursory glance. "By who?"

Before she could tell him she had no idea who was expecting her, the officer's radio squawked with an incoming call. He turned away from the police cruiser and reached for the microphone clipped to his shirt. "Go ahead."

"Eleanor Sinclair is on her way down to meet a special agent from NCIS."

The officer turned and locked eyes with Punky. "A Special Agent Emmy King?"

"That's the one."

"She's here. I'll let her in."

Punky thought she saw the Metropolitan Police officer sag with relief as he shifted into park and stepped out to open the rear door for Punky. She exited the back of the cruiser and looked expectantly at the Secret Service officer. "Who's Eleanor Sinclair?"

"She's the—"

"Punky!"

Both she and the officer turned and saw Connor Sullivan walking down the driveway with an athletic woman in a dark pantsuit with long blonde hair pulled back into a ponytail. She was the exact opposite of what Punky envisioned when she thought of a woman named Eleanor.

"Hey, Connor."

He took in her appearance and the fact that she had arrived by police cruiser, and he frowned. "Are you okay?"

"I've been better."

The Secret Service officer let her through the gate, and Punky shifted her focus to the woman who had the kind of pull to gain her access to the White House in the middle of the night. She held out her hand. "Thank you for seeing me."

Connor took the lead in making their introduction. "Punky, Eleanor is the director of national intelligence. She is the executive head of the intelligence community and oversees all agencies and organizations that conduct intelligence activities."

"I'm glad you came, Special Agent King."

"Please, call me Punky."

Eleanor gave Connor a sideway glance, and again he spoke up. "Eleanor, Punky was the agent who stopped the Chinese from carrying out the synthetic bioweapon attack on the *Reagan*."

The DNI turned back to Punky with a look of admiration on her face. "That was impressive work. I can see you're a woman who does whatever it takes to stop the bad guys from upsetting the apple cart."

Punky ignored the compliment. "That's actually why I'm here."

Eleanor turned and gestured for Punky to follow her. "Let's go see the boss."

Punky was impressed with the way Eleanor walked across the White House grounds and through the historic building's halls as she led the trio to the executive residence. She had never been inside the White House before, and Punky found it next to impossible to keep from gawking at the artwork and items of historical significance that were scattered throughout.

"This way," Eleanor said, leading them from the central hall up the grand staircase. Leaving the ground floor, they ascended the stairs past the state floor to the second floor that was home to the president's private quarters. "He's expecting us in the Yellow Oval Room."

Despite everything she had been through, Punky couldn't help but feel nervous that she was going to meet the president of the United States. It didn't matter that she had been the one to sound the alarm when Viktor Drakov arranged for Adam Garett to be granted a private audience with him during a campaign stop in Fallon, Nevada. It didn't matter that she had been the one to discover that the president's own chief of staff was the person responsible for giving the Russians unfettered access to the commander in chief. He was still the most powerful man on earth, and she was nervous.

They reached the landing at the top of the grand stairs and were met by the head of the president's Secret Service detail. "Hey, Chris, the president is expecting us," Eleanor said.

Punky looked up and saw the familiar face of Chris Albanese, standing resolutely between them and his boss. The last time she had seen him, he was hovering over her while a Navy master-at-arms pinned her to the ground outside the NAWDC headquarters in Fallon.

"Special Agent King and I have a history," he replied.

Eleanor turned to Punky for an explanation.

"That's part of why I need to speak with the president."

Eleanor looked back at Chris as if expecting him to offer some kind of resistance. But he just nodded and turned to lead them the rest of the way to the Yellow Oval Room. "She's been vetted," he said. "But trouble seems to follow her wherever she goes. So, I'll be close, just in case."

Turning into the large central room that looked out on the Truman Balcony, Chris cleared his throat and announced their entrance. "Mr. President, the Honorable Eleanor Sinclair, Mr. Connor Sullivan, and Special Agent Emmy King."

"Thank you, Chris," Jonathan Adams said, coming to his feet and walking across the carpeted floor to greet the two people he had never met before. He shook Connor's hand first, then turned and took Punky's hand, letting it linger there. "So glad to meet you both. Eleanor tells me you have something of pressing importance."

"Yes, Mr. President," Punky said.

He gestured for them to have a seat in one of the plush sofas at the center of the room, then waited until both Eleanor and Punky had taken their seats before lowering himself back into his armchair. "I'm all ears," he said, flashing a smile that was both disarming and disquieting at the same time.

"I'm not sure how best to say this," Punky began.

"Just spit it out," the president replied.

"Samuel Chambers is dead."

The smile disappeared. "What?"

"He was gunned down earlier tonight in Lanham, Maryland."

Jonathan Adams turned to look at his director of national intelligence for confirmation. "Is this true?"

But Eleanor looked just as surprised. "I just saw him..."

"How do you know this?" the president asked, turning his attention back to Punky.

She took a deep breath before replying. "Because he lured me there to kill me."

If his chief of staff's death had surprised Jonathan, her accusation that

Samuel had intended to murder a federal agent was a virtual slap to the face. "To... *what*?"

Connor reached over and placed a hand on her arm to caution her. But she shrugged it off. "I'm sorry, Mr. President, but he admitted that he intended to kill me because of what I had learned about Aurora Holdings—"

"Stop," Jonathan said, holding up his hand to silence her. He locked eyes with Punky for several seconds, then turned to look at the others. "Would you please give us some privacy?"

Chris stepped forward from where he stood next to the door. "Mr. President, I—"

"You too, Chris."

Slowly, Eleanor and Connor stood and followed Chris Albanese from the room. Jonathan waited until they were gone before again locking eyes with Punky.

"What do you want?"

Instead of answering, Punky turned the tables on him. "Did you know about Aurora Holdings?"

He didn't balk. "Not until I met my son two years ago in Nevada."

Punky generally held a high opinion of Jonathan Adams, but she hadn't expected him to be so forthright in answering. But to her trained eye, it looked almost like he felt relief at finally being able to talk about something that had been weighing down on him.

"Samuel told me the Russians were using it as leverage over you." It wasn't quite what he had told her, but it was an assumption she had made based on everything she had learned.

But the president confirmed her assumption and nodded. "They wanted me to stand aside while they recovered nuclear weapons that had been in storage in Ukraine since the Cold War."

"So, it's too late," Punky said, echoing what Viktor had told her.

Jonathan looked confused. "What? No, we stopped them."

"But Viktor—"

Jonathan's jaws flexed with a sudden flush of anger. "Viktor Drakov?"

Punky nodded. "When Samuel couldn't kill me, Viktor tried."

"What happened to him?"

"He's a pile of ashes on Pennsylvania Avenue near the Maryland border," she said. But her mind was still on the nuclear weapons that both Samuel and Viktor had said were in the Russians' hands. "You said you stopped them in Ukraine?"

The tension in his jaw relaxed. "We received confirmation just before you arrived. I would have *never* allowed those Russki thugs to get away with something like that, but Sam thought he could control the situation."

Punky fell silent. If the president was telling her the truth, then the threat of nuclear weapons falling into the hands of jihadis had been eliminated. His traitorous chief of staff was dead. So too was the Russian spy who had been behind it all.

"So, again, I'll ask you…" He leaned forward and rested his forearms on his knees. "What do you want?"

"I want to know why you did it."

"Did what?"

"Why you paid Aurora Holdings to keep your son a secret?"

Jonathan hung his head and let out a long sigh. "I didn't know."

Punky thought the answer was typical for a bureaucrat and beneath somebody like Jonathan Adams. "That's bullshit."

He looked up and stared straight into her eyes. "No. It's not. I trusted Sam when he said he'd take care of it for me—"

"What did you think he was going to do?"

"I don't know," the president admitted. "I thought he was arranging for her to have an abortion. I thought we were paying for her to keep quiet. My opponents would have had a heyday with me funding an abortion when I have been staunchly pro-life during my political career."

"So, it was all about your career."

The president leaned away and straightened his back. "No, it was all about what's good for this country."

Punky shook her head. "Then why? Why was this a secret worth killing for?"

"I didn't—"

She held up her hand. "You didn't, but Samuel did. Why?"

"Because for two decades I made payments to a Russian intelligence officer to hide the existence of my son. I didn't know about him until I met him in Fallon, but that doesn't change the fact that he was later found guilty of treason for divulging secrets to the Chinese. No matter how you slice it, the American people can't lose faith in the office over a scandal of this magnitude."

"It might be too late for that," she said.

Jonathan nodded. "But I want to make it right."

"Maybe there's something you can do."

"Anything."

"I want you to make a call for me."

Jonathan leaned back. "To who?"

"The commanding officer of the Security and Emergency Services Battalion at Camp Pendleton in California."

57

Marine Corps Installations—West
Camp Pendleton Base Brig
Camp Pendleton, California
One month later

The Marine correctional specialist turned the key to unlock the door, then gestured for Punky to walk through. She entered with her head held high and masked the discomfort of her injuries hidden beneath her blue pantsuit. The surprise on Adam Garett's face at seeing her wasn't unexpected. But given everything that had happened since the last time she'd visited; it gave her great pleasure.

"You again?"

"Hello, Garett." Punky took a seat opposite the former Marine corporal and placed a thin manila folder on the table before folding her arms across her chest with a smug and satisfied grin.

He sighed. "What do you want?"

With slow and deliberate movements, she leaned forward and opened the folder in front of her. A photograph was resting on top inside, and Adam's eyes glanced down to it.

"Remember this?"

He narrowed his eyes, then quickly looked up at her. "I already told you—"

"The watch. I know." Punky reached into her pocket briefly, then tossed a watch onto the table in front of Adam. "This watch."

She didn't bother hiding her pleasure at seeing the surprise on Adam's face as he looked down at the elegant steel case adorned with Swarovski stones. He leaned forward and picked it up, turning it over to study it from every angle. Its black leather strap. Its beautiful simplicity.

"Where did you get this?"

"From Samuel Chambers," she said, tapping on the photo. "The man in this photograph. *This* man."

He looked down at the photograph again and hesitated before replying. "I— I don't know who that is."

"Oh, but you do."

When their eyes met again, Punky smiled at him. "He was the president's chief of staff. And you met him."

"I've never..."

Adam trailed off, and Punky could tell he remembered.

"Are you sure about that?"

He was silent for a moment, then shook his head. "No. I remember now."

"What? What exactly do you remember?"

"I remember he was in the room with the vice president when the Secret Service burst in."

"Right before you were arrested," Punky added.

He nodded. "Yes. But I don't *know* him."

Punky could tell there was a memory lingering just beneath the surface that Garett was trying to keep hidden. Maybe he was suppressing it subconsciously, but it was a memory she needed him to recall. She needed him to understand his role in a plot that had almost ended in disaster.

"What happened in that room, Garett?"

"I already told you," he replied. "The Russian forced me to give the vice president a cigar box."

"What Russian? What was his name?"

Adam furrowed his brow in thought for several seconds. "Voronov. Nikolai Voronov."

"And he wore a watch like that one," Punky said, gesturing to the Poljot sitting on the table.

Adam nodded.

"Then what?"

"Then the Secret Service burst into the room—"

"*Before* that."

Punky could tell Adam was replaying the scene in his mind. His eyes glassed over as if he was watching the events inside the NAWDC headquarters unfolding in real time. "The vice president accused the man who was with him—"

"Samuel Chambers," Punky corrected.

"He accused Samuel Chambers of doing something."

"What?"

Adam's eyes focused on hers. "I swear I don't know. He didn't say. He just kept asking, 'What did you do?'"

Punky believed him. She leaned back in her chair and remained silent, waiting to see if Adam could put the pieces of the puzzle together on his own.

"What was in the box?" he asked.

"A secret."

Adam swallowed, then cleared his throat. "What secret?"

This was the moment Punky had been waiting for. How Adam responded would determine whether he would become the asset she hoped him to be or remain an obstacle to her obsession with dismantling the Ministry of State Security's West Coast network once and for all.

"The truth about who you really are."

Adam recoiled as if she had slapped him. "Me?"

She leaned forward and picked up the watch. "I took this off Samuel Chambers after Russians killed him."

Adam shook his head. "Wait. What truth about me?"

But Punky had planned out how this conversation would go, and she kept driving forward. "I took this off his dead body after he tried killing me to prevent the truth from coming out."

In the aftermath of what had taken place in Ukraine and on the outskirts of DC, there had been a major shake-up in the political landscape. Predictably, the powers in Washington had circled the wagons to prevent the truth from shaking the country's foundation to its core. But the damage had already been done.

"After being elected to his first political office in the California legislature, an underage girl in Berkeley gave birth to a baby boy that had the power to ruin Jonathan Adams. But Samuel Chambers took it upon himself to establish a fake business and made regular payments that were then distributed to its two shareholders."

"Who?"

"Mila Smith and Viktor Drakov."

"Who are they?" Adam asked.

"Viktor Drakov is a former Russian intelligence operative and was the person responsible for your kidnapping in Reno. Nikolai Voronov worked for him."

"Who's Mila Smith?"

"Your mother."

Adam recoiled in genuine shock. "My what?"

"Your mother. She was just a girl when Jonathan Adams got her pregnant."

Punky could tell Adam was still struggling to understand the impact of the events that had surrounded his very existence. He opened his mouth to ask her a question, but snapped it shut when nothing came out.

"Mila Smith's real name was Mila Popov—the daughter of two Soviet KGB intelligence officers from Directorate S."

"Was?"

"She's dead."

Adam nodded. "What's Directorate S?"

Hook, line, and sinker, she thought.

"Directorate S was responsible for the Illegals program that put agents in place without an official cover. Their job was to infiltrate American society while doing the Kremlin's bidding. When Mila was born, she was brought into the family business and raised as an American. But their goal all along was to use her to put an American politician in a compromising situation that would make them susceptible to blackmail."

"I don't understand," Adam said.

"When a young, up-and-coming politician named Jonathan Adams got Mila pregnant, her handler, Viktor Drakov, saw another use for you. Instead of exposing the California assemblyman, he poured money and influence into his political career and helped mold him into a congressman, senator, and finally the president."

"What was his use for me?"

"He arranged for you to be placed into the foster care of agents from China's Ministry of State Security."

The surprise on Adam's face disappeared.

"You knew, didn't you?"

"I think I need my attorney," Adam said.

Punky shook her head. "No, you don't. You've already been convicted of treason. You've already been sentenced to spending the rest of your life behind bars in Leavenworth. When you leave here, you will cease to exist, as far as the world is concerned."

"I have nothing else to say."

She had expected him to stonewall her and had prepared for this. "I'm your only chance at tasting freedom again."

He shook his head.

"Your adopted mother is dead."

Punky saw genuine tears welling in his eyes. But he remained mute.

"And your adopted father has forsaken you."

Again, he shook his head.

Punky reached across and delicately picked up the photograph of Jonathan Adams and Samuel Chambers and moved it to the side. Underneath was a second photograph, but one she knew Adam had never seen before.

He held her gaze, openly defying her by refusing to give in to his curiosity.

"Have a look, Adam."

Reluctantly, he looked down and the expression on his face said everything.

"Yes, that's your adopted father, He Gang." She paused to let everything sink in. This was the moment when he realized he was utterly alone. His biological father was a disgraced politician. His birth mother was a dead Russian spy; his adopted mother a dead Chinese one. And his adopted father was alive and well and playing in the front yard of his childhood home with a little girl and her dog.

"Who is she?"

"Her name is Shen Li," Punky said. "Her mother was also a Chinese spy. When she was arrested after trying to carry out a synthetic bioweapon attack on an American aircraft carrier as part of your father's plot to invade Taiwan, your mother stepped forward and claimed to be her grandmother."

"Why are you doing this to me?"

Punky took no pleasure in the heartache that was clearly apparent in his voice. But just like every other person in Garett's life, she would use him to achieve her own aims. "Because if you want my help to shorten your sentence, you need to tell me everything you know about your father."

The tears that had been growing in his eyes finally spilled over and ran down his cheeks. She had succeeded in breaking him and bending him to her will.

At last, Adam nodded.

EPILOGUE

San Jose, California

Punky sat behind the wheel of a government Ford Fusion sedan and watched the chaos unfolding around her. Flashing red-and-blue lights reflected off neighboring houses, trees, and streetlamps, giving the scene an eerie glow. Everywhere she looked, men and women milled about, wearing navy blue windbreakers with "FBI" printed on the back in gold block letters.

"Are you sure you want to do this?" she asked.

The man and woman sitting in the backseat looked at each other and nodded. "We're sure," he answered for both of them.

Punky smiled. She was pleased she had thought of this and fast-tracked the required approvals through the State Department. She hated the thought of taking Shen Li from yet another home but knew the couple in her backseat would take care of the girl and raise her in a loving one. She wouldn't have to fear being pimped out by the Russians to ensnare a politician in a sordid affair or forced to spy for the Chinese Ministry of State Security. She would be free to be nothing more than a little girl with parents who loved her.

"I'll be right back," Punky said.

She opened the driver's door and stepped out onto the dark street. Several FBI agents turned in her direction, and those who had known her Uncle Rick nodded at her in silent greeting. She nodded back, knowing that in their eyes, she was no longer the token niece of a federal law enforcement officer, but a respected special agent in her own right. A different agency maybe, but they fought on the same team in the battle against foreign adversaries who sought to steal their secrets.

Punky crossed the street and approached the front door, just as two agents escorted He Gang in handcuffs from the simple mid-century house. The man's arrogance was plastered on his face, and he glanced at her only briefly, before deciding that she didn't warrant even a fraction of his attention. It was a moment of satisfaction for her that she had been the one to bring his entire world crashing down around him. And he hadn't thought her worthy of even a sneer.

"Enjoy prison," she said, not bothering to hide the contempt in her voice, then sidestepped him and walked into the house.

There, in the center of the living room and surrounded by several federal agents, was Shen Li. The black mouth cur she had adopted when her mother had killed the dog's owner stood protectively in front of her, neither growling at the officers nor backing down from her role of protecting the little girl.

"Hi, Cher," Punky said, bending down to hold her hand out for the dog to sniff.

Immediately, the cur's tail began wagging, and Punky reached up to scratch behind her ears. Shen Li looked up at Punky with worry etched on her angelic face, and Punky smiled as she knelt beside her, still scratching the protective dog.

"Shen Li, my name is Emmy King. Do you remember me?"

The girl nodded, but her face still wore a mask of concern.

"I'd like to introduce you to some friends of mine. Would you like to meet them?"

Shen Li looked at the agents on either side of her, then let her eyes settle on Cher's wagging tail. Punky suspected the girl knew she didn't really have a choice in the matter, but seeing how relaxed Cher was with the newcomer seemed to put her at ease.

"Okay."

Punky stopped scratching Cher's head and reached out to offer her hand to the little girl, who readily accepted. Almost immediately, Cher took her place at Shen Li's side, pressing up against her diminutive form as Punky guided her from the living room to the front door.

"Where will I live now?"

The question broke Punky's heart. She knew that Shen Li's father had been killed by the Chinese Communists for working with the CIA to prevent a deadly bioweapon attack. And she knew her mother had been arrested for her role in perpetrating that attack. Newly orphaned, she had been taken in by He Gang. But Punky knew he had only sought to mold her and twist her into a tool for the Ministry of State Security.

In many ways, Shen Li and Adam Garett had much in common.

Punky gave Shen Li's hand a reassuring squeeze. "Let me show you."

Together, with Cher at their side, they walked through the front door and crossed the yard to the street that was still buzzing with law enforcement. Punky guided her through a throng of FBI special agents and crossed the street to the waiting Ford Fusion.

As they neared, the rear doors opened, and a man and woman stepped out and smiled at the little girl. Shen Li clutched Punky's hand tighter, and Cher pressed herself closer. The woman held an infant protectively in her arms and knelt while keeping her eyes fixed on Shen Li. The man circled around the car and stood next to his wife.

Shen Li stopped walking while still out of reach, but Cher continued and sniffed the strangers. Her tail was drooped with caution, but after a few seconds, it started wagging with apparent approval.

"Shen Li, I'd like you to meet my friends, Jenn and Andy Yandell."

"Hi, Shen Li," Jenn said.

"Hello."

"Is this your dog?" Andy asked.

She nodded.

Punky gave her hand a squeeze again, then guided her closer. Shen Li seemed reluctant at first, but then approached Jenn and Andy and held out her hand. The couple traded glances before Jenn shifted the infant in her arms and graciously accepted the little girl's outstretched hand.

"We would like for you to come live with us," Jenn said. "Would that be okay?"

Shen Li looked up at Punky before responding. "Can Cher come?"

"Of course," Andy replied.

Punky watched the little girl's shoulders droop as she looked around the chaos unfolding on the street. Her eyes found He Gang, sitting in the back of an unmarked police cruiser. And when he noticed her looking in his direction, he turned away. She sighed.

"Yes," she said, looking back to Jenn. "That would be okay."

"Then let's get you home," the former flight attendant said.

Punky released her grip on Shen Li's hand, knowing that the little girl would be loved and cared for. She knew the former Navy pilot and his wife would protect her and keep her safe and give her the kind of home she deserved.

"Is that your baby?" Shen Li asked.

Jenn looked down and smiled at the infant cradled in her arms. She nodded. "Her name is Hope."

Command and Control
Book #1 in the Command and Control Series
By David Bruns and J.R. Olson

As a string of unexplained attacks push superpowers to the brink, the clock is ticking toward the start of World War III.

Don Riley, head of the CIA's Emerging Threats Group, has never seen anything like this.

Riley and his team are tasked with identifying national security threats before they become tomorrow's bad news. But shortly after an Iranian vessel delivers a surprise attack to a US Navy Warship in the Arabian Gulf, a series of seemingly unrelated attacks crop up around the globe.

The US military is rapidly being drawn into full-fledged shooting wars on multiple fronts. Now Riley must sift through the layers of deception in time to discover who—or what—is behind these events...

...before the clock reaches zero hour.

Get your copy today at
severnriverbooks.com

ACKNOWLEDGMENTS

First and foremost, I want to thank my wife, **Sarah**, who has been by my side for over two decades. First as a Navy wife, then as an airline pilot's wife, she has sacrificed her time with me so I could serve a greater cause and pursue my dreams. Now, as an author's wife, she continues to raise me up while doing the heavy lifting in raising our three amazing children—**Tre**, **William**, and **Rebecca**. I would be nothing without my family. Thank you.

For ten years, I have been fortunate to work for a company that feels more like a family than an employer. From the men and women at headquarters to my union brothers and sisters out on the line, you are why I still look forward to going to work. I only wish I had the chance to thank each of you personally. Over time, maybe I will.

To **Ray Porter**, I was a fan before I even began writing this series. It gives me goosebumps when I hear my words coming out of your mouth, and I can't thank you enough for breathing life into Colt and Punky. This series would not be what it is without you.

To my agent and friend, **John Talbot**, I am thankful for your keen eye and constant support. To **Andrew Watts**, **Cate Streissguth**, **Randall Klein**, **Lisa Gilliam**, and the unsung heroes behind Severn River Publishing, thank you for giving me a home and helping to mold this story into a finished product I am incredibly proud of.

Lastly, to you, my readers. Thank you for continuing to give up your most precious commodity to spend time with Colt and Punky. I hope you enjoyed this adventure and look forward to the next one. I know I look forward to delivering it to you.

I'm out.
Farley

ABOUT THE AUTHOR

Jack Stewart grew up in Seattle, Washington and graduated from the U.S. Naval Academy before serving twenty-three years as a fighter pilot. During that time, he flew combat missions from three different aircraft carriers and deployed to Afghanistan as a member of an Air Force Tactical Air Control Party. His last deployment was with a joint special operations counter-terrorism task force in Africa.

Jack is a graduate of the U.S. Navy Fighter Weapons School (TOPGUN) and holds a Master of Science in Global Leadership from the University of San Diego. He is an airline pilot and has appeared as a military and commercial aviation expert on international cable news. He lives in Dallas, Texas with his wife and three children.

Sign up for Jack Stewart's reader list at
severnriverbooks.com

Printed in the United States
by Baker & Taylor Publisher Services